"YOU ARE MORE OF A ~~REGA~~ THAN I THOUGHT."

Eden drew in a sharp breath. "There is no reason for you to be rude, Mr. O'Connor. You mustn't take that tone with me."

Shane stared at her in disbelief. She spoke to him as if he were an insolent servant. Her tone both irritated and aroused him. He couldn't for the love of God guess why.

"I do expect my dagger back," she continued.

Watching the moonlight dab shadows upon her elegant face, Shane compressed his lips even tighter. The light, lingering scent of gardenias reached his nostrils, made every muscle of his body tighten. Damn it, *no,* he told himself fiercely. She was spoiled, pampered—and absurdly dauntless. He didn't want to take her case; his wolf-keen instincts screamed an alarm in his head *not* to take it, and yet he found himself reaching for her, his powerful fingers closing like a bracelet around her slender wrist, and he tugged her close, ignoring her little cry of protest.

"You," he said gruffly, "are coming with me."

Bantam Books by Maureen Reynolds

TEMPTING EDEN
SMOKE EYES

Tempting Eden

MAUREEN REYNOLDS

BANTAM

New York   Toronto   London   Sydney   Auckland

TEMPTING EDEN

A Bantam Fanfare Book / September 1993

ISBN 0-553-56435-8

Published simultaneously in the United States and Canada

Bantam Books are published by Bantam Books, a division of Bantam
Doubleday Dell Publishing Group, Inc. Its trademark, consisting of
the words "Bantam Books" and the portrayal of a rooster, is
Registered in U.S. Patent and Trademark Office and in other
countries. Marca Registrada. Bantam Books, 1540 Broadway, New
York, New York 10036.

PRINTED IN THE UNITED STATES OF AMERICA

RAD   0 9 8 7 6 5 4 3 2 1

For my mother, Frances C. O'Brien, who, with her Irish "gift of gab" enraptured me with her lively storytelling as far back as I can remember. And for my father, Richard Patrick Reynolds, who introduced me to his love for books with those Saturday visits to Johnson's second-hand bookstore where I discovered the magical power of words that would forever be written into my heart. Thank you.

CHAPTER ONE

New York, 1883

IS ESTATE WAS MAGNIFICENT. SEVERAL ACRES OF lush emerald grass sloped up to a stunning three-story mansion built of rose-colored brick and dotted with several chimneys among steep-pitched roof-tops. Tucked like a Scottish castle upon a seemingly endless stretch of impeccably landscaped grounds, the imposing structure was offered an exquisite view of the bay from three directions. Sunlight glistened off turrets and towers and the hundreds of panes of glass in the mullioned windows. Surely, Eden Lindsay thought as she gazed through the locked wrought-iron gates and up the long, winding drive to the front of the mansion, this was one of the most beautiful estates on all of Long Island. Unfortunately, it was also the most impenetrable.

She tilted her head back and narrowed her eye
against the hot late-August sunlight, studying th
tall, formidable gate and the high ivy-covered stor
walls towering above her. Both were designed t
keep out intruders, she was certain. An invulnerab
fortress. The proprietor had even posted guards
various points about the estate. Guards, for the lo
of heaven! Of course Eden couldn't blame the ma
—her dramatic nature even appreciated the for
thought—and she supposed that for a man in h
profession—one in which he was forced to risk h
life continuously, often in extremely dangerous situations, no precaution was too great. No doubt h
enemies would like to see the elusive, international
reknowned, extraordinarily successful private inve
tigator, Shane O'Connor, dead.

Eden shuddered at the thought. Slipping unno
ticed by the front gate, she moved quickly towar
the back of the estate. She was wearing an old pa
of boy's breeches and shirt, her thick white-blon
hair tucked up under a cap. Of course her attire wa
not appropriate for meeting a man of M
O'Connor's caliber, but she had brought a change
clothing along in a carpetbag and would slip into he
dress as soon as she had scaled the wall. That wa
her only option, and she had made the three-hou
trip from the city of New York with the intentic
clearly in mind. There was no way she was going t
turn back now.

As she trotted toward the far end of the estat
where a thick copse of trees shaded the land, sh
heard Uncle Monty's voice ring clearly in her ear
Monty was a family friend, not a true uncle, bu
Eden had fled to him as soon as she decided sh

needed the name of the best detective in town. Though he had told her Shane O'Connor was the best, Monty had warned her about him.

"O'Connor is tremendously wealthy, dear," Monty had said in his dry, droll voice as they sat in his parlor the previous evening. And Monty would know, Eden had thought, for he owned one of the finest homes on Fifth Avenue. "As O'Connor should be," Monty had added. "He caters exclusively to a wealthy clientele." Monty had touched a corner of his handkerchief to the tip of his bulbous nose. "I hear he frequently charges one hundred thousand dollars—" Eden had gasped, but quickly collected her wits as Monty continued. "But it is money well deserved, as his work is exceedingly dangerous. It is reputed that the man will go anywhere in the world —and has—to solve a case, and has outwitted many, many criminals. For all that he's Irish"—Monty gave a sniff—"he's remarkable, girl . . . and nigh near impossible to reach. One needs a connection—a personal contact, perhaps—if one wishes an appointment with the man."

Monty's efforts to discourage her were for naught. Eden, with her thirst for drama and adventure, was instantly intrigued. The nobility and chivalry of O'Connor's profession fired her vivid imagination, and she knew it was best not to reveal her interest in the man to Monty, for he already regarded her as too wild and impetuous. Part of his assessment of her, she knew, was that she, a young woman with background and breeding, horrified Society by leading a second life as a stage performer. Of course, Society was too *cultured* to confront her about her scandalous behavior, but in luxuriant ballrooms and at various social affairs, Eden had heard the vicious whispers about her "vulgar inclinations" and how she had shamed her mother. *That* was one reason why, they said, her mother was so sickly, so frail. Eden, on the other hand, knew her mother had always been so, since Eden's father had died. Her Norwegian father had been a highly respected international businessman, and just to speak his name was an honor. His name was what really protected Eden from the rumors, the gossip Society spread about her. It helped that a few members of the upper echelons were enchanted by her and had taken her under their wing, no matter that others whispered about what a shame it was about the wild children her father had produced.

Of course, those whispers were countered by the ones that blamed Eden's grandfather for her unorthodox ways. Rake. For the love of heaven, his name told all. Years earlier, after her husband had died, Eden's mother had sent Eden and her twin brother to Texas to live with Rake on his vast, sprawling ranch. There, the twins had grown up with unlimited freedom, and performing for audiences—mainly the ranch hands—had been one of those freedoms. Though her brother had left the ranch at age fifteen for New York, where Mama had bought a house on Fifth Avenue, heartbroken Eden had stayed behind in Texas, loving her wild and free life-style too much to part with it. Though her mother had summoned her every summer to New York since that time, and they often vacated to Newport from there, Eden had never lost the desire to perform. Becoming quickly bored at their Newport beach house, she would leave after a couple of weeks and return to the city invariably to join a theater troupe that she stayed with until shortly before Christmas. The past three years, though, Mama had remained in London, spar

ng Eden the long-suffering looks and sighs over her
daughter's unconventional behavior.

She could only think, as she sat across from
Monty, that Mama might be proud of her actions
now, as she planned to take matters into her own
hands. Then again, she mused, studying the troubled
look on Monty's florid features, perhaps not. It took
much to please Mama, and Eden had given up long
ago. All she knew was that she had to gain an appointment with the elusive and highly unattainable
Mr. O'Connor.

She leaned forward eagerly in her chair. "I can
raise one hundred thousand dollars, Uncle Monty. If
I have to sell the house, I will—and some property—"

It was Monty's turn to gasp. He waved his hanky
under his nose as Eden cast him a questioning look.
"Have you taken leave of your senses?" he demanded.

She patted his hand consolingly. Monty was
Mother's friend, and in some ways they were strik-
ingly similar. They tended to overreact to the sim-
plest matters. "I will do anything to help Philip,
Uncle Monty. Surely you know that."

Monty lifted his nose with distaste. "Yes,
well . . ."

Eden didn't allow Monty's attitude to discourage
her. Philip's escapades exasperated everyone he
knew, except Eden, of course. "An irresponsible ras-
cal" was what Monty called her twin in lighter moments. But Monty really had little patience for
Philip. Of course, Monty had known Papa, and
there was such drastic comparison between father
and son that Monty considered there was no comparison at all. Damned shame, he muttered every
time Philip entered a room.

As Monty walked Eden to the door, he tried agai to discourage her. "You'll need an appointmen dear. O'Connor will never allow you past his fror gate."

Eden only smiled at him. "Then I'll have to try th back, won't I, Uncle Monty?"

He sighed. "Yes, well. And plan to pay an *exorb tant* fee. *If* the man even lets you near." Once mor Monty looked down his nose, clearly dismayed the notion of her wasting a penny on Philip. "It rather absurd, don't you think, that you are willin to *sell property*—" Monty actually wheezed the la: and pressed the handkerchief to one nostril, unabl to continue.

Undaunted, Eden stepped onto the front step. " feel rather strongly, Uncle Monty, that there is notl ing absurd about any of this. Although I am not liberty to discuss the circumstances that surroun this emergency, I can assure you that I feel Philip life is in danger." When Monty's faded blue eye widened, she continued. "I will explain later. Whe the time is right."

"When the—time—" Monty was spluttering a she flashed another smile at him. "Girl, you are im possibly dramatic." Still, he smiled back at her, tak ing both of her hands in his. He'd known her sinc she was a baby and he could never stay exasperate with her for long. "You know," he said, "I am re turning to London not only for business, but be cause your mother is doing so poorly. You migh consider coming home, dear, and offering her som consolation—"

Eden's soft, almost self-conscious laugh stoppe him. "Oh, Uncle Monty, we both know that neithe Philip nor I has ever offered Mama much consola tion. Agitation is more like it."

He looked flustered, for she spoke the truth. "But she really has taken a downward turn." He shook her hands lightly as she began to protest. "Just give it some thought, dear, would you? You might want to return to London for Christmas this year."

Eden stifled a sigh. Thinking of her frail, insipid mother lying on her pillows, as she always thought of Mama, she wondered how she could have produced two animated, hot-as-pistols children who could set a town on fire with their antics. "I'll think about it," she promised Monty. "And I'll send you a telegram regarding Philip." Though, Eden ruefully admitted, Monty hadn't asked for one. "And I'm certain O'Connor will take my case."

"Hmm." Monty's gaze ran over her face. "If you say so." He stepped back to allow her access to the coach, and as she settled herself he scribbled two more names on a piece of paper. "To have in the event O'Connor won't grant you an appointment."

Eden pushed the paper back at him, her smile wide and sunny with optimism as the coach jolted off to a start. "Nonsense! I won't be needing those!" And she waved good-bye as the coach wheeled down the drive.

Now, however, Eden had her doubts. The sun beat down on the back of her neck, and as she skirted O'Connor's estate, her heart pounded so hard it was all she could hear—save for the ragged gasps of air she dragged into her laboring lungs. At last she stopped running, pressing her back to the wall and a hand to her thundering heart in effort to slow its wild hammering. "God's teeth!" she whispered. Perspiration trickled down her back and between her breasts, dampening her shirt so that it stuck to her skin. The day was suffocatingly hot! As her breathing evened, she could hear the waves lapping rhythmically on the shore. Any other time she would have been tempted to explore the beach, but there was an urgent matter at hand.

She caught her breath and glanced up, frowning, as she measured the high stone wall. "Well, this is going to be quite a climb," she muttered aloud, even though no one was there to respond. Even when she didn't have an audience, she imagined that she did. It was good practice.

"Well, here I go." She brushed her damp palms on the seat of her pants, then glanced down at herself and grimaced. Good thing she *had* brought her dress and petticoats, for her breeches and shirt were streaked with dust and sweat. Grandpapa had taught her always to make a stupendous first impression, and she had carefully selected the perfect clothes in which to meet Mr. Shane O'Connor. Now she stepped away from the wall and tossed her carpetbag over it. She heard the heavy thud as the bag hit the ground and she winced, visualizing her dress of pink taffeta and ecru lace emerging with a myriad of wrinkles. Shrugging, she reached up to secure a foothold.

The wall was covered with ivy that clung all the way to the top. Eden tested it with her full weight and it held. She was lithe and slender and scaled the wall with ease. When she reached the top and swung one long leg over, she held her breath at the sight below. Her world tottered. Never fond of heights, she felt increasingly dizzy but could not tear her stare from the beauty of the lush green lands surrounding her. She was as high as the treetops. Her world spun. She slipped. Her fingers clutched wildly, but she was making a fast descent straight toward hard, rocky ground that most certainly would kill her.

"Ohh!" Down the wall she slid, branches snapping at her, scratching her soft skin. Once she caught a foothold, but she was moving so fast, it proved disastrous and made her crash landing all the more ignominious.

"Oww!" she howled indignantly, stars shooting across her eyes as she landed hard on her rump. Her teeth snapped down on her tongue and she tasted blood. She lay against a tree trunk, the blue sky spinning crazily above her through the treetops. Well, at least she wasn't dead. Tears of pain smarted her eyes, but she sat up gingerly and tested for broken bones. Uncertainly, she stood. When she didn't immediately collapse and the stars disappeared from her vision, she began to strip.

"*What,*" came a cold, outraged voice from behind her, "in the bloody hell do you think you are about?"

Eden whirled, her petticoats spinning around her, and focused on a long-faced, long-nosed, clearly furious middle-aged man. Her heart pumped hard, and she felt a sudden surge of adrenaline hone her senses. It was time for an act. She didn't miss any opportunity, and now it was certainly called for—perhaps to save her hide. Not for the first time she thanked heaven for her special talent for dropping easily into any role required, or that which was liable to help her out of trouble.

She gasped and widened her blue-green eyes, knowing full well the powerful effect her sultry gaze had on the opposite sex. "Sir!" she cried, appropriately outraged. "Have you no decency! How dare you approach a woman in a state of dishabille!" Eden clutched her dress to her half-bared breasts.

The man was shocked. He took a step closer, apparently unable to believe his ears or to trust the sight before him. *"You,* miss, are in a state of"—he gave her a quick once-over, then sniffed—*"dishabille* on private property!" He looked freshly incensed. "And seeing that the estate is thoroughly guarded, you would be well aware of that." His eyes narrowed as he started toward her. "How did you get in here?"

Eden clung to her dress as if it were a shield. "Do not come one step closer!"

The steel-haired man stopped. "Madame!" he snapped, his blue eyes like flint. "You are trespassing. I am going to have you arrested!"

"That is all well and good," she snapped back. "But before you have me arrested, will you allow me to clothe myself?"

Simon Peterson, distinguished assistant and faithful right-hand man of Shane O'Connor, had never in all his life come across such a creature. Enjoying a rare stroll about the grounds, he'd heard the crash and howl of the woman who now stood half naked before him. He watched, mesmerized, as the dappled sunlight cascaded like liquid gold over her bare shoulders, diving into her glorious wheaten hair. God, she was magnificent. And she spoke with the dignity of a queen. Who was she?

He was about to ask, when, before his stunned gaze, she neatly produced a bowie knife, its gleaming blade reflecting the sunlight shining into his eyes. Simon opened his mouth, then brought his incredulous gaze up to hers, which glimmered with shards of light.

"Do not force me to use it," she warned him, and he could feel the hot blood rise slowly up his neck. Bested by a simple woman! Be damned! He drew in a long, calming breath.

"Are you threatening me?"

"Yes, of course I am."

He stiffened, but Eden was growing too impatient
worry about his male pride. "Please," she said,
back up ten paces, and then you can ask me any-
ing you'd like."

The man did not move, but continued to stare
oldly at her. "Did you come here to kill
'Connor?"

Eden almost laughed, then caught herself, realiz-
g her disadvantage. The man was clearly angry. An
gry man could not be trusted. "I will state my
asiness as soon as I am dressed."

They stared at each other for a moment, then the
an obliged her and backed up five strides. When
e lifted her chin at him, silently reminding him
e'd asked for ten paces, he narrowed his eyes at
er. "You'd be wise to hurry, madame, for I have
ry little store of patience, and it is sorely at its
nit."

Eden ducked behind a tree and wiggled into her
ink dress. The taffeta crackled on the hot August
reeze. "You really should have the grounds better
atrolled!" she called out gaily.

"I assure you," he intoned, "that Mr. O'Connor
as the estate *very* well manned."

"Yes, well, how do you explain my easy entry?"
he leaned down to wriggle a slim foot into a kid
ipper. She could almost feel the ice in the air gen-
ated by the proper gentleman on the other side of
e tree.

"I'm waiting for *you* to explain it."

She sighed and leaned down to put on her other
oe. "If it weren't so impossible to obtain an ap-
ointment with him, I would have gone up to Mr.
'Connor's front door and knocked, just like any
her reasonable—oh!"

She had been so engaged in the chore of making herself presentable, clutching the knife, and keeping up her end of the conversation, she was caught off guard by the man sneaking up behind her. He grabbed her arm, bending it and forcing it up between her shoulder blades. Eden cried out in pain and fear. He loosened his hold a bit, but still managed to slip the bowie from her hand and force her ahead of him.

"Now," he said in a very unpleasant voice, "move. Straight ahead." He gave her a little shove, and she stumbled, crying out again. She quieted when she felt the tip of her own knife pressed to the hollow behind her ear. "And no tricks. I'm sure Mr O'Connor will be very interested in hearing your explanation as to why you found it so necessary to force your entry onto his estate . . . with dagger in hand."

Eden struggled against him, against the force of his strength. *This* was not the stupendous impression she wanted to make on O'Connor at all! But there was no doubt in her mind that she would make an impression.

"Unhand me! Your behavior is exceedingly rude!"

The woman's voice echoed in the great hall, and the servants ducked behind doorways and whispered among themselves. What in heaven's name was happening? Mr. Peterson was shoving an outraged woman into the house—and at knifepoint! Had he captured a villainess? Had she penetrated the grounds? They exchanged alarmed looks and shuddered. If either was the case, Mr. O'Connor would mete out just punishment, and he would have

patience or mercy for her pleas. They quailed to
nk of it.

At the end of the long, majestic front hall, behind
air of handsomely carved mahogany doors, in his
ok-lined, multiwindowed study, private investiga-
Shane O'Connor frowned with dark annoyance.
hat the hell—

"Loose me! Let me go!"

In three quick strides Shane was at the doors. He
ng them open just before Simon burst through
m with a wildly disheveled woman in his merci-
s grip. There was a moment of frozen silence as all
ree stared, stupefied, at one another, then Simon
oved the woman into the room and slammed the
ors behind him, cutting off the servants' gapes.

Breathing hard, Simon passed a tremulous hand
rough his straight gray hair. "She came to kill you,
"

Eden glared at him, rubbing her arm. "I did not!
u lie! I told you—"

"Then explain the dagger—assassin!"

Holding on to her temper with superhuman ef-
rt, Eden gritted her teeth and scowled at the su-
rcilious snoot. "If there's an assassin anywhere in
is room, sir, I'm looking at him, for you have just
ne a fine job of assassinating my character!"

He snorted.

"That dagger, *sir,* was for *my* protection. And I
viously needed it, as you had no intention of leav-
g once you found me in a state of undress!"

Her comment drew the first evident reaction from
Connor, albeit a slight one. Until that moment, he
d been watching her in stillness, emitting a burn-
g energy that charged the air around him. Eden
t it, felt him, a forceful presence that tugged at
r, like a current that drew her with inexorable

force. As she faced him straight on, the first thi that struck her was the raw power of the man, rea ing out to envelop her.

His face was cold, rigidly set, the strong bor and aggressive angles chiseled so lean and so ha that the overall effect was brutal, and utterly co pelling. He was not a handsome man—certai nothing like the pampered, almost pretty-faced m who graced Society's ballrooms and dinner parties but his face held a brooding quality that she fou oddly attractive. It was saved from severity by strong, sensual mouth, which now quirked alm imperceptibly. Her gaze shot up to his eyes, whi were such a piercingly bright silver in his dee tanned face, they were a shock. For an instant Ed could not breathe, impaled on his gaze like a bird an arrow.

He was, perhaps, in his mid-thirties, dressed exquisitely tailored black trousers, his crisp wh shirt undone at his throat and fastened with sa phire studs, his ice-blue satin waistcoat hangi open to reveal his solid, muscular middle. He w tall, lean, and rangy hard, not an inch of wasted fle on him. The muscles were powerful across the aw some width of his shoulders and down the lo length of his legs. His thick hair was slightly cur though it looked as though he had taken pains smooth it off his forehead, as if annoyed with t soft waves. It was a dark, rich brown, the color coffee, and the sunlight caught dark gold strands its depths.

He was nothing like she had envisioned. She thought he'd be older—a nondescript type—not t suave, magnetic, intensely male creature. He w watching her, too, with a look of keen speculati that made her feel as if he'd stripped her. There w

re to his inspection than just the customary male
essment, and she felt like prey that had passed
close to an open trap. Her pulses rapped under
skin in a quickening rhythm, and her palms be-
to sweat. And then, as if he were suddenly disin-
ested, his dark lashes fell to veil his eyes.

He gave her a final dispassionate glance before he
dressed the other man. "Did she have a gun?"

The older man straightened as if a steel rod had
en inserted in his back. "Not that I know of, sir."

Shane quickly dismissed the idea of the woman
lling a gun on them now. He trusted his instincts
d they were telling him that she was weaponless,
d she had come for some reason other than to kill
n. Though, admittedly, the knife had been a sur-
se. She had certainly given Simon a scare; Shane
d never seen the man so shaken. Of course, that
uld be due to something else altogether. . . .

He liked this woman's looks, as he was certain
st red-blooded males who crossed her path did.
ough she was dressed in a gown of pink taffeta
ged with froths of lace and flounces, there was
nething sultry and disheveled about her. With her
de pink mouth and slumberous, heavy-lidded
es, she had an openly sensual face, a provocative
ra that lured and charmed despite the dirt and
atches on her cheeks. With mild amusement
ane realized she most likely had no idea that she
esented a less than perfect picture. Thick strands
her white-blond hair straggled from a lopsided
ench twist, and twigs and leaves decorated the
ffure. Under flyaway brows her eyes were not
ge, but they were heavily lashed, and the striking
or of aquamarines. Her eyelashes were thick, sur-
isingly dark, yet gold-tipped. Her nose was
aight, but for the ever so slight tip at its end.

His gaze slid down her body, noting the so[ft]
swells of her breasts revealed above the deep flounc[e]
of her bodice, her small waist, and the rich, fir[m]
curves of her hips that beckoned for a man's hand[s]
upon them. Under her disarray was a faultless el[e]-
gance, her demeanor conveying that she was a quee[n]
and expected to be treated like one. Shane frowne[d].
Spoiled, he thought with contempt. Most like[ly]
blueblood-rich. She was just the type of helples[s]
highborn, pampered woman he had learned [to]
avoid. This type was flighty and haughty, vain an[d]
frivolous—a gaggle of whining, simpering, clingi[ng]
nuisances. They created distastefully embarrassi[ng]
public scenes, couldn't form an original though[t],
dared not act without approval from the promine[nt]
man in their lives, and were just generally excrucia[t]-
ingly dull.

Shane's frown deepened. Oddly enough, thou[gh]
this woman wore all the trappings, something did[n't]
fit. Her coloring in a less vibrant woman would ha[ve]
suggested insipidity, a lack of spirit, but he could s[ee]
that she was robust and healthy, sparkling with [a]
magnetic appeal that said "look at me!" In a wor[d],
she was delectable.

Keeping his expression impassive, Shane consi[d]-
ered the disconcerting society woman before hi[m],
appreciating her frank stare as she tipped her ch[in]
up, her gaze seeming to demand answers. This, to[o],
intrigued him. She did not coyly lower her lashes [or]
fan her face as one might expect a woman of h[er]
station to do. Fire. He saw it in her, and, despite [his]
annoyance, was curious.

He glanced at Simon. "Where did you find her[?]"

Simon drew himself up. "At the west end of t[he]
estate, sir."

"And what was she doing at the west end of the
ate?"

Simon spared Eden a cold look. "Preparing to
ltrate your home—undoubtedly to gain access to
."

"Oh, for heaven's sake!" Eden burst out. "I insist
u stop defaming my good character this instant! I
ne here without malicious intent, and this is the
st ridiculous—" She stopped her tirade in mid-
eam, silenced by O'Connor's steely gaze flashing
her. Her heart seemed to stop, then she shook
self, annoyed for feeling such jolting alarm. "If
u ask *me* what I was doing at the west end of your
ate, Mr. O'Connor, I would be more than happy
state my case. You might do me the courtesy of
king *to* me, instead of past me," she added.

O'Connor, however, obviously had no intention
giving her any such courtesy. He continued ques-
ning Simon as if she hadn't interrupted them, as
indeed, she were not even present. "Was anyone
e with her?"

"Not that I know of, sir." Simon frowned at Eden
disapproval. "However, her state of dishabille
uld have been a decoy. She could be working with
neone else, sir. But if that is the case, I would
pe the guards would have that situation under
ntrol by now. As for how she gained access to the
ate, sir, she scaled the wall."

Eden rolled her eyes. "Yes. Yes, I did! And I'd do
again—a hundred times—if I wished to reach the
possibly *inaccessible* Mr. O'Connor!"

Though O'Connor was watching her with a quiet
ensity, it was Simon who answered her. "If one
shes to speak with Mr. O'Connor, a meeting is
ually arranged through the proper channels."

Honestly, Eden thought, the aristocracy in En-

gland did not look down their noses half so well a
these two! O'Connor moved then, with the grace o
a tiger. His gaze upon her, he stepped back to lea
against a wall, his weight slung on one hip, his hand
in his trousers pockets. Though there was an air o
composure about him, Eden also sensed a subtle b
distinctive force.

He kept watching her, but once again spoke pa
her. "Have you informed the . . . ah . . . *lady,* S
mon, what type of reception our unexpected gues
might anticipate? Especially," he added in a so
tone, "those who scale the estate walls and . . .
. . . shed their clothing?"

Eden stiffened, her face hot with color. He
made it sound as if it were commonplace for wom
to scale his wall and undress. She felt her temp
flare when she caught sight of Simon, who showed
trace of humor as he gazed at his employer. "Ah, n
sir. In the melee, that particular formality slipped n
mind."

"Hmm." Shane's gaze drifted over her, and Ed
relaxed slightly, allowing her own gaze to drift ov
him too. It lingered on the patch of curly dark ch
hair that was displayed through his open-throat
shirt, and she found the sight oddly arousing. S
brought her gaze back up to his and smiled slight
The men's moods seemed to be softening. Perha
they would offer her a drink of something cold. S
was terribly thirsty, her throat parched from the h
of the summer afternoon.

O'Connor tipped his head at her, a wicked glint
his eye as he continued to speak to Simon. "Do y
suppose we should strip her first, or just tortu
her?" He ignored her gasp of outrage. "And p
cisely what type of torture shall we have Dugg
carry out?"

"*What?*" Eden exclaimed.

O'Connor lifted his eyebrows, and in a voice nged with mockery he asked, "Would you rather e just arrest you, madame?"

"Sir, with your attitude it is a wonder you have a ractice at all!"

His features tightened. "It is a wonder," he said oldly, "that you are still alive, madame. You're a amn fool to risk your neck as you did. Men have een killed for attempting what you actually pulled ff, and it's a wonder you weren't killed too."

Instead of feeling alarm, dismay, or remorse for er actions, Eden brightened. "Then I am to be ommended, am I not? Congratulate me, sir, for ac- omplishing such a feat!"

O'Connor stared at her as if she were daft. He xchanged a brief look with Simon, but she scarcely oticed as she continued.

"And for mastering such a feat, you should be ore than willing to give me your time, lend an ear –please!" she cried when she saw the implacable ardening of his features. "Please, just listen to my tory! I promise I will pay you handsomely for your me!" She was frantic about her twin, alarmed that omething dire had happened to him. She hadn't een so afraid of anything since she was five years ld and her father had died and Mama had dumped er and Philip at their grandfather's Texas ranch. *hilip,* she cried silently, her heart wrenching, *I romise I'll find out what has happened to you.*

But as her eyes met those of the aloof, hard-faced an whom she desperately needed, Eden felt hope eep out of her. He appeared so coldly remote. At er impassioned plea there was no softening in his hiseled features, or in his stony gaze. In a final at- empt she gave him her most imploring look, and almost regretted it immediately. The light in his eyes suddenly burned brighter, a feral gleam that as sessed her, and found her sorely wanting. It was as i he knew her game. Perhaps, Eden thought, feminine wiles were not the approach to take with this man Well, that suited her fine. She had never been much for wiles anyway. The direct, straightforward ap proach was more practical from her perspective.

"State your business," O'Connor bit out.

"But sir," Simon interrupted, "I really don't think she deserves—"

"I'll handle this for now, Simon," O'Connor said in a voice that brooked no opposition.

Flustered, Simon straightened his shoulders and glanced at Eden, his expression one of disdain. "Yes, sir."

She had to curb the urge to cast him a smug grin He dutifully retreated, closing the door behind him

Now she and O'Connor were alone, and suddenly the open, airy study seemed stifling hot, though light, pleasant breeze lifted the curtains at the ope windows.

He eased away from the wall and crossed to hi desk, his long strides brisk and purposeful. Eden watched him arrange some papers, then he looked up, piercing her with those steel-colored eyes. queer thrill shot through her, clutching her stomach Her legs felt weak and shaky.

"Sit down."

His voice was low, but it held a curt note of au thority. Eden lifted her voluminous skirts and moved toward the burgundy leather chair in front of his massive mahogany desk. When she had settle herself, she looked up at him.

"Your name," he demanded.

"I am Eden Victoria Lindsay."

English, Shane thought with a jab of emotion. He
ad his own set of biases about the English, and
aring his youth his feelings had been very bitter.
ver the years, however, his bitterness had miti-
ated somewhat, and he'd learned to judge people as
dividuals. After all, a person couldn't help what he
as born. Still, this young woman and her unfortu-
ate ancestry brought up some unpleasant, shardlike
emories of Meggie. Damn if he would ever forget
er.

He concentrated on the woman before him, a
ost of a smile curling his lips. "And what has Miss
den Victoria Lindsay come to see me about?"

Eden again stifled her rising temper. He spoke in
aperior tones that offended her considerable pride.
till, she needed him. Before they got started,
ough, she had to correct him. "Mrs."

Surprise flickered in his eyes. "And why hasn't
our husband accompanied you?"

"He's dead."

Only a slight tightening of his mouth showed his
eaction. Eden shrugged and sighed. "It *was* sad
hen Wilbur passed on, but he was quite well into
is years, and half expected to die. Not," she added
astily, "that I don't miss him."

O'Connor didn't comment. Instead, he opened
ne richly carved wood box on his desk and ex-
acted a long, elegant cigar. Glancing at her, he
aised a brow in polite inquiry.

Eden continued. "So you see, Wilbur couldn't
ave possibly accompanied me here—or anywhere,
or that matter."

O'Connor stopped in the motion of lighting the
heroot, then continued and blew out the match. "I
ee."

She sighed and smoothed her skirt, watching the

wrinkles flatten under her hand. "Yes, well, you are probably wondering why I'm not wearing widow's garb." Actually, he didn't look as if he was wondering at all, but she hurried on to explain. "It was Wilbur's express wish that I wear gay, bright colors and even though the very *notion* of wearing cheery dresses horrifies my mother and her cronies, I simply must do what Wilbur asked." She smiled at O'Connor. "Of course, Wilbur's express wish was really mine. He just adored me. Oh! I don't mean that with conceit. I adored him too." She tipped her head to one side. "He was the sweetest man, but he *did* spoil me."

Through the wreath of blue smoke between them she saw O'Connor smile briefly, looking as though she'd just told him something he wanted to know. She didn't pause to wonder what that could be, but leaned forward in her chair, suddenly curious. "Are *you* married, Mr. O'Connor?"

Fascinated, she watched his face become immediately shuttered. Quite like a stage curtain dropping at the end of a scene.

"No."

And that was that.

"That's too bad."

"Is it?"

It was odd, she mused, how a strange breathlessness assailed her whenever she met his eyes. It happened now, and she found herself staring openly at him, fascinated by his rugged masculine features. She began to fidget. She wished he'd sit. His size and forceful physical presence intimidated her, and Eden was not easily intimidated. In fact, she could not remember a moment in her life when she had been. To break his stare, she glanced out to the bay. The sun cascaded down on the rippling water, sca

ing diamond sparkles across its blue-gray surface.
e could hear the gentle lapping of the waves on
e beach and she emitted a little sigh. "You have a
ectacular view of the bay," she murmured. "And
e sound of the surf . . . It must be heavenly to
l asleep at night with that soothing—" She broke
f, catching his expression of unconcealed annoy-
ce.

"Madame," he said, removing the cheroot from
s mouth, "please go on. I am pressed for time."

"Oh, yes! I apologize. I have a tendency to di-
ess." As she spoke, she noted that his gaze flicked
t the window, almost as if he didn't trust that she
as simply admiring the view. She watched him nar-
w his eyes against the sun's glare and scan the
ach as if he were looking for something—or some-
e. "I need you to find my twin brother."

He turned quickly, his brows raised. He stood
oking at her so long and so penetratingly that she
lt the need to repeat herself.

"My twin," she whispered, and felt herself go still.
nly her heart, punching her chest, let her know
is was real.

Shane frowned. "You have a twin brother?"

"Yes, I do."

God help the world, he thought with grim humor.
e had made a quick surveillance of the beach and
en nothing unusual, but when she had made her
le comments about the view and the sound of the
rf, his instincts had sounded a shrill alarm. Maybe
e *was* an assassin, and was working with someone.
enerally Simon was the one to worry about life
reats. Shane simply considered the perpetual
reat of danger a sideline of his profession. That
sh of danger was part of why he loved his work—
e thrill was in his veins, his blood, as addictive as a

narcotic. But he found, on this hot summer afternoon, that he'd like to live the day out. Perhaps it had something to do with *her*. In any case, he was prepared.

He leaned down to crush out his cheroot, watching her closely. "Why do you need me to find your twin?"

"Because he's missing, of course," she said in a mildly exasperated voice.

A humorless smile touched his lips. Ask a silly question . . . *"Why* do you need me to find him? *Why* do you think he is missing, and not"—he lifted one hand to knead the bridge of his nose—"on some drunken spree and, ah . . . entertaining the 'ladies'?"

Impressed by his questions, Eden sat forward, eager to help him out. "Well, Mr. O'Connor, that's very astute of you. Excuse me, do you have a headache, sir?"

He lowered his hand and opened his eyes to look at her. "Not yet," he murmured.

Feeling that she was somehow responsible for his tone, she hurried on, explaining. "Actually, I might agree with you that Philip could be on a drunken spree, but the circumstances surrounding his disappearance don't match that observation."

Shane lifted one eyebrow, silently urging her to continue.

"You see," she went on, becoming more upset as she related her story, "Philip *does* spend a good deal of time in the brothels, and there are three in particular that he frequents. But the madames of all of them told me they haven't seen him for several days."

Shane gave her a strange look. "You went into a brothel?"

She frowned. "No. I just told you I went into
hree. And Philip wasn't in any of them." She
hought she caught a flicker of amusement in his
yes, then quickly dismissed the notion. She
loubted the man had a drop of mirth in him.

"What," he asked, "do you mean by the circum-
tances matching the observation?"

Eden sighed. She was losing her patience with
im, then realized she had not produced her evi-
ence, which would lead him to the same conclusion
he had reached. She favored him with her most
harming smile. "Please turn your head, Mr.
)'Connor."

"Like hell."

Though her heart thudded hard, she kept her
mile intact. "But you must! You have to!"

She saw amazement register on his face, followed
y a hard frown. "I don't *have* to do anything I
on't damn well please, madame."

Her smile broke, and she twisted her fingers agi-
tedly in her lap. "Please, Mr. O'Connor," she said
oftly, and came to her feet. Tears started to fill her
ves. "I—I brought some evidence I think might
elp you with the case—that is, if you take it. But it's
. . I had to carry it under my skirt."

Faintly amused, Shane inclined his head toward
er, then shifted his gaze out toward the bay. Out of
ne corner of his eye he saw her whisk around, hoist
er layers of skirt and petticoats to her waist, and
umble with something he could not detect. He felt
ne back of his neck tighten. But if it were a gun, he
ould have smelled it. No, Eden Victoria Lindsay
ad carried *something* under her skirts, and he was
amned curious to find out what.

She turned around again, her skirts spinning.
ith that artlessness and dramatic flair that he was

beginning to understand was a natural part of her
she opened the chamois bag she had tied to the
waistband of her pantalets, grabbed his hand, and
plopped a huge cut diamond into his palm. Taking
his other hand, she plunked down another gem—an
extraordinary dark green emerald as large as the
enormous diamond.

At her touch, Eden felt him stiffen, felt an electric
current leap between them. Was it the shock of the
gems, or something else? Hot, sweeping, exhilarat-
ing, her response to him lit a vital heat within her
She was sure he felt it, too, for she saw his jaw
tighten, saw a strange light kindle the centers of his
eyes.

Abruptly, he shuttered those eyes with his lashes
and looked, once again, detached and impersonal
"Where," he asked in a hard drawl, "did you get
these?"

"That," she said, "is what I've come to tell you.

CHAPTER TWO

HE HELD THE GEMS IN HIS LONG FINGERS. FOR A moment Shane and Eden could only stare at the diamond's brilliance, its dozens of facets flashing rose and blue fire in the sunlight. "Perhaps a hundred carats," he said in a low voice.

Eden looked up, surprised at his knowledge. "Yes."

"Most exquisite," he murmured. His voice was as dark and rich as rum, and she felt its power rumble through her, a strange sensation rippling down to her core. With shaking fingers she pushed her hair from her eyes, and looked back to the diamond, mesmerized. "Very rare," he continued. "Extraordinary. Some would think these are well worth killing for."

Her gaze jerked to his face. She caught the touch of sardonic humor at one corner of his mouth, but his eyes did not smile. He sounded accusing, suspicious, but she shrugged off that silly notion and peered closer into his eyes, trying to read them. They revealed nothing. "Have you some experience with jewels, Mr. O'Connor?"

"Some."

"And those that kill for them?"

His stare was chilling. "To be sure," he said, and his voice was ominously soft, disturbing sensual, tinged with a brogue that caught her by surprise. He narrowed his eyes at her. "Where did you get these? How is it that they are in your possession?"

She gave him a curious look, not quite understanding his tone. "I found them in Philip's bedroom suite," she explained. "And believe me, the sight of them was a shock. I live with Philip on Fifth Avenue—we have the house to ourselves, since Mama lives in London. Philip and I both lead very busy lives, but we don't let two days pass without letting the other know of our whereabouts or plans. If we don't see each other, the servants inform us of the other's doings. Please, bear with me, Mr O'Connor," she added when he turned away to the sideboard and poured himself a shot of Irish whiskey. She thought he had grown bored by her story and she very much wanted, *needed* him to be interested. Still, if he was going to have something to drink, she might as well too.

"Excuse me, sir, would you mind pouring me glass of water—oh!" Her sudden exclamation caused him to jerk around, his body coiled like tight spring. Eden, however, was only staring in dis

ay at her reflection in the ornate gold-framed mir-
or that hung over the sideboard. Her face was
reaked with dirt and grime. Scratches marred her
heeks and chin, and twigs stuck out at odd angles
ll over her head.

"I look a fright!" she cried, upset by the impres-
on she must have made. And judging by the subtle
musement lurking in O'Connor's eyes as they met
ers in the mirror, she knew he agreed with her as-
essment.

"You do," he murmured, and turned to bring her
he water. She quickly took it from him, then
lunged her hand into her décolletage and whipped
ut a lace-edged handkerchief. She dabbed her face,
incing as she ran the handkerchief over her cuts,
hen pulled the pins from her hair. The thick mane
billed down her back and shoulders, and she fluffed
, trying to shake free the twigs and leaves. Hearing
strange noise from O'Connor, she glanced at him,
er arms poised above her head. Seeing his mouth
ghten, she smiled sheepishly.

"Sorry," she murmured. She quickly drank her
vater, then seated herself again.

"Now, where was I?" she wondered aloud. "Oh,
es. I was explaining the facts to you because I want
ou to realize that Philip is *missing,* and not simply
etained. He's been absent for three days, and I've
bund nothing, not a trace of my twin. Nor do the
ervants know anything of his whereabouts. Yester-
ay afternoon I went to his wing of the house and
nocked on his bedroom door. When he did not
nswer, I took the liberty of entering his room. On
is bed was an open valise—half filled. Some of his
lothing was still folded on the bed, as if he had
een interrupted in the act of packing." A small
rown puckered her eyebrows. "Philip rarely travels,

and when he does, it is usually with me. I began t
go through his portmanteau, and came across th
chamois bag with the gems—and you can imagin
my shock."

"Why hadn't the servants learned of his disap
pearance before you did?"

"Because," she said, leaning forward conspirator
ally, "Philip told Charles, his valet, and the maid
that he wanted to be left in peace. That isn't s
uncommon. He keeps odd hours, and, sometimes
very odd company. You see—" She paused, reluc
tant to share the information she knew she must i
order to find her brother. "Philip's a gambler. Yo
know—he frequents the gaming halls, places bets—
all of it."

O'Connor made a low sound in his throa
"Why?"

"You ask that question a good deal, don't yo
Mr. O'Connor?" When his gaze narrowed on he
she hurried on. "And a very good question it is in
deed!" She flipped her hands up in a careless ges
ture and said, "Philip likes to take risks."

"Well," O'Connor drawled, his gaze flicking t
the magnificent stones on his desk. "I'd say he too
a very calculated risk this time." He took a sip c
whiskey, watching her over the rim of the glass. "T
whom do they belong?"

Eden decided she did not like his tone
She straightened, looking directly into his eyes. "
know as little about those gems as you do, M
O'Connor."

"Is your brother a jewel thief, Mrs. Lindsay?"

Though Eden tightened her jaw, she had to thin
about it. "I certainly hope not, Mr. O'Connor." H
was watching her so intently, she felt compelled t
add, "But he could be."

Shane's dark brows drew together. He took an-
her swallow of whiskey, then set the glass down
d walked toward her. "You, Mrs. Lindsay, are sit-
g on a potential powder keg. How did you get
re?"

She looked startled. "Why, I took the ferry. A
vely—"

"And no one followed you?"

"Well, I don't know. I . . ."

Shane compressed his lips into a tight line. She
s more reckless than he'd thought. "You're lucky
one has seemed to caught on to the fact that you
e in possession of the gems. When they do—" He
t himself off. "Well, you're here now, and alive."

ry much alive. Vibrantly, exquisitely, lusciously
ve. Purposely, he kept his gaze on her face so he
uldn't be distracted by her lushly curved body.
er face was a lure in itself, though. Annoyed by his
raction to her, he concentrated on her brother.
o Philip is a gambler and a jewel thief—"

She glared at him. "You cannot assume that!"

He inclined his head toward her, his attitude
ntly deprecating. Still, he respected that she stood
r ground. She was not the whining, simpering,
ak-spined ninny he'd initially thought her.
'rue," he said. "Never assume." She gave him a
lf-satisfied smile, and he hid the unwilling twitch
his own lips as he half sat on the edge of his desk.
Iowever, we know that he's involved somehow
th the jewels. But that may not be why he is miss-
g. His disappearance *might* be connected to gaming, or something else entirely. Does he owe
oney to anyone?"

"Always."

He stared at her. "You sound certain about that."

She nodded. "My mother disinherited him for his

lack of . . . good judgment. And—" She bit h
upper lip. When it slipped free of her teeth she
out a resigned little sigh. "Philip's debts had becon
so great, he turned to lenders of money. Have y
ever heard of El Dagger? Or Sly Camponelli? (
Stealth MacGuire?"

"*All* of them?"

She nodded miserably.

Shane considered her carefully. She looked t
embarrassed to be lying. "Rough crowd," he mu
mured.

She smiled weakly at him. "Yes," she admitte
"but I've never known Philip to do anything"—s
paused, giving Shane a tentative glance—"*un
vory.*"

"Like gamble?" he said, and almost smiled at h
indignant expression.

"*Every* man has some vice, Mr. O'Connor. *Sor*
men," she added pointedly, "have several."

This time he had to lower his head to hide h
smile, and when he caught sight of her bare fo
tapping the carpet, he could only stare. "You'
missing a shoe," he said, "and stocking." And l
was shocked to realize the sight of her slim, elega
foot was arousing him to an uncomfortable degre

She lifted her foot, studying it as she pointed h
toes toward him. "I know. I didn't have a chance
put them on and was forced to leave them behind
the copse of trees where I fell."

"You fell?"

"Yes, that wall is rather high, you know." S
smoothed her skirts and tucked her slim foot und
her petticoats again. "It was very difficult to scale

"That's the point."

She shrugged. "I was able to get only one sh

," she further explained, "when your horrid man-
rvant—"

"Simon," Shane interrupted, unable to under-
and why he felt like laughing when she managed to
thoroughly annoy him.

"Yes," she said. "Simon. When he seized me and,
knifepoint, dragged me here, much to my acute
nbarrassment."

"You mean—with *your* knife."

Her eyes widened. "Oh, yes. *My* knife." She
emed to have forgotten that part. She shrugged.
Well, I'll have to retrieve my belongings on my way
it of here."

There was a discreet knock on the door. Shane
ist an irritated glance that way, then leaned across
e desk to open the top drawer and place the gems
side. Straightening, he called for the intruder to
iter. His butler swept open the doors and an-
ounced, "I apologize for disturbing you, sir. Miss
atricia Alexander is here to see you."

Shane nodded curtly. "Show her into the sitting
om, Spencer. And tell Jamie to come in."

Jamie, one of his guards, stepped into the room.
e was a huge man, at least six feet four inches tall,
d muscle-bound. He looked like a Viking, fierce
d mighty, with pistols strapped to his chest and
aist.

"Please escort Mrs. Lindsay off the grounds, Ja-
ie," Shane said. When Eden whirled on her chair
look at him, he continued, his gaze remaining on
e guard. "Make certain she's safe."

"Yes, sir."

"But—" Eden felt a wild panic. She stood, her
nees weak, a hopeless, sinking sensation in her mid-
le. Was he just going to dismiss her? She could see
at he was becoming cold and unapproachable

once more as he crossed the room to the doors. [
was something he could do quite effectively, almo
as if he were able to erect a shield of ice arou
himself. And no amount of chipping away at it cou
melt him. But melting people was one of the thin
Eden did best. He just *had* to take the case.

Desperation made her go to him. She swept acro
the room and grasped his hard forearm, feeling t
steely muscles flex beneath her fingertips. "M
O'Connor—"

His icy eyes silenced her before he spoke harsh
"Let go of my arm and back up to the desk."

She recoiled, feeling as though she had just con
mitted a crass breach of etiquette. Jamie quick
made his exit, leaving her to settle the matter p
vately with Shane. She backed up only a few pac
unable to move any farther.

"If I decide to take the case," O'Connor conti
ued tightly, "I will inform you within twenty-fo
hours."

There was hope! Eden immediately brightened

"In the meantime," he said brusquely, "do not
back into your twin's room, and instruct the servan
to keep out also. Nothing more should be disturbe
There are several possibilities here. If someone a
ducted Philip for the jewels, he's going to be awa
by now that Philip does not have them in his posse
sion. And that means they will be looking for the
—and one of the most logical places is Philip's re
dence. Also yours."

Shane was growing increasingly annoyed by t
moment. He had given this woman more th
enough of his valuable time, yet he was now alertin
her to the dangers and risks to which her broth
had exposed her, while his beautiful mistress w
waiting for him—most likely with indignant imp

tience—in the sitting room. Why did he feel this protective sense for a woman he hardly knew? A damned exasperating woman too.

"I want you to make a list," he continued, "of all the people who might be connected to your brother's sudden disappearance. Your brother," he murmured, "associates with the most dangerous men in town."

She sighed. "I know."

Shane frowned as he watched her push a thick strand of hair from her eyes. She knew this, yet was risking her neck for him. "It is very noble of you to want to find your brother," he said, and watched her brighten. He saw that she rather fancied the idea of nobility. He kept his own expression neutral, though he, once again, felt that infernal urge to smile. "However, you have also behaved with reckless stupidity."

Her expression swiftly changed to one of affront, and he lifted a dark eyebrow at her.

"You dispute the fact?" he asked. "Carrying those priceless gems with you and riding the ferry unguarded, then throwing yourself over the wall of my heavily armed estate was not exactly a cautious plan. And in the future, madame, I would, if I were you, have a man tend to your affairs. At least those of this nature."

Her eyes flashed at him. He'd obviously stoked her temper. "A man!" she cried as if that were a most unseemly notion. "Why should I have a man do what I am perfectly capable of doing? I got here, didn't I? I managed to be granted the honor of your time, and I secured your services!"

"Not yet, you haven't." He leveled a hard stare on her.

"If I decide not to take the case, I will send Simon

to your home tomorrow evening—with the jewels. It's much safer if I hold them for now. And if I do take the case—"

She cut him off. "Please," she said. "Send anyone but Simon."

He ignored her request. "If I *do* take your case," he repeated, walking toward her, "it will cost you forty thousand dollars—to start."

She looked horrified, as he'd expected, and he smiled with satisfaction.

"I expect only twenty as a retainer," he added, and felt her stiffen as he slid his hand under her elbow, intent on escorting her out of his study.

"Only is right!" she said, startling him and jerking her arm from his grip. "Is that all my twin is worth to you? I would think you would want to charge at *least* fifty thousand—"

Shane stared down at her, convinced she was demented. "Madame, forty thousand dollars is no small sum. If you'd rather pay it all up front, I'll allow it, but—"

"No, no. Never mind." She tossed her head. "I know when I've been insulted."

Usually when women babbled like idiots, Shane, a practiced seducer, knew exactly how to silence them. This one he wanted to throttle. *And* kiss into sweet surrender. She was infuriating, yet fascinating. Standing so close to her, he was suddenly intensely aware of her scent—heady lily-of-the-valley—and he found himself wondering where she had put it on her skin, where he would like to run his tongue over it. An explosive heat poured through his body, and he cursed its staggering power. It was intolerable that she could produce such a savage response in him. She was outlandish, bombastic, extravagant. Shane loathed superficiality in anyone almost as much as he loathed weakness of character. He could not stand hypocrisy either, and because of her high-born station, so opposite from his own, he was determined to find those faults in her, determined not to like her.

Yet, she was wild, vibrant, free. He had labeled her reckless and stupid, but her very dauntlessness stoked admiration in him. He found himself wanting to test her, perhaps as he already had with that comment about letting men handle her affairs, just to see how she would respond, yet he felt a sense of self-contempt for wanting to bother with her at all. Irritated with himself, he tightened his lips and asked her where on Fifth Avenue she lived.

"Just north of Fifty-second Street—"

"Near the Vanderbilts?"

"Why, yes! I'm sure," she added softly, "you will make the right decision."

And then she was gone.

Guilt! She was attempting to manipulate him into taking the case through guilt. Frowning, he crossed the room in long strides, finding he needed a few moments alone before he faced his current mistress. He poured himself another shot of whiskey, his eyes narrowing thoughtfully as he stared into the glass. Something about Eden's spirited appeal for assistance tugged at him. She was doing this for her brother, after all, and Shane could understand how a person would do just about anything for his or her family. But then, he had learned never take a woman at face value. Eden Victoria Lindsay needed to be investigated.

He raised his glass to the light, watching the liquid glint in the sun, before tossing the whole shot to the back of his throat.

Still, even the smooth Irish whiskey couldn't erase

his frown. He was surprised at the intensity of the impression she had left on him. It was not so much physical—he had encountered many stunning women in his life. But she was . . . different. True, her seductive looks pulled at him, but it was not merely that. It was her fire. When she moved, light seemed to follow her, shimmering in her wake, even after she had left the room. Her scent lingered now in the gentle breeze. Who was she—really? A dramatic, disarming creature, and could this all be a setup? There were plenty who wanted his hide. Might she work for long-time enemies of his, might she not be a lure? She was a damned powerful one to be sure, he thought, cursing the effect she'd had on him.

Even if he didn't take the case—and that was a strong possibility—he wanted to learn more about her. If she had been sent to kill him and failed, he wanted to know that. He had been set up before by a woman, and he vowed it would never happen again. His fingers tightened on his glass.

"Simon!" he barked.

Simon, never far from hearing range, appeared in the doorway. "Sir?"

"Follow her."

It was hot, infernally sticky-hot. Even by evening, when the sun was setting in a burst of red and Eden had reached the theater, slightly late for her rehearsal, the heat had not subsided. Here, in the city, there was no breath of fresh salt air, no balmy sea breeze to relieve the sweltering heat.

Worriedly, she caught her bottom lip between her teeth and opened the stage door. Warm, musty air enveloped her, stirred only by the rotating wooden fans overhead. As she made her way down the narrow hallway to the dressing rooms, she could hear the muffled voices of her fellow performers onstage as they rehearsed. She knew she'd better hurry, or she'd delay them all. After all, she thought ruefully, it was difficult to perform *Lysistrata* when Lysistrata was nowhere in sight.

All she could think about, though, was Philip. And Shane O'Connor. Would he take the case? She could not bear it if he did not. She felt pressed, as if time were crushing the breath from her. *Where was Philip?* Had someone killed him? No! The thought was too awful even to be suggested.

Blinking hard to staunch the tears that scalded her eyes, Eden pushed open the door to her dressing room. She inhaled deeply, and the familiar smell of greasepaint embraced her like an old friend. She did not have to change clothes to rehearse, yet she set down her carpetbag and fumbled around inside it for her hairbrush. The ferry ride had mussed her hair, and she needed a good face-scrubbing again. Peering at her mirrored reflection, she decided she could use a bit of color in her cheeks too. As she found her brush, her hand touched the papers she had stuffed into her bag before she had started for O'Connor's residence. Along with the jewels, she had discovered the papers, tied with a ribbon, but she hadn't had the chance to peruse them. She had been back on the ferry before she'd remembered them, and by then, of course, it had been too late to show them to O'Connor. Oh, well, he had the jewels, and that was enough. If he took the case, she'd show him the papers later. If he was such a fine detective, he didn't need anything more anyway, she thought petulantly.

"Twenty thousand dollars! Hmmph!" She unpinned her hair and let it fall, and remembered suddenly how O'Connor had looked at her as she fixed her hair in his study. He was so intense a man, dominant, confident, and assured. And decidedly, one of the most vital, virile creatures she had ever seen. Even his aloofness added to his forceful magnetism. She was certain that not only was he immensely masterful in the field of investigation, but in the boudoirs of women as well. Just thinking about him caused a curious trembling in her mid-region, and never much impressed by any man, she wondered at the tremulous feelings he unleashed in her.

She also wondered if she had unleashed any such feelings in him. He was so unreadable, she'd bet that if he were a gambling man, he'd be the type to wager several thousand dollars without a flicker of emotion on his face. Sighing, she leaned forward to dab color on her high cheekbones, and found that she was frowning. On her way out of O'Connor house she had noticed the "appointment" for whom he'd all but shoved her out. Patricia Alexander was a voluptuous, raven-haired beauty with grand violet eyes and creamy skin. Well, if *that* was what it took to get the man's attention . . .

"You Lysistrata?"

Eden jumped, screamed, and whirled.

The woman who'd had the misfortune to interrupt Eden's musings clapped a hand to heart and leapt back a foot herself. "Gawd a'mighty! Jump back into your skin, would you?"

Eden stared at the young woman, tall and slender, with cinnamon-colored hair that was gilded throughout with long, individual blond strands. Her eyes were enormous, pale green and dark-fringed. She stood with her back to the door, palms flat gainst the panels. Eden had never seen her before. Who are you?"

"I'm Myrrhine—or, rather, I'm playing the part of Myrrhine."

Eden blinked. "Where's Mary?" Mary was the actress this woman was apparently replacing.

The young woman shrugged. "I heard she was called to her ailing uncle's bedside up in Boston. They needed a replacement for her."

Curious, Eden studied the newcomer. She was about Eden's age, even slimmer, but with a high, full bustline and a gamin's face that was at once both mischievous and appealing. Her mouth was long and full, and her nose, though definitely feminine, was marred by a slight bump just under the bridge, as if it might have been broken. Her eyes were truly extraordinary, and, as if she were uncomfortable under Eden's scrutiny, she dropped her gaze to the pots of paint on the dressing table. What an interesting face! Eden thought. She could play a variety of parts with such striking features.

"You don't need the paint," the woman said in a soft, husky voice. She glanced up to Eden again. "You've got color enough."

She had a slight English accent, and Eden was enchanted. "Have you ever lived in England?"

The young woman's gaze sharpened. "How'd you know?"

Eden shrugged. "I'm half English—my mother still lives in London."

The woman hunched a shoulder at her. "The director is looking for you. Blimey, but he's good-looking."

Eden laughed. "That's Franklin. Yes, isn't he?"

"Well, he sent me back here to look for you. He seems in a dither that you're not onstage."

"Franklin is rather dramatic! Come." She looped her arm through the young woman's and felt her stiffen. Eden only laughed again and pulled open the door. "What's your real name, Myrrhine?"

"My nickname's Sparrow," she muttered as they walked down the narrow hallway. "You can call me that."

"Sparrow!"

"That's right. When I was a kid I was very skinny. Other kids used to tease me about it and called me Sparrow. So that's my stage name." Eden raised her eyebrows. "No surname?"

Sparrow laughed, a low, rich laugh that to Eden sounded mysterious. "None," she said. "And that's how I like it."

"Well," Eden said, smiling as they entered the right wing offstage, "though I'll miss Mary, I'm certain you'll make a lovely Myrrhine. Welcome."

Sparrow looked startled, then she sent Eden an arch look and glanced across the stage. Eden followed her gaze toward Franklin. "And," Sparrow said, "somebody thinks *you* make a lovely Lysistrata."

Eden had to smile. It was true; Franklin thought she could do no wrong. When he caught sight of her he rushed forward to take both of her hands in his. *"Darling,"* he all but purred, "where have you been?" Eden grinned at him. "I had an appointment, *darling.*"

The handsome, curly-haired director flushed. He was blatantly enamored of his leading lady. "Only a few minutes late, but the show must go on."

"I'm sorry," Eden apologized. "It was rather an emergency." She cast the onstage actors an apologetic smile. "I'm ready now."

But she wasn't, not really. They rehearsed for

ours, and Franklin, who never became exasperated
with Eden, was actually tugging his hair by ten
o'clock. She had faltered too many times over her
lines, had missed cues, had spoken before her turn.
Her mind was obviously elsewhere.

"Let's call it a night," Franklin finally said. "And
let's go to Max's Café and get something to eat."

The thespian life-style she led allowed her unlimited liberty, and this was one benefit Eden fully appreciated. Though by Society's standards she was
one of their own, she was, in her heart, a true free
spirit. With most of the cast she headed for an open
café on Broadway, where they sat outdoors and
sipped wine, nibbled on fish and crackers, and chat-
ted and laughed as small public stagecoaches rattled
up and down the stone-paved street. Eden had her
own carriage and driver parked alongside the café,
and her friends affectionately teased her about her
"high station" and pampered ways. Still, they were
aware of the dangers the young heiress could draw
to herself simply because of her station and curious,
liberated life-style.

That night, though, Eden was not her usual radiant self. They could all see that she was troubled,
though she tried to hide her glum spirits with her
smile. At last Franklin, leaning close, whispered,
"What is it, little sugar-angel?"

Eden smiled at his endearment. "Oh, Franklin,
not to worry. I'm certain my troubles will evaporate
by the end of the week." She spoke with much more
confidence than she felt, but she didn't want to ruin
the others' evening. "I promise you I will be in fine
form at tomorrow's rehearsal."

A couple of hours past midnight Franklin set her
in her carriage, kissed her cheek, and sent her home,

with the reminder that if she needed a friend to tal
to, he would be glad to assist her in any way.

By the time the carriage rolled up to her three
story mansion on Fifth Avenue, Eden was ha
asleep. Tilton, the driver, helped her alight. Sh
waved him off drowsily, then went up the wide
graceful front steps, slid her key into the lock, an
slipped inside to the spacious front hall. Because c
her late hours, she had an understanding with th
servants not to wait up for her, and all she had to d
was tug a bell cord if she needed to summon he
maid.

She tiptoed up the long staircase and down th
thickly carpeted hallway to her bedchamber, the
pushed open the door. She froze at the sight tha
greeted her. Her bedroom suite had been ransackec
Furniture had been turned over, drawers had bee
yanked out, and the clothing that spilled from ther
looked like startled ghosts in the pale moonlight tha
shafted in through her open window. There the cu
tains billowed, and Eden's heart pounded. Was th
intruder lurking out on the balcony? Alarm bur
geoning inside her, she raced to the window an
slammed it shut. In the stillness she stared in horro
at the debris strewn across the floor and on the bec
Precious figurines had been shattered, books ha
been hurled, and it appeared that every piece of jew
elry she owned—including her grandmother's pear
earrings—were gone.

Eden let out a little cry. She felt violated to he
core, as if hot knives had slashed her insides, he
heart. On shaky legs she walked over to her dresse
and ran her fingertips over the bare top, staring i
numbed disbelief at the violent mess around her.

"The only 'ladies' I know that run about this tim
of morning," drawled a deep voice from the shad

y depths of her room, "are strumpets, courtesans,
d entertainers. Which of the three are you?"

Jarred bone-deep by the insulting words, Eden
un to face the intruder. A tall, wide-shouldered
an loomed like Lucifer in one corner of her room.
e screamed. And screamed and screamed. She
dn't even know she *was* screaming until she felt
m behind her, his callused hand clapping over her
outh.

"Quiet, you little fool!" he whispered near her
r. "Do you want to rouse the servants?" When she
uggled against him, he tightened his grip. "It's
e," he said through his teeth. "O'Connor!"

Immediately Eden stilled. Her first impulse was to
ng her arms around his neck with immense relief,
it, of course, that would not do. Even if she were
inclined, he spilled her from his arms as if she
ere contaminated. She saw that he was breathing
rd, but his quick movements had hardly exerted
m, she was sure. And then she realized she was
eathing rapidly too. Perhaps it had something to
 with the fact that she still felt the impact of his
anite-muscled body against her back and bottom,
s heat pressed into her like a seductive second
in. Even his scent clung to her, a subtle tang of
icy cologne that was utterly male.

His narrowed eyes gleamed a light silver in the
oonlit room. They measured each other like cats at
ating time, but before either of them could speak,
ere was a rapid knocking at her door.

"Miss Eden! Miss Eden!" her maid called franti-
lly. "Are you in peril?"

Eden darted a glance at Shane, who merely lifted
 eyebrow at her. "No, Alice!" she called. "I—I'm
acticing for a role!" She ignored Shane's expres-

sion as *both* his eyebrows shot up in admiration f
her improvisation.

"Do you need me, miss?"

"No, Alice, I'm fine, really. I apologize—I did n
mean to alarm you." She shot another look at Shan
"I'll scream more quietly now."

They heard Alice's footsteps retreat down t
hallway, and Eden turned to Shane again, who w
staring at her with amusement. "That will be inte
esting to witness. How, may I ask, does a pers
scream quietly?"

Eden shrugged. "My servants understand my ha
its."

He considered this, then his face tightene
"What the hell, woman, were you doing out at th
hour? I thought your rehearsal was finished hou
ago."

Eden narrowed her eyes at him. "You know! Y
know I'm an actress!"

He was silent.

Incensed, she strode over to him, putting her fa
up close to his. The pearly moonlight glanced off t
slanting planes of his face, the high, harsh chee
bones. He stared down at her implacably, his ey
glowing like a cat's.

"There was no reason," she said, "for your earli
remark about courtesans and entertainers. You we
spying on me!" A smile flickered across his mout
"Spying is my business."

She let her gaze rake over him. "Oh, yes, ho
could I forget? And is it your business, too, to hi
in women's bedrooms?"

Only the slight narrowing of his eyes revealed th
he even considered her pointed barb. Eden foun
his proximity so disturbing, she moved away to lig
the small glass lamp on the night table. When sl

ed back to face him, she couldn't help but stare.
was stunning in elegant evening attire of raven
k, including his waistcoat and cravat. Only his
ted white shirt broke the severity of his clothing,
it contrasted sharply against his bronzed skin.
hands were in his pockets, and the light illu-
ed him in mellow gold, touching the same soft
l in his dark hair.

Why are you in my room?" she demanded. "You
uldn't be up here at all."

Jot in the habit of explaining himself, Shane
vned. "Earlier this evening I had a dinner en-
ement. Simon was actually the one spying on
, and he sent word to me about your . . . er,
iation to the theater. My curiosity got the better
ne, and I came here—"

I'm sure your 'engagement' appreciated that,"
interrupted with wry humor.

Ie ignored that. "I'm in your room, madame, to
more spying—to watch your reaction to this
os. I assume you were escorted back here after
r . . . rehearsal?" His tone implied he doubted
had been rehearsing all this time, but her gaze
left his to survey the damage in the lamplight.
sank slowly to the edge of her bed, staring at the
ris around her.

My God," she mumbled, "who could have done
?"

Good question. I—"

Ie stopped as Eden fell supine across her bed.
ne felt every muscle in his body tense as his gaze
pped to her rounded breasts, pushed up entic-
y against her décolletage. He tore his stare from
tempting sight, sure she was trying to manipulate
in some way. But to his shock he saw that she
crying. Not hysterical sobbing as he might have

expected from such a dramatic creature, but qui
her eyes closed, tears slipping from beneath
thick lashes.

Shane stared helplessly. Emotional scenes
gusted him, and tears were the worst emoti
scene with which a woman manipulated a man.
evitably tears drew a cold reaction from him.
Eden was crying as softly and openly as a child,
in all honesty, he could see it had nothing to do
him. He felt his chest constrict with the odd nee
take her in his arms and soothe her, just as he wo
a child.

She sat up suddenly, though, before he even ha
chance to resist the urge to go to her. Damn, but
was unpredictable! He watched her sweep ac
the room to her bureau and riffle through one of
drawers.

"How *could* they?" she exclaimed, and raked
hands through her hair. "How could they
Rake's gold watch?"

"Rake?"

She spun around, her eyes glittering with te
"My grandfather. He gave me the watch as a ke
sake."

Her gaze drifted out the window, and Sh
stared at her in bemusement.

She was a study of contrasts, to be sure. That
was an actress too disturbed him. In his experier
women came fully equipped with guile and wi
and this woman was most likely well practiced at
art of those distasteful qualities. He tightened
jaw as he wondered again if she was toying v
him? She could have conjured many a scheme
whatever reasons suited her. He did not trust I
and he had come there with every intention of t
ing her that he was *not* going to take her case.

le'd found this destruction, though, and, despite
better judgment, waited for her. For hours. What
d of mad creature was she to test the stringent
rictions placed upon females of society? A
nan of her class and station a common stage per-
ner? He was quickly learning that she was in-
ely individual and not the most exemplary
del of conventionality. A troublemaker. A woman
caused people to gossip about her—and who
n't care. All of this intrigued him. He started
ard her.

tartled out of her reverie, Eden glanced at him as
le had suddenly made up her mind about some-
g. "You'll have to leave," she said. "In fact, you
st admit, Mr. O'Connor, that your presence in
bedroom is extremely . . . forward . . . and
nd—" She swallowed as he continued his ap-
ach, moving with a quiet power, that animal
ce. Compelled by the stark intensity of his being,
whole attention focused on her face, Eden went
still as a statue, waiting . . . for she knew not
at.

le stopped just a foot from her, and she felt en-
ped in heat. His eyes burned on her. She
pped her own gaze and caught sight of a pearl-
dled pistol he'd stuffed into the waistband of his
sers. Her mouth went dry.

I have a note," he said quietly.

ler gaze jumped back to his. "A note?"

le nodded. "The intruder left a note."

Well, let me read it."

That's my job, not yours."

ler heart leapt. Was he taking her case? "But if
y left it for me, why can't I read it?"

What would you have done if you had come
n the intruder?"

She tossed her head. "If I had had my bowie
your faithful assistant stole from me, I would
used it, of course."

"Then you're more of a reckless little fool th
thought."

Eden drew in a sharp breath. "You may thinl
Mr. O'Connor, but I do plan to retrieve my b
knife. And I do have every right to read that ne
She hated a mystery. She liked everything to be
ble, where she could examine every facet. She th
her hand out, waiting for him to give her the n

O'Connor, however, had no intention of r
quishing it. "The note," he said, "is merely a
mand for the gems. And since they didn't find
gems here, the abductors will be after you."

"Well, then there really is no reason why I
have a look at that note, is there?"

His stare was chilling.

She sighed. "On the other hand, I can wait."
she glanced at his splendidly tailored black jac
wondering how she could search his pockets v
out his taking offense. It wasn't right that he'd
ten his hands on the note meant for her and
keeping it from her. Just who did he think he
Realizing abruptly what he had said, she lookec
at him again. "Abductors?"

"Someone," O'Connor said with exaggerated
tience, "is holding Philip hostage."

Eden bit her lip and squeezed her eyes shut
to deny his words.

"And if they had found you here," he contin
inexorably, "there is no telling what they might
done to you. I really don't see, Mrs. Lindsay,
you and your bowie could have defended your li

She opened her eyes and blinked at him. He re
was a supercilious know-it-all, she thought.

hen, he *was* unable to make a sound judgment on her knife-wielding abilities. She had been taught how to use her knife by an Apache. "Rattlesnake would not appreciate your lack of faith in my prowess."

"Rattlesnake—" Shane couldn't even begin to fathom her incomprehensible response. He shook his head and brought his hand up to rub the knotted muscles at the back of his neck. Most women would have gone into a dead faint at the merest suggestion of murder. She was an anomaly. And what was this cursed responsibility he felt to protect her? For the love of God, he had just met the woman. Perhaps it was because she was so damned trusting and could so easily walk straight into an ambush. She hadn't a lick of horse sense, and no doubt would get herself neatly caught within hours if he didn't take her case. But he didn't need her hanging like an albatross around his neck either. What in the hell was she doing, staying out until two in the morning? It was amazing she hadn't gotten herself killed before now.

Her voice interrupted his thoughts. "Please leave, Mr. O'Connor. I'd like to be alone for now."

Dangerous notion. Shane gritted his teeth as she turned from him and her scent, sweet and intoxicating, drifted to his nostrils. He felt a cold displeasure at the sudden course of his thoughts. Dammit, *no,* he told himself fiercely. She was spoiled, and pampered—and absurdly dauntless. He'd be a fool to take her case, to become involved with her on any level. His instincts screamed an alarm in his head *not* to take her case, yet he found himself reaching for her, his fingers closing around her slender wrist. He tugged her close, ignoring her little cry of protest.

"You," he said, a steely thread of warning in his voice, "are coming back with me."

CHAPTER THREE

"ARE YOU OUT OF YOUR MIND?" EDEN WAS ALMOST yelling as Shane pushed her, struggling and indignant, ahead of him into the luxurious confines of his carriage. "I cannot come and live with you in your home!"

He ignored her protests and nudged her back against the soft leather squabs, then settled onto the seat beside her.

Yes, Shane thought as the carriage started off. He *was* out of his mind—unequivocally, categorically insane to be taking her with him. How else could he explain his throwing clothes into a valise for this woman, then all but carrying her out of her house while warning her baffled servants—politely, of course—not to interfere? From the start she had thrown him off center, and now he questioned his objectivity. The very notion that he was questioning his motives unsettled him, for he was never given to self-doubt. The uneasy feeling settled like acid in his gut. And she was storming like a summer squall beside him.

"I could have you arrested!"

"You could."

"This is totally improper!"

"Most likely it is." He glanced at her in the shadowy coach. "But somehow I don't think you're overly concerned with what is proper and what isn't."

Eden glared at him, thinking how the light of the carriage lamps cast his harsh features into diabolic contours. "You can't force me to come with you."

"You've been forced," he said, his voice quiet and dry.

She couldn't argue with his logic. She settled down, but popped upright again, nearly elbowing him in the ribs when she realized that they were headed for the docks, and he was truly bent on absconding her to his home. Dismayed, she said, "Sir, surely you cannot carry this farce to completion! Please, I beg you, turn this coach around this minute. We hardly know each other. This is a ludicrous plan—" Suddenly a thought came to her, and she brightened. "Besides, the ferry is not running at this hour."

"I have my own boat and slip." He stretched out his long legs and settled back for the ride. He looked so unaffected by her distress that Eden wanted to punch him!

She was silent for a few minutes, then said calmly. "Well, this is good news."

Her complete turnabout clearly caught him off guard. Almost warily, he asked, "*What* is good news?"

"It's obvious, since you will be harboring me in your home, that you will be taking the case."

He grunted, but he didn't dispute her.

"And more good news."

He glanced at her.

"I'll be getting my bowie back."

He smiled faintly. "You'll have to wrestle Simon for it."

"I'm very good at wrestling." She caught his look of surprise, and his reaction pleased her. It showed, at least, that he was paying attention. Suddenly a carriage wheel hit a pothole, throwing her off balance, and she lurched against him, gripping his hard thigh. She felt his muscles flex beneath her fingers and drew her hand back as if stricken.

"Sorry," she muttered, thankful that he couldn't see her flushed face. He was so male! She felt a strange desire to curl against him, to give in to the compelling power and heat he emanated. Glancing at him, she saw a hint of sardonic amusement in his eyes and quickly looked away. She stared out the window until the docks came into view.

When the carriage stopped, he swung out of it with a lazy grace that entranced her. He reached for her, and before she could protest, he grasped her by the waist and lifted her down. As soon as her feet touched ground she started her protests again. "Mr. O'Connor, I insist you take me home." Her legs were slightly unsteady as he pulled her forward, curling his long, powerful fingers around her upper

m. "There is no need for you to bring me to your
tate—"

He stopped suddenly, and she stumbled against
m, feeling as though she had run into a mountain
rock. In the pale moonlight his face looked as if it
ere etched in rock, his lips a straight, compressed
e. "The decision," he said, "has been made. Now,
) you want me to find your brother or not?"

Properly chastised, she lowered her gaze. "I do."

"Then you come with me."

He turned abruptly and helped her into the boat.
ne armed driver, gripping her valise in one hand,
llowed, and soon they set sail, off to the island.
nere was a slight breeze, and the bow of the boat
ade a soft slicing sound as it parted the dark wa-
rs.

"Now that we're comfortable," Eden said, settling
rself on the hard seat, "tell me, sir, do you have a
an?"

Shane stared at her. "A plan?"

"Yes. You know, to get my brother back."

His gaze flickered over her upturned, expectant
ce. She had to be joking. "I will," he said dryly.

She looked disappointed. "You mean you don't
ve one yet? Well, how can you expect any help
om me if you haven't even formulated a plan?"

He gave her a wintry smile. "I promise you, Mrs.
ndsay, if I need your assistance, I will ask for it."

She settled back with her arms crossed over her
iest, looking a little petulant. "I don't see how I
n be of any assistance at all if I don't know what's
that note."

He was incredulous. Did she ever give up? "Go to
eep."

"I will not. I want to see the note."

Shane glanced at the armed driver, then, in a de-

liberate snub, leaned back in his seat, stretched o
his legs, and closed his eyes. He adopted the ind
lent pose simply to silence her, and most peop
would have obliged him. But not this one. He cou
sense her temper sizzling and he almost laughed
himself. Damn, but she had spirit.

She nudged his booted foot with her toe. "I
not believe for a moment, Mr. O'Connor, that y
are asleep."

He folded his arms across his chest, continuing
ignore her. Though he knew he appeared lazy an
relaxed, his senses were keenly attuned to the sligh
est noise or movement. That was why he w
stunned to feel her hands upon him, searching h
pockets. Disbelief made every muscle in him tighte
No one ever caught him unaware. Worse, his bo
was responding to her touch, impersonal as it wa
and he felt heat ignite in him like a hot flare, searir
him from the inside out.

His hand lashed out to grasp her wrist. Staring
her, he snarled, "What the hell do you think you'
doing?"

Eden tried to twist away from his powerful gri
then froze when the driver whirled, his gun draw
Not only was she stricken by the sight of the gu
pointed at her, but her heart pounded with alarm
the cold fury in O'Connor's face. His anger co
fused her.

He jerked his head toward the driver, who lov
ered his gun, then looked back at her, his eyes na
rowed and glittering. "You're lucky," he said in
low, furious voice, "I didn't draw my gun. I usual
shoot first, ask questions later."

They stared at each other. The night was so siler
they could hear the other breathe. Only the stars ar

moonlight dabbed their faces with light, giving
m both an odd, phantomlike glow.

"You're wise, then," Eden whispered, "to have
yed unmarried. How unfortunate it would be for
ır wife to reach for you in the night and find
rself shot."

She thought she glimpsed a flash of humor in his
es, but it was quickly gone.

"Fortunate indeed," he murmured. "For more
ısons than one."

He released her wrist, and she rubbed it, her gaze
ched to his. "Mr. O'Connor, there must be more
ıst between us."

"Trust?" He uttered the word as if he had never
ard it before and did not know its meaning.

"Yes, trust! You can't suspect every action I take,
ery word I say. I assure you I am no more danger-
s to you than a flea, yet you seem to think I pose
serious a threat to you as any criminal might. You
ll just have to get over that fear. You can't expect
: to work with you if you continue to jump at me
every tiny transgression!"

"I don't expect you to work with me. I ask you
estions, and you answer them. That is the extent
your input." At her disgruntled expression he
ıwled. "Now get some sleep."

She stretched like a cat and felt his body stiffen
ce again. "I'm really not all that tired."

"That wasn't a suggestion. It was an order."

Eden sighed. He really was much too sure of him-
f—a characteristic she thought he might need to
ep in check. She told him so, then added, "Sir,
ı cannot *order* a person to go to sleep!" She al-
ıst laughed at the absurd notion. "One falls asleep
nply when they are tired, and not on command."

He rubbed his eyes with one hand. "It is three-

thirty in the morning," he said tightly. "You've be
back and forth between the city and the island on
already, and now you're headed back again. I'm te
ing you, woman, get to sleep!"

Now he had her ire up. She ignored the sudd
interest they had drawn from the driver and angl
away from Shane on the seat. Putting her hands
her hips, she prepared to give him a piece of h
mind. "Sir, I did not pay you good money so y
could boss me any which way you please, any fi
time you like. Now I demand that you stop treati
me as though I am a schoolgirl and let me fall asle
when I wish—not a moment before! I'm sorry I ca
not oblige you by feeling the slightest bit weary, b
I just do not."

For a moment the only sound was the gentle sl
of the water against the boat. Then O'Connor sa
in a low, taut voice, "You're right."

Eden straightened her spine, pleased that she w
right about something. But what? Her brow fu
rowed in a confused frown. "What am I rig
about?"

"You did not pay me good money. You have n
paid me any money at all."

She digested this. "Well, there goes my argumer
but I still insist you treat me with more understan
ing. I cannot fall asleep on command. And I will p
you the first chance I get."

"I'm not concerned about it."

"You should be. What if I have no intention
paying you—"

"I have the gems as collateral."

"But they're not mine!"

"Rest assured, though I am taking you to n
home, I do not do any cases out of charity. You w

ay, for your coming to stay at my estate is strictly
or professional purposes."

She smiled, happy he had no ulterior motives. Yet
he had second thoughts when he shifted beside her
nd his iron-hard thigh pressed intimately to hers.
he felt scorched, on fire. Her body was suddenly
iffused with a delicious yet alarming heat.

O'Connor seemed oblivious of what his touch did
> her, though. He'd settled back again, as cool as
iountain water on a summer day, and seemed to
ave completely forgotten her presence—or hoped
>. But Eden felt jumpy, his musky, cologne-tinged
:ent driving her to distraction, and she fidgeted on
ie seat.

"Stop that," he said after a few minutes.

"Stop what?"

He opened his eyes, and they were like ice in the
ioonlight. "You either sit still or I'll find the means
> make you."

She glared at him. "You are a horrid boss."

And she was close enough to kiss, Shane thought.
' she were any other woman, he would have kissed
er. But she wasn't, and his lips tightened at her
rave words. "It seems," he said, "you have some
ouble recognizing the proper respect one should
iow the boss." He ran one finger down the peach-
oft side of her face. "Shall I teach you, Mrs. Lind-
ay?"

Seemingly paralyzed by his touch, she stared at
im wide-eyed. He was about to see how far she'd
t him go, when she blinked and pushed his hand
way. "Sir, what is this talk of bosses?" she said,
ughing lightly. "We're partners in this effort, and it
ould be wise to remember that in our endeavor to
nd my brother."

Was there no end to her outrageous persistence?

Shane wondered. Seeing her bright, optimistic ex
pression made something cold clench his vitals. Per
haps the wisest thing he could do would be to tur
the boat around and forget he had ever seen her.
She wasn't even intimidated by his coldest, mos
threatening look which had sent grown men run
ning. "I think," he said, "it would be best if you jus
relieve yourself of the notion once and for all tha
you will be helping me investigate this case. And
would be very wise if you shut your eyes and went t
sleep!"

He shouted the last. Cool, unflappable Shan
O'Connor was shouting. He was on his feet, as
sitting next to her was too nerve-racking to tolerate
His driver and the boat captain were staring at hin
as if they had never witnessed such a sight.

Eden blinked. "Heavens, Mr. O'Connor, there i
no need to shout. I'm only trying to help. Two mind
are always better than one, don't you think?"

He leaned over her, his hands gripping the sea
back on either side of her, his face barely a breat
away from hers. "Not," he said harshly, "when on
of those minds is totally lacking in logic, is com
pletely twaddled, *daft*!"

For a moment she stared at him, then pursed he
lips. "I can see you have a very high opinion of you
own mind," she said. "I see I'll just have to prove t
you that I am not the typical brainless female wit
whom you evidently associate."

He swore softly, pushing himself away from he
and straightening. Exasperated, he shoved both hi
hands through his hair. She was thick-skinned too
There was not a damn thing left to say. Withou
another word he thrust his hands into his pocket
and strode briskly away from her to go talk to th
boat captain.

They arrived at the estate shortly before dawn, nd the armed guards at the entrance swung open e wrought iron gates.

"If your estate is so protected," Eden asked as the rriage rolled up the long, winding drive, "then hy didn't you take guards into the city with you?" he asked the question somewhat tentatively, given s earlier mood. When he looked at her, though, he saw his eyes had softened and that faint lines uched the corners of them. Suddenly she yearned see that humor in him, and she wondered what d make him laugh.

"O'Hara there," he answered, "doubles as my odyguard and driver. Actually, the estate guards re Simon's idea." He smiled slightly. "In the past e've had many an argument about the necessity of uards. I feel that if a man wants to kill me, he'll find way to do it. But Simon thinks it only fair to allow e the privilege of sleeping with just one eye open stead of two, knowing the place is guarded."

Buoyed by his sudden loquacious bent, Eden miled. "It's refreshing to know that a person can in an argument with you, even if that person is imon."

He merely lifted an eyebrow in response. She nought he looked especially intense with the nadow of a dark beard roughening his face, sur-ounding his well-defined mouth. His mouth was urprisingly sensual, firm and full, in contrast to the ggressive angles of his face. She wondered what his nouth would feel like pressed to hers, then chased he forbidden thought away. Obviously, she was too eary to think straight.

"I need some sleep," she murmured, and slumped deways, falling into an instant, deep sleep.

"What the hell?"

Shane quickly leaned over her and shook her. S[h]e swatted at him, then groused and shifted as she trie[d] to find a more comfortable position. Less than [a] minute later the carriage stopped in front of t[he] house and O'Hara swung open the door. Sha[ne] scowled at the other man's grin.

"Well, boss, you finally found a way to shut h[er] up."

"Dammit, man, she fought sleep all the way hom[e] and now she's practically unconscious!"

O'Hara's grin spread. "The best way to get her [into] the house, I'd say, is to carry her."

"Like hell."

O'Hara was chuckling now. "Boss, I'd say you'[re] a mite jumpy around the woman. What's she got—thorns?"

"More than any rosebush I've ever seen."

"I do not!" Eden shot upright like a startled dee[r]. The last had apparently penetrated her consciou[s]ness, and through sleep-blurred eyes she glared fro[m] one stunned man to the other. "Have your mothe[rs] never taught you it is rude to stare?"

"Were you feigning sleep?" Shane demanded.

She gave him a queer look. "Why would I do su[ch] a thing? I just had a little catnap. It took the ed[ge] off."

With that she put her hand out, waiting f[or] O'Hara to help her alight. He took her finger[s], shooting a wary glance to Shane. When Shan[e] climbed down, the bodyguard whispered, "She's a[n] odd one, she is."

Shane merely sauntered after her, his han[ds] shoved into his trousers pockets, wondering at h[er] game now. For he was sure it was a game; no on[e] could be so mercurial. He watched her sweep ahea[d] of him, watched the graceful, provocative sway [of] her hips as she ascended the wide front steps. She turned, poised on one foot—for effect, he was certain—and tilted her head to one side. That, too, he decided, was intended for provocative effect. Given the instant tightening of his loins, her ploy worked damn well.

"Mr. O'Connor."

She flurried back down the steps toward him, ignoring O'Hara's openly curious stare as he stood behind his employer, her valise in one hand. "You *do* have gardenia scents, do you not?"

Shane stared at her, hiding his growing confusion, frustration, and impatience. "What?"

She widened her eyes and touched his forearm. "Perfume scents. You know, for my bath. You certainly don't expect me to get into bed before a bath, do you?"

He eyed her dubiously. "I'm not quite sure *what* I expect."

"Well? Have you gardenia scents?"

"Actually," he drawled, "I prefer rose scents in my bathwater."

She laughed. "I suppose that means you don't." She sighed. "I'm going to miss Alice's ministrations after my bath. Do you have a maid who will rub body oil into my skin?"

The power of her words slammed into him. Shane's eyes narrowed as the vision of her nude, oiled, lusciously curved body flashed into his mind. The tightening in his loins was becoming damned uncomfortable. Damn, she was a practiced flirt! But she seemed blithely unaware of her effect on him as she once again swept up the front steps and waited for O'Hara to open the door. Shaking his head, Shane followed. Once inside the huge foyer, he instructed O'Hara to tell the maids to prepare to assist Mrs. Lindsay.

Now eager for the sleep she had denied needing a couple of hours earlier, Eden followed O'Connor up the wide, curving mahogany staircase that swept in a graceful half circle from the foyer to the second floor. He walked ahead of her, across the second story balcony, to a splendid suite of rooms which, decorated in emerald green and gold, overlooked the bay. She glanced outside to the white-maned waves that raced one after the other to shore, then back to the man who still stood by the door, watching her. It seemed as if he were waiting for her stamp of approval.

"Thank you," she said. "This is lovely."

He nodded tersely, then led her to the adjoining bathing room. Awed, she stared at the rose-quartz-marbled walls and floors and at the huge sunken tub in the center of the room. Through a round skylight high above, early morning sunlight poured in, glinting off the gold faucets and the quartz-veined marble.

"You've never seen a bathing room?" O'Connor asked.

She shook her head. "No, I—" She lowered her lashes, suddenly feeling self-conscious. "I've always had a bath sent up."

"Well, you may use this room, or have a bath sent up if you prefer."

Enraptured by the luxury of the room, Eden smiled at him. "Oh, no. I'm certain I will want to use this room. I may never come out!"

"When you do," he said with a hint of sarcasm in his tone, "meet me in my study."

Befuddled by his abrupt dismissal, she watched him turn and walk out of the room. Really, something had to be done about that autocratic manner of his, she thought. But right now she had more important matters to attend to.

The bath was heavenly. After a long soak—*sans* the perfumed oils—she sank into a deep, dreamless sleep on the enormous satin-covered bed. When she awoke, brilliant afternoon sunlight beat through the sparkling windowpanes into the sweltering room. She rolled over, her hair sticking to the back of her neck, her heavy-lidded eyes straining to open.

It was so hot! She dragged herself upright, then left the bed, crossing swiftly to the window. She opened it, letting the barest breath of a breeze cool her naked body. Hearing a shout below, she leaned out and saw O'Connor, big and powerful, swing off a horse as magnificent as its rider. She caught her breath, and as if he'd heard that noise, he looked up and saw her at the window.

He froze, and Eden did too, forgetting her nudity as she was spellbound by his raw virility, the sweat dampening the front of his white shirt. He stood with his legs braced apart, his hands planted on his narrow hips, and only when his harsh glare intensified did she remember that she was as naked as a baby. She glanced down at her puckered pink nipples, and heat flared in her cheeks, for certainly the stableboy helping Shane had seen her bare breasts too.

"Oh, dear," she murmured, and ducked back into her bedroom.

Eden dressed quickly, wearing only a sheer shift under her pale blue sprigged muslin dress. After putting her hair up, she flung open the door and all but flew down the stairs and almost straight into Shane's arms. She put her hands up to stop herself from blundering into him, and they pressed against his broad chest. His shirt was still half open, and the feel of hard muscle, naked skin, and crisp chest hair made her recoil as if burned. His heated body produced strange quiverings within her, and despite her confusion, she longed to run her palms over his smooth bronze skin again. She could see by his icy gaze and tight face that he was furious, but she hadn't an inkling why.

"Do you realize, Mr. O'Connor," she asked, slightly breathless from her downward flight, "what time it is?"

Without a word, and under the stunned stares of various servants, he grabbed her arm and hauled her into his study, slamming the double doors behind them. He released her so abruptly, she stumbled before she righted herself. Turning, she glared at him, intent on giving him a setting-down for his boorish behavior. The words stayed trapped in her throat, though. He stood with his broad back against the doors, his eyes slicing through her like sabers. Sweat trickled down his sideburns to curve over his lean, hard jaw, and her heart thumped wildly as she was strangely aroused by the sight. She drew a quick breath to calm herself and changed tactics.

"You have horses?"

For a cold, unnerving moment he simply continued to stare at her, then he pushed himself away from the door. "I have horses," he said as he ambled across the room to the sideboard. "I breed horses. I have a ranch in Saratoga." He poured himself a drink, and she watched as his long, tanned fingers wrapped around the crystal glass and lifted it to his lips.

She smiled at him. "You ride very well." He rode like a god.

He gazed at her over the rim of the glass as he

ok a sip. When he said nothing, just kept looking
her, she let out a loud sigh. She did not like this
t-and-mouse game.

"I need to go to the city," she said. "I have a
hearsal."

Something like humor flickered in his eyes. He
alked over to his desk and perched on the edge,
vinging one leg. "Tell me," he said, his gaze finally
aving hers to move ever so slowly down her body,
vhy you were standing at the window"—he paused
his gaze lingered on her breasts—"bare-
easted?"

Her face flamed. The word "breasts" coming
om this excessively virile man horrified her. "Mr.
'Connor, I am shocked."

"Can you imagine my shock when I saw them?"
: asked with a sardonic gleam in his eye.

Her face became even hotter. She thought it
eadfully rude the way he continued to stare at her,
strange, unfathomable smile quirking one corner
' his mouth. Defensively she put her chin up. "I
ways sleep naked."

Shane's eyes narrowed. Her remark, he was sure,
id been calculated to stir his blood. "I'll keep that
mind," he murmured. "But not in this house, you
on't."

"I beg your pardon?"

He stood, knowing he was being unreasonable,
t also knowing how impossible it would be for him
sleep during these sweltering nights while her de-
:ious naked body was just a short distance from his
:droom. What he had glimpsed of her from the
rd below had been enough to set any healthy
an's blood on fire. She was as lush and ripe as he
id imagined, and since meeting her he had imag-
ed plenty. "You heard me." He set down his glass

and walked over to her, stopping just inches awa
"You will *not* sleep naked in this house."

"You cannot dictate to me what I might ar
might not wear in the privacy of my sleeping qua
ters. Frankly, sir, it is none of your business!"

"You made it my business when you came to tl
window."

"You weren't supposed to look."

That amused him. "I have a sixth sense about b
ing watched."

Eden wanted to back away from him but couldn
He was so damned attractive—even more so u
close. The contrast of his light eyes against his da
skin stirred her irrepressibly. He smelled of hor
and sweat and leather mingled with the faint scent
salt sea air. She felt hot and weak, perspiration form
ing on her skin, making her undergarments cling
the most intimate places. Unable to bear the thic
electric tension between them any longer, sl
stepped away—even though it galled her to be tl
one to move first.

"Mr. O'Connor," she said as she faced him, "yc
cannot govern my personal habits when I am behin
closed doors. In the future, you, sir, will have r
idea whether or not I am retiring with or without n
clothing. Now," she went on, satisfied that she ha
made her point, "I must leave for town. I have b
minutes if I'm going to make my rehearsal in tim
Could you have a carriage ready, please, to bring n
to the ferry?"

"No."

She stared at him as if she hadn't heard correctl
"Excuse me?"

He walked away from her, all the way behind h
desk. Looking absorbed in some paperwork and t
tally unmoved by her dramatics, he said in a bu:

sslike tone, "I've already sent a missive to your
ector informing him that you will miss this after-
on's rehearsal."

"What! How dare you!"

He glanced up from his work, regarding her im-
ssively, and continued in a clipped voice that rang
th implacable authority. "In fact, you will not per-
m until this case is resolved. I can't have you run-
ng around the city as an open target. And I have
ore important things to do than to cover you while
u pursue your . . . ah, attraction to the stage."

She sucked in a sharp breath. He made her pas-
on sound obscene!

"I'll have you know, sir, that my 'attraction' gives
any people pleasure. And you have no right whatever to put a stop to it."

"I do and I am."

"Oh, you horrible man! You cannot keep me
om performing. It's—it's my life's blood, my
urce of excitement, my reason for living!" She
ced agitatedly around the room, then dropped
o the leather chair in front of his desk.

Shane's gaze raked over her. The woman was cer-
nly given to drama. "Mrs. Lindsay, you don't need
stage."

She sat up, looking intently at him. "Have I just
en insulted?"

Turning to hide the smile that tugged at the cor-
rs of his mouth, Shane reached for a piece of pa-
r and pen. "Even though we know the thieves
ve your brother, it is wise to pursue all other ave-
es in the event the note was a ploy." He looked at
r again. "You *did* come up with a list, didn't
u?"

"Oh, of course I did. In between riding the ferry
me, rehearsal, and riding back with you, I've had

all the time in the world to do so." She sat forwa
and glared at him. "I am not so *twaddled,* sir, tha
can't think of a list of names off the top of
head."

Without answering, he picked up a pen and be
his head over a piece of paper, waiting for her
begin. Instead, she said, "You must have been a h
rid little boy."

Though her tone was teasing, he lifted his head
stare stonily at her. "I beg your pardon?"

"You must have always had to have been King
the Mountain."

For a long, still moment he held her gaze, th
said almost gruffly, "I didn't have much time f
that sort of thing." Once again he looked down a
started scratching out some notes.

Puzzled, Eden studied him. All little boys play
King of the Mountain. She and Philip had play
often, and she had beat him too. She tried to pictu
this remote, sophisticated man before her as a chil
and could not.

"Well?"

She jumped, startled. "Well, what?"

"The list," he said tightly.

"It's going to be a long one."

He waited.

"Philip had a lot of . . . disgruntled people
his life."

"Give me the name of one."

"Well, there's Mama, but I'm sure she would
kidnap him."

Not a muscle moved in his face as he stared
her. "A legitimate suspect, Mrs. Lindsay."

"I can't think on an empty stomach."

Irritation flashed across his face as he stood.

ree long strides he was at the bell cord, and he
ulled it, summoning the butler.

"Refreshments, Spencer, for the lady."

She grinned at him. "I'll be sure to let folks know
hen I get out of here that the O'Connor stronghold
eds its prisoners."

He obviously did not share her humor. Instead,
e studied her as he remained standing, his hands in
is pockets, his gaze arrogant and aloof. She was
sed to men's stares. Shane's, however, was strictly
npersonal, and it was beginning to annoy her. Hav-
g a healthy dose of vanity, she wanted him to look
her as any man looked at a pretty woman. Maybe
e did not find her appealing. Since that notion did
ot sit well with her, she was determined to learn the
uth, and change it if need be.

"You know," she said, "Philip might have re-
rned home by now."

"He hasn't. I planted a man there, and so far
ere is no sign of your twin."

"Oh." She tried to squelch the panic and bitter
isappointment within her as she felt tears sting her
yes.

Shane frowned. "Don't cry," he snapped more
arshly than intended, but he didn't like tears, espe-
ially hers. He felt completely at a loss when he saw
hose blue-green eyes fill with water. But now they
ere flashing at him like jewels, and he almost
ughed at how swiftly her mood could change.

"Well, excuse me, sir, for feeling a bit of loss over
y only brother. I will cry if I so choose, and now
hat you've chased *that* desire away, I will tell you
hat you simply cannot tell a person how to feel. If I
el a certain way, I shall act on it despite your
tuffed-up highbrow attitudes about emotion. Is that
lear?"

Spencer, the butler, opened the door at the end of her lecture and was stopped cold. He glanced at his employer, who looked unperturbed by his dressing down from this mere chit, but Spencer had never known anyone to talk like that to O'Connor and live a normal life afterward. Quickly composing himself Spencer stepped into the room with Eden's tray of food, making a concentrated effort to keep his eyebrows level, his gaze averted. When he had set the tray down, he turned to Shane.

"Will that be all, sir?"

"Yes, Spencer. Thank you." Again Shane's attention was drawn to Eden as she let out a squeal of delight at the lunch set out before her. Shrimp and lobster salad was her appetizer, and beside that was a plate of thinly sliced cold beef and a small bowl of gravy. A basket of bread and rolls was kept warm with a linen napkin, and there was a fine selection of cheeses and fruit. All of this was finished off with rich pastries.

"Oh, I'm *famished!* Thank you, Humbart!" she called after the butler, who stiffened as if she had put a hot poker to his skin.

"His name is Spencer," Shane said.

"Oh, well, yes . . ." She sent the butler an apologetic look as he closed the doors, then she delved into her meal with relish.

Shane watched her pop a bite of roll into her mouth, followed by a forkful of salad. She appeared to be famished, as well as to have forgotten he was there.

And that was just as well. He couldn't believe it but watching her *eat,* for God's sake, was arousing him, and to an uncomfortable degree. She ate voraciously, as if she hadn't seen food in a week, and he marveled that she could put it all away and re-

ain so slender. Most well-bred women he knew ate
aintily, pushing this away and that aside, pretend-
g they weren't hungry. Eden, however, possessed a
sty appetite and made no secret of it. He won-
red if her appetite in bed was as lusty.

His eyes narrowed. Though she was clean and re-
eshed, her hair twisted into a thick chignon at the
ase of her neck, she still had that tousled, sensual
ok about her that made him want to possess her
mediately and intensely. She was appropriately
amed, as maddening a temptation as the forbidden
uit offered to Adam in the Garden of Eden, and
ery bit as luscious.

"Look at the size of these strawberries!"

He did look, and regretted it instantly. His gaze
stened on her lush pink lips as they pursed and
alled the strawberry into her mouth. An uncontrol-
ble surge of lust gripped him, and he silently
arsed its intensity.

"Mmm!" She chewed and swallowed the ripe red
uit. "Do you know what strawberries *do* to me?"

Shane clenched his jaw. He knew damn well what
ey were doing to *him*. Before he could respond,
e reached for a peach and bit into it, the juice
ickling off the golden fruit.

"They're so juicy!"

Spinning around, he strode to his desk and sat
own quickly. Eden looked up, surprised.

"I'm glad you finally decided to be seated." She
ached for her napkin and delicately wiped her
icky hands and mouth. "It's much more comfort-
ble, don't you agree?"

"Much."

"There's nothing I like better than fruit."

"Nothing?"

His voice held a peculiar note of testiness, and it

occurred to her that she had been extremely rud
She smiled at him and plucked a tart from the tra
"I apologize. I was so ravenous I ate everything u
without offering you anything." She held out th
pastry to him. "Do you want some?"

"No."

The word was cold and short. Eden frowned, hu
that there seemed to be nothing she could do t
please him. She was finding it a challenge to dec
pher this man.

"Now, may we proceed, madame?" He was gla
ing at her, and Eden lifted her nose.

"I wasn't under the impression that I was thwar
ing the procession, Mr. O'Connor. Elizabeth Towr
send."

His brows lowered in a thunderous scowl. "Wh
the hell is that?"

She looked at him all wide eyes and innocenc
"You asked for a name and I've just provided yo
with one. Elizabeth Townsend."

"Who is she?"

"I don't see any reason why you have to spea
through your teeth, Mr. O'Connor." When he mac
to rise, she hurried on. "The woman claims Phili
has made her . . ."

She faltered, and he leaned across the desk towar
her. "Made her what?"

Eden's face flamed. "Pregnant."

"God."

Eden glanced out the window, down at her lap
over to the bookshelves, anywhere but back a
O'Connor. "Really, sir, I do not see the reason to g
on. Why do you need me to detail Philip's life? Yo
already know that the jewel thieves are holding hir
hostage."

He rubbed his forehead. "I just finished tellin

ou that we must consider all the possibilities, espe-
ally when a scoundrel like your brother is in-
olved—"

"You're calling my brother a scoundrel!"

"And that's a damned compliment, I'm think-
ig!"

They stared at each other, both stunned by his
rogue.

A sudden pounding at the doors disrupted them.
Come in!" O'Connor snapped.

"Sir, what is all this racket—"

Both Eden and Simon gasped at once, furious,
dignant, and fired by the sight of the other.

Simon pivoted to glower at his employer. "Have
ou lost your mind, man? You brought her *here*?
ou're taking her case? Do you know what this
ight mean to your sanity?"

"I'm beginning to realize," O'Connor drawled,
d Eden whipped around to glare at him. For the
rst time she saw real amusement in his silver eyes.
Ie leaned back in his chair, linking his fingers be-
ind his head, and the muscles in his upper arms
velled against his shirt-sleeves. His deceptively lazy
rawl could not conceal the danger and the power
f his body, or the raw sexuality he radiated.

"Do not, either of you," she warned, "start with
is nonsense again of speaking past me as if I am
ot present." She speared Simon with a glare. "And
ive me back my dagger!"

"In a pig's eye!"

"Oh!" Her temper was rising fast, but she quelled
, and cast Simon a look of cool hauteur. "Very well,
that's the way you'll have it. Two can play this
ame. Since I am now a guest of Mr. O'Connor's, I
ave access to his home, and your quarters. I will, I
romise you, steal upon you like a thief in the night

—you'll not have an inkling as to when—and take that knife from you. But I warn you." She paused dramatically. "That knife has a curse on it for those who have stolen it from their rightful owner."

"I'll be quaking in my boots until that moment." He looked past her toward O'Connor. "Sir, I have some information for you."

Eden surged to her feet. "Is it about my brother? Is it?"

Simon continued to stare past her.

"Sir," she said in a gentle tone so that he was forced, out of sheer propriety, to bring his gaze to hers. "I hate to be the one to inform you of this, but"—she dropped her lashes as if embarrassed—"your . . . trousers are . . ." She blushed, unable to go on.

Horrified, the proper Simon looked down, and saw that he had fallen prey to her trick. His trousers were buttoned as they should be. He lifted his head, his face flushed, and pointed at her while addressing Shane in outraged indignation. "She is no lady, sir! I told you, any woman of her status playing on stage—"

"And I'll thank you in the future to—"

"Enough!" Shane stood abruptly, silencing them both. The two of them were acting like unruly children. He looked at Eden. "Stay put. I'll be right back."

She raised her brows at him as he walked past her. "And where do you think I might wander off to as you're guarding the door?"

He only shot her a cold look, and she rolled her eyes, her own patience at its limit.

She paced for a few moments in front of a book-shelf, casually reading the titles. Then she saw O'Connor's jacket, the one he had been wearing the

evious night. The one she hoped still had the note
it. Odd that he was so impeccable and the jacket
d been casually tossed over the back of a chair.
rhaps he had fallen asleep there after they had
rived that morning. At any rate, Eden was just glad
have found it, and now was the perfect opportu-
ty to search for the note. When she found it in the
cket's inner pocket, she read it quickly:

Bring the jewels to Pier 9 off South Street on the
East River tomorrow night at eleven o'clock if you
want to see your brother alive again. No cops—no
tricks. It is a fair swap, don't you think?

She shoved the note back into Shane's pocket, her
art pounding heavily. Her palms felt clammy cold.
amn Shane O'Connor! How in the name of
aven, if the abductors were summoning *her* to
op the gems, was he going to manage looking like
woman? How was he going to execute this plan
ithout her?
Staring out the window, she gnawed on her bot-
m lip. Eleven o'clock. Pier 9. She knew where that
as. Philip would be there. She thought very
ickly. Shane would take the jewels, so she would
ot have to carry them. She could simply meet him
ere on the pier, and it would be too late for him to
otest.
She grabbed a pen and swiftly wrote him a note of
r own, that she'd left to take a stroll on the beach.
y the time he read it, she would be gone, on the
iblic ferry, while he, no doubt, would be starting
f on his own. Damn him. How dare he keep this
tal information from her!

She turned and lifted a leg over the windowsi squeezed her eyes shut tight, and dropped sever feet to the ground. There was no question in h mind about what she had to do. She *must* be on Pi 9 at eleven. Her brother's life depended on it.

CHAPTER FOUR

$\mathcal{T}$HE NIGHT AIR WAS HEAVY WITH THE ODOR OF FISH and tar and brine. Eden stood alone at the head of the pier behind several crates and barrels. Water lapped against hulking vessels that were docked, and the diffused light from far-off streetlamps cast an oily glow over everything.

The heat was oppressive, the air thick, bringing with it the stench of dredged harbor muck and rotting wharves. Eden took small shallow breaths, unable to inhale deeply without gagging. Her fingertips brushed her thigh, touching her bowie where she'd trapped it under her skirts. After she'd climbed out the study window earlier that afternoon, she'd skulked into Simon's quarters and retrieved it. Now she was glad she had. The night was eerie, sinister and she was alone.

Far down the empty dock were more crates and barrels and a large ship, but there was no one in sight. She was early, however, and had fifteen minutes before the swap was supposed to happen. She had arrived in the city with time to spare, and had dashed over to the theater to see Franklin, explaining to him that her life was a bit tumultuous of late but promising him that she would be at the next day's rehearsal.

"I hope so, Eden," he'd said, a troubled look in his dark eyes. "This play goes on in less than a month, and we need to practice. You know I much prefer you as Lysistrata than Jacqueline, your stand in."

She had left him reassured. There was no way Mr. Shane O'Connor was going to stop her from performing. She had a life to live, for the love of Pete.

She heard the pier creak and whirled to see a tall man standing several feet away from her, his broad shoulders blotting out the faint light behind him.

"Mr. O'Connor!" Her whisper sounded like the crack of a bullwhip on the deserted pier. O'Connor spun on his heel and swore so quietly and profusely that she was stunned into momentary silence. Lightning-swift, he was at her side, a muscular arm clamped tight around her waist and his hand hard over her mouth.

"Damn you, woman, what the bloody hell are you doing out here?"

"Mmph—ffmmph!"

"That's no goddamn excuse! Did I not tell you to stay put? Didn't I?"

"Mmph-phh!"

"No arguing with me, dammit! That's all you've one since the second I laid eyes on you, lady, and m damn bloody well tired of it!"

"Arww-mmph!" She clutched his wrist, trying to ull his hand away from her mouth, but he held her st. He was muttering and swearing through his eth. She wriggled against him, striving to get free, nd felt his body tense.

"You think *that's* going to soften me up?" he said. Hardly, darlin'. Now is not the time to use femi- ine wiles. I am *not* distracted in the least, do you ear me? Christ," he swore with pure disgust, "I ught to stuff you in one of these barrels and push ne lid on tight until this is all over!"

That did it! He was rude, overbearing, and so rrogant, his manner bordered on being cruel. She upposed he was used to countless women throwing nemselves at him, but *she* was the exception—at :ast for then. Angrily Eden reached up and grabbed fistful of his perfect hair, pulling hard. He swore chly and released her so abruptly that she spilled in heap at his feet.

She scrambled upright and glared at him. "You re, by far, the rudest—"

"Save it. And shut up. Unless, that is"—he let his vords linger ominously—"you don't mind these cul- rits cutting you up and using you for fish bait."

She tilted her chin up. "You don't scare me!"

He was upon her again, one hard arm circling her nroat, cutting off her breath. His voice, by her ear, asped with steel. "This is *nothing* compared to what bey will do to you if they capture you, sweetheart."

Eden felt dizzy, light-headed, and somehow cold s ice. She could hear, could feel his harsh breath- ıg, the frightening power of his strong body behind

her. She grabbed him and said his name faintl
"Shane . . ."

The sound of his name from her lips hit him like
blow to the chest. Shane dropped his arm an
hooked it once again around her slender waist, pul
ing her in close. The woman was the most madden
ing—and provocative—creature he'd ever had th
misfortune to meet.

"Do you know what kind of danger you've pu
yourself in, woman?" Stupid question, he though
She didn't know the meaning of the word dange
Reckless, impetuous little fool. He shook he
slightly. "The slightest sound will alert these villain
Do you understand that?"

"I am not an idiot."

He gave her a look that doubted her statement.
thought you went to take a walk. I left the islan
thinking you were in your room."

She smiled smugly, but winced when his finger
tightened on her upper arms.

"I should have known," he muttered. "What th
bloody hell did you think you were doing, climbin
out the window? Are you some kind of monkey tha
scales walls and vaults out windows?"

She stared straight at him, her eyes rebelliou
"The note clearly specified that I deliver the jewel
not you, Mr. O'Connor. How, may I ask, are yo
going to make yourself look like me?" She gave hir
the once-over and shook her head.

"You read the note."

"Of course I read the note! You had no right t
keep it from me!"

His mouth tightened. "Dammit, lady, if you liv
through this night, I am going to make you unde
stand one thing—"

He stiffened, and his hands tightened on he

ickly, he pulled her deeper into the shadows and
ished her. The smell was truly rank, and Eden
inkled her nose, but over it all she caught the faint
int of him, and moved closer to his tall, rugged
dy. "What is it?"

'I said *shh,* dammit!"

She scowled at him. "I should be out there, Mr.
Connor, on that dock, in plain sight with the jew-
You did bring the jewels, I take it? It's almost
ven, and they'll be looking for me. I know you're
y clever, but I *really* cannot see how you will be
e to disguise yourself as a woman—"

'You're going to get him killed."

'I beg your pardon?"

'You'll be begging it plenty, all right, I'm think-
, if you don't shut your mouth. If the abductors
ir you talking to me out here, do you think they'll
sitate to harm your twin?"

His frank words chilled Eden's blood. He jerked
head toward the open area of the pier and said,
here's your woman."

Puzzled, Eden followed the direction of his gaze
d let out a soft gasp. A tall, lithe woman with hair
white-blond as her own stood alone halfway down
pier. She seemed to be unaware of Shane and
en, and looked apprehensively about her.

Eden felt an immediate hot stab of jealousy.
Who is she?"

"That's Camille, one of my assistants."

Eden decided that she did not like the warm, pos-
sive tone he used. Nor did she like seeing her
uble. There was only one Eden Victoria Lindsay,
d Miss Camille was taking unforgivable liberties
th her personage. "She's an impostor!" Eden
ed.

Shane looked at her in stunned disbelief. "That's

the whole point, woman!" He closed his eyes,
lently beseeching the heavens for patience. "She
here for *your* protection."

That immediately comforted her. At least
wanted to protect her. "Is she wearing a wig?"

Deciding the best way to shut her up was not
respond, Shane ignored her and reached for
pearl-handled pistol tucked into his waistband.

"Surely, sir, *that* is not necessary." Her vo
quavered, and he realized with some humor that s
had the wrong impression.

"I do not intend to use it on you, Eden. Please
beg you, try to keep silent for a few minutes. Tl
woman out there"—he nodded toward Camille—
taking a colossal risk for both of us."

That quieted her, and it was a good thing, for t
men suddenly appeared at the end of the dock ne
the large ship. Camille backed up a few steps.

"Let's see the gems!" called a rough voice.

Camille lifted the chamois bag with both han
"Now let me see my brother!" she called back.

"Drop the jewels first."

"No! I want to see my brother."

Eden held her breath. Her thundering he
sounded like torrential rain pounding in her ea
She gripped Shane's forearm, digging her fing
into hard muscle. She could feel his body tense as
waited to make his move. A thrill of raw fear shi
mied up her spine. Where was Philip? Was this a
farce? Did they even *have* her brother? Was
dead? She closed her eyes tightly, praying, th
opened them wide to see one of the burly thu
striding toward Camille.

Camille called out, "Do you take me for a fo
Show me Philip!"

The burly man turned to look back over his

ulder. His accomplice disappeared behind the
ge ship and reappeared with a tall man.
"Is that your brother?" Shane asked.

Eden strained to see. "I can't tell from here."

"Damn."

"Bring him closer!" Camille called.

"Drop the jewels," growled the abductor. "And
p 'em fast. You'll get your brother back when
y're in our hands."

"But that's not fair—"

"Drop 'em!"

Eden could feel the taut expectancy in Shane's
dy. She knew he scented danger; his powerful
scles were coiled tightly, and he was ready to
ing. The thug was moving closer to Camille. She
k a step back, but stumbled over a loose plank.
r wig tumbled off.

"It *is* a wig!" Eden cried, her voice immediately
rting the assailants. She heard Shane's vicious
se, felt the sudden absence of his body near hers,
rd the crack and pop of gunshots exploding
und her. *Ping!* A bullet hit a crate near her head,
l she ducked and squealed. Then anger flooded
. How *dare* they! How dare they kidnap her
ther, steal all her jewelry, expect the stolen gems
k, and *now* try to shoot decent people!

Acting on instinct, she reached under her skirts,
sped her bowie, and leapt out from behind the
tes and barrels. To her shock and horror, there
re more armed men than she had expected. And
ane had already kicked two of them into the
rky water. She had never seen anyone fight like
. She'd grown up amid tough Texan ranch hands
l an Apache who could take any of them, but
ane was different. While the men lunged and
ew hard punches, he easily deflected them. His

fighting was brutal and clean, both beautiful and te-
rible. He used his powerful body like a weapon,
rattler-fast he was but a blur of action.

"Dammit, Eden—run!"

She was so stunned by the drama enacted bef
her, though, she could only watch. Camille was
where in sight, obviously having fled.

"Look out!"

She felt rather than saw the man come at her fr
behind. She whirled, lifted her arm, and flung
knife. It struck its target with satisfying speed a
accuracy, and the thief howled, clutching his sho
der.

Shane's voice was a hoarse growl. "Run, da
mit!"

Weaponless now, she finally did as he order
She ran as if the hounds of hell were after her. S
didn't know in which direction she was headed, b
heard Shane behind her just seconds after she h
left him. Bullets whizzed by their heads, and
grabbed her hand, pulling her with him as he ma
a crazy zigzag pattern along the waterfront. As th
dodged the bullets, they could hear the footsteps
their pursuers and kept running. Eden's thr
burned. Air tore in and out of her tortured lungs,
Shane did not break his pace.

"Quick, behind this building," he rasped, a
dragged her into an alley that stank with rotting g
bage.

"Ohmigod," she panted, and held her nose.

"Shh!"

"I—have—to—breathe—"

"Not so loud, you don't."

They were coming closer. Shane heard th
shouts, their running feet. And Eden was yakk
like an old lady who hadn't had company in

onth. He figured he had only one option. Without
other thought he hooked an arm around her waist
d dragged her in close to cover her mouth with his
vn. He meant only to silence her, but her full lips
:re so velvety soft, he deepened his kiss, the pres-
re of his mouth opening hers and his tongue slid-
g inside to taste her. Shock waves rocked his body,
d the world faded. She was hot and she was sweet,
e melted honey, her mouth acquiescent to his, as
her whole concentration was on the feel of him.
:r body softened in his arms. Shane made a primi-
ve sound in his throat and pulled her in closer, his
ngue a searing scorch against hers as she twisted
e a flame in his hands.

Eden heard only a distant rush in her ears, like the
nd, and felt heat, his heat, branding her. Never
d she been kissed so! She met the ardent demand
his tongue as it thrust in and out of her mouth in
compelling rhythm that left her helpless under his
ntrol, dominated. Her fingers twined through the
ick hair that curled at his collar. She didn't—
ouldn't—even think why he would kiss her in some
ick alley, with villains in wild pursuit. She only
ent with the moment, taking and giving of the
veetest potion in which she had ever indulged.

But shots rang out. She stiffened, and Shane
agged his mouth from hers. Their breathing was
bored and ragged, and Eden knew it had little to
) with the running. As if he were angry with her for
e kiss that he had initiated, he grabbed her wrist
d none too gently tugged her down the alley.

"We're going to fly now, so you better keep up,
oman."

"F-fly?" She was weak-kneed—*limp!*—and he ex-
ected her to fly? She supposed he did, for he was
erally dragging her across the putrid garbage, past

half-starved, mangy-looking mongrels sniffing
food. The taste of him lingered in her mouth, ting
on her tongue. To be kissed by a man so practic
and skilled had been a heady experience, and s
grew dizzy as she kept pace with him.

It seemed he had no such reaction, though. S
could have sworn he thought her nothing but a n
sance as he gripped her hand in a relentless vise
steel while they raced on. They wove in and out
the city's streets, stopping only briefly so that Ed
could catch her breath. Shane's pace was inexorab
grueling, and it stunned her to realize that he kne
this city like he would the back of his hand. Wh
they had finally managed to lose their pursuers a
Shane had flagged down a hack, another realizati
struck her.

"Did you call me Eden back at the docks?" s
asked as she climbed into the carriage.

Shane settled himself beside her. Stretching out
his customary fashion, appearing indolent when
body was still taut with tension and energy,
closed his eyes and ignored her.

"You did," she insisted. "I heard you. You said,
do not intend to use my gun on you, *Eden*.' And y
said, 'Dammit, *Eden*, run!' " Immensely pleased, sl
settled back and smiled at his stony profile.

His drawling voice dashed her high spiri
though. "Eden was a whole lot shorter to say th
Mrs. Lindsay when we were under attack."

She felt a little jab under her heart. Why did
have to be so cool and composed when they had ju
come through such a hair-raising episode, and t
umphed? But then she brightened once more. "V
weren't under attack when you called me Eden t
first time."

He didn't respond, and with his eyes closed, sl

k the opportunity to study him. She wanted him
kiss her again. She wanted to reach and trace her
gers over the rock-hard planes of his angular face.
persistent throbbing began low in her belly, a
asant, achy feeling that moistened and heated her
she remembered his tongue thrusting into her
uth, exploring. Her cheeks burned. He had done
cking things with his tongue . . . which she had
ed *very* much.

The hack stopped in front of the grand Fifth Ave-
e Hotel, and Shane stepped down before her. He
d the driver and, ignoring her confused expres-
n, grabbed her hand and tugged her out of the
ck. Realizing his intention, Eden drew back, scan-
lized.

'You can't bring me in there."

He turned to look down at her. "Why not? Don't
l me you're concerned about your reputation.
u're an actress." His voice was dry and mocking.

She stared up at him, stunned she would even
ve to explain to him. "Mr. O'Connor, it is quite
e thing to spirit me away to your estate and keep
: in seclusion, where no one but our servants
ow my whereabouts, and quite another to expect
: to register in a hotel with you."

His big hand slid under her elbow to propel her
ward. "It's necessary," he said in way of a terse
planation.

She pulled back. "I don't see how."

They stopped on the front steps, and she could
: by the tensed muscles in his jaw that he was fast
ing his patience. "It is not your place to 'see how,'
d frankly, madame, I don't care what you see. You
ve managed to turn this night into a catastrophe. I
n't even know if Camille is wounded, or worse.
d it's because you felt you should be there on the

docks tonight. Did it accomplish anything but bloody disaster? Did it?"

Her lips grew pinched. "You are, once again, ra[ing] your voice at me, sir. You are beginning to dr[a] attention to us."

She could almost hear him grit his teeth. [H]leaned his face close to hers in a pretense of in[ti]macy, and despite herself she drew back. "You," [he] said, his voice low and hard, "are to follow my [or]ders from here on in, is that understood?"

For a long, tense moment she kept her stare [on] his, then she raised her nose primly. "Perfectly."

He nodded curtly. "Good. Now, we are regist[er]ing as husband and wife, and I don't want you [to] open your mouth."

"But we're going to look very silly without lu[g]gage." She felt him tense beside her and realized [he] did a good deal of that. She thought it wise not [to] mention that, though, given that his features h[ad] fallen into their familiar implacable lines.

Of course Eden *had* brought up a valid point, b[ut] the desk clerk did not comment on their lack [of] luggage, for Shane paid him double to keep h[is] mouth shut. After that, the man became subservie[nt.]

"Anything you like, Mr. O'Connor, anything [at] all. Just say the word. And that goes for"—his ga[ze] slid toward Eden, and his look was dubious—"yo[ur] wife."

Eden gave him her most blinding smile in retur[n.] "A hot, *perfumed* bath would be nice," she sai[d,] ignoring Shane's scowl. "With gardenia scents."

"Oh, yes, yes, of course, madame." The clerk[']s scrutiny showed that he thought she looked [as] though she could use a bath, but Eden simply toss[ed] her head and sashayed ahead of her "husband."

The bedroom suite was glorious. Done in ivor[y]

lue, and gold, the room was the epitome of stately
egance. Diaphanous blue curtains lifted gently at
he open windows, and they could hear the muffled
oise of city traffic far below. A huge bed covered in
ory and gold silk dominated the room, and Eden's
aze slid from that to the French doors that opened
ut to a balcony, ringed in intricate wrought iron.

Once they were inside, Shane closed the door and
aned back against it, staring at her, his arms folded
cross his chest. For a moment all Eden could do
as stare back at him. He was, truly, a magnificent
xample of manhood. His hair was tousled and a
ruise colored his left cheekbone, but for that he
ardly looked like he'd been touched. She sensed
here was much to this man—a boiling caldron of
motional depth and passion which he kept carefully
ashed under his frosty, brooding reserve. Still, his
egant appearance could not conceal the ever-burn-
g fires of intensity in his searing eyes.

Though his forceful presence set her heart to
eating erratically, she smiled brightly at him.

"How," she asked, "do you do it?" When he
erely raised an eyebrow, she said, "In this heat,
fter that mad chase, you still manage to look as cool
s a slice of watermelon on a hot summer day. As
," she added with a laugh, "you've just been for a
isurely stroll. Look at me!"

She turned to the huge ornate mirror that hung
ver the massive fireplace. With her fingers she
ombed her hair away from her eyes and made a
ace at her reflection, marred with dirt smudges; a
ng scratch on her cheek added to those she'd ac-
uired the day before from her fall onto his prop-
rty. "I'm a mess." She could feel his stare on her
nd turned to look at him.

A taunting smile played about his mouth as he

asked casually, "How do you expect to take a bath in my presence?"

Her mouth fell open. "Oh." She hadn't thought of that."

Before she could say another word, the maids arrived to fill her bath. Shane inclined his head toward her and strolled out onto the balcony, "for smoke," he said.

Really, Eden stormed internally as she plunked herself into the heavenly hot scented bathwater moments later. He acted as if she were the most trying person he had ever come across in his whole supercilious, arrogant, *perfect* life! And he seemed a great deal more concerned with his precious Camille than he was with *her*! Of course, the woman *had* risked her life, but it seemed logical that an assistant of Shane's *would* risk his or her life. After all, that was their business.

Wearily Eden leaned her head back against the rim of the tub and closed her eyes. *Philip, Philip,* she thought with a pang in her chest, *I'm sorry. Sorry you're in this mess, sorry I only made things worse tonight. Where are you, where are you? Please come home.*

Suddenly she was bawling like a baby. Outside on the balcony she heard Shane curse, and remembered how he hated tears. But she couldn't stop.

"What," he asked icily, "are you crying about now?"

He said "now" as if she cried continuously. She whirled in the tub to see only his shadow, beyond the silk dressing screen, out on the balcony. He was staying carefully out of view of her naked body, and she didn't know whether to be insulted or flattered.

"You are not responsible to soothe me every time I cry, so you can relieve yourself of that burden, Mr

'Connor! I realize how it weighs so heavily on those broad shoulders of yours."

Shane remained half turned away from her, fixing his gaze heavenward in exasperation. And yet he was laughing. She was so damned dramatic, it was comical.

"Are you *laughing*, Mr. O'Connor?" She nearly screamed the word "laughing" at him. "I have never once heard you laugh, and I cannot believe you would be so callous as to laugh at my distress now. I'm beginning to think you are a deranged man, Mr. O'Connor. Very deranged indeed."

"I'm not laughing," he half laughed, half growled. "Now, will you hurry the hell up and get out of that tub so we can go to sleep?"

"I don't like to sleep. There's always so much happening that I feel I'm missing when I sleep. Besides, it's much too early to sleep."

"It's those entertainers' hours you keep," he observed dryly.

"Do you think so?" She lifted a shapely leg and squeezed the sponge over it. Shane could see her silhouette against the silk dressing screen and thrust his hands in his pockets. His cheroot was long gone, and he wished for a shot of brandy now. He tore his gaze away to look out across the city, its thousands of winking lights. "Mama said I never slept much as a child. She, too, was annoyed by it."

Shane stiffened. He doubted she was aware of the wistful note in her voice when she mentioned her mother.

"I didn't say I was annoyed by it," he said, and he laughed. The woman switched moods so fast, it was fascinating.

"Oh, but you are. Mr. O'Connor, have you stopped smoking?"

"Yes. How did you know?"

"You are not pausing to inhale, and the smoke ha[s] dissipated." She laughed again, as if guessing his sur[-]prise. "See? I would make a half-decent investigato[r] myself."

His response was a noncommittal grunt.

"It was Philip who slept like a rock," she went o[n] in a desultory tone. "I remember nights in Texa[s] when we were small and I used to try to wake him s[o] we could run outside and watch the fireflies." Sh[e] smiled. "But it was no use. I used to watch the[m] alone, or with Rake, and—sometimes even with Rat[-]tlesnake."

Shane shook his head. It could be the traffic tha[t] had affected his hearing but he was certain she ha[d] said Texas, Rake, and Rattlesnake all in one breath[.] He remembered that Rake was her grandfather, bu[t] what did that have to do with Texas, and who o[r] what was Rattlesnake?

"You lived in Texas?"

"All my life practically. Except after I turned fif[-]teen when Mama summoned me to Newport in th[e] summers. I grew bored of that and returned to th[e] city to join a theater troupe, performing until Christ[-]mas, when I usually returned home to Rake." Sh[e] laughed sadly. "Yes, Philip and I were left with Rak[e] after Papa died. My sickly mama could not raise tw[o] wild savages like Philip and me."

Hearing a note of loneliness, even desolation, i[n] her voice, Shane wished she'd stop reminiscing. H[e] didn't want to know about her past, didn't want t[o] acknowledge her as anything more than his client[.] Yet her revelations had stunned him. Though Simo[n] was running a background check on her, it too[k] some time, and Shane had been under the impres[-]sion that she'd grown up a pampered brat on Fift[h]

venue. This picture of her as a parentless hoyden
idn't fit her at all . . . except, perhaps, for that
:ckless streak. "You better get out of that tub."

"I know. I'm as wrinkled as a prune." She stood,
nd he clenched his teeth as he heard water run off
er in rivulets. Purposely, he turned his attention
nce again toward the city, and surprised himself by
king, "Is Rattlesnake an Indian?"

Eden raised her brows, surprised by his question
o. "Yes. Apache. He was caught as a boy of fifteen
nd brought to my grandfather, who raised him as a
and. Rattlesnake liked it at Rake's ranch well
nough, and he showed me many Apache tricks."

"Ah. Like how to use a knife?"

She preened. "You noticed?"

"I'd better warn Simon."

She laughed, then caught her breath as his tall,
road-shouldered frame stepped through the
rench doors. "I—I'm not dressed yet, sir."

His eyes raked over her towel-clad body. His ex-
ression was indulgent and amused, yet tinged with
at perpetual trace of cynicism. "I know. But some-
ne is coming."

"How—" A knock on the door cut off her ques-
on, and she stared wide-eyed at Shane as he
rossed the room. His senses were as keen as a
olf's. She watched him open the door to a young
an who spoke with him in low tones. The thick
air at the nape of his neck had curled, probably
om the humidity, and looked so tempting to touch.

When the man left, Shane closed the door and
rned to look at her. "She's alive."

Eden blinked. "Who?"

His lips tightened. "Camille," he said shortly, and
rode across the room to pour himself a brandy.

"You remember. The woman who shielded yo
from the danger in which she placed herself."

Eden bristled. She was not so insensitive as h
would like to believe, but she refused to give him th
satisfaction of showing him that side of her nov
"Yes, it *was* unfortunate the wig fell off. Now th
kidnappers know they were going to be duped. An
my brother's in just that much more jeopardy."

"Pity that."

Eden frowned, confused by his harsh tone. Mo
ments ago he had been almost warm, conversationa
and now he had slipped back into that cold, una
proachable persona. Softly she asked, "Did you sen
a missive to her?"

He nodded curtly, then tossed down his brandy i
two swallows. He poured another.

"I'm glad she's alive."

He turned slowly and his cynical gaze locked o
her. Lifting his drink at her, he drawled, "Good t
know you can feel for the 'underlings' of the world.

Eden drew herself up. "You're being deliberatel
rude, Mr. O'Connor, and I refuse to stand here an
listen to you."

He laughed shortly. "Seeing as we're locked int
the same room for the night, I don't see how yo
have much choice." He threw himself down on th
divan, loosened his cravat, and cradled the brand
snifter in both hands. "Do you plan to sleep in th
towel tonight, or will you sleep, as is customary fo
you, naked?"

She glared at him and clutched the towel tighte
between her breasts. Normally she would have bee
able to change into clean clothing after her bath, b
this situation made that option impossible. And h
knew it. What choice had she other than the obvio
one of redonning the dusty, damp clothes she ha

orn there? The thought made her wrinkle her
ose. Impudently, she met his hard gaze, ignoring
e heat that washed through her at the intensity of
s stare. "I don't see why it makes a difference to
u, Mr. O'Connor, exactly how I sleep—nude or
herwise. And another thing I want to know. Why
d you kiss me?"

He sipped his brandy, then said laconically, "It
as the fastest way to silence you, me darlin'."

Eden moved a step closer to him, trying to detect
e lie in his eyes. But she couldn't. He had dropped
s lashes in that peculiar way of his, and his gaze
as inscrutable. Still, she challenged him. "You
ssed me because you wanted to, Mr. O'Connor."

He smiled disagreeably. "I kissed you, madame,
silence you. You flatter yourself to think it was
ything more."

Eden felt curiously disappointed, confused, and
mehow hurt. It had seemed that he'd lingered
nger than necessary while "silencing" her, and had
und it difficult to pull away. Yet what did she
ow of such things?

"But why—" She broke off, catching her bottom
in her teeth. She remembered the hot, hard
rusts of his tongue, and shuddered. Just the mem-
y made her breasts swell, her nipples tighten into
gid points. Slightly embarrassed, she turned and,
eling as if she were walking a high wire, made her
ay to the bed. She sat carefully on its edge and
uared her shoulders. "I would like it, Mr.
'Connor, if you would please not use that annoyed
ne with me. We are here, as you mentioned, with-
t much choice in the matter, and I would like to
ake our stay as pleasant as possible."

Lounging back on the divan, his long legs extended and crossed at the ankles, Shane looke amused. "You would like that, would you?"

"Yes, very much."

Shane let his gaze drift down to the temptir swell of creamy skin that rose above the towel, tl cleft between her breasts, her beautiful shape shoulders and smooth, slender arms. He felt a gri ping urge to go to her, to sweep the towel away fro her seductive body and have her twine those arr around his neck as he crushed her close. He wante to push her down on that bed and enter her with long, slow thrust, to feel her sleek, moist, satiny fle surround him, grip him. She would be passiona and responsive, as she was about everything in life—he could almost hear the soft sounds she wou make as he possessed her. He was nowhere near unaffected by her kiss as he wanted her to believ Her full, soft mouth had responded to his with fe vor, and he wanted to taste her again. Now.

He shifted uncomfortably on the divan. She w turning out to be surprise after surprise. Thoug there was definitely a regal air about her, and sl fancied herself a queen of sorts, she was also gut and courageous and a whole lot more intellige than he had credited her. Yet . . . how much her was play-acting, how much of her was real? Sl certainly cared enough about her brother to pa with her money and risk her life. She had kept that ruthless pace he had set on the streets witho ever once whining. And he had kissed her. One the greatest damned mistakes of his life, and he ha made very few. For he knew now that she was woman who would leave an imprint on his soul if l let her. She was fire, and he was a torch, and t gether their heat was combustible. He woul scarcely have taken the chance of "silencing" her that particular fashion if he had known of her drugging power.

Yet he had known, instinctively, from the moment she had stepped into his office.

He brought his gaze back to her unforgettable green-blue eyes. "Blow out the lamp."

"What?"

Shane frowned with irritation. "Regardless that *you* seem to require very little sleep, I'd like to catch some. So blow out the lamp." *Then I won't have to look at you.*

Eden did, muttering about *his* being closer to the lamp, then she slipped into bed, draping the towel over a bedpost as she pulled the covers up to her chin. She lay still for a moment, sinking into the luxurious pillows, and felt only slightly guilty that she had the bed, he the divan. She supposed she should be more apprehensive about sharing a hotel room with a strange man—Mama would have been absolutely horrified—but Eden shrugged her mild misgivings away. Oddly, she trusted him. Of course, she was trusting of almost everybody, expecting the best out of people, but Shane O'Connor had made it clear that he was totally uninterested in her as a woman, that kiss notwithstanding. No harm had come to her while living briefly under his roof, and if his intention had been to force himself on her, she supposed he would have already done so.

Thinking back over the events of the past two days, she sighed. "I suppose my dagger's lost for good now."

"It would seem that way," he said in a mild tone. "Wouldn't have lost it if you weren't there."

She glared at him in the dark. Only it wasn't as dark as she would have preferred. She could see him stretched out on the divan. He had shed his black brocade vest and white shirt, and the moonlight spilled across his muscled chest, bare, sinewy shoulders, and powerful arms. The faint light dappled his tan skin in silver-white, making him look like a savagely beautiful sculpture. Her heart began to thud hard. It took her a moment to find her voice, and when she did, the anger had seeped out of it. Still, she was piqued. "You constantly bring up that moot point, Mr. O'Connor."

"I don't see how you can call it moot. If not for your interference, madame—and my having to look out for you—I would have had your brother safely delivered to you by now. Case closed."

Eden couldn't decipher whether he sounded annoyed because he hadn't yet closed the case, or because he would have been rid of her if he *had* closed the case. She turned over on her side and stared out the French doors. Somewhere out there in that huge city was her twin.

"I don't think that was Philip," she said softly. Immediately she could sense Shane's alertness, like a prowling mountain cat, all of his senses keenly aware.

"Why not?"

Her fingers toyed with the covers. "I think he would have called out to me—or who he thought was me," she finished dryly.

"That's a good point."

"I do make them sometimes."

"Mmm," Shane murmured. "That means they still have him hostage somewhere." Or they had killed him. "Damn," he added aloud. It struck him that he had not yet asked Eden for a description of Philip. He had assumed, because they were twins, that Philip was blond and blue-eyed, but they might not be identical. "Describe your brother to me." He waited. "Eden?"

Her name had slipped out again unbidden, but it didn't seem to matter. From what he could tell, she was fast asleep. It amazed him how she could be carrying on a perfectly normal conversation one moment and drop off unconscious the next. Especially when he was lying awake in the dark with his body uncomfortably tight and hard, in a state of acute arousal. From the corner of his eye he could see her beautifully turned hip, draped in silk, and he wondered how her breasts would feel in his palms. All he had to do was go to the bed, turn back the coverlet, and find out. The image of it made moisture break out on his forehead. He punched a silk pillow and closed his eyes, waiting for sleep to steal over him, but sleep did not come. He lay awake, memories and desire haunting him till the first light of morning showed in the city sky.

Eden woke with sunlight falling on her face. For a moment she lay staring at the ceiling, remembering last night.

It was still hot. Even the bedsheets clung to her skin. She started to stretch, then stopped when she caught the faint scent of soap on the air. Her heavy-lidded eyes trailed across the room to where Shane was shaving over the enamel washstand, which stood beneath a mirror. His back was turned toward her, and she was instantly mesmerized. He wore only trousers, and she could see the roped muscles of his back and shoulders rippling, bunching, and flexing with every movement he made. Her heart went weak as she watched him lift the razor and stroke it along his jaw. Such a masculine act. It aroused giddy sensations, a pulsing ache.

Hardly breathing, she allowed her gaze to drift lower, to where his black trousers hugged his perfect backside, and she clenched her hands, wanting to put them on him. Her mouth went dry. How beautiful he was, made of copper flesh, and sinew, and long, lean strength. She wanted to touch him, run her palms along the hard swell of muscles that rode his body like a dream, a forbidden dream.

He leaned down to rinse his face and swab it with a towel. When he was done he straightened and ran both of his hands through his coffee-colored hair, slicking it back to where it curled damply at his nape. Eden's heart was beating so hard, she felt faint. She watched him drape the towel around his neck, then he turned.

When their eyes met, she couldn't look away, or pretend that she hadn't been staring at him with an almost painful appreciation. Even now her gaze drifted down past the towel, stark white against his tan skin, following the dark hair that shadowed his chest and ran in a thin line down the plane of his stomach to disappear under the waistband of his trousers. Her breath caught when she saw the scar—a vicious jagged scar that cut from his abdomen to his side and curled like a serpent around to his lower back. She wanted to ask him about it, but thought it might embarrass him. She wanted to touch him with soothing fingertips, though she doubted he would want any comfort from her. Somehow, she thought, the scar only added to his dangerous appeal.

She glanced away from it, but unfortunately her stare dropped to the rising bulge of his manhood. Instantly her gaze flew up to his face, to his eyes, which were shielded once more by his thick, dark lashes.

"You're up." How long had she been studying him? Shane wondered. Under her open, searching gaze his body had stirred, had grown to full, heavy arousal. He damn well better do something about his burning need, and fast, too, if he knew what was good for both of them. Time to visit his mistress, though she had become exceedingly boring of late. The thought brought him great displeasure. Odd, how every woman he had ever known, no matter how sophisticated or beautiful, seemed bland in comparison to this candid, open, and astonishingly sensual creature. She lay half reclined upon the pillows, her flaxen hair tumbling wildly about her bare shoulders, her heavy-lashed turquoise eyes smoky from the last vestiges of sleep.

"Yes, I'm up." She smiled at him. "I see you are too." She flushed vividly as she realized the double entendre of her words. "I—I mean—"

"I've been up for a while now." As her cheeks became even pinker, he couldn't help smiling. He shrugged his shirt on. "You fell asleep as I was questioning you."

"I apologize. What was your line of questioning?"

He turned to the mirror to fasten his cravat, then looked back at her. "I was asking for a description of your brother."

She began to climb out of bed. "Oh, he looks like me, except he's six feet tall and has hazel eyes." She froze, obviously realizing that as she had flung the covers off, she'd given him a brief but thorough glimpse of her nude body. She squealed and dove back under them, only her nose poking out. "You have to hand me my clothes and leave the room while I dress."

Shane bowed mockingly. "Yes, madame." He grabbed her clothes and tossed them on the bed. She wrinkled her nose. "I hate to put them back on."

"Don't, then."

Her gaze flew to his, and he smiled. "With a body like yours, you could stop traffic—not to mention possibly starting a riot on the streets."

His backhanded compliment seemed to astonish her, and she did not think to speak again until he was already stepping out into the hall.

"Wait!" she cried, and he stopped, glancing back at her. "I'm starving! Can you order us a huge breakfast?"

He frowned, remembering her lusty appetite and how it aroused him to watch her eat. Absurd, he knew, but he'd fallen into the habit of equating food with passion. "We have to keep moving. I already made arrangements to breakfast elsewhere."

"Where?" she asked, inching out from under her covers.

"Camille's," he said, and shut the door.

CHAPTER FIVE

WHY," EDEN ASKED, HURRYING ALONGSIDE SHANE AS they strode up Broadway, "do we have to go to Camille's?"

Shane compressed his lips, fighting the urge to tell her that he regretted having to take her with him at all. Even early as it was, the sweltering heat streamed down on them, glancing off the stone-paved street, soaking their clothes, beating down on their bare heads. Shane was alert, squinting against the harsh glare of the sun as he watched for potential assailants. He kept his hand pressed to the small of Eden's back, shielding her with his body and urging her ahead of him. "You have asked that question at least a dozen times since we left the hotel."

She glanced up at him. "Yes, but you haven't answered me."

He led her to the back door of Camille's flat and knocked once.

Eden tried again. "They had a perfectly lovely breakfast at the hotel. And I'm starving." She put the back of her hand to her brow. "I do believe I might faint." When Shane frowned down at her, she added, "It's the heat—and my hunger."

"Don't provoke me, Eden."

She bristled just as the door opened, and Camille greeted them with a warm smile. Eden's heart sank. Camille was even more beautiful than Eden had imagined, with doe-brown eyes, creamy skin, and rich, dark brown hair. It seemed dark-haired women appealed to Shane, and she had further proof of that when he leaned down and gathered Camille into his arms.

"You *are* all right," Eden heard him murmur, and did not understand the tangle of emotions burgeoning within her.

Camille smiled up at him, her eyes bright with warmth and affection. "Oh, Shane, you worry too much. Of course I'm fine. I just regretted leaving you in a bind like that. But I lost my weapon and knew I would do you more good if I ran. It seems I had a bad case of clumsiness," she added ruefully, "and the jewels ended up in the river."

Eden caught her breath. With all the commotion and her worry about Philip, she had forgotten about the jewels. Now they had no collateral to use with the thieves in exchange for Philip's safe return. But Camille was smiling to reassure her.

"Don't worry, they were glass replicas. Shane had em duplicated—right down to the volcanic rock." Eden's eyes widened and the compliment was out fore she could stop herself. "How clever of you!" Shane seemed suddenly alert. His piercing gaze ll on her, and she wondered if he thought she was asing him. She wanted to assure him of her sincer-, but he turned to look at Camille again. "This," said, his voice rumbling-low and with the barest ace of amusement, "is my client, Mrs. Eden Lind-y."

Though Eden graciously stepped forward and ok Camille's hand, she felt a hot ache in her chest Shane's impersonal introduction. Of course, she asoned, it was a perfectly normal way to introduce er, but she felt slighted at his addition of the word client." "I apologize," she said, "if I jeopardized ur life last night. Mr. O'Connor tells me I did."

"Oh, Shane!" Camille turned to scold him, and ain Eden felt that absurd flash of jealousy that amille could call him Shane when he had insisted e call him Mr. O'Connor. "She was only trying to lp."

Shane lifted an eyebrow. "I'm surprised, Camille, at you would come to the defense of someone who arly got you killed."

Eden whirled to glare at him, but her mouth fell pen, for standing behind him was a tall man with air as red as a rooster's crown. His freckled face roke into a broad grin and he clapped a huge hand n Shane's shoulder. "Well, me foin friend, causin' ouble with the ladies as usual, I see."

Shane turned to regard him with a wry expres- on. "They're joining forces against me, Liam. What ave you to say about your wife's close brush with eath last night?"

His wife! Shocked, Eden watched the big Iris
man shrug his broad shoulders and stroll across th
kitchen to put an arm around Camille, who smile
up at him. "All in a day's work, me friend. All in
day's work." He turned his bright green gaze o
Eden. "An' who might be this bonny-faced lass?"

His brogue captivated Eden. It was, of cours
more a lilt than a brogue, for she knew that in Ame
ica, one survived best without accents. He looked
be older than Shane, perhaps thirty-six or so, but h
face was open and boyish, his eyes glimmering wi
the legendary Irish twinkle. She couldn't help b
smile back at him. "I'm Eden, Shane's helper."

Liam threw his head back and boomed wi
laughter. Shane, however, ran a hand over his fa
and shook his head, muttering something as h
strode to the kitchen table and pulled out a chai
"Forgive my manners," he said as if there was n
help for it, and dropped into the chair before th
women were seated. "Mrs. Lindsay," he said, glan
ing at Eden, "I present to you my good friend an
assistant, Liam Dougherty. Liam, may I present th
woman who . . . ah, made a marked difference i
the course of events last night."

His tone was faintly insulting, and Eden glowere
at him. Liam, though, who was correctly gauging th
tension between the two, chuckled softly. Well, s
that's how it was, he thought, watching Shane wit
shrewd eyes. In all the years since a rich society bitc
had practically ruined Shane's life, Liam had neve
seen his friend come undone. But now, despit
Shane's imperious, aloof exterior, Liam could se
that he was ruffled indeed. Always impeccabl
Shane had shaved, of course, but had missed h
upper lip. Liam doubted Shane was even aware tha

was absently rubbing the shadow of stubble
ere.

"Growing a mustache, eh, friend?" Liam asked,
ding his smile.

Shane glanced at him, frowning. Eden distracted
m, though, by dragging out a chair opposite him
d flounced onto it. "Mr. O'Connor insists on call-
g me Mrs. Lindsay, but that's silly, don't you
ink?"

Amused, Liam looked at Shane. " 'Tis."

Shane's frown intensified.

Eden gave Liam a beaming smile. "I'm glad you
ree. Sometimes he can be so unreasonable." She
anced down at her clothes, her brow wrinkling in
wilderment. "For instance, he would not let me
op at my home first and change my clothing. You'll
st have to pardon my appearance. He didn't seem
find the need for me to look presentable."

"An ogre he is sometimes," Liam said, grinning.
e and Shane went a long way back, and since Liam
as the older of the two, he felt he some rights that
one else in the world would dare take with Shane
'Connor. Liam liked this woman, too, and was in-
nt on seeing Eden's perspective at least. "So tell
e, Eden," he said, winking at his wife before he
rode across the kitchen to take down bowls and
ates for breakfast, "did you enjoy your stay at the
fth Avenue Hotel last night?"

Eden's cheeks grew warm. She glanced at Shane,
ho merely gazed back at her, then she looked at
iam. "Mr. O'Connor forced me to room with him,
u see. I had no choice in the matter."

Liam shook his head and gave Shane a mock
owl. "Brute. I hope he behaved as a gentleman at
l times?"

Eden's face grew hotter. "Well, yes," she said i
breathless rush. "He's *always* a gentleman."

The note of disappointment in her voice ma
Liam look at her curiously, and he hid his amu
ment as he started to prepare pancakes. "Shane
that," he said, "a gentleman to the core."

Disgruntled and not even knowing why, Eden
back. Shane was staring at her, his gaze cool a
remote. She should be able to read such eyes, s
thought, so light were they, but he was a master
probing without revealing any information of
own.

"And I would know that," Liam went on, mixi
batter by the cookstove. "About his bein' a ge
tleman, that is. His ma taught him well. I've kno
him since we were no higher than the countert
here, an' workin' in the coal mines in Pennsylvani

Eden's jaw dropped. "You worked in a mine?

Liam hooked his thumbs in his waistband, tilt
his head back to look up at the ceiling, and laugh
"Were ya thinkin' he lived all his life in the lap
luxury, mavournin? Ah, no, though it appears th
way, I'll give you that. The boyo has manners equ
to the aristocracy of this here foin town. But no,
were once urchins runnin' in the streets, weren't v
friend?"

Though Eden half expected the very priva
Shane O'Connor to be angered by Liam's dive
gences, she was stunned to see a smile touch h
eyes, crinkling them slightly at the corners. His tee
were very white and even, startlingly attracti
against the weathered tan of his features. His w
the most riveting smile she had ever seen, and
erased the harsh cynicism from his face, making
appear unguarded. Even his eyes had warme

ming like the sun on a winter day. Eden was
ivated.

That's right," he said in a slow, easy drawl she
never heard from him before, "and I saved your
more 'n once on these mean streets, old
d."

His voice held a trace of a brogue that made her
er. The accent was rolling, almost musical, and
Shane O'Connor, unequivocally seductive. It
ld be, she thought, a strange warmth unfurling
in her, the voice he would use in the night with
oman in his arms. And as she listened to him and
ched him, she wondered what it might be like to
hat woman. Her own thoughts horrified her, but
could not seem to stop them, or the tumult of
tions warring inside her.

Like the time O'Malley had a knife to your
oat," Shane went on. "Remember that?" He
ghed softly.

Ah, no, me memory fails me," Liam said with a
epish glance toward his wife. "Don't you believe
, me darlin'."

ut Camille was laughing too. "I've never known
ne to lie," she teased.

Ah, but he exaggerates his abilities."

den didn't think so. The way he had fought the
t before had been brutal, vicious . . . and nec-
ry. The man was extremely competent, and le-
. But she kept silent, feeling much the outsider in
tightly knit circle of friends.

Camille cast her husband another teasing look as
made the coffee. "Ah, but I'm sure you've 'saved
hide' on more than one occasion, have you not,
darling?"

iam began to peel potatoes. "Ah, yes. Like the

time I pulled him clear of that runaway dray.
member that, me mate?"

Laughing still, Shane slouched even lower on
chair, linking his hands behind his head. Again E
saw the white flash of his teeth. "No."

Liam looked indignant. "Ya save a man's life
that's the thanks it gets ya." He cut up the pota
with a vengeance, until Camille removed the k
from his fingers and put the potatoes in a pan to
Liam didn't even seem to notice as he turne
Shane. "Ah, but I was better at stick ball than
were."

"Well, you always found the best broom han
for our bats," Shane said, and laughed again w
Liam swore.

"Excuse me language, lass," he said to Eden, v
was watching all this with delight. "But the man
dragged in here this mornin' is a damned blo
liar."

His scowl grew fiercer when Shane laughed n
heartily. Eden could hardly believe this was the s
man who treated her with such cold arrogance a
for the most part, insulting indifference. With
friends he was warm and amiable, at ease, able
show a wonderful, wry sense of humor. Though
basked in the warmth of his rare smile, she felt h
that he could not—would not—share this side
himself with her. Ridiculous, she knew, yet the l
lingered.

"I *did* save his life," Liam said, drawing her att
tion back to him, "when the brat was but nine y
old an' deliverin' milk by horse cart. Little fool
into the street, almost got killed. I yanked him ou
the way by the scruff of his neck, and"—Liam s
denly gave a shout of laughter—"I know why
bloody well don't remember. You turned on me

rnered cat and near pummeled me to death be-
I could even catch me breath. Ungrateful little
a were even then." Grinning, he turned back to
tove and put on sausage to fry.

remember, Liam," Shane said. His voice was
r, and his eyes held an odd glint, as if he saw
elf back on the streets. "You brought me home
ur mother that night and fed me mutton stew."

am looked over his shoulder at him. "She
ted ta keep ya fer one of her own. Shoulda
d," he muttered. "But ya had too much
ned pride even back then."

silence fell between them. Only the sizzle of the
g potatoes and sausage cut through the still air.
dd ache seemed to permeate the kitchen, filling
Eden. Then Liam said, "Maybe 'twas a good
g, since she died so soon afterward."

amille put a hand on Liam's forearm. "You were
g Eden about the coal mines."

Oh, yes!" Liam's face cleared. "We worked in
fer two years, then couldn't stand the pit of the
h any longer, and came back to New York to run
a wild pack of boys."

den's eyes widened, and she looked at Shane.
For a while," he said quietly.

But it was long enough, wasn't it, boy-o?" Liam
with great verve, oblivious of Shane's darkening
ression. "Long enough to learn the streets, and
to stay alive."

Was that when you learned how to fight so
?" Eden asked.

iam nodded. "We had a very mean-spirited man
d One-eyed Jack who taught us some very dirty,
, I must say, helpful survival techniques." He
ured with a big hand toward his best friend.

"An' this sophisticated gent was ol' Jack's best
pil."

A silent exchange passed between the two
like a dark secret, shared horrors from a war. I
looked from one man to the other as she took
cup of coffee that Camille set before her, then
gaze settled on Shane.

"But what had your mama to say about su
wild boy?" she asked.

A hard light came into Shane's eyes, and the
cles in his jaw flexed. "My mother did not kno

"You kept it a secret?"

"My mother would have turned over in her g
that is, if she had one, if she knew what had bec
of me. I was an orphan when I set foot on t
shores. My parents died en route."

As if he had revealed too much, he stood to v
his hands at the pump. He was angry. She coul
it in the set of his big shoulders, the tightness i
face. Liam whisked the plates to the table wi
flourish and grinned at her.

"You'd never know it to look at him now, w
ya, mavournin? Who woulda guessed that little
fian would become one of New York's richest, i
powerful men? But—" Liam made a rueful
"He never was able to turn his blood blue, wer
me boy?"

"Nor would I ever want to." He sent Eden a
ting glance, and she lifted her nose in response

"One cannot be held accountable for their bl
lines," she said.

Liam cleared his throat. "No matter, that, fo
wines and dines and deals with the biggest and
of 'em . . . when he so chooses. Funny thing, t
He doesn't really *like* the rich, doesn't much lik
rub elbows with 'em."

"I find it interesting," Shane said with a warning dare for his friend, "that you've analyzed my character so precisely."

Liam winked at Eden. "Don't listen to 'im. He's shy, he is, and most modest. But don't let him fool a, Miss Eden. All he ever did—the hard work—the fortune he made—he did it all for Meggie."

The name froze in midair. Catching sight of Shane's hard, shuttered face, his feral, glittering eyes, Liam went white. In his exuberant mood he had said too much, and there were boundaries with Shane that even Liam dared not cross.

"If I were not civilized," Shane said slowly, "I would call you out, friend."

Eden could not bear to look at Liam's face. That he should be so humiliated before her, and his wife! "Shane!" she exclaimed, hurting for Liam. Shane's gaze sliced across the room to her, chilling her. She had used his first name again, she realized too late, but she didn't care. "You mustn't be so serious! We don't care about your past women—"

"Enough!" he said. That one word was like ice. Camille and Liam looked away from him, but Eden was glowering at him as he crossed the kitchen and sat back down in his chair across from her.

"Ignore him," Eden told Liam. "He's a horrid bully."

To her surprise, Liam laughed. "That he is, lady, that he is."

"And terribly ungallant."

"He is that too."

The tension was broken. Still, Eden would not forgive Shane his rudeness. Between bites she pinned him with her most murderous glares, until even he became casually amused.

"Have you ever seen a woman eat like this one?"

he asked at length, and laughed when she speare
him with another furious glance.

"Aye, an' it does me heart good ta see it," Liar
said. She swallowed and flashed him her most rad
ant smile. "Have more," he added then, his red eye
brows shooting up as Eden heaped on severa
hotcakes. "How you can eat like that and stay s
slender?" He sat back to watch her with awe.

"Mama has always been horrified by my appe
tite," she said, and wrinkled her nose. "She think
females should survive on as little food as possibl
But Rake raised me to trust my own appetite and no
what others deemed right for me." She paused t
give Shane a pointed stare, then she smiled again a
Liam. "And you are a fine cook, Liam Dougherty—
rare trait in a man—to cook, that is."

He nodded, pleased. "Who, may I ask, is Rake?

"Her grandfather," Shane answered. "Fror
Texas."

"I don't see why," she said, not bothering to la
her fork down, "you think you have the right t
divulge *my* private life before strangers when yo
can't even allow memories of your own to be dis
cussed among friends, Mr. O'Connor."

Liam waggled his eyebrows. "She has a poin
Shane."

Shane scowled. "She hasn't a point at all, dam
mit."

Liam laughed. "Oh, but I think she does, don'
you, Camille?"

"I have to agree with my husband, Shane."

"You weren't agreeing with him before."

They had all sat back now, lingering over thei
coffee—all but Eden. She didn't mind their stares
and was especially impervious to Shane's narrowe
gaze as she popped a biscuit into her mouth. Sh

new without looking at him that he was as intensely aware of her as she was of him. Some kind of torrid undercurrent burned between them, and she wondered that the others didn't feel it too. When she had chewed and swallowed the biscuit, she said, "Usually before breakfast I'd go out riding with my grandfather. I miss that."

"Ah, ya had horses, did ya?"

"Oh, yes! Rake's ranch was a horse ranch, you realize."

A look of mischief crept over Liam's freckled face. "No, I didn't realize. You have somethin' in common with Shane here. Did ya know that, Shane, boy-?"

All he got in response was a lethal glare.

"I realize that we have that in common," Eden said, "but Mr. O'Connor seems to find it distasteful to talk to me about anything he considers personal."

Liam fingered the handle on his coffee mug, his eyes dancing as he glanced at Shane. "Why do you suppose that is? I find it nothing but rude meself."

Shane had put on a look of boredom, but that didn't stop Liam. He was enjoying himself immensely.

"Yup," he went on, "this man's got two passions—and horses is one of them."

"What's the other?" Eden asked, falling right into Liam's plan for the course of conversation.

"He hasn't told you?" Liam's eyebrows shot up as he shook her head. "Why, it's the theater. He's fascinated by it."

Eden drew in a quick breath. Her gaze flashed to Shane, who was scowling at Liam. Liam was still undeterred, enjoying his role as devil's advocate as he sat back in his chair, one ankle propped on the opposite knee.

" 'Tis true," he continued. "When Shane was ju a sprite, he'd slip into the theater—without payi mind you—and watch the shows, utterly fas nated."

"Really." Anger flared through Eden. His derisi comments and total disdain for her "hobby," as l had so neatly put it, had put her on the defensi with him almost from the start. To learn that theat was one of his "passions" made his rejection of h "hobby" all the more personal . . . and she felt the more wounded.

"And," Liam went on ruthlessly, "passion for th ater runs in his family, it does. His great-uncle was famous stage performer in Ireland, and even h da—"

"I think," Shane interrupted in an icy tone, "th my personal *passions* have been discussed nauseaum."

"But it was just getting interesting," Eden cou tered, delighting in the sight of the muscle twitchir at the corner of Shane's mouth. "You didn't tell n any of this, Mr. O'Connor, and frankly, I find th obviously deliberate omission quite absurd." Sl leaned forward on her elbows, gazing at him with purposely guileless expression. Still, her brea caught when she met his eyes, which were like sli ers of ice.

"My family," he said tautly, "is my business."

An uneasy silence settled in the kitchen. Eve Liam was quiet.

"Shall we move on," Shane said after a minut "to the matter at hand—the reason we are here i the first place?" He paused effectively, then shifte his gaze to Camille. "Were you able to detect th man they identified as Philip?"

Camille put down her coffee cup. "It was hard t

, Shane. He was tall, of course, but I couldn't see
his hair was light. I couldn't even make out his
.tures."

Shane was silent. Seeing the harshness in his fea-
es, Eden felt discouraged. A hot ache rose in the
ck of her throat, and she swallowed hard.

"Maybe they never had Philip," she said. "Maybe
neone else—"

"I think they have him—or did," Shane inter-
oted her, his voice grim. "They know you want
ur brother back. They also know you've hired me.
the future they'll be more cautious . . ." And,
ost likely, he added silently, a good deal rougher
her brother. "Their primary aim is to obtain the
ms and get your twin off their hands." And it was
to Shane to make certain they didn't kill Philip, if
ey hadn't already. He wondered if the thugs knew
e gems were lost in the river, and hoped they
ln't, that it had been too dark to see. If they did
ow, then Philip was as good as dead.

"I think," he said, "there were too many men last
ght for them all to be the thieves. No doubt they
re hired by the thieves, and threatened by them
at if they returned without the jewels, they would
killed." He saw the color drain from Eden's face
d tightened his lips. "They know to either contact
e or you—and the most likely place to contact you
ould be at the theater." When her face lit up, he
rned, "Don't get any ideas."

But Eden had already "got" them. "I can't think
a better place to wait for word from Philip." Her
ile grew wider. "So when are we headed for
ere?"

"*We're* not."

She frowned at him. "*I* hired you, sir. It is my
od money—"

He cut her off again. "We have been this ro
before," he said as he stood up, bracing both han
on the table and leaning toward her.

"Oh! I forgot once again! In all this furor I ha
yet remembered to write you out a check." S
glanced at Camille and Liam. "No wonder he's
touchy. I have yet to give him his measly twen
thousand-dollar retainer."

She was oblivious of Camille's and Liam's start
looks, but Shane felt obliged to say to his friends,
know that I will get paid. I will escort Mrs. Lind:
to her house to get the check later in the day. I
going to the Fulton ferry now, where I have an a
pointment with a . . . er, rather unsavory lender
money who could have an idea about Philip. I
might even be able to tell me something about t
jewels." As soon as he said it, he knew he should
have.

"Are you going to see Sly Camponelli or El Da
ger?" Eden asked. "Which one is it, Mr. O'Conno
I have a right to know. Or is it Stealth?"

Shane's lips tightened again. "Camille, keep I
here. She is not to leave the premises. Understood

Eden took offense. "I am not a child!"

Shane didn't even bother to look at her. "She is
be monitored. It's all for her own good."

Eden's eyes were blazing. He straightened to I
full height, and she tilted her head back to glare
him. "And I find it interesting that you, M
O'Connor, profess to know what is for my ov
good."

He kept his gaze on Camille. "I'll be a couple
hours at most, then I'll take her off your hands."

"Stop talking past me as if I weren't here!" Ed
exclaimed. To Camille and Liam she added, "M
O'Connor must curb this tendency of his to rega

as an inanimate object when in the company of
…ers."

'You really must, boyo." Liam gave his friend a
…ong look of reproach.

Shane ignored them both. He raked his hands
…ough his hair, smoothing it back off his forehead,
…l continued to address Camille. "Make sure she
…es not move out of your sight—" He stopped in
…dsentence as he saw tears spring to Eden's eyes.
… felt a strong wrench in his chest, and cursed.
…or the love of God!" he swore, angrier at himself
… his reaction than at her. "Not again!"

But Eden was wailing now. "I want my brother
…ck!"

Camille rushed over to her and threw Shane a
…k of rebuke. "Shane! Stop being so heartless.
…is is her twin brother we're trying to rescue! Of
…urse she is going to be upset. There, there," she
…d, patting Eden's shoulder. "He's just a bear
…en things don't go his way—"

Shane was close to the point of shouting. "She's
… actress, for God's sake!"

Liam was glaring at him now as well. And he *did*
…ut—or bellowed. "Well, anyone can bloody well
… those tears are real, man!" He took two long
…ides toward Eden and laid a massive hand on her
…posite shoulder. "There, there now, me darlin',
…ona worry, me sweet. He's a ruffian, but 'tisn
…led the best detective in the East for nothing."

"He's the most heartless." Eden sniffled, then
…sed her head to pierce Shane with an indignant
…k.

"Yes, yes," Liam agreed. "That he is, but 'tis a
…lt we must overlook."

Shane was staring at them all with sheer disgust
…d complete astonishment. Had his closest friends

taken leave of their senses? The woman was impos-
ble! Yet she had so effortlessly swept up these d
friends of his—but strangers to her—disarmi
them with her obvious, *affected* charisma. And ne
her tears. He swore silently, refusing to be lured
well, and walked toward the door. "Keep her lock
in." At their horrified gasps he turned and look
straight at Liam. "I'm warning you, friend, she
trouble with a capital T."

Furious now, Eden surged to her feet. Mimicki
his position from moments before, she placed l
hands on the table and leaned over it, intentiona
displaying the full curve of her breasts. With sm
satisfaction she saw his gaze flick down. He was a
so indifferent. "I want my brother back. I want
change my clothes, go to the theater, and—much
I hate to admit it—pay you!"

Their eyes clashed and held; his piercing-brig
hers defiant. Then she lost her breath as his fier
burning gaze swept over her, both intimate and d
passionate at once. "You seem most eager to 'p
me, madame," he said, the cynical smile that s
hated hovering around his lips. Deliberately,
dropped his gaze once again to her full bosom a
let his stare linger. "I wonder why that is. . . ."

His meaning was not mistaken. Eden stiffene
"You," she said coldly, drawing herself up to her f
height, "are a despicable man."

He laughed. Then, in that sensual brogue th
made her skin tingle, he said, "You don't know t
half of it, darlin'."

She squelched the hot wave of temper that rose
her, but felt it flush her cheeks. Tears had dried
them, making them sticky, and suddenly she realiz
the reason for his surly behavior. "It's my tears, is
it?" she said softly.

"What?"

She smiled at him, certain no man could be as ensitive, or hide it so well, as Shane O'Connor. She as beginning to like him. But she found him most xasperating. "Really, sir, I told you already, you ust *not* concern yourself with my tears. They are st an expression—a release—of sorrow—fear— ustration—"

"I know what tears are," he said stiffly. "And I now how many ways a woman can use them."

She was outraged again, and planted her hands on er hips. "I will follow you to Fulton if I please."

Shane took one threatening step toward her. He asn't sure what he was going to do with her when e had her, and putting her over his knee seemed a ound notion. But Liam insinuated his way between em, and Camille wisely led Eden down the hall- ay, advising her to rest.

"Calm down, man," Liam said, grasping his arm. You insulted her. How do you expect the woman react? And you don't really think she'd dare fol- w—"

"She'd dare anything." Though he spoke with ir- tation, there was a grudging admiration in Shane's ne too. He heard her wail then, and he swore. She is the most—"

Liam hid his grin. "Here, change your shirt."

"My shirt?"

"Yes, here's one of mine."

"I don't want one of your shirts, Liam. Hell, that oman is—"

"Yes, yes, I know." Liam held a blue cambric irt toward Shane.

"No, no, you don't know. Don't let Camille leave er for an instant. Check her now. I'll wager you e's already slipped out of Camille's clutches."

"Put the shirt on, man. You're missin' half ye studs."

Shane frowned. "What the hell?" He looke down at his shirtfront to find that indeed, it was onl partially fastened. His frown intensified. "How th hell did that happen?" But he knew. Eden. Damn, the woman wasn't distracting. He remembered he on the bed that morning, her sunny hair spilling ove her bare shoulders, and he understood why he ha left the hotel half dressed.

He took the shirt from the grinning Liam an shrugged into it. As he was fastening the cuffs, C mille returned to the kitchen, smiling. She froze however, when she saw Shane's expression.

"Dammit, Camille," he said. "You didn't leav her alone, did you?"

Camille rolled her eyes. "Shane! For the love c heaven! She was exhausted and needed some res Trust me, that woman is going nowhere."

"It's not you I don't trust, Camille." He set o toward the bedroom, tucking Liam's shirt into hi trousers as he went. When he got to the doorway h stopped abruptly, stunned. There was no doub about it. Eden was curled up on the bed, soun asleep, looking as innocent and peaceful as a baby

CHAPTER SIX

$\mathcal{S}$HANE TOOK LONG STRIDES TOWARD THE DOCKS. Hands shoved into his pockets, his sharp gaze scanning the streets, he was glad he was wearing Liam's work shirt. He blended in with the fishermen and merchants as he neared the fish market. His rendezvous at the market was not foremost on his mind, however. Eden was.

Damn the woman. He had allowed her to muddy his usually keen thinking, and he had only himself to blame. He should have never taken the case; from the start all his instincts had screamed a loud, distinctive no. She could exasperate a saint. And he was a far cry from a saint. Worse, just thinking about her made his muscles tense, and he was spoiling for a fight. It had been years since he had allowed anyone to get under his skin, years since he'd used his fists to release tension, but he was as tense as a caged wildcat, and he was ready to spring.

He arrived at the market and spotted Camponelli, smoking by the pier. He was a small, mean, and ugly man, and Shane had dealt with him before. Shane glanced back over one shoulder, half expecting Eden to come bounding up behind him. He had never had so much trouble keeping a client protected in all his years of practice. He had even stood over her for several minutes before he had left Liam's, just to make certain she was actually sleeping. Liam and Camille had stared at him as if he were daft, but he knew they would learn in time.

Seeing no signs of Eden, Shane approached Camponelli, his face purposely hard, his smile cold. They were virtually alone. Only a slim boy wearing a cap sitting on the dock and an old bum were nearby, and neither showed any interest in Shane or Camponelli.

Sly Camponelli looked up at Shane, his black eyes slitted. He looked, Shane thought, like the rat he was. Before Shane even spoke, Sly whined, "I don't see why I should give you anything on that worthless piece of life." He was referring to Eden's twin. "Wastin' a busy man's time you are, O'Connor."

Shane slipped him twenty dollars, and Sly immediately pocketed it. Shane passed him a cheroot, and Sly lit it. "I agree," Shane said, his gaze flicking over the wooden warehouses on the pier, the ornamental iron crest rails on the roof of the Fulton Ferry Building. He looked back at Sly. "But I've got a client that needs to locate him."

Sly tensed, suddenly predatory. "Oh, yeah?" He

haled on the cheroot, then exhaled the smoke in a
nort. "Who might that be?" He lifted his face, gaz-
ng off to the side, and the sun reflected dully off his
itted skin.

If Shane told Sly about Eden, he'd be on her trail
ke a hound on a hare. "When did you last see
im?" he asked instead.

Sly hunched his shoulders. "I ain't seen the weasel
1 a month. But when I catch up to him I'm gonna
reak both his legs—and shoot his kneecaps. He
wes me so much dough, it'll take him years to pay
1e off, and I heard he had it and spent it in one
ight. Ya know, I thought he was a good risk, I did,
vin' up on Fifth Avenue and all, but—"

As Sly babbled on, Shane's gaze drifted to a group
f boys that had wandered toward them. They were
hedding their clothes to kick up their heels in the
vater that washed over the lower docks near the
varehouses. Out of the corner of his eye he saw
he lad on his right sidle toward them.

"I ain't got years worth of patience," Sly was go-
1g on. "An' as far as I see it, he's got two choices.
Come work for me, or die. He sure as hell ain't
onna come up with the loo—What the hell—"

In a rattler-swift move Shane lashed out and
lamped a big hand around the slim lad's arm. A
quick jerk and the boy's cap tumbled off. A cascade
f thick wheat-blond hair spilled out, and Sly let out
sound that was half hiss, half wheeze.

"Holy sh—"

Shane was so furious, he didn't trust himself to
peak. His fingers tightened around Eden's arm, and
he winced. "You're hurting me."

"You're lucky," he said between his teeth, "I'm
ot killing you." Still, he let go of her, not trusting
imself to touch her.

"A woman!" Sly exclaimed, and ran his gaze up and down the slender form clad in boy's garb. "What—who—"

Eden was rubbing her arm and glaring at Shane, undaunted by his formidable expression. Looking away from him, she bestowed upon Sly a brilliant smile and extended her hand toward him. "Mr. Camponelli, it's a pleasure to meet you."

Sly, totally dumbfounded, took her hand.

"A pleasure!" Shane roared, and people turned to stare. "Do you know who this man is, you little fool?"

Eden turned to frown at him. "I beg your pardon, Mr. O'Connor—"

"You'll be begging a lot more than my pardon, lady, when I'm finished with you." He reached for her again, but she adroitly escaped him, ducking behind the totally baffled Sly.

"Please, Mr. Camponelli, tell him to get control of himself. He has a vicious temper, and I—"

Sly tried to get a glimpse of her, but she stayed out of his sight, dancing from one foot to the other behind him. "Are you one of his pretties, miss?" He craned his neck around to see her.

She looked horrified. "Pretties? Heavens, no! Mr. O'Connor can barely tolerate my presence. He positively seethes whenever he sets eyes on me! See, look at him."

Sly glanced at Shane's rock-hard face, his chilling eyes, and had to nod. "Yes, I do see. O'Connor, didn't know you beat yer women."

Shane swore in disgust. "Eden, you have to the count of three to get your impertinent little butt over here, or I'm going to sling you over my shoulder and carry you that way through the city."

"You wouldn't."

"One."

"Please, Shane, I need to talk to Mr. Camponelli—"

Sly scratched his head. "Why does she need to talk to me?"

"Two—and call me O'Connor."

"Shane, you are the biggest bully—and you just called me Eden again. Please, be patient for a moment and let me talk to this man about my brother—"

Shane pounced. She let out a little scream, but he had only slung a heavy arm around her waist and hauled her against him. She found the intimacy extremely uncomfortable. Looking up, she met the fierce blaze of his eyes.

"I would tell you to shut up," he said, "but you've already managed to give this man information that, as you can see, is making him froth at the mouth."

She glanced at Sly, who was grinning ferally at them both.

"I didn't know the kid had a sister."

Shane narrowed his eyes, staring hard at the small man. "You even think of touching her, of even walking down the same side of the street she's on, Camponelli, and your balls will be shark bait. Got it?" He felt Eden stiffen beside him at his crude choice of words, but Sly understood. He'd gone pale. He knew Shane never made idle threats.

Shane tightened his grip on Eden, who'd begun to squirm against him. "Move."

"But there are boys up there."

He glanced at the nude boys frolicking in the water. "Yes."

Eden looked mortified. "They're naked."

"Yes." He began to force her forward.

"Some are young men."

He looked down at her. Her cheeks were stained with color. A faint smile tugged at his lips. "And they have nothing you haven't seen before."

Her cheeks grew brighter. "You're going to make me walk past them."

"It's preferable to standing here all day in the broiling heat."

"Hardly."

"If you didn't trail after me like a tenacious bird dog, you wouldn't find yourself in embarrassing situations like this."

"And if I didn't trail after you, I would be kept in the dark."

"A good place to keep you, I'm thinking."

Eden moved with as much poise as she could muster, averting her eyes. Still, helplessly fascinated, she found her gaze straying to a young man of about nineteen. Her husband hadn't looked like *that*—young and hard and tautly fleshed, smooth muscles flexing and bunching as he moved. She felt a queer pull in her belly, something primitive stirred up by the sight and sounds of the male youths, and couldn't resist stealing another quick peek. How wonderful to be so wild, so free! She remembered the sultry, lazy days of her own youth in Texas, when she would shed her clothes on the banks of the river near the ranch and swim away the afternoons. How uninhibited she had been, until her body had begun to change, to develop. Then everything changed. How unfair that even as boys grew into men they could remain uninhibited. They had no qualms about stripping out in the open, while women had to relinquish such freedoms at a much earlier age.

"Perhaps," Shane drawled, "you would like to photograph them for further reference."

Eden's gaze flew to him. She was scandalized that

had caught her staring—and with such open curi-
ty! But she quickly rebounded and chased after
n—as usual he was walking slightly ahead of her,
e an arrogant Apache who expected his women to
low close at heel. "I was just thinking," she said,
ow unfair it is that males can strip out in the open
thout thinking twice, while women are not al-
wed such liberties!"

He glanced at her, his expression wry. "I think
st men would be happy to allow women that in-
lgence." He continued walking, taking long
ides, his hands shoved into his pockets.

"Allow!" she repeated, frustrated. "That's the
oblem, don't you see? We shouldn't need permis-
n! Why is it that men have the final say in every-
ng?"

Shane slowed to smile at her, an arrogant, purely
le smile. "Because we're bigger and stronger than
men are."

Eden still smoldered with the unfairness of it all.
hen she glanced up again, she saw Shane's gaze
d become warm, thoughtful, and her breath
ught at the flame that had leapt into the centers of
e silver depths. "Mrs. Lindsay," he said, "you can
ip and play in the water too, when you return to
y estate. I give you permission."

Shane wasn't surprised when anger flashed in her
es. They were equally blue and green, he noticed,
eming to darken and lighten like water that
anged as a cloud passed over it. He actually
pped in the street to stare down at her, mesmer-
d—not so much by her sensual appeal, but by the
pressions that chased across her face and surfaced
her open gaze. His own gaze drifted to her velvety
roat, lingering on the hollow, where a fine sheen of
rspiration traced her skin and the sun glimmered

gold. He saw her pulse pick up there, where he su
denly—urgently—longed to press his mouth. Fu
ous by the potent need pumping through him,
frowned and started to walk again. Dammit, she w
the most *un*inhibited woman he had ever know
and she wanted to be more so. The thought of h
naked on his private stretch of beach was too da
gerous for any healthy, normal man to entertain.

"I don't *want* to go back to your house," she sa
as she caught up with him.

She sounded dejected, and Shane didn't know
he would ever be able to keep up with her moo
The sooner he located her brother, the better—
she'd give him a bloody moment to do it! "T
bad."

She bristled at his curt tone. "There you go aga
snapping at me. Do you have to be so surly? Ca
you understand that even though I like the oce
and your home is quite lovely, I really need to stay
the city so I can go about my own life and try
keep my mind off Philip?" She was running alor
side him now, like a lapdog after her mast
"How," she panted, "can you protect me if you'
eight steps ahead of me!"

She shouted the last, and he stopped dead in h
tracks, turning to pierce her with a look that wou
have warned any creature that valued his or her li
But Eden stood with her hands on her slim hip
ignoring the curious stares of passersby, an obstina
tilt to her chin.

She heard him hiss something obscene under h
breath, then he took the four steps back to her, h
height and powerful shoulders suddenly formidab
instead of attractive. Eden fought down the inexp
cable alarm shooting up her spine. She could s

w that under his tautly controlled façade Shane
as burning with anger.

His big hands clamped down on her upper arms
d he dragged her away from the crowded sidewalk
to an alley between two buildings. She didn't even
ve the sense to struggle. He was forceful, indomi-
ble. In the alley he pressed her back against a
uilding, and she could feel the cool stone through
r damp cotton shirt.

With his hands still gripping her arms, he leaned
ose, and she could see the harsh determination
rved into every masculine feature, the unmitigated
ry in his eyes. She shuddered.

He shook her—lightly—and pressed his hard
dy to hers, flat against the building. His hands
amped around her wrists and he held her arms
ove her head, so she was crushed under him like a
crifice. All their parts touched—her pliant breasts
his stone-hard chest, his steely thighs to hers, fem-
ine, lithe, and slender. He was one hard plane, like
slab of wood, but warm, and pulsing, and real.

"Look at me."

Even his whisper was harsh—and sexual. Raw vi-
lity burned in him, and she could not meet his
aring eyes, could not reveal to him her fear—an
solute cold fear of herself. Of her want, of the
mpant emotions that charged through her like
mething untamed.

"I said look at me."

He shifted his body against her, and she could feel
s force, his energy, humming against her, singing
her veins, her blood. She met his gaze, alive with
tensity and heat. He shifted again, and her eyes
idened; his muscles were hard and intimate, press-
g into her curves. Her throat was locked up tight,
d she could not make a sound—could only watch

him, fascinated by the harshness in his taut feature
the tiny scar under his left eye that she had not n
ticed before.

"Now that I have your undivided attention," I
said in a voice that was phantom-soft, "I'm going
ask you a question. Do you think you can answer
without drama?"

She puffed up, but he stiffened against her, for
ing her to be still.

"Did you not hire me to find your brother?"

If he would just back off a few inches! She cou
feel his warm breath upon her skin, and inside sh
felt a curious melting that made her voice trembl
"Well, *technically* I haven't hired you yet because
haven't paid—" She broke off, wincing as his finge
tightened around her wrists. "Yes," she breathe
and immediately his grip loosened.

"Then," he said even softer, "you either allow n
to do my job in peace and my way, or I walk awa
now. Do you understand that, Mrs. Lindsay?" H
tone promised dire consequences if she did not.

Eden lowered her gaze to his mouth. She couldn
help it. His lips were hard and full, and madly, sh
wanted him to kiss her again, wanted to feel th
compelling warmth of his mouth on hers, and fc
him to take his time about it.

"Answer me."

She raised her gaze to his again and found it odd
beautiful, and dangerous. She tried to steady he
voice. "If you would please let go of me, sir . . ."

"If you don't give me your word now, then
walk."

A desperate panic lanced through her bod
"He's *my* brother! I want to help. I need to be ce
tain you're doing all you should be doing—"

"What you *need*," he interrupted, "is to stay aliv

u *need* to stop blundering into dangerous situa-
ns, and you *need* to do what I tell you." He let go
her as he continued speaking in a low, seething
ce. "Have you any idea what kind of man Sly
mponelli is? Dammit, woman, you can't be traips-
 after me like some inept puppy dog, always get-
g under my heels!"

Glowering at him, Eden rubbed her arms and her
ists where his touch still burned. Though he'd
pped away, she could feel the imprint of his body
 hers, and she longed to feel it against her again.
t she was angry now too. He was insulting her,
d she was going to put a stop to it. "Mr.
Connor," she said icily, "I'll have you know that I
ve *not* been traipsing after you, but that I have
ived in both meeting places—last night *and* this
rning—before you! Who's the inept, hmmm?"

For a long moment he only stared at her. His
uth opened, and she lifted her chin, daring him
 come up with a better argument. He let out a
ise sigh, ran his hand over the back of his neck,
d shook his head.

"Now that that's settled," she began, but his eyes
crowed on her, cutting off any further words.

"You think so?"

She raised her eyebrows.

"Tell me, Mrs. Lindsay," he continued, "what
kes you think you're safe from a vulture like
mponelli?"

The way he uttered Camponelli's name made her
udder, but she answered with a sniff. "Any man
 be reasoned with."

"Because you're beautiful, and a woman, you be-
ve that."

Eden caught her breath. His statement was cold,
rsh, and she thought he must have known many

beautiful women who would compromise the
selves simply to "reason" with a man. Oddly, she
a knot in her throat, and swallowed. "No," she s
on a taut whisper. "I just have faith in men's bet
qualities."

Surprising her, Shane tilted his head back a
laughed—softly, though, chillingly. His eyes w
cold with cynicism when he looked at her aga
"You really are living in a sugar-coated world, are
you, honey?"

Was that what he thought? "I—" she began, l
he was already striding out of the alley, his har
shoved deeply into his pockets. His pace was
surely instead of brisk, and she caught up to h
easily. He was chuckling still, as if at some priv
joke.

"You're rude," she told him. "And arrogant." l
she wore her own secret smile, for she hadn't giv
him her word. "Oh!" She looked up to catch si
of the confectionary shop across the street. "Tr
fles!"

Before Shane could stop her, she had darted in
the road, narrowly missing being hit by a passi
dray. By the time he had caught up with her, l
clerk was tucking six truffles into a small tissue-lin
box.

"I can't resist them," she said, smiling winsom
as she reached across the counter for the box. "l
the man, Shane, will you? I left my money at hom

He wanted to protest, did not want to subj
himself to another seductive eating session, but l
clerk was waiting expectantly and Eden had skipp
back out to the sidewalk. "Damn the woman,"
muttered, digging for change, He handed it to l
clerk, who gave him a knowing grin.

Outside in the bright sunlight he came up behi

r. "You just ate breakfast. How can you be hun-
y?"

She whirled to face him, catching a bit of choco-
e on the tip of her tongue. "I can eat truffles any-
ne, night or day," she said with pure delight, and
ld the box under his nose. "Want some?"

She was generous, that was for sure. She always
fered him some of what she was eating.

"No."

A frown flitted across her brow, then she was
iling again, and she let her tongue make lazy
irls into the buttery center of the truffle she was
ting. Shane felt a flare of hot lust, and he tore his
ze from her to stare out at the street. But her soft
clamations were a major distraction. "Mmm.
re? This is delicious."

"I'm sure, dammit."

Eden shrugged and plucked another chocolate
m the box. As she bit into it, though, he scowled,
d the treat settled in a cold lump in her belly. She
uldn't understand why her eating truffles had
orked him into such a state—a subtle state, but a
ate just the same. She shrugged and walked along-
le him as he began to cross the street. "Aren't you
ing to ask me?"

"Ask you what?"

"Ask me how I got to the docks before you." By
s long silence she guessed he *wasn't* going to ask.
e shrugged and told him. "I took a trolley. Know-
g you would check on me before you left, I pre-
nded to be asleep." She furrowed her brow. "You
vered over me for the longest while, Mr.
Connor."

"I should have known you were faking."

His irritated growl delighted her. "I am a good
tress, aren't I?"

He looked down at her, his scowl even dark
than before. "You are," he said shortly.

"Well, you should have taken the trolley too.
would have got you there much faster."

"I like walking."

Glancing up at Shane, she saw his gaze was draw
to a painted woman standing in his path. She look
him over, liked what she saw, and offered him h
wares with a quick gesture. His assessing ga
passed briefly over her, and he gave her a crook
half-smile. Then, much to the woman's obvious d
appointment, he brushed past her.

Eden felt a plummeting sensation in her stomac
Why couldn't *she* hold his attention as so ma
other women could? She didn't understand it. T
strumpet had been dark-haired too, with very whi
skin. Perhaps that *was* the problem. All her life sl
had received compliments on her coloring, b
maybe Shane O'Connor just found her too blan
He also seemed drawn to women who played fa
and loose.

"Besides," he went on as though there had bee
no interruption, "I saw no reason to race you ther
Hell, I didn't think you'd *be* there."

She laughed. "Next time, perhaps, you'll weig
the matter more carefully."

"Next time," he said, his voice soft with a sill
menace, "there'll be no need to."

He sounded so certain, Eden couldn't stifle tl
surge of disappointment she felt at his words. F
had made it perfectly clear that he considered h
nothing but a nuisance. To counteract her sinkir
spirits, she popped another truffle into her mout
then stared down in dismay at how fast she'd eate
them. "There're two left," she said, and returned tl
smile of the apple vendor on the corner. Her spiri

ere quickly restored. "Are you sure you don't want
ne?"

"I do not like truffles." His eyes narrowed on hers
s if he dared her to challenge his remark. "Got
hat?"

She stared up at him as if he had two heads. "I
on't believe you for a moment, Mr. O'Connor.
hat is the most ridiculous statement I have ever
eard any person make."

"Then you have been sorely deprived."

"You don't like truffles?" she repeated.

"I don't." He took off again at a brisk stride,
urning the nearest corner and not even looking be-
ind to see if she had kept up.

She polished off the last two truffles, got rid of the
ox, and trotted up alongside him. "And you don't
ke other people to like truffles either, is that it?"

"Can we drop the subject, for crissake?"

"It's true, isn't it? It bothered you that I enjoyed
hat chocolate so much."

"Mother of God in heaven!"

He stopped dead in his tracks. Eden, who was at a
lose clip behind him, barreled smack into him and
lundered so that he had to grab her to keep her
rom hitting the ground. Abruptly, he released her
nd tore both hands through his hair, his breath
oming hard. "Woman," he snapped, "don't you
now when to let go?"

Rather than being disturbed by his exasperated
one, Eden brightened. She had proved she could
rouse impatience in him, and that was a good sign.
f she could arouse *some* emotion, maybe she could
et him to notice her feminine attributes.

Running her gaze over him, she thought how rug-
edly appealing he looked in Liam's work shirt. The
ky-blue linen made his coppery skin appear darker,

his eyes lighter, and though Liam was broader and heavier than Shane, the cloth hugged the spread of Shane's shoulders.

"I hate to be the one to inform you, Mr O'Connor, but if you continue to tear your hand through your hair that way, you'll be bald in no time. It's a wonder you aren't already." When he took a menacing step toward her, she hastened to answer his previous question. "And actually, no, I don't know when to 'let go,' as you so eloquently phrase it. Stubbornness is truly one of my most serious faults. But you, as an Irishman, should understand that!" She smiled and moved on, passing him with her nose in the air.

"I liked your friends, by the way," she added when he quickly caught up to her. "Liam and Camille are both so charming. You are very different."

His mouth quirked at her subtle barb. "My friends are not going to be happy with you. You duped them."

She sighed. "I suppose one could look at it that way. But I felt what I did was in the best interest of my brother. I left them a note, after all. And how is it that you and Liam were both in America as youths and he still has a brogue?"

"He relaxes around friends. He can speak perfectly unaccented English when the occasion warrants it."

"Hmm. And who is Meggie?"

To hear her name from this virtual stranger's lips made Shane feel as though she had pressed a hot poker to his chest. For a moment his breath was cut off, as he was suddenly, painfully, swamped with memories. "None of your business," he bit out.

"I *know* that, but tell me anyway."

He stared straight ahead, his fists shoved into his

ockets, his muscles tensed. Fragmented pictures of
is past, like shards of glass, splintered into his
mind, cut into his heart, as he remembered her.

"She is someone I prefer to forget," he said, but
e couldn't. He would never be able to forget Meggie.

Eden touched him, and he went very still. He
rowned down at her, at the slim, elegant fingers that
ested on his forearm. "You must have loved her
ery much," she said softly.

His expression hardened. He didn't owe her any
explanations—he owed her nothing. She was his client, and she was too nosy for her own good. But she
vas staring up at him with those wide, jewel-blue
eyes as if she really cared. "She is nothing like you
re thinkin', mavournin," he said softly. "Meggie
vas my little sister."

Eden sucked in a sharp breath. "Your sis—" She
vas obviously shocked, but she dared another ques-
ion. "Is she alive?"

Unable to look at her, Shane started to walk
gain. For years he had covered the wound, enabling
aim not to think of her too intensely. Eden's ques-
ions pricked the wound, though. He began to bleed
nside, just from the wondering. "I don't know. I
aven't seen her since she was a baby."

"Please explain. I'm curious."

"Yes, you are." So why was he bothering to tell
er about Meggie at all? Meggie was private, per-
onal, off limits. But perhaps, he told himself, be-
ause he was making certain that Eden Victoria
Lindsay would remain *impersonal* to him, it didn't
eally matter if he told her at all.

"I was nine years old when I crossed the Atlantic
with my family. I had three brothers, a sister, and

Meggie, born en route." He paused, frowning as he thought back to that dire trip. He remembered distinctly, even after so many years, the roll and pitch of the ship, fighting off violent attacks of seasickness, the filth and the squalor below decks. It hadn't mattered then that the O'Connor family could trace their bloodlines back to the first kings of Ireland. They were just like all the rest—wretched and gripped with the fever and racking coughs as their ship tossed upon turbulent seas to reach America. "The English were, of course, the reason we left."

Eden bristled. "I am not responsible for England's occupation of Eire, Mr. O'Connor. And I am not in the least political."

"Mmm." His brooding gaze flickered over her face, then he went on. "I watched my family die one by one, of one thing or another. First Padraic, a year younger than me. He died of cholera—a horrible death. Then Seamus. I . . . was closest to him. He was my older brother. Then Colleen, and my da. Then my baby brother, Danny, and finally Ma. She hung on for a while after she had Meggie, but she was so bloody weak."

His jaw tightened as he remembered his mother with her haunted eyes, once so beautiful, green-eyed, and blond. A cough had racked her and, in the end, taken her forever. He remembered the sight as if it had happened yesterday—still in death, her eyes closed, holding baby Meggie in her arms. It had torn his heart from him.

"Only Meggie and I survived," he went on, his voice husky with emotion. "My ma asked me to look out for her—made me promise to put the baby in an orphanage until I could save enough money to raise her myself."

"And you were nine? Shane . . ."

"Yeah. Once I hit these streets, I wondered why
e had left such green hills for America. I did work
rd, even moving to Pennsylvania for a while with
am to find more steady work in the coal mines. I
sited Meggie as often as I could, and sent money so
e would never want for anything." A grim smile
shed across his face. "She was everyone's favorite
the orphanage."

He closed his eyes, remembering. Clawing out a
ing in the pit of the earth at ten years old was a
orse hell than anything he could imagine . . . ex-
pt losing Meggie. He was doing it for her, he
uld remind himself daily, for Ma, for his family.
e wanted to be a family in the worst way. He was
ed of living in tents, on the streets, sleeping on the
ound at night, shivering in train cars. He was tired
short visits with his baby sister. She was adorable,
e angel of the orphanage with her dark blond
rls, large, pale eyes, and impish personality.

"Well, the mines got to me after a while, and
hen I turned twelve I came back to New York to
ork at various labor jobs." He narrowed his eyes
ainst the sunlight, against the pain that lanced
rough him. "But she was gone."

Eden gave him a blank look. "Gone?"

"The nuns gave her away. They'd found a home
r her—someone wealthy, someone who could pro-
de for her as—let's face it—I would never have
en able to. At least not until her childhood was
er. I . . . never saw her again. They wouldn't tell
e where she went, who'd adopted her." The mus-
es flexed in his jaw. He swallowed. "They de-
royed all records and documentation concerning
e adoption, thinking it was for my own good that I

not know. It's as though she disappeared off the fac of the earth."

"Oh, my God." Eden felt numbed by the stor stricken. She thought of him at nine years old, arri ing on the cold damp shores of New York with a infant in his arms. She imagined the little urch finding an orphanage for the baby, looking for wor trying to be a father to her, a big brother, a family a in one. In her mind's eye she could see Liam pullir him out of the way of a careening dray—he'd prob. bly been exhausted from hunger and hard physic labor—and still, Liam had said, Shane had foug like a cornered cat. No wonder he had never playe King of the Mountain. A tender pain tugged at he heart for the child he must have been. All this, alor on the streets, with no warmth, no love, still survi ing, and only God knew where.

Hot tears flooded her eyes. Poor baby, sh thought, poor little lost boy. She had grown up vi tually parentless too, but at least she'd had Rak and her twin, and had grown up under a vast Tex; sky. Shane hadn't any of those things.

Her vision dimmed, and she tried to will away th burning sensation in her eyes. She knew how h hated tears. He would hate her pity even more. Sh blinked her eyes, clearing her vision, and felt a flas of relief at the familiar sight ahead.

"Oh, the theater," she said, and hurried on ahea of Shane, grateful for the opportunity to hide he painfully deep emotions from him.

Shane stopped on the sidewalk and stared afte her, ice forming around his heart. He cursed himse for having told her anything at all, for having bough her caring act. He should have known she was to shallow to understand something that had haunte him his entire life—something he had never share

ith anyone but Liam. Watching her dance away
ke a fairy princess, he felt the old familiar contempt
reep back into him. He should have trusted his
itial instincts about her. Eden Victoria Lindsay did
ot give a damn about anyone but herself.

CHAPTER SEVEN

*S*HANE WATCHED EDEN FROM THE DOORWAY OF TH[E]
dressing room, one shoulder propped against th[e]
frame. She was in her element, flitting about like [a]
fly around a honey pot, laughing, flirting, chattin[g]
with several other—he assumed—members of th[e]
troupe. She was the star, her blond hair flying, h[er]
brilliant eyes alight as she hugged her friends, an[d]
they welcomed her back, expressing their variou[s]
concerns.

"But where's Franklin?" he heard her ask.

"He stepped out for a bite to eat—be back in [a]
moment," piped up a raven-haired blowzy woma[n]
from the corner. She was seated at a dressing tabl[e]

ffling a deck of cards, and watching Shane with
n dark eyes.

Eden turned toward the door and saw Shane. As
ays, he radiated that air of regal elegance and
ogance, like a dark prince. Yet even as he lounged
olently against the doorway, his weight slung on
e hip, his hands in his trouser pockets, a primitive
ce throbbed around him, something untamable,
al. His face was unreadable as always, but his eyes
de her heart stop. They were splintered ice, and
y were assessing her as if he found her distasteful.
w ironic, she thought, that he could emanate
:h heat and at the same time freeze a person with
nere flick of his eye.

Turning quickly from him, she flashed her best
ile at her friends. "Everyone, I'd like you to
:et"—oh, dear, how would he want her to intro-
ce him—"my friend," she finished triumphantly.

"Huh!" snorted Sparrow from her right. Eden
nced to her in surprise; it seemed she had
erged from the shadows. And she wasn't buying
e introduction.

Eden smiled hesitantly and tried again. "Well, ac-
lly, he's a cousin."

Sparrow tilted her head back and hooted irrever-
tly. The others began to chuckle too.

Eden sighed. "All right, he's—"

"I'm her bodyguard," Shane said from the door-
y, and a collective gasp sounded in the room.

"Why d'you need a bodyguard, Eden?"

She looked at them all helplessly. She didn't want
worry them needlessly, and she didn't want to
vulge any information Shane might want to keep
:ret. She assumed by his silence, though, and by
 own introduction, that she could tell them about
 r missing twin. So she did.

All of them were wide-eyed when she finished

"My gawd, that's excitin'!" Sparrow exclaim then she raised her chin when Shane's hard g flicked her way.

Noticing his swift, intense perusal of Sparrow f lowed by the sudden shielding of his eyes, Eden v reminded of her own first meeting with him. P haps, she thought, he searched for Meggie in ev woman within her age bracket. Perhaps it had I come an unthinking reaction in him. She watched he nodded slightly to Sparrow.

"It's more of a nuisance than exciting," he sa blandly.

"Well, for you maybe. But this sort of thing is common for folks like us." Suddenly Sparr frowned. "You got a problem, mister? You lookin' down yer nose at me as if you was roya and I was a peon of the streets."

"Oh, don't take that look personally," Eden sa "Mr. O'Connor looks down his nose at everyon She didn't realize she had created a horrid blund until several of the cast members laughed, and s glanced apologetically at Shane.

"O'Connor—an Irisher," Sparrow muttered, a Eden held her breath when Shane straightened, I jaw tightening. But the sudden whoosh and snap Lenore's cards broke the tension.

Almost fifty, Lenore fancied herself a Gypsy sorts, and called herself Madame Lenore. She wor low-cut blouse that exposed a good portion of h heavy bosom, and big gold rings in her ears th winked in the light. Shane turned to the woma watching as she arranged the cards in a particu pattern on the table.

"The Celtic cross," he said with a slight smile th

l not reach his eyes. But he did settle back against
e door frame.

Lenore glanced up at him, and Eden said in sur-
se, "You know the cards?"

His silver eyes flicked her way, then back at Le-
re. "My aunt Frances used to read them back
me. It's been years since I've laid eyes on
em. . . ."

"Ah, and you're a skeptic," Lenore said, examin-
g the tarot cards spread out before her. "I've done
s spread for you."

"You shouldn't have bothered," he said dryly.
'm not interested."

Lenore began to read them anyway. "You've had
ard life," she said, scrutinizing the cards. "But the
t twelve years have been lucrative for you, and
u have made—and invested—a good deal of
oney."

Eden, noticing the almost painful look of toler-
ce on Shane's face, came to Lenore's rescue now.
t's true, Shane—"

"But he doesn't like anyone knowing his busi-
ss," Lenore continued. "He's almost reclusive."
e glanced up at him and grinned flirtatiously up at
m. "But ooh-la-la, the women are wild for you."

"Well, it's easy to see why . . ." purred one fe-
ale member of the troupe, who sidled past him,
sting him a coy look from under her lashes.

Lenore went on, despite the tightening of Shane's
atures. "You have highly developed intuition.
ost rare in a man." She looked up again. "You
ould be a detective or a mystery writer. You're
sting your time as a bodyguard."

Eden laughed. "And Lenore should go into busi-
ss, shouldn't she, Shane?" When his cold eyes

flicked her way, she immediately sobered. "I me⸱
Mr. O'Connor."

"And"—Lenore continued as if there had be⸱
no interruption—"you are going to have . ⸱
hmm, how shall I say it? A period of upset. And t⸱
women will . . ." Lenore laughed, looking up on⸱
more. "Well, I see you tearing your hair out, M⸱
O'Connor—does that make any sense to you?"

"None at all," he said in a detached, impersor⸱
voice, but Eden laughed, remembering vividly h⸱
she had caused him to tear at his hair less than⸱
hour earlier. Shane cast her a sour look, but befo⸱
he could speak, a strong masculine voice call⸱
down the narrow corridor.

"Here, here. You're all rehearsing, I hope."

Their director, Franklin, came into view, stoppi⸱
as he confronted Shane's tall, rangy body blocki⸱
the doorway. He frowned until his eyes lit on Ede⸱
"Eden!" He glanced up again at Shane. "Excu⸱
me, sir, do you think you could let me by?"

Shane pulled away from the doorway and ambl⸱
partway into the room. With an irritated expressio⸱
Franklin brushed past him and strode forward, ta⸱
ing both of Eden's hands in his. "I was beginning⸱
worry, Eden," he murmured, and smiled down⸱
her.

"Oh, Franklin, I told you you mustn't!"

Aware of several pairs of eyes on them, Frankl⸱
jerked his head toward the hallway. "Onstage ever⸱
one. I'll be there in a moment."

As they filed out, Eden grasped his hands. "I to⸱
you I'd be here, didn't I?"

His brown eyes were full of warm affection. "Y⸱
did, little one. It's good to have you back. No⸱
finally, we can rehearse."

"She's not rehearsing."

Franklin stiffened at Shane's deep, drawling voice
I turned to face him. "Who the hell are you?"

Shane's eyes were shuttered. "The same person
o sent the missive to you yesterday, informing you
t she was not performing."

Angrily, Franklin turned back to Eden. "Who is
, Eden? A messenger from God?"

Eden swallowed a horrified giggle, but had to ad-
that Shane was so arrogant and commanding, he
ild pass himself off as a messenger from God.
d he exuded such potent masculinity that the
ndsome Franklin paled significantly in compari-
. Eden almost resented Shane for it.

"Eden," Shane said, "is coming home to stay with
"

Sparrow, who was the last of the troupe to leave
room, lingered in the doorway and rolled her
s at Eden. "Lucky you," she said, and was gone.

Franklin, however, saw no humor in the situation.
s face turning a deep shade of red, he clenched
fists and took a step toward Shane, who stood
ind Eden.

Eden grabbed one of Franklin's arms. "Franklin,
ase! Shane, explain!" She was caught between
two men, where the air simmered with hostility.
e could feel the heat of Shane's body behind her,
I dared a glance at him, to meet his cold eyes. Of
irse he had no intention of explaining anything.
"Oh, dear," she fretted aloud, glancing from one
n to the other. "Franklin—"

He cut her off. "Eden, don't you have anything to
about this? You told me you were going to re-
irse with us today."

"I intended to, Franklin, but things have taken a
inge turn."

"*What* things?" His gaze narrowed on Sh
again.

"Oh, it's not what you think, Franklin.
O'Connor is my bodyguard—"

"Your *what*?"

She was trying to pass this off as a light situat
and was failing miserably. And *he* was no help at
If anything, he seemed to be enjoying her frus
tion, and took some perverse pleasure in ri
Franklin, though she couldn't imagine why.
leaned close to her, his mouth nearly touching
ear, his warm breath a soft rasp against her che
and she jumped.

"Remember, you wanted to change your clothe

She sent him a sideways glance and was stun
by his rakish pirate smile. If she didn't know bet
she would think he was attempting to seduce h
and to sully her reputation before her good friend
strange light was smoldering in his eyes, sendin
keen quiver through her. Why was he looking at
like that?

"Eden, haven't you anything to say about this

Franklin's voice snapped her to the present sit
tion. She tore her gaze from Shane, and looked
Franklin, blinking her eyes as if in a daze.

She shrugged and flipped her palms up. "He's
boss, Franklin."

Franklin rubbed a hand across his face. "Damn
Eden, you're my main character!"

"Franklin," she said soothingly, again resting
hand on his arm, "we have plenty of time to rehea
before the show goes on. Shane will find my brot
in no time."

"Your brother?" Franklin looked thoroughly co
fused now.

"Yes, my brother disappeared, and Mr. O'Conn

elping me find him. He's actually a private inves-
ator, *and* my bodyguard."

Franklin shook his head as if trying to clear it.
his is a mess, Eden."

"Yes, Franklin, I know, and I'm sorry." She hesi-
ed, then added, "And if you need to find a re-
cement, feel free—"

Franklin suddenly clutched her hands, looking
nestly down at her. "No! Never! We'll postpone
ening night if we must. Eden, you're my star, dar-
g, the attraction that will pull the audience in!"

"Oh, but Franklin, there is so much other tal-
—"

"No. I—"

"This is a very touching scene," Shane inter-
ted, "but we have a trip ahead of us, and today
uld be a good time to start home."

Franklin frowned at him. "You'll get her in good
e, man." He turned back to Eden, his features
tening as he regarded her. "But what about the
er play, Eden, the one you wrote? We've hardly
d time to rehearse that one."

Eden felt Shane's gaze slash to her face, and she
nced curiously at him. He was looking at her as if
had never seen her before, and when she raised
r eyebrows in question, his dark lashes fell to veil
eyes almost completely.

Drawing in a shaky breath, she forced a smile to
r lips and patted Franklin's hand. "Not to worry.
won't be long. And I know my lines by heart,
anklin, I assure you. In just a couple of days I will
ntact you again. I'm sure we'll have some news on
ilip by then."

Franklin was still uneasy. "All right, darling," he
d at last, "but please, no longer. It's been long
ough already."

He sent Shane a determined look, which Sha
supposed meant he was expected to produce Ed
in a couple of days for the besotted director. A c
ner of his mouth lifted in a slow, curling smile.

"You have yet to introduce me to your . . .
rector," he said, truly not caring if he was ever int
duced to the pompous, lecherous ass, but knowi
he needed Franklin's cooperation.

"Oh, where are my manners today? Sha—M
O'Connor, this is Franklin Pauls, and Franklin, tl
is Mr. Shane O'Connor."

They did not shake hands. Shane inclined his da
head and said, "I trust you have Mrs. Lindsay's b
interests at heart, Mr. Pauls."

Franklin bristled, obviously putting the meani
Shane had intended to his words. That was, tl
Franklin might not have Eden's best interests
heart. The smaller man smiled thinly. "I think
both agree that it is of the utmost importance
keep her safe."

He cupped his hand under Eden's elbow a
urged her out into the hallway. Shane was only
step behind.

"I expect," he said, "that the people involv
with this will be making contact with Eden, and it
imperative that you contact me immediately wh
they do."

Franklin sighed, stopping when they reached t
theater door that led to the street. All the acto
were on the stage, except for the young woman he
spoken to earlier, the one who had been the last
leave the dressing room after Franklin's arrival. Sl
hovered by the door, her big eyes dancing fro
Franklin to Eden to Shane. She was clearly delight
by all the goings-on, and was not in the least intin

ated by Shane's irritated expression. In fact, she
grinned at him.

"Of *course* I would contact you," Franklin was
saying. "But I tell you, the idea of ruffians loitering
about my theater—"

Shane cut him off impatiently. "I have a man
watching the theater. If anyone makes contact with
any of you, he'll know it, and let me know. Here's
my address." He handed a card to Franklin and to
the young actress as well, who was craning her neck
to see the man standing by the streetlamp out front
and down the street a ways.

"That's him," Shane said brusquely. "Now do
you have it all clear?"

Franklin snorted. "We are not imbeciles."

"These men play rough, Pauls. They'd just as
soon shoot your head off before they ask questions."

Franklin paled. "Dammit, do you have to be so
explicit? I don't want any of my people jeopardized.
Thanks to you and your silly little games—"

Shane grabbed a handful of Franklin's shirt and
jerked the director toward him. "How silly will you
think my little games are when they use a baseball
bat on that pretty face of yours, mate?" He ground
out the words, his eyes narrowed and glittering.
With a final disgusted look he let the man go, and
Franklin staggered.

"Shane!" Eden said.

But Franklin had composed himself. He stepped
away from Shane and nodded at Eden. "I assume,"
he said, a dark flush underlying his high cheekbones,
"I will see you in a few days. In the meantime, little
one, try to resist this man's irresistible charms." He
flicked a deprecating glance over Shane. "The vulture just might try to eat you alive. Come, Sparrow,
the show must go on."

Sparrow, whose back was plastered against th door, her pale green eyes huge, offered them both weak smile, but before she could move, Shane re peated, "Sparrow?"

"Nickname," she whispered, "cause I've alway been so skinny." She cleared her throat. "Blime but you scared the bloody hell out of him."

"I think," Eden said quietly, "that was his point.

Part of the point, Shane acknowledged to himsel He took Eden's arm and guided her out the doo "Come on," he said, his tone weary. "Time to hea back."

She descended the marble staircase like a fairy tale princess, ethereal in white and gold.

Shane's breath caught at the sight of her. He ha just come in from the front stoop after a smoke preferring to wait outdoors for her rather than in th stately elegance of her home, and what it repre sented to him. Her house was white Georgian three-storied, majestic, with Corinthian pillars an tall, mullioned windows. Exactly as he'd expected Of course, he'd been in it at night, but had not see it in all its glorious splendor. He remembered star ing up at houses just like this as a little boy, thinkin that they were castles.

A smile tugged at his mouth. His mother used t tell him that he'd had a "writer's" mind, that h could make stories out of clouds, could see huma traits in animals, and animal traits in humans. H did remember picturing faces in the center of flow ers, hearing conversations between bumblebee imagining ants with underground armies, forts, se cret plans. But after a couple of years in America, al that had changed. He saw only reality—horribl

poverty, hunger, sorrow, death. He saw haunted
faces, sunken eyes, squalling babies, more death.
And he had made himself tough because he'd had
to. Because you couldn't survive if you spun stories
from cloud formations . . . if you even looked up
at the sky. No matter, for he hadn't been able to see
angels anymore. Just warriors on great beasts, fighting, fighting, always fighting to survive.

All that had changed again, of course. He had
pretty much resolved his ideas about money. He
liked it; it was power, and it was protection. But he
had little respect for the idle rich. Money was to be
made, invested, shared, enjoyed—not flaunted,
abused, or hoarded. And he had no respect for those
who sat around and waited for it to be handed to
them. That was the picture he had conjured up of
Eden's brother.

And what about Eden? She mesmerized him. No
matter, in that magical moment, that she was one of
the idle rich. She wore a white frock with a diaphanous overlay of silk, gathered in tiers that fell gently
to the hem and was trimmed with pale gold ribbon.
The same color sash wrapped around her small
waist. The neckline was low enough to show just a
glimpse of her breasts and the silky creaminess of
her shoulders.

She had piled her hair in a loose knot on her head,
the thick mane tucked up with combs, a pale ribbon
intertwined. The style made her shoulders and neck
seem all the more vulnerable to the touch of a man's
mouth . . . his mouth. Her hair was so thick, so
soft, he wanted to pull it free, feel it fall over his
hands, crush it to his face and breathe in its fragrance. Her skin was dewy soft, flushed peach-rose
from her bath, and he could smell her—some fruit
and flower scent that made his blood pound madly.

Her eyes, when she noticed him at the landing, lit up. Sea green and sultry with that slumberous essence of passion that was woman, promising hot, erotic nights while promising nothing at all.

Again it struck him forcibly that yes, she was a golden goddess, but behind her rich, elegant trappings he sensed she longed to stretch out, to run free. She belonged on some rough coastal shore, or on the back of a white charger, pounding across glittering desert sands, or against the majestic awe of high cliffs—a dramatic backdrop to match her equally dramatic nature.

Eden slowly descended the stairs, her skirts gathered in one hand, a check in the other. When she reached the bottom step she smiled at Shane and pressed the check into his callused palm. The brief contact was scorching, and she quickly drew her hand back. He stared down at the check, frowning.

"Now you're hired," she said lightly, ignoring the swift racing of her heart. All the way down the stairs she had felt his penetrating stare on her, watched him watch her. She had felt breathless, had felt her body heat, but as always, Shane's face had given little away. And she had taken such pangs to look lovely for him.

He lifted his head, and she saw there was a queer light in his eyes, as if he were looking for something.

"Am I?" he asked.

She'd been so caught up in his intensity, she had forgotten the subject matter. "Are you what?"

"Am I hired?" he asked, smiling faintly.

Hot color bathed her cheeks. She wondered why she found his not-so-handsome face so attractive. And why just the barest trace of his smile—ironic or otherwise—could make her pulses leap. "You're

ired," she said almost matter-of-factly, and brushed
ast him, her skirts whispering.

"Ah, Mrs. Lindsay," he said, shoving the check
ito his pocket and crossing to her in one stride. She
aused to look up at him. "Where are you going?
's time to head back."

"We have to wait for Alice to ready herself," she
iid, referring to her maid. "I thank you very much,
Ir. O'Connor, for allowing me to bring her back to
ur home." She smiled. "I can't expect you to play
.dy's maid, can I? And I *do* so need help—all those
xasperating hooks or buttons up the backs of my
owns." She did not understand the flash of irrita-
on she saw cross his face, and swiftly changed the
ibject. "Tea?" she said, heading for the salon.

"Are you inviting me to tea?" He asked this as if
ie'd just suggested he stay the week.

She smiled again, her skirts swishing as she turned
ie corner to the salon, knowing he followed. "Why,
es, Mr. O'Connor, I thought it a pleasant way to
)end the time while we wait for Alice and the rest
f the servants to pack up. I certainly think that is a
)od idea, and agree with you that it is not safe for
iem here. Some of them are distraught at the
iought of leaving, but I assured them I will recall
iem all as soon as I return—which *will* be soon,
orrect, Mr. O'Connor?"

He had followed her to the doorway and stopped
iere. "I do not drink tea."

She looked back at him, faintly exasperated. "You
id not answer my question. I will not be long at
ur estate, will I?"

"That depends."

"Do you like lemon with your tea, or cream? And
eavens, please do come in and sit down. I can't
ave you loitering there in the doorway." She tried

to charm him with another smile, but he remaine
unmoved.

"I do not drink tea."

She crossed to the tea service already prepared b
the butler. "Let me guess. You don't like tea."

"Good guess."

"Ah." She tilted her head to one side, a finge
resting alongside her jaw as she considered hin
"You don't like tea and you don't like truffles."

"This," he said, his face impassive, his eyes no
even flickering, "has nothing to do with truffles."

"It most certainly does, Mr. O'Connor. It has ev
erything in the world to do with truffles."

Shane was abruptly annoyed that she was usin
his surname instead of his Christian name. Absur
that, since he had insisted they stick to imperson;
formalities. Watching her now, he allowed himse
another fleeting fantasy as she bent over the tea se
vice. She had a lushly curved bottom, and it wa
pointed straight his way. He felt a heavy warmth i
his groin, a low, dull ache.

She turned to grin at him, the teapot in her hanc
and the ache became a searing pain.

"Come in, will you, and stop this foolishness. D
you like lemon or cream?"

His gaze flowed down her body. He had a tast
for something else altogether. He indulged he
though, and strolled into the salon. "If you insist. I'
take mine with a shot of whiskey."

Laughing, she poured him a cup of tea and urge
him to sit. He lowered himself to the edge of th
rosewood sofa, took the delicate china cup from he
and felt ridiculous. Tea, for crissake.

She settled across from him, looking luminou
against the silks and velvets, amid the scent of te
and roses and pungent lemon. Her eyes caught th

unlight and sparkled like green gems. He couldn't
ook away as she brought her teacup to her lips and
ipped. She had luscious pink, soft lips. Only when
he lowered her cup and it rattled slightly against the
aucer did Shane detect that she was nervous.

"Didn't your family drink tea?" she asked. "I
now it's thought of as an English beverage, but
hat's not entirely true—"

"I will not speak of my family to you," he inter-
upted. After her insensitive reaction to his divul-
ence of Meggie, he wondered why she had
nentioned his family at all. Their story was not ap-
ropriate for parlor small talk.

He saw the leap of anger in her eyes, as if she
ound it unfair that he had denied her that right.
'Fine, then, Mr. O'Connor, what is it you'd like to
alk about?"

He didn't answer. Instead, he leaned down to put
is teacup on the low table before him, then sat
ack, cocking an ankle over the opposite knee. She
eld his gaze in silence for a minute, then her mouth
ursed.

"Since you are not forthcoming," she said, "I'll
sk you—what do we do now?"

"Now we wait."

She almost fell off her chair. *"Wait?"* she re-
eated, incredulous. "We're not going to *do* some-
hing?"

"No," he said firmly. *"We* are not."

"But I don't understand."

"You don't have to."

She looked truly distressed, though, staring dis-
nally into her tea and gnawing at her bottom lip
vith her teeth.

"Eden," he said so softly, almost gently, that she
ooked up, startled. It had startled him, too, to hear

the emotion he'd breathed into her name. "We wa
to see what the abductors want now. We'll dra
them out, then get your brother back."

"But we will find him, won't we?" She was pract
cally begging him. "You are legendary in your fiel
have left no case unresolved, have you, M
O'Connor?"

Only one, and he thought of Meggie with a flas
of pain.

"I will find him," he said, "but sometimes thes
things take longer than we desire. In order for me t
expedite my plans, you have to promise me tha
you'll keep out of the way."

She pressed her lips together.

"Eden."

She smiled unexpectedly. "I like it when you ca
me that. You did a couple of times already today
did you know that?"

He smiled in return. "And you called me boss."

She looked down, smoothing her skirts. "I did
didn't I?"

"But you don't really feel that way."

She shrugged. "It pacified Franklin." She looke
up and added, "I apologize for his behavior towar
you. He isn't always so surly. It's just that he's a
artist and gets very temperamental when his work i
disrupted."

"Is that his excuse?"

She flushed. Again, Shane noted, she had avoide
his request that she stay out of his way. But onc
they were at his estate he would have her under loc
and key, and the case would be resolved much mor
swiftly.

"Yes, well." She frowned slightly. "You were aw
fully hard on Franklin. Sometimes he needs to b
treated with kid gloves."

"Franklin," Shane drawled, "is a pompous ass, full of self-importance. He needed to understand the gravity of the matter."

She looked startled at his opinion of her friend. "Well, if you gave him a little time, you would see that Franklin is a very nice man."

The last person in the world he wanted to discuss was Franklin Pauls, but he suddenly remembered what Franklin had said. He leaned back, stretching his long legs out, and watched her intently. "You write plays?"

Eden caught the interest in his voice and felt a quick lurch in her middle. He had never looked at her quite that way. "Yes . . ." she answered slowly.

"For how long?"

"Since as long as I can remember. I used to write them as a little girl—as soon as I *could* write, actually."

"Why?"

He'd asked the question softly, but with growing interest. "Why do I write them?" She had never thought about it before. "I like to. I feel compelled to write, to make up stories and then act them out." She couldn't believe the expression on his face. He actually looked impressed! Because she wrote plays?

He ruined the moment, though, by lowering his brows and saying mildly, "Mmm, fairy-tale world. You mythologize life."

She felt a swift anger. "Not always. I write about murder and mayhem."

"And do you find murder and mayhem exciting?"

She did not like the note of sarcasm in his voice and sat up straight and regal. "Much more so than lying on a divan all day, eating bonbons."

He laughed, surprising her.

"Tell me, doesn't Society hate that you're a stag
performer?"

"Oh, yes." A small smile curved her mouth. "Bu
no one can stop me."

"I'm sure," he drawled.

A slight puff of air blew in through the partl
opened window, bringing with it dust and grit fror
outdoors. The clipclop of horses' hooves on cobble
stone, muffled male laughter and soft women'
voices, the squeals of children, drifted up from th
street, making the salon seem too close, almost inde
cently intimate. Shane continued to watch her wit
that lazy, penetrating gleam in his eye, and she sud
denly remembered the rough, thrilling kiss he ha
honored her with the night before. She wanted t
taste him again, wanted to run her hand there, insid
the collar of his open blue work shirt, to pres
against solid muscle, trace the glisten of his coo
slick sweat.

An earthy, primal pulse throbbed deep in he
belly. What thoughts, she wondered, were behin
his remarkable eyes?

She fanned her face. "Mighty hot in here."

He smiled at her western expression. "Mighty,
he drawled.

Her cheeks on fire, she craned her neck towar
the hallway. "Wonder where Alice is."

Shane said nothing. He seemed to be enjoying he
discomfiture.

"That bump on your nose," she said idly. "Hav
you broken it?"

"No."

"No? Never? That's odd. A man in your profes
sion, and with your background—"

"The bump is part of my face, just like you

reasts are part of your body. There's no changing it
—they are simple facts of life."

As he'd expected, his choice of words made her
olor. But she was not distracted for long. "Well, it's
ery attractive."

Though he felt a startling flash of pleasure at her
ompliment, Shane looked at her as if she were de-
ented.

"As is your new mustache," she added.

"What the hell—" He shot to his feet, glaring
own at her. "You and Liam. I am not," he said
rough his teeth, "growing a mustache."

She shrugged. "If you say so."

She stood also and started toward the door. "I
ink I hear Alice now."

He followed her out into the hall and stiffened
hen he saw the trunk and several portmanteaus at
e bottom of the stairs. Alice stood on the landing,
miling nervously, twining her fingers together as he
owered at her.

He strode forward to face Eden. "Where in the
ell do you think you're going, Europe? What is all
at—that—baggage?"

Eden looked up at him with innocent eyes.
Whatever do you mean, Mr. O'Connor? I told Al-
e that we might be going for an extended stay and
pack sufficiently."

He started tearing his hands through his hair
gain. "Woman, she has packed enough for a year!"

"Oh, Mr. O'Connor, surely you exaggerate—"

Crack! Something hit the windowpane behind
er, shattering the glass. Eden screamed. Before she
ould move, Shane tackled her right to the floor.
eatly, painlessly, but still, her chin hit the polished
ood and she bit her lip. Tears of pain stung her
yes, and she could not breathe. Shane lay on top of

her, his heavy body shielding her from dange
Stunned, she tried to move, to decipher what ha
happened, but he held her there, pinned under him
She felt her world go dark, heard Alice's scream
from some distant point.

"Stay put," he whispered, his order harsh an
grating in her ear. And then he was off.

Did he think she could move? It took great effo
to pull in air as she remained with her cheek to th
floor, listening to Alice and watching Shane sid'
toward the window, his back to the wall, gun drawn
The curtains lifted on a gentle puff of summer ai
She could see he did not want to shoot blindly—
there were pedestrians out there—but he move
noiselessly closer, and with a quick jerk of his head
looked out.

"No one," he muttered. Then, with a quick lung
he was off at a run, the predator after very unfortu
nate prey.

CHAPTER EIGHT

THE ASSAILANT HAD FLED. SHANE MADE A QUICK SUR-
veillance of the area, his animal-keen instincts alert,
body tensed, ready to pounce when necessary,
but he found no one, nothing. People continued to
stroll down the sidewalks, and carriages rolled
swiftly down the street as if a woman's life had not
been in jeopardy just seconds before. It was as if he
had imagined the shooting . . . except for the
crack in the pane.

He took one more quick look about, his nostrils
flaring as if he could scent the danger, and he
palmed his gun. He needed to get back inside, to
Jolen. The shot could have been just a ploy to dis-

tract him away from her. It was best, he thought,
take her out of the city—and fast. Whoever h
been the trigger, he or she was playing a dangero
game. For no reason at all, should *anyone* be sho
ing at Eden, unless it was to alarm *him*?

He tightened his lips. If she had just stayed at
estate as he had arranged for her in the fi
place . . .

He was beyond impatient by the time he was ba
inside her house, and he snapped out orders, expe
ing the servants to jump. They did. He allowed o
one trunk per person, and within minutes they w
speeding toward his private boat. Once home,
made certain Eden and Alice were safely ensconc
in their rooms, and guarded, then he went for a v
orous ride on the beach, taking comfort in the br
liant blaze of late summer sunset, the peace, t
solitude.

He did not see Eden for forty-eight hours. It wa
blessed relief. Simon had informed him of the ma
messages from Patricia. She wanted to see him, w
tired of waiting for him to contact her, when, c
when, would she see him again? He responded w
a message of his own, along with the order for a f
dozen roses to be sent to her home, and that was
unequivocal good-bye. He had tired of her befo
Eden had burst into his life, and he just didn't ha
time just then for Patricia. She had become too c
manding, petulant, and expected marriage of hi
She needed to understand that he had no intentio
of marrying . . . ever.

By late morning of the second day, Shane sent
note up to Eden for her to meet with him in l
study at four o'clock that afternoon. He had al
written that she was invited to use the premises

r liking, as long as she let the guard outside her
oor know where she was going.

"The nerve!" Eden fumed to Alice as she hiked
ack the bedcovers at noon and pushed the hair out
 her eyes. She crumpled Shane's note in her hand.
"First he puts a guard outside my door as if I were a
ayward child, and now he tells me I'm allowed out
 here so long as I tell the guard where I'm going!"

The room was hot and stuffy, and she strode na-
ed to the window to feel the slightest breath of sea
reeze. The sun was blinding bright. The sand
eamed pale gold. She squinted against the power-
l glare reflecting off the purplish bay water. In the
stance she could make out a white-sailed yacht,
obbing on the bay. She sighed, leaning out over the
ll. "So hot," she muttered. She'd never known a
eat wave to last so long. "And I do so want to take
 swim."

"You're certainly dressed for it," Alice said from
hind her. "Here, miss, please. The master will be
ost churlish if he sees you unclothed."

Eden turned. "Oh, it's nothing he hasn't seen be-
re, Alice." When Alice paled, she brushed aside
er comment with a careless wave of her hand. "Oh,
ot *me*, of course." But he had. "He's just a man-
out-town, if you know what I mean. He—" She
owned suddenly. "Did you call him *master*?"

Alice bobbed her head.

The title sounded frightfully imposing. "Good
eavens, Alice, please call him Mr. O'Connor. *Mis-
r*, not *master*. He's just a mister—got that?"

"Yes'm." She glanced around her luxurious sur-
oundings. "It's just that this place is so . . . castle-
ke, mum."

"Yes, I suppose. And he is so like a lord." Eden

lifted her heavy hair off her neck. "The water is to
inviting. I'm going to go for that swim."

And for the better part of the afternoon she di
She strolled the grounds for a time, half hoping sh
would run into Shane, but he was nowhere to b
seen. She wasn't entirely alone, for there was th
ever-present Alice and the infernal guards alway
hovering about. Did they think some stranger wa
going to scale the walls and abduct her? Reall
O'Connor was impossible.

Still, she gave Mr. O'Connor a great deal
thought. After a long, refreshing swim on his privat
beach, where the water felt icy cool in comparison t
the sweltering day, she perched atop a big rock t
gaze out at the sea. While watching raucous sea gul
dive into the ocean and swoop up again into the sk
she contemplated Shane and his attitude toward he
He was not happy with her, she could see that. I
fact, if she were the type to read into a situation, sh
would venture to say that he was avoiding her. An
that note he had sent to her room. She sighed. Sh
supposed that to him she represented only troubl
But he brought trouble on himself. He was so set i
his ways—so controlled. If he just bent a little, h
would see that there were other ways of doin
things. To give him credit, she supposed his way
had to hold some validity, for he was a legendar
detective, but couldn't he at least listen to her *som*
times?

And that was another problem. He seemed to b
holding her responsible for the bullet that ha
cracked her window. He had somehow gotten it int
his mind that she shouldn't have been in her ow
home when that had happened. But he'd said littl
else. A brooder, to be sure.

Mesmerized, Eden watched the waves roll towar

er and crash against the big rocks at her feet. Sea
am curled on the sand, disappeared. Her lively
nagination took hold of the thought that this would
e an ideal spot for a murder scene in a play. She
uld create two antagonists fighting precariously on
e boulders, one with a knife. The villain would
se his footing, fall to his death. . . .

Cold sea spray stung her lips, startling her out of
er reverie. She licked the salt from them, breathed
deep of the tangy air. "Heaven," she murmured,
ut sobered when she thought again of Shane. He
as determined not to like her. And she was just as
etermined to make him like her—at least notice her
a woman. She had that appointment with him at
ur o'clock. She would make certain he noticed her
en.

When the time came, she knocked on the door to
is study.

"Come in," he said tersely, and she pushed open
e doors. He was at his desk, head bent over his
ork, and didn't even glance up to acknowledge her
ntrance.

"Good afternoon, Mr. O'Connor."

He grunted, still not looking up. She frowned.

"Come in and shut the door."

She sighed to herself and did as he commanded,
osing the doors behind her. "I went for a swim,"
e informed him as she crossed the room and sat on
e leather chair.

Again, no answer. She watched him scribble
mething, and her gaze drifted over his broad
oulders, his powerful forearms where his shirt-
eeves were rolled up, and his broad, long-fingered
ands. Impeccable as always, he was wearing an im-
aculate white shirt, crisp and fresh against his dark
kin, and a silver-gray waistcoat unbuttoned at the

middle. But the heat had forced him to abandon hi
necktie and jacket.

"Sit down," he said.

She bristled at his dictatorial tone. "I am seated."

"Hmm. All right, I want to finish this up as soo
as possible. I have an evening engagement."

She felt a little lurch in her chest and squelched it
The man certainly had the right to engagements. Es
pecially since he did not like to spend more tim
with her than was necessary.

He reached for a piece of paper, scanned it, an
frowned. Then, still without looking at her, h
leaned back in his chair, linked his hands behind hi
head, and closed his eyes as if he were very weary
But he looked refreshed—cleanly shaven, his hai
smoothed back, perfectly groomed. The spicy scen
of his cologne drifted to her on the close air, and sh
wanted to move nearer to him, feel his warmth, tha
compelling masculine heat that drew her. Lost in he
thoughts, her yearnings, she jumped when he spoke

"That bullet could have been meant for me a
well as for you."

She watched his mouth as he spoke. She remem
bered those hard, warm lips covering her own, and
she shivered. Damn the heat. Damn him.

"It's safest to keep you here."

"So you keep saying."

"The jewels," he went on, "belong to a man calle
Forrest Steele. He is one of the richest men in th
world, an American who lives in London but own
homes in almost every country. He is a bit of ar
adventurer—dives in tropical waters for treasure
lost in shipwrecks, scouts excavations and expedi
tions to the far corners of the earth, mines gold an
silver, diamonds and emeralds. He is highly re
spected, and the stolen gems have created an inter

ational scandal. Scotland Yard is involved. Steele
as offered an exhorbitant reward for the return of
he jewels—they are the first of a find. And they are,
s you know, exquisite. A reward is also being of-
ered for information leading to the culprits, which
he Yard believes to be a ring of thieves."

Until Eden exhaled, she did not know she had
een holding her breath. "Forrest Steele," she said.
"I've heard his name."

"Is it possible your brother is a member of this
ing of thieves?"

"No."

She said it quickly, angrily, and he finally opened
is eyes and looked at her. He blinked once, then
tared at her as if he had never seen her before.

As rapidly as a tiger springs, he was on his feet.
he held his gaze steadily as he shook his head and
arrowed his eyes.

"Lord, who the hell are you?"

Eden touched her dark wig. She had worn it to
et his attention, since he preferred dark-haired
women, but his reception of her into his study had
een less than desirable, and now she didn't care if
he impressed him at all. He had accused her
rother of something dreadful. "Philip is not a thief!
And you are despicable to accuse him of such a
hing! A few days ago, when you first asked me that
question, Mr. O'Connor, I wasn't sure whether or
ot Philip was involved with jewel thieves, but now,
when we both know that he is being held hostage, it
s a ludicrous suggestion."

Shane circled the desk, still staring as if he could
ot believe his eyes. "It's a wig, isn't it?" He stood
n front of her, a kind of amused wonder in his
leaming eyes. When he reached out to touch, she
erked her head away.

"Apologize!"

He laughed instead, a rich, full-throated laugh that caught at her vitals. His teeth were very white, making his skin look even darker, and when she glowered at him, he laughed even harder.

"Why in the hell are you wearing that wig, woman?"

She pulled it off, and her tightly wound hair beneath it gave Shane a fresh shock. When he started laughing again, she surged to her feet, glaring so fiercely at him that his laughter was irrepressible. "I was play-acting!" she said. "Please, hush. And apologize to me about my brother."

He bowed deeply at the waist, and when he straightened he had schooled his features into a mask of sobriety. "My heartfelt apology, madame. Forgive me for allowing the thought to cross my mind that your scoundrel of a brother could possibly be linked to a ring of thieves." He reached for the wig, but she snatched it back.

"That was *not* heartfelt!"

He didn't answer as his gaze scanned her flushed face. It drifted lower—briefly—then he quickly lifted it back to her face.

"What are you wearing?" he asked. It was some type of cotton blouse, not worn by any woman in the East as far as he knew. It was white with puffed sleeves. The neckline rode the crests of her beautiful shoulders and dipped low enough for him to catch a glimpse of her firm, rounded breasts. He could see a fine sheen of perspiration glistening on her skin there, between the tempting mounds, where he suddenly ached to run a lazy finger. With considerable effort he removed his gaze from that tantalizing view and let it wander lower to her red skirt, which stopped at her shapely ankles. On her graceful, slen-

r feet she wore some type of leather sandals. Even
r toes were sensual. He felt the sweat break out on
 own brow, felt a tightening in his loins, and he
e his gaze back to her face. But her posturing had
n laughing again—one hand on her hip, that hip
ust toward him in a belligerent yet flirtatious
se.

"This," she informed him haughtily, "is a Mexi-
1 peasant blouse called a *camisa*. The sandals are
araches."

He had to turn his back on her. His trousers had
come uncomfortably constricting, and he needed
distraction to ease the sense of fullness in his loins.
t even when he faced the open window, feeling
 slight, sporadic breeze drift over him, his skin
ll felt hot and tight. The suffocating heat did not
lp, but only increased his discomfort. He was hard
d throbbing, yet at the same time, laughter shook
n. When had he laughed so much? He could not
member. Laughter did not come easily to him—he
d lost the freedom of that gift long ago. And, cer-
nly, no woman had ever evoked real humor in him
just cynical humor, dark humor.

His gaze narrowed on the ocean. He did not want
 be affected by Eden, but he was. She was so un-
edictable—a refreshing change from the jaded
omen he had known, practiced seducers, all of
em. But Eden. She was a life-lover, wild, impul-
e, her behavior infectious, an unabashed expres-
n of life. And for all her beauty, it wasn't that that
d him pacing the floors at night or galloping down
e shore on his mount to be rid of the fire that
nsumed him. It was her spirit which burned so
ight, there was no looking away from it. He did
t want to want her, though. Clearly, she was mak-
g an effort for him to notice her, but she was not

his type. Frowning, he realized Eden was not a "type" at all. For the life of him, he could not cla ssify her. She fit no particular mold, nor, he doubte would she ever. Everyone she met—with the exce tion of Simon—seemed both baffled by her and i trigued. Also, he thought, recalling Franklin, s charmed people effortlessly. That thought sober him.

With his back still turned toward her he ask mildly, "You wear that in Texas, do you?"

Crestfallen, Eden fought the hot press of tears her chest. It was obvious that even the dark hair a her seductive pose had no effect on him, except f amusement. Did he find her *comical*? Somehow, th was much worse than his feeling nothing at all. the time she had spent with Shane O'Connor, s had learned that he found very little—if anything to laugh about in life. But she was it, the one sour that could trigger his laughter, and that knowled thoroughly dampened her usually buoyant spiri He found her frivolous.

Swallowing her tears, she finally answered hi "Sometimes." Her voice came out breathy, only s was not acting. It truly had escaped that way. Sha turned to look at her, and she smiled lamely, dete mined to hide her feelings. "Mostly I wear this wh it's hot, like today. I bring cool clothes with me e ery time I come to New York. Though I wear the only in my home."

She sat down abruptly, unable to bear the way l eyes kept flicking over her body. "This time," s continued, "it was a wise decision. The heat, course, calls for cool clothing, and I am wearing th outfit in the play I wrote, as it takes place in t West. I think it will be eye-opening for the childr

see that there is a whole different world outside of
the city of New York."

"What children?"

She blinked at him. The sun fell on his hair, making it shine, and she longed to twine her fingers
through the soft curls at the nape of his neck. "This
heat is too oppressive," she muttered, and stood
again. She crossed to the window where he was and
leaned out to catch what little breeze there was.

"You're hogging the air."

Startled by his dry, amused comment, she
straightened, and promptly banged her head on the
window frame. "Ooh!" She rubbed the crown of
her head, then stopped when she realized how close
they stood . . . and how he did not look as though
he planned to move.

He was inches away, and her skin tingled with
awareness. Somehow, even though he had obviously
washed and shaved, he smelled faintly of horses and
leather. Standing this close, she could see that tiny
white scar again at the corner of his eye, and wanted
to ask him about it. Instead, she stared mesmerized
into his eyes, pale diamonds glittering in his bronze
face, so piercing, she felt the cut deep, deep into her
soul.

"Eleven years old," he said, his voice husky. At
her puzzled expression, amusement lightened his
eyes. "Fistfight with four kids who tried to rob
Sam. We won, but took a beating, and the scar you
see is evidence of that."

Her eyes widened. How had he known . . . ?
She felt hypnotized by his gaze, his heat. Her hand
went to her throat, where her pulse beat rabbit-fast
under her fingertips. "You read expressions very
well."

He inclined his head slightly, mockingly.

"And give nothing away in your own."

Her words broke the spell. His gaze became shuttered, locking her out, and she wanted to curse i frustration. Instead, she stood her ground and sai softly, sincerely, "I'm sorry you had such a roug childhood."

His jaw tightened. "What children were you refe ring to?"

He didn't forget anything. She sighed and leane back, resting against the window frame. She saw h gaze dip to her breasts, and she felt her nipples ti gle.

Mortified, she straightened, for he must have see them harden to prominent points under her thi perspiration-dampened *camisa*. It was entirely to revealing; she realized that now. But then, her boo had never responded this way to a man's *look,* f the love of heaven, and she just didn't understand No man in her life had aroused these keen, tumult ous sensations in her as did Shane O'Connor, ar she wasn't sure she liked it. Nor was she sure sl understood the flash of heat in his eyes. It was mo than desire. It was . . . possessive. That notic both puzzled and pleased her, and she decided put it to the test.

"The children at St. John's Orphanage—" She b gan to answer him, but he cut her off.

"What?"

"St John's—"

"I know what you said," he interrupted aga harshly.

She frowned at him. "Then why did you ask me repeat it?"

He was frowning too. "What in the hell is yo business with St. John's?"

"Why, you act as if you have a personal stake

e place, Mr.—" At the sudden tightening of his
atures, she knew. "Your sister stayed there?" she
ked softly.

He nodded tersely. "And you perform there."

Judging by the stony expression on his face, Eden
asn't certain she wanted to admit to such folly.
Yes, I've been putting on performances there—and
other homes—for years now."

He studied her narrowly as if he didn't quite
now what to think of her. "Why?"

"Why?" She let her gaze rake over him, feeling a
dden surge of temper. "Because it's a free country,
Ir. O'Connor."

His lips thinned ominously. He turned back to his
sk to light a cheroot. As he shook out the match
d inhaled on the pungent cigar, his sharp gaze
turned to her face. "Why else?"

Eden bristled. Tension simmered between them,
d it was more than prickly tempers. It was heat. A
xual, seductive heat that electrified the air, was
pe with a sense of expectancy. But, she realized, he
as determined to ignore it. Now, she thought, was
e time to put him to the test.

"I know," she said, deliberately slipping her finger
der the neckline of her blouse to blot the perspi-
tion there, "that you think I am a very spoiled,
lfish woman who thinks only of herself." She freed
e top button of her blouse. With satisfaction she
w his eyes flick there, then back to her face. "But
lieve it or not, I do have a fondness for children,
d I do enjoy performing for them."

"Or perhaps you just like an enraptured audience,
d children usually are enraptured by stage per-
rmers," he drawled, his impertinent gaze flicking
ce again to her breasts.

She felt another flash of anger. "You have to be

very, very good to hold a child's attentio
Mr. O'Connor. And, for your information, I li
children. They are my favorite audience, an
they—they are such open, honest creatures." Sl
swallowed the unexpected knot in her throat ar
shifted her gaze out over the brilliant water. H
voice lowered. "And since I won't ever have any
my own, they fill a need."

She sensed a sudden alertness in Shane. "WI
won't you have any children of your own?"

She glanced back at him. He looked as arrogant
always, half seated on the edge of his desk, his ey
shielded by a wreath of smoke. She gave him a ti
smile. "Because you need a husband for childre
and I don't plan to ever marry again."

His eyes narrowed. "Why not?"

She lifted her eyebrows and slipped her finger i
side her blouse again, releasing the second butto
She saw his gaze shift there, saw the tensing of h
jaw, and hid a smug smile. "I'm surprised you as
Mr. O'Connor. But I'll tell you, I found marria
very boring. Wilbur was a kind man, but a go
thirty-five years older than I. And he allowed me
perform—as long as I was home in time for dinne
I'm certain he was more lenient with me than mo
women ever hope to see in the course of their ma
riage, but a married woman has very little freedor
No younger man would ever allow me to perforn
and since I've already fulfilled that obligation—ma
riage—I see no reason to remarry. I am free to do
I please for the rest of my life."

"And that is?"

"Acting, enjoying my friends, keeping whatev
hours I please. I am happy with my life as it is." Sl
smiled and stretched her arms over her head, awa
that her breasts were thrust toward him. She wou

ke him notice her if it killed her. Besides, it felt
od to stretch, and the slight breeze caressed her,
sing goose bumps on her skin.

Shane felt everything in him grow tight. Her ac-
n was beautiful, graceful, and in that instant all he
uld picture was her stretched out beneath him on
e hot sand, a bed, anywhere, her arms lifted as he
oved over her, into her, and she watched him with
r heavy-lidded blue-green eyes. His eyes traced
e length of her slender arms. The undersides were
arly—such soft-looking skin. He wanted to run
s tongue over it.

He cursed inwardly, but could not pull his gaze
ay. Her high, upthrusting breasts with their
htly beaded nipples were revealed through the
in *camisa,* needing the touch of his mouth. And,
mmit, she was not wearing a corset! He hadn't
alized that until she stood by the window, the sun
hind her, the breeze molding the blouse to her
rves. Seduction at its best.

He shook off the insistent, throbbing need and
ushed out his cheroot. He longed to fill his palms
th those firm breasts, to pull the aroused pink
ests into his mouth and suck. He wanted her
rcely, desperately, almost obsessively. She dis-
pted his sleep at night—what little he was getting
late. Flashes of her haunted his dreams, of her
ckoning to him, of her in bed with him, twining
r arms and legs around him, pulling him into her,
oving to his rhythm. Hot, wild, disturbing dreams
at left him no mercy. When he woke, his blood
as pounding, the sheets damp from his sweat. He
d never been so mad with longing.

And now she was taking the pins out of her hair,
tting it fall down her back and shoulders. The
lor was lighter than that of sun-ripened wheat. He

clenched his hands into fists, fighting the pelting-[
desire to pull her into his arms and bury his face
that thick mane. When she cast a curious look
him, he tightened his lips and his resolve, det
mined to reject her spell. If she meant never to
marry, that meant she would play the part
mistress. His women ran toward courtesans, r
silly, frivolous actresses. She would not be able
twist him around her little finger as she obviou
did with others. He was not a man to be manip
lated. The experienced women he slept with
played their little games and used their wiles, just
she was doing now. But, eventually, he grew bor
with the lot of them.

Eden, though, was far from boring. This f;
deeply disturbed him. And the orphanage, the ch
dren. He was almost annoyed that she seemed
have some sensitivity, some depth. But what the h
did *she* know about orphanages? What the hell (
she know about lost dreams, desperation, despai

"What about men?" he asked, keeping his voi
disinterested.

She blinked at him. "Men?"

"Male companionship."

"Oh!" She smiled and walked across the study
the sideboard. "I have plenty of male companio
ship," she said, fingering the bottle of brandy.

Lovers, he thought, confirming his unflatteri
opinion of her.

She turned to him, fluttering her eyelashes. "N
O'Connor, I'm sure you did not ask me here to d
cuss my personal life, did you?"

Irritation flashed through him. Somehow, on
again, he had gone off on a personal bent with h
Truly, the less he saw of her, the better. "You a
here to answer some questions," he said.

"Ask away."

"Would you like a drink?" She looked startled,
  she was caressing the liquor bottles as if they
  e going to caress her in turn. Shane's nerves felt
  .

  he smiled at him. "That is an easy question to
  wer." She paused, touching the bottle of sherry.
  ay I?"

  rowning, he went to the sideboard and poured
  a sherry. Handing it to her, he made certain their
  ers did not touch. He watched her bring the
  s to her lips and sip, her eyes on his over the rim.
  "Delicious," she murmured, but wrinkled her
  e.

  hane hid his grin. He turned his back on her and
  de back to the window, shoving his hands into
  pockets. "First of all, did you steal Simon's gold
  ch?"

  he gasped, choking on the wine and spluttering.
  whirled. She had her hand on her chest, her eyes
  ring as she coughed. It took a few moments for
  to draw a steady breath, but when she had
  med, he regarded her with amusement.

  "Was that a yes or a no?"

  he glared at him. "Did that pompous goat accuse
  of theft?"

  Actually, Simon had done a lot more than that—
  d threatened, shaken his fists, stamped his feet.
  nswer me."

  he lifted her nose at him. "I will not stand here,
  bjected to such accusations. If Simon wants to ask
  himself, then let him."

  hane smiled without humor. "Since you haven't
  ied it, I'm assuming you did—"

  "Never assume." She tossed his own words back
  im.

"And since you are a guest in my home," he c
tinued slowly, "I suggest you return the watcl
him immediately in order to secure your posit
here."

Eden gave a most inelegant snort. "Or else wl
My position will be reduced to servant?"

Shane's face tightened. Had he ever met a m
defiant—and dauntless—woman? No man, wom
or child had ever dared cross him as she did—
every turn. Tamping down his temper, he said, "
values the watch immensely."

"As I value my dagger." She smiled. "You
give Simon a message for me, Mr. O'Connor. If
wants to accuse me of stealing his watch, he
accuse me to my face, not through you. And tell I
I'm certain he is valuing his watch a great deal m
now that it is missing."

He wanted to shout with laughter. Insane
sponse to her impertinence, but she was outraged
Silently, he saluted her spirit, her wittiness,
turned to hide the smile that tugged at his lips.

"Now," she continued, and out of the corner
his eye he saw her smooth her skirt, "if that is v
you have summoned me, Mr. O'Connor . . ."

"It isn't." He turned to her again. "But I'm wa
ing you, Eden, you better have returned that wa
to Simon by evening, or you'll have to answer
me."

Eden's chin went up a notch. "You will be g
by evening."

When he took a threatening step toward her,
hurried on. "I do not have the watch." It was nc
lie. She didn't have it on her person, but had hidc
it to teach Simon a lesson.

"I am not going to play games with you."

She offered him a tentative smile. "Don't y

..k, Mr. O'Connor, that whatever bones Simon
..d I have to pick, we should pick them with each
..er?"

"I think," he said in a tone that told her she was
..ining his limited store of patience, "it is a wise
..oice on your part *not* to take on another husband.
..u would, most likely, drive him to an early grave."

She looked down to hide her hurt. He had no way
.knowing, but that was what Society had whis-
.ed about her after Wilbur's death. He had not
..n young, to be sure, but the elite had put their
..ds together and whispered about her having too
..ch spirit for him, too much verve, and it had
..ed him. She didn't believe it—he had had an ail-
.. heart to begin with—but it gave the upper eche-
..s a legitimate reason to gloat. Normally she didn't
..e what Society had to say about her, but this in-
..ved a man's life—or death, so to speak.

Ignoring the sudden tightness in her chest, she
..t Shane's gaze straight on. "Do you care to con-
..ue with your questions, Mr. O'Connor? Or do
..u prefer to continue discussing the fragile nature
.. men?"

He seemed about to smile, but frowned instead
..d ran a finger around his collar. "I want you to
..te a note to that . . . director," he said, his
..ce low and annoyed. "And tell him to stop writ-
.. to you." He picked up a fistful of notes from his
..sk and held them up, then opened his fingers to
.. them drift back to his desktop. "He has sent all
.these to Liam's, and it is becoming a bloody nui-
..ce. Does he think we have nothing better to do
..n to intercept his besotted love letters?"

She froze, her drink halfway to her lips. "Is *that*
..y you called me to your office? I thought you
..re going to question me about my brother."

"Furthermore," he said, ignoring her comment "the notes are stupid, reeking with sentiment, and pointless."

"You read them?" she exclaimed. "You read m personal letters?"

"Oh, Lord." He pushed a hand through his hai and turned to look out at the rolling blue sea. "D you not think it wise that I read *everything* ac dressed to you?" He glanced her way. "Love note and all. Believe me, there was nothing personal i them. What he wrote has been written a thousan times before—by Shakespeare, Tennyson, Emerso all the romantics." He said the last with blatant der sion. "The man does not have an original thought i his head."

Her eyes widened with amazement. "Why, you' jealous!"

He looked at her again, obviously startled, then l put his head back and laughed with real pleasur "Is that what you think, mavournin?" He crossed her in three long strides but did not touch her. I stead, he spoke very quietly. "As long as I am inve tigating this case, you play by my rules. And n rules are that that overinflated windbag of a directe stay out of the picture for now." Now he did touc her, but it was a contemptuous touch, a lazy rasp one finger down her throat. "What you want to with your lover later, of course, is entirely up you."

She drew back swiftly. "He is not—" She stopp when she saw a sudden flame leap into his eyes. W give him the satisfaction of revealing her private li to him? Besides, it wasn't Franklin she wanted talk about, but Philip.

"Please," she said. "Hasn't anyone contacted ye

about Philip yet? Hasn't anyone sent you a message?"

He was silent for a minute, searching her features, then he moved away from her to pour himself a drink.

"No. As soon as I hear, I'll let you know."

Eden felt hot despair wash over her. "Maybe they killed him," she whispered.

She saw his fingers tighten on his glass. Then he lifted it to his lips and took a slow sip. He put his glass down next to hers and she found the sight oddly intimate. "You may go to your room now," he said.

Belligerence stiffened her spine. "I am not a child. I came here under your orders, and I came with great reluctance. I hired you to find my brother. I will, in the future, heed your advice concerning him, but I will not allow you to tell me when to go to my room."

A slow smile curved his mouth, and one eyebrow lifted in subtle challenge. "You will do as I say in my house, madame. I think your room is the safest place for you right now, and I want you to change out of those clothes and into something decent."

She arched her eyebrows. "You don't find this decent?"

"Get upstairs, Eden."

Their eyes clashed in a test of wills. Then Eden whirled, snatched the wig off the chair where she'd dropped it, and strode from the room. She felt his penetrating stare on her back as she crossed the foyer, muttering all the while. As she started up the stairs, she saw out the foyer window a stately carriage in Shane's drive. The coachman was helping a cool and beautiful blonde alight, and Eden felt a slash of jealousy such as she had never known before.

Turning to Shane, she said, "Oh! You're evening engagement has arrived."

His eyes narrowed, but before he could answer, she added, "And, by the way, I'm sleeping on the beach tonight."

She heard his curse as she flew the rest of the way up the stairs, and laughed at him.

"Like hell you are, woman!" he shouted after her just as the butler opened the door to admit the blonde. She stared haughtily at Shane, then lifted her gaze to Eden at the second floor balcony.

"I am!" Eden responded naughtily, delighted that the blonde's image of the perfectly proper Mr. O'Connor was certainly distorted now. "It is too bloody hot to sleep indoors!" She skipped off to her bedroom, laughing at her last glimpse of Shane, glaring up at her in formidable icy silence.

Eden sobered, though, as soon as she entered her room. He had *another* paramour, when he couldn't even bear to acknowledge *her*. Her spirits plummeted, but as she glanced out at the soft yellow pre-evening sky, a realization gripped her, and she brightened.

Shane's new mistress was blond.

CHAPTER NINE

DEN DID NOT SLEEP ON THE BEACH. JAMIE, THE GUARD
at her door, would not let her past. She was to be
served dinner in her room, he told her, and be kept
there for the night.

"Like a prisoner!" she cried, feeling stricken. This
was getting personal now. She tried her most charming smile on Jamie, but he was adamant that she was
not to leave.

Mid-evening she took a bath, and after Alice
tended to her, she had her maid play various roles in
both *Lysistrata* and the children's play she had written. Alice was less than enthusiastic, though, and

Eden noticed a sullen attitude about her usually accommodating maid.

"What is it, Alice?"

"Oh, nothing, mum."

"Of course something is gnawing at you. Out with it."

But Alice did not want to speak. She lowered her eyes until Eden badgered it out of her. "It's about that man's watch."

Eden's eyes widened. "Simon's?"

"Yes'm, that's the one."

"Well, what about it?"

"They're callin' you names in the servants' quarters, miss. Thief, and the like."

"Well, I'm not wounded, so do not concern yourself with it." Still, she could see that the maid was troubled. "Alice, please concentrate on the play. This is very trying for me. We are supposed to put on the children's play next week, and I promised Franklin I would rehearse privately."

Alice gnawed on her lower lip. "You're not a thief, are you, mum?"

"Of course not."

Alice's gaze went to her mistress's throat. "You *are* wearin' a man's gold watch 'round your neck."

"Yes, I am."

Alice hesitated, obviously not wanting to cross the line into impertinence, then she plunged ahead. "Is it his?"

Eden sighed loudly. "Of course it's his. But I didn't steal it. I'm teaching him a lesson."

Alice's face cleared. She was accustomed to Eden's logic and understood at once. The only problem was that not too many others could follow it, and it was becoming a task defending her in the servants' quarters.

"If they bother you again, tell me," Eden said,
and I will straighten it out for you. Now, are you
ready?"

In the end, though, Alice got bored with the rehearsing and Eden sent her on her way. When the
maid was gone, Eden picked up a book to read, but
could not concentrate. She thought of Philip, then
pushed those thoughts away, afraid to think. She
went to the window and leaned out, inhaling deeply
of the night air. The stars were high up, winking
silver. The ocean surf was constant, lulling, and she
ached to run down to the beach and feel the cool
water splash over her bare feet. But she was a prisoner.

She wondered what *he* was doing, then decided
not to wonder. Whereas before she had been delighted his new mistress was a blonde, now she was
discouraged, for he had only chosen that one over
her. She sighed and peeled off her silk nightgown.
No point in wearing that. Taking up her script again,
she began to pace the floor, reading aloud, gesticu-
lating, stopping to scribble notations in the margins.
But the night was torrid. And she was lonely.

She wandered to the open window again and
stared out, her gaze drawn to the beach, where the
waves were tipped silver as they raced together, leaving the sand glistening under the moonlight. As she
allowed herself to be lulled by their constant murmuring, a movement farther down the beach caught
her eye. A horse and rider, and she knew it was
Shane.

He rode like a god in the wind. Thunder and
power and sheer muscle, both horse and rider. She
gripped the windowsill and leaned out farther. In all
her years in Texas she had never seen a man ride like
him, not even Rattlesnake, not even Rake. He was a

part of the horse, fluid and graceful. The moonlight revealed enough so that she could see he was shirtless, and she watched him shamelessly. She wanted to get closer, to hear the pounding of hooves, to smell him, to ride behind him, her thighs hugging his. Crazy, irrational thoughts! But they were there just the same, as were the wild, hot, zigzagging currents that pulled and tugged inside her. Helplessly fascinated, she kept her eyes trained on horse and rider till they were gone from view, then let out a pent-up breath. Her heart pounded, pounded. She grabbed her silk wrapper, intent on watching him up close, at least from the screened-in side porch, and she was determined to con Jamie into allowing it if she must.

But Jamie had left his post. Though she blessed her good fortune, she puzzled about it as she crept down the stairs, then realized that Shane had probably lifted the command since he was home and able to guard her himself. All the gates were guarded, and men were stationed at various points along the walls, so there was little chance of her escaping this fortress anyhow.

The night air was thick and hot. She stepped out onto the porch and felt a slight breeze that lifted her hair and tugged at her wrapper. She sat down at one of the wrought iron tables, but at least a half hour went by and she did not sight him. Disappointed, she was debating whether to go down to the beach for a swim or walk on the shore for a while, when she saw him.

He was walking from the direction of the stables, and he was still shirtless. Cream-soft moonlight poured over his broad chest and shoulders, so that she could see the rigid muscles in them. It was a wonder that a man so lean could be so solidly built.

But he was, and her gaze roved down his chest to where dark hair thinned to a line that disappeared into the waistband of his jeans.

Her breath stalled in her throat. Shane in jeans. What a contrast to his impeccably tailored suits, his customary fastidious attire. In that moment he could have been a hand on her grandfather's horse ranch. His jeans were so worn, they were faded to white at the stress points, the frayed front placket cupping the heavy bulge of his sex. Captivated, Eden couldn't drag her gaze away from that masculine ridge. Watching him, she thought her heart would burst. He came toward her, closer, closer. Not only did he ride like an Apache, but he walked like one, with a silent, savage grace that held her spellbound.

Suddenly, he stopped. He'd caught sight of her. In the shadowy night she could see that his face was taut, the angles hard as stone, his brooding eyes piercing and luminous in the dark. For one frozen, stomach-clenching moment she thought he would order her back to her room, and she knew she wouldn't be able to bear that. But he stood a few feet from the porch, saying nothing. At last he started walking again, and he took the porch steps two at a time.

"What are you doing out here?" he asked.

Watching you. Eden's insides jumped about as she saw that he was damp. His curly chest hair glistened with silver drops of seawater, and the hair on his head was slicked back, gleaming in the lamplight. He must have gone swimming.

He carried his boots, and he set them on the floor with a thump. Pulling out a chair across from her, he cast her a crooked, engaging smile. "I have never known you to be at a loss for words."

He was teasing her, was actually being charming!

And his charm had a dangerous, potent effect on her. Eden told herself to get up and flee. She stayed though, the torment growing within her, the torment of wanting and not being able to touch what she wanted. She had never felt this way about anyone in her life, and it frightened her, alarmed her that she could feel so intensely about this man . . . while he felt nothing at all. Reminding herself of that, she strengthened her resolve to remain as aloof as he. Still, her voice wavered as she asked, "You were swimming?"

Stupid question! She could have kicked herself. But Shane continued to smile that engaging half smile.

"Among other things."

"I know . . . you were riding." She swallowed heavily. "You ride like an Apache."

His lips twisted in a wry grin. "No, I ride like an Irishman with a blood lust for Thoroughbreds." His gaze slid over her, as if he were inspecting *her* lines, and Eden hadn't an inkling of what he thought of them. His gaze drifted to her mouth, then back up to meet her eyes. "Have you come out to sleep on the beach after all?"

Though he seemed amiable enough, she thought it wise to answer evasively. "I couldn't sleep."

"I noticed."

At her questioning look he added, his deep voice slightly sardonic, "I told you to wear clothes in your room at night."

"How did you know I—you were spying again!"

"Spying, hell." He looked up at her window, and she followed his stare. Her room was brightly lit and if she were pacing before the window, anyone on the beach could catch an eyeful. "Who can miss?"

His tone carried an undercurrent of humor, and he brought her gaze back to his. "I'm wearing clothes now."

Shane looked deliberately at the V of her ivory silk wrapper where it was gathered over her breasts. Modestly, she pulled the wrapper tighter under her throat, and his mouth curled in a soft smile. It amused him that she pretended modesty when she had been all but advertising her wares earlier.

He had been riding, trying to ease his mind of his ever-increasing obsession for her, when he had looked up and caught sight of her—and felt as though all hell had broken loose inside him. He had pulled on the reins at the vicious slam of desire in his loins, and his big bay had reared up, whinnying in protest. Watching her pass back and forth in front of the window, he'd felt a sweet flash of pain, his groin muscles tightening so fast that he ached all over. Watching her now, he still ached. The swim in the ocean had done little to cool his raging desire. He was throbbing, lust burning high in his blood, and he wanted her more—a thousand times more—than he'd ever wanted any woman. It shook him, and angered him, that he could feel so intensely about a woman like her. They were opposites—she flamboyant, exuberant, wildly alive, and he reserved, intense, hard-bitten.

He caught her scent on the breeze. The faintest aroma of honeysuckle prickled his nostrils, and he realized she changed her scent often—gardenias, roses, violets, sandalwood. But her own sweet scent was clean and fresh, female.

It intoxicated him.

"That woman," she said suddenly. "The one you spent the evening with. She was not Patricia Alexander of the other day."

His gaze sharpened on her. That she would remember Patricia's name surprised him, and that she would comment on either woman surprised him even more. He passed a hand through his hair. "That's true."

"Hmm. Did you have a nice evening?"

He frowned. What was her game? What the hell did she care what his evening was like? Fact was, he hadn't enjoyed it at all. Lisa was petulant and boring, and it had struck him halfway through his engagement with her that he could think only of Eden. Images of her had flashed through his mind at the oddest times—Eden in silk and ruffles but barefoot, Eden charming his friends, Eden in boy's garb with Sly Camponelli, in Mexican clothing, in virginal white descending the stairs. Eden eating truffles, throwing a knife, fighting with Simon. Eden . . . Eden . . . Eden . . .

He had come home to ride, to pound her image out of his mind, his blood. It hadn't worked. He wanted to shove aside the table that was between them, tear off her silk wrapper, and pull her down beneath him on the porch floor. He wanted to feel her firm round breasts in his hands, feel the nipples turn hard with arousal. He wanted to possess her.

With effort, he suppressed those fiery needs. "It was . . . interesting," he said at last. "And yours?"

Eden smiled at him. "Thank you for asking. I have to admit, it was boring." Her eyebrows drew together in a troubled frown. "I . . . I want to rehearse with the troupe, Shane." Immediately she regretted her words, for he frowned.

"Forget it," he said brusquely.

Her lashes lowered. She made an idle pattern on the table with her finger.

"Eden."

She looked up, hopeful.

"You were shot at two days ago. It's safest for you ʊ stay here."

She sighed. "I suppose you're right—partly." Her aze drifted out to sea. "It's just too difficult to con ɛntrate on my own role when there's no one to ɪteract with. Alice is helping, but she is not much of ɪ actress—" Suddenly she stopped, a wonderful lea sparking in her mind. "Why don't *you* play a ɔle—"

"No."

"Why not? Liam says you have a passion for the ɪeater."

"Liam talks too much."

She laughed. "He does not. I bet you are a mag ificent actor. Why, it's even in your family history. ʼhat uncle Liam mentioned."

"I have a passion as an observer, not a partici ant."

"Oh, nonsense!" She brushed that comment off ith a wave of her hand. "You act all the time as an ɪvestigator. I bet you play different roles constantly. ʼou could play the part of the Apache who—"

"Eden."

His tone broached no argument, but she made ne last appeal. "Not even a tiny part?"

He remained close-mouthed.

She glanced once again to the water. The waves ʊpped silver moonlight, like a million filled chalices ɪrned up to the heavens. She stared in awed won ɛr. "The night is so beautiful."

"And time we went inside."

Oh, but she wanted to stay out there with him! ʼhere was magic in the night, and Shane was part of ⸬. "Please," she said, and her voice was taut, husky.

"I want to stay here for a while." She paused. "I'l pay you extra for it."

He laughed, then nodded obligingly at her, ges turing with an outstretched hand.

"The night is yours, milady."

She couldn't help smiling too. "How much will i cost me?"

Her smile faltered, for the flicker of intensity sh saw in his eyes made her question sound ripe wit sexual invitation. When he answered her, his voic was even deeper than usual. "A veritable fortune, n doubt, mavournin."

The air was swollen with the heavy, hot undercur rent of potent sexuality. Their eyes communicated what words could not. Eden knew now that sh wanted to explore the fathomless depths he had re vealed to her. She suspected, just from the pain i his eyes when he had told her about Meggie, tha under his controlled façade he was immensely sensi tive. That he could keep this from her suddenly di not seem right. Nor did the fact that he hadn' kissed her since that first time. She realized she wa insulted that he hadn't pursued her, and impulsively she asked, "Why haven't you kissed me again Shane?"

He seemed stunned at first at her blunt question then he shrugged, the picture of supreme indiffer ence. "Because I choose not to."

Eden felt a shattering inside, like icicles breaking The pulse in her throat clogged her breath, hurt. Sh felt a sharp pain behind her eyes as she stared acros the table at this aloof man who, she could sense, wa pulling back increment by increment, once agai gaining his taut control. She searched his eyes for flicker of warmth, but they were as impenetrable a

tal. In any other situation she would have pooh-
ohed his cold withdrawal, but she was possessed
unquenchable pride, and it was on the line.

She stiffened her posture and attempted a smile,
t her voice was as sweet and cold as ice cream.
hat explains that." She rose, but his hand shot out
d clamped tight around her wrist.

"Sit down." His voice had the jolting steel impact
a sword being drawn from a scabbard.

With collosal dignity she nodded coolly and sat.
lease let go of my wrist." She met his eyes across
e table, caught the admirable glint in them, and
t both relief and pain when he slowly released her.
She shook her hair back again, calmly meeting his
ze. If he wanted to pretend, she could pretend
o. "The horse you were riding was magnificent,"
e said, and stared out over the water again.

"Yes."

"Do you have many horses?"

"I do."

"And do you race the horses you breed?"

"All over the world. You can ride the horses if
u want to, Eden."

The tenderness in his voice startled her. Some hot,
ght emotion swam up in her chest, squeezing her
art, and she glanced at him. He looked solemn, his
es sober, and she thought this might be his way of
ologizing for the imprisonment—and the rejec-
n. "Thank you."

"You're welcome."

She smiled tremulously. "I can ride bareback."

He leaned back in his chair, stretching out his
gs. His eyes were teasing. "So can I."

"I'll race you sometime."

"Sometime perhaps."

"You said I could have access to everything on tl estate," she went on. "May I use your kitchen?"

He stared at her, obviously surprised by her que tion. "Why?"

"I like to cook. You don't believe me, but I d Rake taught me. At seven, I was flipping the lighte hotcakes in Texas."

"What a rarity," he drawled. "A society woma who cooks."

"But I'm not a society woman, not really. We technically, I am, but not at heart." She grinned him, happy again that he was indulging her the little pleasures that meant so much to her free ar wild spirit. He didn't return her grin, though, b studied her with such intensity, she cast him a pu zled look.

"Why did you marry a man so much older th you?"

The question caught her off guard. She wondere why he hadn't forgotten that about her, and w surprised that he was curious. It seemed he probe at whatever was on his mind until he got to the cor

"I did it for Mama," she said, her voice soft ar low. It was the only thing she had ever done t please her mother.

"Why would your mother want that for you?"

Again, he surprised her. Not so much his que tion, but his voice. It was hard and cold, as thoug he didn't think much of her mother. She smiled him. "Mama wanted to increase my wealth. Ma rying Wilbur did that. When he . . . passed on"- she swallowed, remembering what everyone had sai about Wilbur's death—"I was left very comfor able."

A gold digger, Shane thought. But even as I

ught it, he knew it didn't fit her—it fit her
her. What a selfish woman, to expect that bond-
for her lovely daughter. "Did it leave your
her comfortable too?" he asked sardonically, but
n apparently missed the darkness in his voice.

Oh, yes! But Mama was plenty rich to begin
. She had my father's money, you see."

I see." He saw all too damn well. "And that
n't enough for her? She had to marry you off to
e old lech—"

Oh, it wasn't that way at all! Mama is sickly—
been since Papa died. She has a very weak heart,
see, and needs long spells of bed rest. She
ted to make certain we were all cared for, and
bur *was* a dear man. In a way, marrying Wilbur
the best thing to happen to me at that time of
life. Imagine if, at twenty-three, I still hadn't
rried. I'd be a spinster and it would only strain
ma's heart."

Imagine that," he drawled.

he glanced at him with curiosity, then she
led. "It does sound silly, I agree. But Mama had
own rules, and my marriage pleased her."

Did it please you?"

den lowered her lashes. "I already told you how
lt about Wilbur. I made an old man happy—for a
le, anyway. Although, if it had been up to me,
sure I wouldn't have married. Too bothersome."

looked up at him again. His hair was drying
v, and he smoothed it back with both hands, a
nnerism she had begun to find endearing. "What
ut you, Mr. O'Connor? Why haven't *you* mar-
d?"

Tell me why I should," he responded with
used indulgence.

"Why, for love . . . or money," she add
pragmatically. "Of course."

"Of course." His gaze drifted down her bo
roving boldly over her breasts. "But neither is
good enough reason."

She sighed. "I agree. But most people don't." S
hesitated. "But don't you ever get lonely?"

He looked even more amused. "For women?"

She blushed. "No, you don't seem to be lonely
women." She tapped her fingertips on the tablet
studying him intently. "What about children?"

"What about them?"

"Do you want any?"

His face hardened. "I'm too busy for a fami
And I would imagine that my chosen professi
would be hell on children. A wife too." A faint sm
touched his eyes. "Now," he said, his voice softe
ing, "if you are finished with your questions, I su
gest we go indoors."

He stood, but Eden could not move. She
across from him and saw, at eye level, the vicio
scar that snaked from his abdomen to his low
back. She drew in a sharp and audible breath, a
his gaze sharpened on her.

"Do you see what I mean?" he said, smiling a th
smile. "Not the nightly reminder a wife wants to li
with, is it now?"

"What happened to you?" she asked, her voi
shaky.

"What happened was in another time, anoth
place—and too ugly for your pretty ears to he
Now, come. It's time to go in."

She stood on weak legs, stricken by the agony
must have suffered. It was a knife wound for certai
and that was somehow more revolting, in that h
assailant had to get very close to him to hurt him li

hat. She lifted her gaze to his. "It looks like some-
ne tried to kill you," she said.

"Someone did."

And his tone warned her not to question him any-
ore about it.

CHAPTER TEN

$\mathcal{T}$HE NEXT MORNING, EDEN'S MOOD HAD CHEERED CON
siderably. The night before, after the house w
quiet and she was certain Shane was asleep, she h
crept back out onto the screened porch, settled on
cushioned, wrought iron settee, and drifted off
sleep as the sea-misted breeze caressed her skin. S
had opened her eyes to a bloodred sun that h
risen slowly over the green sea. Of course, the bea
was guarded as well as the estate, so she did r
worry about endangering her life—not that she d
anyway. Really, she thought as she slipped back ir
the house, Shane should have no objection.

On the way up the stairs she brightened ev

re as she recalled Shane's words when she had
ed him why he did not kiss her. "Because I
ose not to," he'd said. Not "I don't *want* to," but
ause he simply *chose* not to kiss her. Judging by
 way he had looked at her the night before, he
nted to kiss her very much indeed.

Her mood soured when she opened her door and
nd her room had been searched. Very surrepti-
usly, but her belongings had definitely been
ved through. "For the love of heaven!" she cried,
iding forward to slam shut the top drawer to her
reau. And she knew the identity of the culprit.
non. Or one of Simon's patsies. "This," she de-
red out loud, "is war!"

She heard footsteps outside her door and ran to it.
nging it open, she saw one of the housemaids
rrying down the long, carpeted hall.

"Come back here, missy!" Eden shouted, in-
sed, but the maid was gone.

Obviously, Eden thought, she would have to clear
r good name among the staff.

Later that morning she went down to the kitchen
 set matters straight. Servants scurried about,
opping vegetables, rolling out dough on wooden
les, stirring concoctions in bowls. A red-cheeked
ddle-aged woman stood by a six-foot-high brick
eplace, stirring something in a kettle. She looked,
 Eden, like the head cook. Positioning herself in
e middle of the huge room, Eden propped her
nds on her hips and addressed them all.

"I understand," she said, glancing from one
und-eyed face to the next, "there are some of you
o think I am a thief."

She smiled, reached into her décolletage—an ac-
n that caused the males to gape—and pulled out
non's gold watch. Many of the servants gasped,

audibly, and she let the watch drop between h[er] breasts. She strode smartly before them, smili[ng] pleasantly while her pointed words made their i[m] pact. "I am not a thief. I have no reason to ste[al,] have never stolen a thing, and would rather be jail[ed] than steal."

"You have the man's watch 'round your neck[,]" said a tall man by the corner.

Eden turned to him. "Your name, sir?"

The man paled.

"Come now," she said, holding out her han[d.] "Let's have it."

"Mike O'Downey, miss."

"Mike O'Downey, I'm pleased to meet you." H[er] smile widened when his mouth dropped ope[n.] "Very astute man, you are. And yes, I have Simon['s] watch around my neck. But—" She paused for [ef]fect. The servants leaned forward to hear. S[he] leaned forward to accommodate them. "Simon is t[he] thief."

A collective gasp filled the room. The red-cheek[ed] woman cried, "You defame his good character!"

"Good character!" Eden exclaimed. "He stole [a] dagger right out of my hand and he had absolute[ly] no intention of giving it back to me. When I r[e]turned to the brutal city, I was left defenseless! [If] anything, my dear lady, he is defaming my goo[d] character to all of you! I am only attempting to tea[ch] Simon a lesson, that if you take from others, i[t's] bound to happen to you." She nodded once for e[m]phasis. "My grandfather taught me that."

The woman peered at her. "But, pardon my i[m]pertinence, miss, a woman of your good standin[g,] what were you doing with a dagger?"

"Impertinence pardoned. My grandfather gave [

me years ago. I carried it with me in Texas, and
er since."

"Texas?" asked a wide-eyed young man who had
opped kneading bread dough to hear all this.

She turned to study him. "Have you an interest in
xas?"

He blushed. "I've always wanted to visit there,
a'am. Jes' weren't meant to be, though, I guess."

"Well, my goodness, don't ever give up! If it's
ur dream to visit Texas, hang on to that dream, sir,
d do not let go of it, ever. You'll get there yet."

The man beamed. "Well, jeesh, miss, do you
ink, sometime—" He broke off, embarrassed with
mself for his lack of manners.

"Yes," she said warmly. "I will talk with you
out Texas. Under one condition." She turned in a
micircle to appeal to them all. "Mr. O'Connor is
owing me to cook in his kitchen—"

At their horrified gasps she held up her hands. "I
ze to cook. I've lived much of my life with my
andfather, and he taught me how. If you would be
kind as to share your kitchen during my stay here
which will be brief, I assure you—I would be
ost delighted."

And they were most delighted to have her. It was
mazing how quickly they took to her, but Eden was
ppy with their response.

"And," she informed them, "after I visit the other
rvants and set them straight on this trumped-up
cusation of theft, we are going to cook a meal like
r. O'Connor has never eaten before." They all
oubted that, she could see, and hoped she hadn't
advertently insulted them. But they *would* see. She
d every intention of keeping her word. "But Mr.
'Connor won't let me venture off his estate—he
inks he is protecting me, you see, on a very per-

sonal matter he won't let me talk about—and I really
do need some special ingredients I am sure we can
obtain only in the city."

"I'll go into the city for you, ma'am," the
breadmaker said eagerly, nearly tripping over himself to rid his skin of the flour.

The red-cheeked woman glared at him. "First
things first, Neddie! The bread, the bread!"

"Oh, sure." He grinned sheepishly at Eden.

She, too, was disappointed. She had hoped that
one of them might be able to escort her into the city.
She was due for a visit to Franklin and the troupe.
But the head cook's next words sealed her fate.

"Now, pretty one," she said, coming over to pat
Eden's hand, "if the master says you are to stay here
on the estate, he has a very good reason for it. They
don't call him the best investigator for nothin'."

Eden smiled weakly at her. "I suppose you're
right, Mrs. . . ."

"Leahy. But you can call me Frances, dear. Would
you like a cookie?"

Eden shook her head, thanked her, and after a
quick and successful visit to the servants' quarters
below, she hurried back to her room to write out an
extensive list for Neddie.

It turned out to be quite a search for the needed
ingredients. Late that afternoon Neddie came back
crestfallen that he hadn't purchased everything she
needed. She assured him that he could try a few
other markets the next day, and maybe he needed
her help. But Mrs. Leahy, who seemed to be able to
read Eden's mind, assured her that Neddie would
find the remaining ingredients with *her* help tomorrow. Eden, forced to postpone her special meal, decided to head for the stables and find one of Shane's

·ses to ride. Turning to leave the kitchen, though,
ran smack into Simon.

They recoiled off each other like polarized mag-
s.

"You!" both cried in ominous and indignant
·ces, and their audience in the kitchen watched
·m in frozen horror.

·ust as Eden opened her mouth to give him the
·down of his life, Simon caught sight of his watch
·und her neck.

"This," he shouted, fury turning his face red, "is a
·ody outrage!" He reached for the watch, and
·en Eden stepped back, his face turned purple.
·ive me back my watch, you conniving little—"

"*Mister* Peterson!" broke in Mrs. Leahy. "You are
·aking to a lady."

His icy eyes left Eden's to slice a path to the cook.
·en thought he might spit he looked so angry.
·rs. Leahy," he said frigidly, "*this* is no lady! She
·a bloody thief! You can see for yourself she is
·aring my watch—"

"You leave her be, you wretched man! She is a
·ly and Mr. O'Connor's guest."

Simon couldn't believe his ears. Just hours ago
·se people were building up a healthy animosity
·ward Mr. O'Connor's "guest." What the bloody
·ll had happened? "For the love of God, woman,
·e has stolen my watch and is blatantly wearing it
·ht under my nose! What would *you* call that?"

"An eye for an eye," Eden said, and gave him her
·oulder. "I find it interesting, Mr. Peterson, that
·u felt it perfectly fine to hold on to my bowie knife
·en you stole it. Now, if you want your watch
·ck, you'll have to use your ingenuity, won't you?
·ithout," she added, glaring at him, "searching my
·om."

The kitchen help gasped.

"This is preposterous!" Simon said.

Eden smiled at him. "You need to be taught lesson."

"Mr. O'Connor will hear of this."

"He already has. And he decided to let you fin way to deal with the problem yourself."

Simon tried to wear her down with a furious gla but she matched it with a haughty one of her ov Feeling outnumbered, he spun on his heel a stalked off, the heat of his anger like a tangible wal

"He needs a wife," Eden muttered, and the s vants roared with laughter.

As it turned out, it took quite a while to gather her ingredients, and Eden was not able to prepa her meal until two days later. In all that time she not catch a glimpse of her "protector." She was w aware of being watched by several of his bodyguar as she swam and rode and slept on the porch, b she wondered what work kept him shut away such long hours in his study that he couldn't ev come out for meals. She fretted that he would come out for hers. She had fussed all day over a fie pot of chili, tamales, enchiladas, and more, all to served with a bottle of cold red wine or iced be She was certain he would like her southweste meal. Neddie certainly did. In fact, he was the o one in the kitchen who didn't need to wash down as soon as it was in his mouth. The ent kitchen staff was in near convulsions, tearing a wheezing and howling, half drunk to boot. Th were laughing as they dared another mouthful, th poured more wine and beer down their throats.

"Not only does she steal valuables," Simon sa from the doorway when all the howling drew curiosity, "but she is trying to poison the help."

Eden turned to him. "It's my grandfather's special
ze-winning recipe."

Simon snorted. "Is that why these people are cry-
;?"

She giggled. "That's the hot peppers. The hotter
: better."

"Try it, old chap," Neddie encouraged, clearly de-
hted at the notion of downing the food, but Si-
n turned his back on them as if they weren't
rthy of his company.

Seven o'clock approached and it seemed nothing
uld lure Shane out of his study. Eden had encour-
ed the butler to tell him dinner was a surprise, but
: haughty servant had returned to tell her Mr.
Connor was otherwise occupied and had no inter-
in dinner.

Eden sighed. "Well, thank you, Higgins. We
ed."

The butler straightened as if he'd been slapped
tween the shoulder blades. Eden frowned at him.

" 'Is name's Spencer," Mrs. Leahy whispered, and
len offered him an apologetic smile.

"Oops. Sorry, Spencer. I don't know why I'm
ving trouble with your name."

She wondered if Shane was entertaining a woman
his study. What else could keep him in there for
long? By the time eight o'clock came, she made
her mind to bring a tray to him herself.

"Oh, no, miss," Mrs. Leahy protested, " 'tisn't
ht you be waitin' on him like a servant. Bad
ough you cooked the meal."

Eden ignored her, bustling about and setting up a
ıy. "Don't be silly. Go get Smithers to announce
ıner and I will bring him the tray. Has he eaten
ything in the last forty-eight hours?"

"Not to my knowledge, mum. But he does this

sometimes—when he works especially hard on
case—shuts himself in there to work."

"And since it's my case, I insist. Now, hurry a
fetch Smithers."

"Spencer. The butler's name is Spencer, Mis
the cook gently reminded her.

Minutes later Eden was following Spencer ir
the study. When he bowed out and closed the dc
behind him, she scanned the room. No sign of
male company.

"I brought you some dinner," she said tentativ
when Shane didn't bother to look up from his wo
How could she forget that barely leashed sense
power that simmered around him, even seated?

"I told Spencer to forget dinner."

"Oh, but you have to eat!" She began to fuss w
the tray, but stopped, looking up when she felt
stare on her. Her breath caught. The dove-gray sh
he wore made his eyes look more slate-tinged, b
still like a lake on a winter day.

"You are not my caretaker," he said.

Immediately her light spirits were dashed. S
stuffed the hurt that surged through her back do
and lowered her eyes. "I know that. I—you—" S
took a breath and lifted her gaze to his again. "Y
said I could use your kitchen. I did, and here's
results." She turned and headed for the door.

"Eden."

She stopped, squeezing her eyes tight against
tide of warmth that flooded her at the sound of
deep, rich voice uttering her name. She turn
slowly to look at him. The wind that blew in t
open window behind him fluttered his dark ha
lifting it and settling it, so that not all of his smoo
ing could tame the disheveled waves.

"I will eat."

Her smile was radiant, and Shane cursed its power. She was like a beam of sunshine pouring into the room, flooding it with light and warmth. To hurt her with sharp words was beginning to hurt him, and he didn't understand it. She was a nuisance, a burr, and from what he was hearing, a real bane to Simon, his superb assistant. Shane wanted no part of her, yet she seemed a permanent fixture in his mind.

He hadn't been on the estate the past few days, but in the city. He'd wanted to chase away a gut-old dread, the dread that he'd have to tell her her brother was dead. He needed to find answers, and without her tagging along and getting underfoot. So, with explicit orders for every guard on the estate and Simon, who'd bristled at the assignment, to keep her constantly in sight, he'd set off, free to investigate on his own. He found little. No unclaimed, unidentified bodies. He'd met with El Daggar and Stealth MacGuire, just to ask them if they knew anything about any new deals Philip had made with anyone. Nothing. He visited the brothels Philip frequented and still came up with very little. The man was a scoundrel, no doubt, a card cheat and womanizer. A rakehell. He wondered if Eden knew her twin as well as the underworld did.

He'd watched her theater troupe for a while too. He couldn't gauge much, but he had qualms about *something.* That would not score him anything in the history books, he'd thought grimly on his ride home.

Now Eden stood before him, nervously twining her fingers. He'd never known her to be nervous. Though dusk had fallen, he had not yet lit a lamp. She was cast in purplish twilight shadow, and the room was fragrant with the scent of her . . . and of spicy chili.

He glanced at the food. There was beer in a glass

on the tray. He reached for it and took a swig, clo
ing his eyes as the icy treat settled in his bell
"Damn, that's good."

"I didn't cook *that*."

He was smiling before he could stop himself.
was getting easier to do that all the time . . . sin
she had come into his life. That notion made hi
frown. Damn, he wanted to settle this case, and fa
Get her out of his life once and for all.

"What is that photograph?"

"What?" He was startled by her question, by ho
quickly she had crossed to his desk and picked u
the photograph. She had entered the room
abruptly, he had forgotten to shove it back in h
desk drawer, where it had been for years. He didn
know what had possessed him to pull it out. He w
angry with her nosiness, yet . . . he waited eager
for her reaction.

Eden's brows drew together in a puzzled frow
The photograph was old, curled at the edges, and
sepia tones. It was of a boy and a baby. The boy w
about eleven, holding a cloth cap in one hand an
the hand of the baby, who looked about two, in th
other. The baby was cherubic, with huge eyes an
lots of light, curly hair. She was grinning into th
camera, but the boy offered the camera only a sh
heart-tugging half-smile. His short jacket and tro
sers were threadbare, yet he wore them as thoug
they were of the finest quality. He was thin, har
faced, with an alert look, all his senses alive. Only h
mouth showed a hint of sensitivity, and his eyes, fu
of fire, so striking, so eloquent, Eden felt she kne
him. And then she realized she did.

"The boy is you," she said softly.

The only sounds in the room were from the lig
breeze sifting in and the surf. She looked up fro

e photograph to see those same beautiful eyes, so
uch wiser, so much older, yet still keen with the
ral fire that made her heart dance. She swallowed,
d her throat hurt. "And Meggie?"

His shoulders were tensed, his face like granite.
And Meggie."

She couldn't help it; tears scalded her eyes. She
w Shane's startled expression and cursed those
ars, knowing he hated them so much. She set the
otograph down, though she was reluctant to re-
ase it. She wanted, suddenly, in the worst way, to
uch his face. To smooth away the harshness, the
in. But she could only offer lame words. "There is
thing to say about something like that."

Shane looked down at the photograph. He re-
embered the day the newspaper photographer had
me to the orphanage to take pictures of the or-
ans, for those westerners who wanted to adopt.
ster Superior had asked for a photo of Meggie and
m, one he could keep for himself, to look at while
was away from her. It was the only photograph he
d of her. Later, after she had been taken away,
'd wondered if they had carted her west. But
thing in his search for her indicated that.

"Nothing to say, to be sure," he murmured. No
ords. Just incredible gnashing pain when he al-
wed himself to think of his little sister, which
dn't, in the past few years, been often. For some
d reason, with the arrival of Eden in his life, he
as thinking of Meggie more. Perhaps because Meg-
e would be just about Eden's age. There was no
e in torturing himself over memories, though.

"Well, thank you for the meal."

Eden looked at him, startled. "Aren't you going to
mple the food?"

He stared at her as if she were the most tryi
person he had ever met, but he picked up the for

She watched him heap it with chili, raise it to h
in a mock salute, and put it into his mouth. Ho
that procedure could start strange quiverings insi
her, she did not know. But to watch Sha
O'Connor chew was like watching him talk, wal
smile, and move in every way. A pure sensual d
light. He swallowed, and a pleasurable ache hit h
stomach.

"Very good," he said.

She was disappointed at his modest assessme
"Hot?" she prompted.

"Quite."

No fanning of his mouth, though, no tears,
wheezing. Damn, how hot did it have to be f
Shane O'Connor? She sat on the edge of his des
smiled, and said, "Rather than sneak out of he
tomorrow, I thought I'd just tell you that I ha
decided to go into the city."

He reached for his glass of beer and drank slow
"You mean you can't think of a way out of this fo
tress."

"That is not what I mean at all. Where there's
will there's a way."

He tilted his head to one side, eyes warm wi
humor. "You've certainly proven that."

She blushed. "I have been held here captive lo
enough."

She noticed, with pleasure, that he was still drin
ing his beer. Hot, all right. Perfect. Though it a
peared he'd rather die than let her know.

Shane put the glass down. His mouth was on fi
"And do you plan to see your precious Franklin?

She looked annoyed. "He is not my precious, a
it is silly of you to say so. I need to practice. We ha

erformance at the orphanage in little more than a
ek, and I want to please the children."

Shane's face tightened, as did his fingers on his
ss. If his mouth would cool off, he could shoot
r wheedling proposal right down, but as it was, he
uld barely clip out, "I'll see what I can do." He
ended to do nothing but continue to keep her
ere until her brother was found.

She glanced at his empty beer glass. "Would you
e more beer?"

He stared at her, wondering if she had planned all
ong to paralyze his vocal chords. "Yes, ring for
re beer." As she turned to pull the bell cord, he
ded, "A person could get very drunk on your
ili."

She laughed, the sound like a shake of sleigh bells
a winter afternoon. Her laughter gripped him,
d he had to use iron control to stay seated, not to
after her, pull her into his arms, and crush her
uth to his. She danced out of the study and was
ne, seeming to take all the light from the room
th her.

CHAPTER ELEVEN

$\mathscr{Y}$OU *PROMISED*! EDEN ALL BUT SHOUTED AS S
bounded into Shane's study the next afternoon,
terrupting him and Simon as they compared no
on the case. Shane had left explicit orders with
servants that he was not to be disturbed, but she h
waited long enough, Eden thought, for his respon
to her request that he escort her into the city to s
Franklin. As he rose from behind his desk, thoug
he looked positively lethal.

"First of all," he said, his tone frigid and seve
"I promised you nothing. Second of all, so help
God, woman, if you ever barge into my study li

s again, I'll lock you in your room and throw away
key."

Eden stood her ground, her hands knotted into
all fists at her sides. "You *did* promise! You said
1'd see what you could do. And I waited all morn-
; for your answer. Now half the day is gone! That
s your plan, wasn't it? To make me wait, and then
would be too late to go into the city at all!"

His mouth hardened. "Actually, no," he said,
at wasn't my plan at all. I had no plan for you
ing into the city, so you can just put the idea right
t of your head. And get out of my office. I have no
ie for this." He apparently expected her to de-
irely bow her head and back out of the room, but
'd forgotten who he was dealing with. She flew at
n, grabbing a pillow on the way and flinging it at
n. He neatly ducked aside, and the pillow went
ht out the window. She leaned over his desk, put-
g her face, flushed with anger, close to his. "You
nnot *do* this. I paid you good money to find my
other, not pen me in my room like a woman with-
t a wit about her, a brain in her head!" She caught
non's smirk and whirled on him, his gold watch
ing out of the front of her shirt and almost smack-
; him in the face. "Have you no decency, no cour-
y, Mr. Peterson? Can you not see that this is a
ivate conversation?"

Simon straightened in his seat, looking down his
se at her. "Private, madame? The entire island can
ar your bellowing."

She ignored him, turning the full lash of her fury
ck on Shane. He further incensed her with his
and expression and shuttered eyes, completely im-
une to her desperation. "You are hateful, mean,
d despicable, and I refuse to stay your prisoner
ie more moment."

"Go upstairs and get some decent clothing You look," he added, letting his gaze ride slo over her, loitering on her breasts, "like a vagabon

That he could single that issue out now frustra her. "This is my exploring-the-beach outfit." wore a boy's white shirt, a pair of dark blue cot knickers, and her huaraches. In deference to heat, less fierce than it had been but uncomforta nonetheless, she had foregone corset and stockir "Give me my money back! I'll find Philip mysel or go to another investigator that won't impris me."

"The money is mine," Shane said. "And I am in the habit of leaving a job unfinished."

Her eyes blazed into his. In a silent battle of wi they glared at each other, and valiantly, Eden thr her jaw forward. "I am leaving these grounds witl two hours. Try and stop me."

But he already had. Jamie was looming in doorway, ready to take her away.

"Mrs. Lindsay," Shane began with exaggera patience.

"Oh, we're back to that, are we? Well, fine, *Mis* O'Connor. You think you can bully me into stay here, but I am determined to get into the city— have to fly there."

His mouth curved in a contemptuous sm "You'll have plenty of time to decide how to do t while you remain in your room for the next f hours." The smile left his face, replaced by a co stony mask. "I do not have time for this, Eden. I warned you plenty to stay out of my way, but y insist on insinuating yourself in places you don't long. This is the final warning. Don't push me t far, or I really will have to use strongarm tactics keep you subdued."

"You truly act as though I am a child—or miscre-
at!" she said as Jamie crossed the room to her.
You can't keep me in my room. Is that your idea of
unishment?"

"Furthermore," he went on in that implacable
ne that only raised her ire, "stay out of my sight.
ou have hundreds of acres of land to play in and
t you are constantly underfoot."

She squelched the hot pain of his searing rejec-
on. His words were a slap. She watched him dis-
iss her, sit to scribble something on a tablet, that
mnable calm of his making her throb with anger.
e acted as if she were not even present. "I want to
home," she said, softly now. "I want my brother
ack." Childlike wishes, she thought, cries for the
ars, the moon. Her pleas fell on deaf ears. Slowly,
e walked from the room, Jamie on her heels, then
e fled up the stairs to her room, slamming the
or shut in the hope that Shane would hear the
mphasis of her anger.

She collapsed on the huge bed, but she was too
utraged to cry. Hot anger swam through her, and
e jumped off the bed to pace the floor and come
p with a plan. Her gaze slid to the door. She knew
mie was on the other side of it, standing guard. A
ow smile crept across her face. No one was outside
er window. She made haste, tying bedsheets, tow-
s, and some of her clothing together to construct a
ain long enough to reach the ground. That done,
e tied one end of the makeshift rope around a leg
f the heavy bureau, then leaned out the window.

"Oops!" She had almost forgotten a change of
othes. It was one thing to walk about the estate in
ich casual dress, and quite another to parade into
e center of New York. She tossed a dress and un-
ergarments in her small valise and hailed it out the

window. She heard its thump, nodded her head wi
satisfaction, and swung her leg over the windowsi

Inch by inch she made her way down, grippi
the knotted cloth in her moist palms. She was ter
fied. She dared not look down, and her stoma
pitched when she once lost her grip.

"The bloody tyrant," she muttered, fiery ang
continuing to plague her as she wriggled down t
rope. Her shirt was damp with sweat, clinging to h
skin, and wisps of her hair stuck to her neck ar
cheeks. Her hands slipped again, and she let out
startled scream as she dropped several feet. Catchin
herself, she swung against the warm brick of h
cursed castle. She moaned softly, her stomach twis
ing as she caught a quick glimpse of sand and gra
and beach below. She closed her eyes, felt puls
beat behind her lids, and uttered swift prayers
find the courage to continue her downward route

It seemed to take her hours, though it must hav
been only minutes, before her toes touched th
safety of ground. She wanted to fall to her knees ar
kiss the earth, but opted instead to lean her forehea
against the rose brick of the mansion. Her heart wa
pounding, roaring like the surf in her ears.

"You nearly killed this bloody tyrant with that fl
ing missile, your valise."

Eden screamed. She barely had the strength
whirl and glare at him, but she managed. He wa
regarding her with an expression of exaggerated pa
tience.

"I thought you might try something like this," h
said.

She put her hands on her hips and scowle
"Then why," she demanded, "did you wait until
landed?"

He lifted one eyebrow, as unmoved as ever. "Yo

emed determined . . . and obviously needed the xercise. You have an unquenchable amount of en-gy." He seemed amused. "Those are some rather olorful verses emitting from your pretty society-dy's mouth."

She smiled snidely at him. "Yes," she said, "color-l indeed. I've picked them up along the way. My ordid stage friends' influence, you know."

"No doubt," Shane murmured, but there was old mockery in his eyes. He glanced to the valise at had missed him by inches. "You might want to ke that back upstairs."

Eden bristled. Composed now from her daunting imb down, she wiped her palms on the seat of her reeches and stalked past him to grab her valise by s handle. She straightened, looking directly at him. I might not."

He smiled slowly at her, but the smile did not uch his eyes. "You will. And now."

She raised her chin. He was standing with his ands in his pockets, the picture of imperious arro-ance, expecting her to follow his command—im-ediately. At that moment Eden hated him. She felt warted beyond belief, in bondage, his prisoner. nd he was amused by the notion of her as his cap-ve. She could see it in his eyes. He was going to eep her there until he found Philip, and he didn't are if she died of boredom or frustration in the rocess.

She shoved the valise away from her, and it ounced piteously off the ground. She longed to ress the heels of her hands into her eyes, to stop the narp pain of tears that burned there, but wouldn't ive him the satisfaction of showing how he affected er. She'd thought he had a heart. She'd thought, at ast, he would make her time there less of an incar-

ceration and more of an amicable adventure—wit
him as her new friend. But, it seemed, Shar
O'Connor had little use for the likes of her. He'
had it in his mind that she was a brainless nuisanc
and she was beginning to think this was all a sor
mistake. Once she had suffered his arrogance th
first day, she should have hired another investigato
one who did not make her feel things she had nev
felt in her life.

A wild aliveness surged through her whenever sl
saw Shane, even if from a distance. She burned wit
some empty yearning—she didn't quite know wha
—while she lay restless at night, first on her be
then on the porch, where the calls of the sea and th
wind, tangling her hair like a lover's fingers, bot
calmed her and excited her. She wanted his roug
fingers on her, his mouth to coax her, woo her, tak
her. She wanted to press herself into his bare ches
run her palms over his hard muscles, smooth flesl
dark, crisp hair. Wanton, she knew, but could not l
to herself. But he wanted none of this from her. H
wanted nothing. She wanted him to take away th
fearsome, haunting loneliness that even riding an
swimming and acting and writing could not driv
from her blood, her heart. She put it up to the lo:
of Philip, but knew that it was more, much, muc
more. It was everything.

Looking up at him, she tightened her jaw. "Yo
win," she said. "But I will not return to my room.
She gave her valise a little kick. "Have one of th
servants bring it to my room. I'm going for a ride.
She paused, one brow raised. "That is, sir, if I hav
your permission."

Shane measured her for a moment, captivated b
her queenly airs, which he knew were not affecte
this time, but real, her dignity almost majestic. Eve

er boys' clothing could not detract from the regal
quality she radiated. He wanted more than anything
to tear off those ridiculous clothes and pull her under him, to watch the sunlight pool in her lovely
feminine hills and hollows. He reined in his passion
and gave her a slight bow. "As you wish, madame."

She let her gaze run over him coolly. "It's my
belief, Mr. O'Connor, that if I were to cut you, you
would bleed pure ice water."

With that she broke into a run, her hair flying
behind her, her long, graceful legs flashing in the
sunlight, her perfect, luscious derriere a taunt that
made licentious, decadent images streak through his
mind. He stood in frustrated need, fighting it, yet
wanting, *aching* for just one long night with her, a
night drenched in erotica, a night spent tasting,
touching, coupling in every way, a night steeped in
passion thick and hot, this man with ice for blood.

Eden didn't return until after dark. A bodyguard
followed her down the length of the shore for miles.
At first she rode hard and fast, wanting to lose him,
but he kept pace, always a distance behind her,
shadowing her. She hated this. She hated restriction
of any kind, and even a guard made her feel cornered, tied to *him*.

When the sun set, she stopped to watch it. The
sky was ablaze in red and gold. Autumn soon. The
leaves would be changing colors, and soon after that,
as was her custom, she would be heading home to
Texas. But things were different this year. She didn't
even know if she would be able to perform. At least
not by the time Society returned to the city. Philip,
she thought with a swift pang, please, please come
home.

She returned to Shane's estate and slipped up stairs without eating supper. She wasn't hungry. More than that, she was depressed, a rare thing for her, and she didn't quite know how to push the blues away. Alice tried to cheer her, waving chocolate and sweets under her nose, but Eden curled up on the settee and gazed wistfully out the window. The beautiful bedchamber seemed unbearably oppressive, and it wasn't the heat that made it so. It was knowing Shane was in the house with her, and they were worlds apart. It was knowing he wanted to keep it that way.

She slept restlessly that night, once again on the porch. Thinking it best to keep out of Shane's sight she avoided him all that day and the next. Why, he wouldn't even know if she was alive, if not, she was certain, for the daily reports from his guards. She ached to nag him about Philip, wanted to beg him to do something to bring her brother home, but she supposed he knew what he was about, and would tell her if he received word on Philip.

During the afternoon of the second day after their falling out, she occupied herself by diving off the high rocks into the sea and swimming. As she rested on the boulders, watching the occasional sailboat bob and dip on the bay, she longed for a companion. Eden loved life, and loved those who colored it with their motley personalities. She missed the troupe and wondered how they were doing. She thought of her new friend, Sparrow, and wished she'd had more time to become acquainted with the intriguing young woman. She missed the handsome Franklin, and Lenore—all of them. And she really needed to get to Franklin and tell him she wanted to continue acting in *Lysistrata,* but she wouldn't blame him if he'd found a replacement.

Sighing, she stretched out on the hot, wet rock, letting the sun and wind caress her skin. It was already four o'clock, and she wondered if Shane missed her just a tiny bit. Sighing again, she pushed herself to her feet and shoved her hair out of her eyes before she headed back down to shore to mount her mare. She would study her lines for a while, then take a walk on the beach. Perhaps even Alice would stroll along with her. Anything for company.

She rode at breakneck speed back to the estate. When she glanced back to see if the bodyguard had kept up, she thought for a hopeful moment she had lost him, then saw him as a mere speck in the distance. Disappointed, she headed for the stables. After leaving her horse with the groom, she strode off toward the house.

As she neared the double French doors that led in from the porch to the library, she felt a sudden heaviness in her heart. Knowing that Shane was avoiding her as she was avoiding him did not hoist her spirits. Worse, if she happened to run into him, she would have to suffer his cold detachment, and suddenly she was beside herself. She could not go on like this. They would have to call a truce or she would have to insist that she leave and find another investigator—the expense be damned.

She gave a little sigh and stepped into the house, her bare feet soundless on the hallway carpet. Muffled voices from Shane's study drew her attention. Curious, she moved in that direction, pushing her tangled hair out of her eyes. She glanced down at her cut-off breeches and boy's shirt and grimaced. She knew she looked like a hoyden, but the pull of her curiosity was too strong to resist.

As she reached the open doors of his study she

heard a woman's soft laughter. "Oh, Shane!" the woman said. "You grow more charming every time I see you."

Charming!

Forgetting all caution, Eden bounded through the doorway, her mouth open with astonishment. There were five people in the room, including Shane. The others, two men and two women, were all strangers to Eden. They were staring at her as if she were some wood nymph come to spirit them away. The women looked appalled, the men intrigued. And Shane, lounging back lazily in his leather burgundy chair, looked amused.

He was dressed for visitors in a pearl-gray suit with a dark blue waistcoat, the elegant cut emphasizing his broad shoulders and lean waist. He appeared to be totally relaxed, his legs crossed, a glass of whiskey in one hand. Yet beneath his indolent pose Eden sensed a simmering awareness, a primal sixth sense that throbbed just below the surface of his aloof exterior. Tiger, tiger, she thought, when will you spring?

He let his gaze flick up and down her figure in quick, arrogant appraisal. "Well now," he drawled in a horrid voice, "what an honor for your highness to grace us with her presence."

Eden flinched as if she felt the bite of a whip on her skin. Why was he so contemptuous? What had she done to deserve such biting sarcasm from him? She opened her mouth to respond, but the beautiful blond woman at his right spoke first.

"Shane sweetheart," she said, looking down her nose as if she smelled something putrid in the room. "Who *is* this woman?"

Shane smiled, and Eden thought it was not pleasant smile at all. "That's no ordinary woman,

e said. "This, my dear audience, is the reigning
ueen of theater. Every moment is a performance.
nd I have the honor of protecting her. She is my
harge." He lifted his glass to his lips, and his eyes,
ver its rim, were like shards of crystal cutting her
nto pieces.

The women snickered, the men laughed. If he had
tripped her naked in front of them all, he couldn't
ave humiliated her worse. Eden felt a shattering
nside; it spilled into her heart and eyes. He touched
er in soft, secret, vulnerable places where no one
ad ever touched her before. Places that hurt. Places
hat felt ravaged by his words, his annoyed looks, his
oldness. Blinded by tears, she turned swiftly and
an from the house. She heard his curse and a crash
ehind her, a woman's gasp, and she ran faster. She
idn't want him coming after her. She wanted to die.
he wanted the earth to swallow her. She never
vanted to see him again.

Over the hot, glittering sand she ran, her feet
urning as sobs burned in her throat. Tears
treamed down her cheeks, ran into her mouth,
alty, hot, bitter. The ocean lurched before her as
he raced on. She heard him behind her.

"Eden!"

She ran faster. She didn't want him near her,
lidn't want to see his face, those brilliant, condemn-
ng eyes. She didn't want to smell him, didn't want
o ache to put her hands on him. She hated him,
ated him. She chanted it like a litany under her
oreath as she kept on running, away from there, out
of his life. But he was hard on her heels and coming
loser. She heard his breath, his lurid swears, his
anger.

"Goddammit, woman!"

"Leave me alone!" she screeched.

Shane swore again, reached for her, snagged a arm around her waist, and brought her to th ground. Under him she fought like a cat, cryin scratching, until he pinned her down with th weight of his entire body.

"Be still," he commanded, "or I won't let yo up." Her sobs were wrenching his gut, and he swo again. "Shut up."

"I—hate—you—"

She buried her face in her arms and wept. Shan felt a curious burning in his own eyes, his locke throat. Jesus. He ran a hand down his face and gri ted his teeth.

"If I let you up," he said, "do you promise not t run?" She stilled beneath him. A good sign. Slowl cautiously, he stood up. She lay like a broken doll o the ground, her hair in beautiful, wild wind-tangle her slender body jerking with sobs and need for ai What the hell was he doing to her? Trying to brea her spirit, he knew. Bastard. He was a bastard. H fought her potent spell like a man possessed, and h wanted to win badly. The more she filled his minc his thoughts, his wants, the more he wanted to pus her away, the colder and harder he became towar her. To fall into her clutches, he was sure, would b like dying a slow death. So he fought her by erectin a wall, keeping her out, hurting her. Judging by he piteous form on the ground before him, he was once again, a blazing success. He felt a hot wave o self-contempt.

"Edie." He reached a hand to her in entreaty.

She couldn't possibly have seen it, but she rolle away from him, coating her body in damp sand. "G away!" she screamed, and broke into sobs onc more.

The sounds tore at him, ripped his heart. He too

step toward her, but she stunned him by springing
o her feet.

She was beautiful, as she had been in his study
with the sunlight cascading around her like warm
gold. Disheveled, half dressed, insanely tantalizing.
Her drenched eyes were storming with fury, brilliant
with color. She was robust, glorious, a stormy little
world-shaker. She wore her heart on her sleeve.
Shane had never known anyone like her.

"I hate you!" Eden cried again, her voice breaking on the last word. Impotent with fury, she picked
up a nearby seashell and flung it at him. It glanced
off his broad chest. She wanted to incite him to anger—she would rather have him furious with her
than bland and uninvolved—but he only stood
watching her with sober eyes, stone-faced. She broke
into sobs again, shaking, shuddering, sick with anger
and the pain of rejection. "You are a wretched snob
—a *snob*—do you know that, Shane O'Connor?"

This time he flinched.

"That's right—you—the rich man who shuns the
rich—self-made Irisher—" She jumped back as he
took an angry step toward her. "Irisher!" she
screamed to the heavens. "So proud—so stubborn.
You must have descended from kings, Shane
O'Connor, for you have the bearing of the most arrogant of royalty!" She laughed as she watched his
face tighten, go hard and fierce. "I *hope* you're angry! It's refreshing to know you feel that at least!
You have a heart of stone. You know why you like
the theater so much, Mr. O'Connor? Because you
are feeling vicariously through it!"

His eyes were ablaze with anger. His jaw worked
tensely. His fists clenched at his sides.

She laughed at him, the sound brittle and shrill.
"Yes," she cried, "you are an arrogant, arrogant

snob. And I bet *no one* has dared talk to you li]
this before. They wouldn't risk the terror of exper
encing your *cold freeze*."

And just like that his eyes shuttered. Ice chips in
face of granite. It infuriated her. She flew at hir
and she was sure he thought her demented, but sl
had lost all caution. She put her face within inch
of his and made him stare into her eyes. His wei
breathtaking, and totally unreadable.

"Is there anything inside you, Shane? How is
that you can hide so much behind your eyes? C
maybe there's not so much to hide at all!"

His lashes dropped lower. She had the uncann
sensation that he was looking into her own so
while she could see nothing of his.

She balled her hands into fists and screamed up a
the sky, "Why won't you let yourself feel?" Sh
glared at him, but he was already turning his bac
on her, heading for the house. "No!" She grabbe
his arm, leapt around in front of him, even as h
continued to attempt walking away from her.

"Coward!" she yelled. That made him stop
"Only certain women meet your criteria, don't the
O'Connor? Not actresses—never actresses! Wors
an actress with English blood!" She paused to dra
in a quick breath. "Well, I don't want you eithe
You're a brute. And I'm going home."

"Good."

If he had struck her, she could not have felt mor
agonized. Still, she pushed the pain away and con
tinued. "But before I go, Shane, I want you to knov
one thing. Actresses have feelings too. And what yo
did to me in there, in front of those people, wa
unforgivable."

She blinked, but Shane saw the pain in her eyes
shining and keen. Again he felt that God-curse

rch in his chest. He reached for her just as she
roke into a run. This time he was faster. He
rabbed her from behind, one steely arm locked
round her slender waist, pulling her hard and fast
gainst his body. "Edie," he groaned, dragging her
o him.

"Don't!" she cried, struggling. "Don't call me
at—"

But he already had her and he could not let her
o. His big hand was splayed along her jaw, his
humb under her chin, tipping it up and back, forc-
ng her to meet his open mouth. She made a small
newing sound, fighting his rapacious kiss, but he
eld her firmly against him, her full, rounded bot-
om crushed to his hardness and heat.

"Edie."

He whispered her name with a raw ache in his
oice, and heat roared through Eden like an inferno,
weeping her away in his kiss, his animal-wild desire.
he had to grip his hips to keep her balance, yet she
till could not meet his kiss fully. Her head dropped
ack to his shoulder, exposing her throat to the sun,
is touch. He laid his open mouth against her neck,
naking her shudder and sag against him. His thumb
an up and down the length of her neck, then across
er jaw to her open mouth. His finger slipped inside,
nd they both groaned as he turned her around,
heir bodies still crushed together.

His mouth came down hard over hers, almost
ruising. With a low cry of pleasure she felt the
hrust of his tongue, plunging deep, exploring the
leek velvet of her mouth. The exquisite pleasure
tunned her, and she curled into his hard body,
naking him groan. His tongue delved deeper into
er mouth, and he pulled her closer, between his
ard-muscled thighs, forcing her to feel the turgid

bulge of his arousal. She stiffened, shocked by h
size and potent power, then, instinctively she arche
up into him, easing the unbearable pressure, th
sharp, aching throb between her own legs.

She was swamped in him, his rich scent of leathe
and tangy cologne and man. The whiskey taste of h
plundering mouth made her hunger for more . .
more. Under her palms, against her thighs, the int
mate shift of his muscles was both scorching an
heady, and her own muscles quivered and ached
She gripped his hard shoulders, then her arms sli
up and around his neck, her fingers sliding into th
thick, soft hair at his collar.

"Shane, Shane," she whispered into his mouth
and the sound made him growl deep in his throa
He palmed her bottom, locking her intimately close
to his steely body. It was too much. She tried to tur
away, to breathe, to relieve herself of this heady
wild sensation that pummeled her blood. But h
filled her mouth with his tongue, plunging deepe
and deeper so she could scarcely breathe. He wa
fierce and he was wild. He was devouring her, eatin
her alive, and she was branded by his heat, by hin
He ground his hips against her, and she let out a so
cry. She melted into him, her body weak and lim
and surging with life. Her hands slid down his broa
back to his tight buttocks. She pressed her palms t
the hard hollows, feeling the muscles there tense an
flex as she pulled him against her.

"Christ," Shane muttered. Did she know what sh
was doing? He was intoxicated, drunk . . . on her
Her mouth was open and ripe and sweet female silk
Her velvet tongue danced against his in perfec
rhythm. He was dizzy with the taste of her, with hi
want and need.

Edie, Edie . . . Her name swam through hi

ead like an aphrodisiac as he thrust his fingers into
er hair, the veil of satin he had imagined swirling
round his naked body in the depths of sultry, black
elvet nights. She was as wild and impetuous as he'd
nown she would be. No simpering, snooty airs with
er, no pretense of shock that he dare touch her so.
he was just as eager as he, searingly passionate,
inging to him as the fever between them climbed
igher and higher.

She pressed against him, and his kiss became
ore intense, open, hungry, passionate. He brought
ne hand up her back to the nape of her neck, his
umb caressing the delicate skin there even as he
nprisoned her, locking her into his kiss. His other
and slid up her torso to cup her breast. She purred,
d the sound drove him half mad with desire. Her
reast was soft and warm, firm and full, the nipple
ard. He pushed the swell of flesh up higher, mas-
aging it till she fell against him. He tore his mouth
om hers and put it to the side of her neck, biting
ghtly.

"Shane!" she gasped, and he fastened his mouth
n hers again. With both hands in her hair now, he
ressed her down gently. Mouths clinging, they sank
o their knees, then he pressed her backward until
ne lay on the hot sand beneath him and he was
neeling between her legs. Bending his head, he
ontinued his assault on her mouth, and then, oh,
God, on the curve of her shoulder, where he'd
ulled her shirt down. Quickly, deftly, he unbut-
oned her shirt, and it was open, baring her beautiful
reasts to the sun.

"Oh, God, Eden," he groaned. Her breasts were
ull, the hard nipples flushed a deep rose with desire,
athed in sunlight. He lowered his head and took
ne into his mouth, pushing her firm flesh up,

squeezing with his fingers so that the nipple was su
rounded by his lips. He sucked and tugged on
hearing her gasp, then he rasped his tongue over t
sweet, turgid flesh. It was warm from the sun, fr
grant with her scent, swollen with arousal. As he w
swollen, so swollen he thought he would burst. F
moved to the other breast, his mouth closing hot
over her tight flesh. She cried and arched into hi
but he carefully kept his hips from hers, knowing t
danger if they touched. He would take her sure as
breathed, there, out in the open, where anyo
could see. And he wouldn't care.

Still, he was unable to resist moving lower, slidi
his lips down her slender body to the waistband
her knickers. Somewhere a gull cawed, but that, t
tumble of the surf on the shore, and the wi
sounded distant. Everything was distant but h
Blood pounded in his head as his lips caressed h
and he closed his eyes, unable to bear looking at t
beauty of her skin. Gold shimmered in it, even b
fine blond hairs catching the gift of the sun.

Eden was lost, lost in him. This was indecent, pr
miscuous, but there was no stopping it. She w
helpless against the hot, thick heaviness that w
surging within her, making her arch toward him.
frantic longing seethed inside her, and she hovere
balanced on a very fine edge. Shane was magic, an
she throbbed for him, a totally new sensation, f
she had never throbbed for any man. She wanted l
mouth on her . . . everywhere. The sight of his b
hands on her breasts was shocking, electrifying, an
she only wanted more. His tongue on her abdome
made her insides stretch tight, then relax to a w
ribboning flow that centered in the most privat
pulsing part of her. His powerful arms were tren
bling on either side of her—she could feel witho

ouching. She wanted to feel his heart against hers
gain, the most violent thunder, the pounding in his
owerful chest . . . no heart of stone had he.

His mouth moved lower, his warm tongue sliding
nder the waistband of her breeches. The sensation
as so exquisite and so unbearable, it brought tears
o her eyes. She reached for him, her fingers touch-
ng his jaw. He whispered something she could not
ear, something that warmed her. She watched him
ith glazed eyes, watched his dark head, and felt a
uickening, a forbidden want, between her legs.

"Shane, don't—" she whispered, and before she
new it her hand slid between them to cover her
ntrance.

The sight of her slim hand there stopped Shane
ith a cold shock. He stared for a moment, breath-
ng hard. What the *hell* was he doing? He lifted his
ead to look at her, and something jerked in his
hest. She looked both exquisitely seductive and
uietly terrified. Her soft mouth was puffy from his
ough kisses, and he dragged a finger over her trem-
ling bottom lip. Her eyes flickered, eyes that were a
moky blue-green of distant mountains surrounded
y mist. He swallowed hard, his chest so crowded
ith feelings, he could not speak. His hand left her
outh to drift across her cheek. He felt her flinch
nd cursed himself. Slowly he eased off her as if she
ould shatter, rolling away from her to sit in the
and.

"Lord," he breathed. He felt ravaged, as if he had
ought in some long war and was just getting his
earings. He had never wanted a woman more, and
ad never stopped himself when he was so close to
onsummation. Women had been offering them-
elves to him since he had barely been past child-
ood. He took them for pleasure, period. Why

could a look in *her* eyes stop him cold? And wh
after such fiery passion, *had* she stopped him?

"Shane?"

Her fingers touched his arm, and he stiffened.

"I—"

"Don't. Don't say anything." There was nothin
to say. He sure as hell wasn't sorry for what they ha
shared, he just regretted not finishing it. When, goo
dammit, had he developed a conscience? Especiall
for a woman who had been offering herself to him i
a variety of ways for what seemed a lifetime now
But her silence was making his stomach tighter
"Edie," he said hoarse and low, "run inside now
Before it's too late."

She didn't answer for a moment, then she reache
for him again, touching his shoulder. "Shane," sh
said, "you're using my pet name."

He jerked his head around to look at her. He
hair was wild, her eyes smoky green. She had alread
buttoned her shirt, but it was askew. She ran the ti
of her tongue over her well-kissed mouth, and h
clamped down on the fresh surge of desire washin
through him. "What?"

"It's true," she said softly. "Papa used to call m
Edie, and Philip does too."

At the mention of her brother's name, Shane's ja
tightened. "I received a note from the jewel thieves.

She was suddenly alert, on her knees and leanin
toward him. "Philip's alive!"

"It appears that way."

"When did you hear?"

He exhaled heavily. "This morning. The messag
was sent by that woman, Sparrow. There's to be an
other dropoff in the city." There was something od
about the message, though, something he could no
identify. He frowned and rubbed the knot of tensio

n the back of his neck. When he looked at her again
ne saw the hopeful expression on her face. His voice
roughened. "Yes, they want *you* to drop the gems,
and I've been warned not to make an appearance or
they will slit your throat."

Eden paled.

"Don't worry, mavournin, I've no intention of letting them within twenty feet of you. I'll take you
with me, all right, but I'll leave you at Liam's and
again work with Camille."

Eden pouted. "Then what's the point of taking
me at all?"

A smile curled one corner of his mouth. "So you
won't get any alternate plans in your head, and con
the servants, the guards, and the ferry driver with
that peculiar brand of charm you possess."

"Can I visit the troupe?"

"We'll see."

When she became even more petulant, Shane
wondered how it was that when Lisa pouted it was
annoying, with Eden, seductive. Frowning contem-
platively, he pushed himself to his feet and shoved
both hands through his hair as he stared down at
her. The rawness inside him made it hard to speak.
"Eden, I am not the man for you."

She looked startled, even stricken.

"What we've just done here is played with fire.
And honey, you're sure to get burned."

Eden felt a hot ache behind her eyelids. "Why are
you so certain of that, Shane?" When he tensed, she
smiled at him despite the growing tears. "I will no
longer call you Mr. O'Connor, not after this."

He returned her smile, though his was slightly
mocking. "I'm sure you can guess my history with
women, Mrs. Lindsay."

Her heart contracted with a sharp pang. She was

sure he'd called her that deliberately, perhaps to prove how easily detached he could become. "You *do* have a good many women in your life, don't you sir?" He didn't deny it, and she added, "Are . . . are they all beautiful?"

Shane took in a sharp breath, and he felt some strange, unidentifiable emotion lock in his throat. It would be kinder to be cruel, he thought, and tell her, yes, they are all beautiful as well as sophisticated and practiced bedwarmers. But he could only stare at her. *Eden,* he thought, *already I've let you get too close.*

"Oh, I know they are," she said when he didn't speak. "I've seen your women with my own eyes." She grinned. "You are careful, I'm sure, to not let the women see each other."

"That meeting you disrupted," he said, not sure why he was explaining, "was a business meeting. An old friend bringing me clients."

"Then you'd better get back to your meeting. They'll wonder what happened."

His mouth curved in a slight smile. "They had only to step out to the porch."

Her face grew scalding hot. He thought her blush was charming . . . and rare.

"So," she said, "do you think we'll get Philip back this time?"

"I hope that we do."

"So you and I say good-bye?"

He ignored the sharp stab in his heart and simply stared at her.

She twisted her fingers together. "I see. And in the time I have remaining here, you choose to ignore this . . . this . . ." She glanced out to the sea then brought her gaze back to his. "This passion that is between us?"

His silence was his affirmative answer.

"I can't," she whispered.

He took a step toward her, then stopped. "We must."

"Why, Shane, why?" She turned her imploring eyes to his.

"Don't call me that. It only makes things worse."

"Why do you deny what is between us?"

"I don't deny it. I just plan to do nothing about it."

His words slashed at her insides. In other words, Eden thought, she was not a good choice, as opposed to his other women. But what did *she* want? Not an affair. Not to be his mistress. A stolen kiss here or there? That was silly. Then the awful realization struck her that she wanted Shane to *care* about her. She might as well try to catch the wind.

"Fine," she said. "We will go about our business until the case is solved. I will stay out of your way, and you will stay out of mine."

He smiled without warmth. "I do stay out of your way."

Her chin nudged up. "Maybe we'll have Philip back by tomorrow and can say good-bye then."

"Maybe."

She shuddered, hating his cold detachment. How could he turn from hot branding fire one moment into ice the next? "Now, if you are finished with me, may I leave?"

He was silent for a moment, then nodded. She responded with a slight curtsy.

"I will be ready at what time tomorrow?"

"Ten o'clock sharp," he answered.

She backed away from him. "I will meet you in the foyer at that hour. I'm going back to the house now."

She glanced at him once more before turning away, wishing he would pull her into his arms and take her again to that sweet wild world where only he and she existed. But he was going to do nothing of the sort. He was wearing that tautly controlled expression again. That was why, when she took a stride away from him, his voice startled her.

"Please, I'm begging you, honey, put some clothes on."

She turned to grin at him, caught the humor in his own faint smile, then walked on, well aware of the scorching power of his eyes on her all the way up to the house.

Alone, with the wind whipping his hair about his head, his clothes about his body, Shane frowned. Logically it was unwise to make her his mistress. He was fascinated by her—she was like a cyclone, wild, swirling, tempestuous—and he hated to admit it, but he actually *liked* her. He wanted no emotional involvements in his life, though, and she was brimming with emotion. Kissing her was as far as he was willing to go.

Yet, as he watched her disappear from view, Shane knew he was only fooling himself. He was already emotionally involved with her—and it was far, far more than to his liking.

CHAPTER TWELVE

EVERYTHING WAS DIFFERENT NOW. ON THE WAY TO
[Ma]m's, on both the boat and in the hired hansom
[cab], they rode in silence, the air between them in-
[fus]ed with a charge of sexual energy that was raw,
[ner]veracking. Eden kept watching Shane, fighting
[the] warm, tingling stirrings inside her. Though he
[pre]tended to be relaxed and oblivious of her, she
[wa]s aware that from under his thick lashes he
[wa]tched her too. In the close confines of the carriage
[she] could smell him, delicious, disturbing. He was
[cle]an-shaven, and the sunlight fell across his hard,
[ang]ular face, highlighting the chiseled and lean bone
[stru]cture. His thick hair was smoothed back and

gleaming. She could see a few dark gold stra[ ]
among the walnut.

He was so beautiful, she thought with a ris[ ]
ache in her throat. Looking at him was painful so[ ]
how, yet she couldn't drag her eyes away. Her h[ ]
gry gaze slipped down over his wide chest to his [ ]
belly. Lower her gaze slid, to the front of his tr[ ]
sers, and she remembered with sharp clarity t[ ]
part of him pressed intimately against her on [ ]
beach the day before. Her heart began to po[ ]
violently, and she had to look away, out the wind[ ]
to focus on passing omnibuses and hacks, phaet[ ]
and pedestrians. Her stomach was jumping, her s[ ]
prickly. The naked, frightening truth was that [ ]
was in thrall of him.

Leaning back on the seat, Shane watched her. [ ]
sat across from her, purely a survival move. See[ ]
her today was worse than it had ever been, a[ ]
what they had shared yesterday. She had come do[ ]
the stairs that morning looking radiant and eleg[ ]
in a day dress of watered green silk, the green [ ]
exact color of her eyes. To look at her was an exp[ ]
ence in pure sensualism. He felt his instant respo[ ]
in the basest part of his body.

He wanted to go to her now. He wanted to ta[ ]
the fragrance of her silky skin, put his tongue to [ ]
flesh, fill his palms with her firm, full breasts. [ ]
wanted to experience every part of her, inside a[ ]
out, wanted to explore her secrets, her passions. [ ]
wanted nothing more than to lift her skirts and s[ ]
into her tight heat, hard and fast and deep. And [ ]
watch her eyes as he was inside her.

He damned himself and his desires. Where wo[ ]
it lead? Nowhere. She was the kind of woman w[ ]
would haunt him forever. Once he had her, [ ]
would be in his blood, and he would never be a[ ]

ree himself of her staggering impact on him. He
w this deep in his gut, and in all the years since
blood had been spilled on the life-sucking streets
New York, his gut had never failed him. He was
fool. Once his job was done, he would send her
her way, and fast. And he would hope never to
her again.

He stared out the window, forcing himself to con-
trate on her brother instead. Philip must still be
e for the thieves to know where to contact Eden.
: thieves couldn't extract information from her
vants, for she had dismissed them all temporarily.
erefore, Philip must have told them that Eden
; a member of the troupe.

cotland Yard was cooperating with him, allowing
1 to pursue the case as he wished, without their
erference. When the thieves were captured, they
uld be sent to London and incarceration in that
intry. The Yard's undercover agent on the job
uld be in touch with him as soon as was neces-
y. Forrest Steele, he had been told, had the ut-
st faith in him, having heard of his reputation,
l the millionaire adventurer was on his way to a
ith American expedition. That was faith, Shane
ught with some irony.

The carriage stopped at Liam's, and the door was
1g open immediately. Eden was enveloped in the
at Irishman's warm bear hug. After the way she'd
the couple last time, she hadn't been sure of her
eption. But Liam swept her gallantly inside, and
nille was full of bright smiles as she set down a
ner of corned beef and cabbage.

"I'm famished!" Eden exclaimed.

Liam grinned. "We were counting on that, ma-
urnin."

They sat down to the hearty meal. After finishing

a healthy portion of corned beef, Liam sat back
addressed Shane.

"Well, boyo, this is, what, the third trip into
city you've managed without a bodyguard? Ho
that trussed-up old man Peterson handlin' the si
tion? He don't like it a bit when you risk y
neck—"

Shane shot his friend a warning glance, but E
was already fixing him with an accusatory stare.

"You've been in the city? Without my kno
edge?"

Liam looked like he had swallowed a goldf
"Oops." He rose, a plate in each hand. "Des
anyone?"

Shane cast him a wry smile, but Eden was
manding a response. His light eyes flickered on h
"I do not have to answer to you, Eden," he s
"I'm doing what you hired me to do. I'm investi
ing the case."

He said this so quietly, she settled down, thou
she did pout a little. "You were rather sneaky ab
it."

A faint gleam of amusement lit Shane's eyes. "I
learned it's the best way to go about matters wh
you are concerned."

Liam and Camille exchanged looks. "Wh
this?" Liam said. "Are we on a first-name ba
now?"

His comment, and the burning intensity
Shane's stare, drove hot blood into Eden's chee
Liam was giving her a penetrating look, too, a
Camille's eyes had grown warm. Eden was sure th
could both read on her face what she and Shane h
shared on the beach yesterday. Her cheeks burn
hotter.

"A first-name basis is easier," Shane drawled,

ere was a warning note in his voice that told Liam back off.

"Hmm" was all Liam said, and went to cut the e. "Camille, don't Eden look the foin lady today, essed in that beautiful gown?"

Camille smiled at Eden. "She does. She is absotely radiant."

Liam set a piece of pie in front of Eden and nked at Shane. "Isn't it a pleasant way to spend an ternoon—in the presence of two grand, beautiful men?"

Shane wore a skeptical expression, and Eden ushed again. Forcing a bright smile to her lips, she ickly changed the subject. "Shane thinks we will ve Philip back by the end of the day. I do hope all es well." She looked at the other woman. "Caille," she said softly, "I thank you for risking your e for my brother. You did it once before and I did t thank you properly, but now I want you to know at I feel you are giving me a gift."

Camille touched her hand. "Oh, my friend, it is y pleasure. There is nothing in all the world more portant than family."

Tears glistened in Eden's eyes. She was uncomrtably aware of Shane staring at her and tried to nore him just as she tried to ignore the tension etween them. "And I apologize about sneaking out e window last time I was here. You were kind to ave me, but I was distraught over Philip. This time will stay put."

"You sure as hell will," Shane growled.

She turned to him. "I left them a note!"

"And a nice note it was," Liam said.

Shane wore a look of pure disgust. "Don't defend er, Liam. She's full of tricks and wiles. Just when

you think you might trust her, you find her climbi
out windows, bribing the guards . . .''

Eden leaned across the table toward him.
wouldn't have to resort to those measures if y
didn't keep me under lock and key like a prisone

"And I wouldn't have to keep you under lock a
key," he answered, "if you abided my wishes."

"Your wishes are unreasonable."

"My wishes are sound. To stay on the prope
and out of the line of fire."

"Your wishes are not wishes at all, but co
mands."

Liam broke in here. "My God, man, you're kee
ing her guarded, and under lock and key? Tha
barbaric."

A ghost of a smile touched Shane's lips. "Y
know nothing of the circumstances." He sto
abruptly. "Time to head out, Camille."

Liam looked baffled, Camille bemused, by
sudden shift. Eden, however, was still seething. F
was watching her with those icy eyes, that arroga
almost aristocratic hauteur freezing her where s
sat. There was not a hint of emotion on his face. O
she would like to kiss him now! To prove to him th
he wasn't so indifferent, so cold where she was co
cerned. She would like the others to see the heat
his gaze, hear his groan as he crushed her to hi
passionately.

She must have shown some frustration, for
amused expression crossed his face. "I trust you w
keep occupied while I'm gone."

"Oh, certainly," she said lightly. "I'll write
whole new play. Liam can help me act out the par
When I tire of that, I'll drill Liam for all the person
facts of your life." She grinned impudently as

hot her a dark look, then he took Camille by the
lbow and steered her toward the door.

Sombered abruptly at the realization that they
vere leaving to rescue Philip, she stood, wringing
er hands before her. "Do you have the gems?" she
sked. "And a wig?"

Camille lifted up her new blond wig and the
hamois bag that held the glass replicas.

Shane opened the door, urging Camille through

"And you have the right location?" Eden asked.

Shane looked exasperated, his lips compressed
ightly. "Yes, Eden, we have the exact location. Sit
ight until we return."

If they returned, she thought. "Be careful." The
vords were out before she could stop them, and his
yes glittered queerly with some emotion she could
ot identify. Then he nodded to Liam.

"Watch her like a hawk, friend," he said, then
hey were gone, closing the door on sunlight and
lust motes and street scents.

The room seemed stifling, close, and Eden walked
lazedly back to the table.

"You going to be all right, lass?" Liam asked.

She lifted her head and smiled at him. He was so
ull of warmth and affection, so gregarious, it was
ard to believe he was Shane's friend. She began
emoving plates from the table. "I'm really not
lressed for dishwashing, but let's get these done."

Liam was horrified. He snatched the plates out of
er hands. "Like hell—I mean, no dishwashin' fer
ech a foin lady as yerself."

"Oh, Liam, don't be ridiculous. It'll keep my
nind off things."

He relented, but allowed her only to dry. As he
slunged his hands into the soapy dishwater in the

basin, he said, "Every time Camille goes out on tl streets, and vice versa, we just pray, m'vournin'."

She glanced up at him, surprised. "You pray?"

His great, booming laugh rang through tl kitchen. "I know I look like a heathen, but, yes, n girl, I have a chat with the angels ever' once in while." He winked. "In what little time I had wil her, my ma brought me up right."

She laughed. "I can see that, Liam."

He sighed. " 'Tis a rough life that man of you has chosen. But he loves it—'tis his life's blood."

She looked down, rubbing a dish dry with tl towel. "He's not my man. And you know that."

"But you wish that he was?"

Pain welled in her, a hot pressure building behir her eyes. She glanced away from Liam's sharp gaz "I'm a fool to wish."

"Ah, no, lass, no." He lifted his hands out of tl water and dried them. "Those need to soak." I took Eden by the elbow and led her to a chair in tl sitting room. She sat, looking morosely out the wil dow, but Liam pulled up a chair and forced her t look into his eyes. "Yer brave to wish, mavournil brave to feel for that man. I kin see how ya love hir by the way you look at him with that light in ye eyes."

Eden was horrified. "Oh, but I don't love hir You're—you're mistaken, Liam."

Liam's gaze was soft and kind. "Am I, little one Don't be afraid—you can't hide it."

Tears burned her eyes. "Oh, my God, I do lov him." She buried her face in her hands and wept.

Liam was beside himself. He was standing ove her in an instant, pushing his handkerchief into he hand. "Oh, you mustn't cry, melove," he crooned patting her shoulder, utterly at a loss as to what t

do with her. Camille never cried. This woman was
weeping as if there were no end to her tears. That
damned Shane. Liam loved him like a brother, but
Shane was a born heartbreaker. Couldn't he see that
this was no ordinary woman? She was a treasure, she
was, and it had nothing to do with her looks. She
was lively and spirited, full of love and warmth, not
one of those cold bitches Shane always took to his
bed and then, eventually, left. Shane always left his
women. And more than anyone, Liam knew why.
But this time it was different.

He watched Eden compose herself. She sniffled
and looked up at him, trying to smile. "Are you all
right now, me sweet?"

"Oh, yes, I'm fine. How refreshing it is to cry and
not to be condemned for it."

Liam was amazed. "Why would I condemn you?"

"Shane hates tears. He thinks I cry buckets—un-
necessarily."

Liam sat back down in his chair. "Ah, no, Shane
cannot abide a woman in tears."

Eden laughed. "That's putting it mildly."

"But if you need to cry buckets, do. Don't let him
stop you."

"I don't let anyone stop me."

Admiration lit his eyes. "I'll bet that's true, mavournin." But then he sobered, musing as he ran a
forefinger across his upper lip. "Let me tell you why
our Mr. O'Connor don't like tears. Women have
used tears on him countless times, countless ways."
He started to chuckle. "It's been a long, long time
since he has run into a female that sheds real ones.
And I'd venture to say he isn't quite sure how to
handle them."

Eden wrinkled her nose. "He doesn't have to handle them. He just has to let me cry without deridir me for it."

"Ah, but that's the point, lass. He feels he *has* handle the situation when he thinks it's comir apart in front of his eyes. He's a man who value control . . . should have been born royalty for th way he runs his life, his empire. Or haven't you n ticed?" He smiled at her. "And when he's cold an unreasonable he's most scared—or angry—and bot are good signs where you are concerned."

Eden sighed. "I have never met anyone colder. Except when he was kissing her. And she knew, sh just *knew* that he had a soft spot under all that ic "What do you mean, good signs?"

"If anyone can read Shane O'Connor, 'tis me," h said proudly. "An' you, Miss Eden, he likes."

She was stunned. "No, Shane does *not* like me. annoy him beyond belief."

"Another good sign."

She looked at him blankly.

"You've got to understand one thing about Shan He does not have a high opinion of women, I'r sorry to say. There's only one I know of he likes, an that's my Camille." Liam looked truly rueful abou that. "This is not exactly comfortable fer me, yo see, talking about my good friend in his absence, bu I like you, lass, and I think you would be good fc the boyo. He's always preferred sophisticatec worldly women, women he pays for, women he ca leave when he is, ah, done with them. If you've nc ticed in the time since you've stayed at his home, h does not have women in his bedroom, but take them off the estate to, ah, enjoy their company." Oł Liam was getting in deeper and deeper, and Shan would throttle him if he found out he was divulgin his secrets. "Simply stated, lass, he uses women fo self-gratification, that is all. He has never loved any of them."

"Liam," Eden said, laughter lurking in her eyes, "are you trying to make me feel better for loving this type of man?"

Liam's face colored. "Not doing a good job of it, am I? The point is, he beds these women so he can stay the jaded cynic that he is."

Eden's brow puckered in confusion. "But why would he want to be that way? He hardly ever laughs, Liam. Why does he have to keep in such control? He's only hurting himself." She paused. "I know he had a hard childhood, and he lost his little sister—"

"He told you about his Meggie?"

She grinned at him. "Well, actually, you offered me that entrance, and then I badgered him about it."

"And he told you."

"I am good at badgering."

Liam laughed. She was wonderful. "I suppose it started with Meggie. Or maybe even before that. He was such a little tyke, runnin' around the streets of New York. To look at 'im now, ya wouldn' known he was a small kid, but he was, and was lost as a kitten when he first got here." Liam puffed up his chest. "Good thing, 'twas, he met up with me. Learned how to use his fists real fast, and I taught him how ta steal." Liam's eyes misted as he thought back to those times. "Damn, but he was a tough little—" He remembered Eden, cleared his throat, and went on. "But he was full of pride, even then. Wouldna accept charity, no. He insisted on workin', and when he couldna get work, he always put back what he stole from folks. He had a real thing about honor. Anyway, he refused the shelter of my home and for a while lived in a cave in Central Park—"

At her gasp, Liam broke off.

"A cave?" she repeated.

"Yep. I joined him when Ma died. Bloody frigid those caves are, and dark. We stayed only one winter, couldn't take it after that."

Eden shuddered. In the heat of the afternoon she felt cold, aching, numb. A huge knot of emotion constricted her chest. "Poor little boy," she murmured.

"But he's a tough one. Look at 'im now."

"Yes."

"An' he was the one in the gang with the grandest sense of humor."

"Shane?" She couldn't believe it.

Liam's shoulders began to shake with laughter. "Oh, yes, Shane. He played pranks that would make us laugh for days afterward. When we worked in the coal mines, he found a way to get the boss drunk so he mixed up his days and paid us fer Sunday when we didn't work 'tall. He was the smartest, the fastest, the hardest worker of us all. He always said he was goin' to be rich, and none of us ever doubted him."

"But he was doing that for Meggie, wasn't he?"

Liam sobered, his eyes taking on an odd sheen. "Oh, my God, yes, little Meghan. He was saving money for the little bairn, would brag about the flat he was going to move her to soon as he had saved enough. But they took her from him, and I swear to you, Eden, I thought he was going to die. Twelve years old and world-weary. Meggie had been everything to him. With her gone, he felt he had nothing left. And at the time he didn't, really. I remember his nightmares. He missed her so bloody much." Liam lowered his eyes. "Our gang was all he had left—we were family, me and Shane, Tim O'Reilly, about seven more of us, and Kyle."

On the last name his voice broke, and Eden's gaze sharpened on him.

"He was like a brother too," Liam added. "But I'll let Shane tell you about Kyle, lass, and about the woman that betrayed them both."

Eden leaned forward in her chair. "Oh, but he won't, Liam, you know that."

Liam gave her a beseeching look, his palms turned up. "You know enough fer now, melove. 'Tis only right he tell you. But I do want you to know this. He changed after that night and has never turned back. He wants you to believe he's cold, but he's not. Remember, he's not one to reveal his heart—that's his own, and in one piece. To show emotion fer him is a sign of weakness, and to show weakness is to give another power. He believes that. He used to feel everything intensely, an' I don't believe a person can lose that, d'you? Don't let him fool you. You exasperate him, and that's good. Unfair as it is, he finds women silly creatures and made for only one purpose. He's hardly indifferent with you, though, as he pretends."

"The scar," Eden said suddenly. "Did it happen before or after Shane became a detective?"

Liam's face went hard. "He damn near bled to death that night." He closed his eyes briefly, then opened them. Seeing her stricken features, he gentled his voice. "Before, melove, before. But that night was a contributing factor that led him to his profession."

She wanted to wheedle the story out of Liam, but that was unfair. She could see that he was already suffering pangs of guilt over having spilled enough information to whet any curious woman's appetite.

"Thank you, Liam. I'm glad you told me about him. I can see how much you really care about him." She thought about all he'd told her and marveled that Shane had done so well for himself, after a life so empty of warmth and love. It pained her to recognize her own love for him, but Liam had helped her ease that pain. She smiled affectionately at him. "Might we go for a walk?"

Liam looked at her warily. "Oh, no, Miss Eden, please, no tricks."

"Tricks?" she repeated, insulted.

"Yes. You told 'im you were going to stay put."

She waved off that remark with a flutter of her fingers. "Oh, Liam, no tricks. Just a short walk to the theater, that's all. I want to tell them I will most likely be returning soon."

Liam was shaking his head. "Ah, no, no, m'vournin. I canna do that. Here now, don't pout. Do ya like checkers? We'll have a go as we wait fer them."

But the wait was much, much longer than either of them had expected. Eden beat Liam soundly for many matches, then accused him of not concentrating, or of letting her win. Liam scowled fiercely at her, but still could not beat her. When it was past ten o'clock and they'd had no word from Shane or Camille, they both began to fret. Eden asked Liam to play the piano for her, which he did, while singing bold ballads she begged him to teach her. When they tired of that, he regaled her with more tales of his and Shane's youth. He further demonstrated Shane's soft heart when he told her that when Shane was ten and could barely feed himself, he came across a litter of stranded kittens. They were cold and shivering, as he was, but he brought them back to the cave and managed to find scraps for them, and make a home there. When he moved to Philly to work in the coal mines, he left the cats at the orphanage, where the nuns made them their pets.

It was after midnight when Eden pulled Simon's watch out of her bodice and frowned at it.

"If they aren't back in five minutes, I'm going out after them," Liam growled.

"You know where they are?"

He nodded. "Dammit, anything could have happened." When he saw her troubled expression, he cleared his face. "That's an odd way for a woman to be carryin' a watch."

"Oh, it's not mine."

Liam's red eyebrows shot up in arcs. "Whose is it?"

"It's a long story. I'll tell you when I'm not so worried. You're going to let me come with you, aren't you?"

Liam could see by the set look to her jaw that he was going to have some trouble with this. "I want you to stay here in case they come back."

"But we can just leave a note—"

The front door swung open, and Shane and Camille filled the doorway. They all stared at one another a moment, then Liam thrust himself out of his chair, crossed the room, and gathered Camille in his arms. As they embraced, Shane looked at Eden, his gaze like a sizzling touch.

"It was a no-show," he said somberly.

Eden's mouth dropped open. "A what?"

Shane's lips tightened. "We waited for hours at the location indicated, and no one appeared. No one."

Liam drew Camille to his side, one arm circling her shoulders. Eden wished Shane would do the same for her, but he strode across the room and flung himself into a wing chair, wearily rubbing his eyes. "I knew there was something odd about this time, but couldn't figure it. It's almost as if . . ." He frowned, his gaze sharpening on Liam. "You say the woman—what the hell is her name—Robin?"

"Sparrow," Eden said.

"Sparrow. She received the note?"

"Yup." Liam drew Camille across the room and seated her on the sofa. "A drink, melove?"

His wife smiled up at him. "A drink would be lovely, Liam. Water is all."

His eyebrows shot up. "Brandy, I'm thinkin'."

"No, no, it wouldn't be good for the babe."

Liam went white. Every red freckle stood out on his face as he gaped at Camille. "B-babe?"

She smiled beatifically and patted her stomach. "I knew you wouldn't let me go tonight if I had told you earlier, and it is important to help our friends."

Liam whirled to fix murderous eyes on Shane, who was staring at Camille as if she had lost her mind. "You *knew*?" Liam roared. "You knew my wife was carrying my firstborn and you let her— Why, I'll—" He took a menacing step toward Shane, but Camille's calm voice stopped him.

"Oh, heavens, Liam, of course Shane didn't know. He would *never* have allowed me to accompany him if he knew his little godchild was lying in wait with his mother."

"Mother of God." Shane dropped his head back against the chair and closed his eyes. "Camille, if you weren't Liam's wife and like a sister to me, I would bloody well turn you over my knee."

Camille only laughed. She seemed to find it hilarious that two big strapping men were making such a fuss. Her big brown eyes dancing, she turned to Eden. "Aren't they silly? Don't you think the little one will have to get accustomed to such a life if his mother and father—"

"No," both Shane and Liam growled at once.

But Camille was still laughing. "Liam, please, the water. I'm dreadfully thirsty."

Instead, Liam dropped on his knees before her. He grasped her hands and stared at her with pure, unabashed love. "Oh, me darlin', a babe," he said, and put his head in her lap.

Camille stroked his hair, and Eden watched, a lump rising in her throat. To feel such love, and to be so open about expressing it, was a gift and a joy she feared she would never have. She glanced sidelong at Shane, who was also watching his friends and smiling warmly.

"Congratulations," he said softly. "And from now on, Camille, you are off duty."

Camille shook her head. "There's no harm in doing my job."

"You took a great risk the other night on the rocks."

Liam paled. "Oh, Camille—"

"I am fine, Liam, and the babe is too."

"Camille," Eden said, "you are brave, but I have to agree with them both. The danger for you is too great."

Camille's eyes softened. "I'm sorry we did not find your brother, Eden."

A great warmth flooded her, and immediately Eden could see how these two men could love her. She was kind, thoughtful, and concerned about a virtual stranger, when she herself was carrying her first child. Eden felt ashamed over her initial jealousy toward this woman. She went to her now, edging Liam, who reluctantly went to fetch the water, out of the way. She took Camille's hands in her own.

"Don't worry about my brother, Camille. Shane will find him." She thought she saw him tense, but went on, smiling at her new friend. "I'm so happy for you and Liam. I got to know your husband quite a bit better tonight, and he is a fine man."

"And she's a foin woman!" Liam boomed from the kitchen.

When Liam returned with the water, Shane asked him if Sparrow had given a description of whoever had dropped the note at the theater.

"Nope. Not to me," Liam said. "Guess you'll have to ask her."

Shane frowned. He ran a forefinger over his upper lip reflectively.

"What is it, boyo?"

Shane glanced at Eden. He did not want to speculate in her presence, but nothing slipped by her.

"Do you think something went wrong?" she asked. "Do you think Philip might have rebelled on the way to the site and they killed him? Or perhaps *he* killed *them* and . . . and . . ." She drifted off, twisting her fingers.

Liam raised his brows at Shane. "No one can say she doesn't have an imagination."

Shane stood. "We need to get down to the theater tomorrow first thing." He scowled when she brightened. That damned Franklin again. "We'll talk to this Sparrow and see what she can tell us." He didn't say any of Eden's guesses could have been accurate. Anything could have happened.

"You weren't followed here?" Liam asked.

"No. That's half the reason we took so long to get back. Made the route impossible to trail."

Liam yawned. "Let's catch some sleep, then." He sent his wife a mock frown. "We have some serious business to discuss."

She laughed as he helped her to her feet, then she nced at Eden. "You can use the spare bedroom, en, and Shane, you'll have to take the sofa. It's all have. Come, Eden, let me give you a nightgown wear. I'm sure it'll fit. We're about the same size."

"Doesn't matter," Shane drawled, a wicked spar- in his eyes. "She doesn't wear anything to bed." smile curled the corners of his mouth as he tched her turn pink to the roots of her hair.

She whirled to appeal to Liam and Camille. "That not what it sounds like. He's deliberately goading he's—"

"We know, we know, mavournin," Liam said, tting her hand. "Come now, time for sleep."

"But—" She stopped to fix Shane with her rcest glare, but he only laughed softly and turned ay, hands in his pockets as he strolled outside for moke.

CHAPTER THIRTEEN

*M*ORNING CAME, AND WITH IT A HUGE BREAKFA[ST.] Eden was famished, and polished off a whole sta[ck] of pancakes before reaching for a bowl of fruit.

"Ah, it does my heart good to see a woman e[at] so," Liam said, clapping a hand to his heart. Seei[ng] Shane frown, he laughed and said, "Not much sle[ep] last night, mate?"

Shane didn't answer.

"Strawberries!" Eden dove at the plump red be[r-]ries and popped one into her mouth. "Have on[e,] Shane."

He stared at the berries as if they were poisono[us.]

"Oh, I know. You don't *like* strawberries." S[he]

ughed, glancing at Camille and Liam. "Do you
ow Shane doesn't like truffles or tea?"

Liam looked astounded. "Why, I've not ever
ard of anyone disliking truffles."

"Oh, but it's true!" She laughed again. Amazing,
e thought, how attractive Shane looked when he
as glowering at her. "He never accepts what I of-
r."

Liam cleared his throat and Camille smothered a
ggle behind her hand.

"Why, I bet if I offered him chocolate and cream,
'd turn his nose up at that too." She popped an-
her berry into her mouth, almost giddy under
ane's intense, disapproving perusal.

"Eden," Shane finally said, "loves strawberries.
ou don't know what they do to her."

"Better eat up, then," Liam said, filling the bowl
ith more strawberries. "Season's almost over.
ime's running out."

The words took on a double meaning, and sud-
enly Eden lost her appetite. She lowered her lashes,
nable to swallow past the heavy, hollow feeling in
er chest. Yes, time was running out, for her, for
hane, for her brother. She pushed the bowl away,
d Liam leaned toward her.

"Something I said?"

She looked up. "I think we ought to be on our
ay now." More than anything, she wanted to go to
hane and hurl herself against his chest, feel his
rong arms around her. She wanted to rest her head
the curve of his shoulder, to kiss his warm neck.
ut she would find no comfort in his arms. He just
anted to find her brother and be rid of her. She
uld see it in his eyes.

As Liam and Camille walked them to the door,

the men paused to speak in low tones. Camil
caught Eden's arm and pulled her aside.

"I know you love him," she whispered.

God! Eden's heart lurched. Was she *so* transpa
ent?

It did not seem to bother Camille, though. "R
member, even when he is cold with you, Shane is a
intensely sensitive man. He's not the loner that
pretends to be." She smiled at Eden's doubtful loo
"Once he longed for what we all long for—a fami
and happy home. A close union with a woma
though he would never admit it. Be patient, Ede
He is just mistrustful of people."

Eden still questioned Camille's words as sh
hugged her and Liam good-bye, thanking them f
their hospitality. She wondered if she would ever s
them again, then she and Shane were off. The
hitched a hansom cab to the theater and rode i
brooding silence much of the way.

Eden finally spoke when they were almost ther
"I suppose this means, till we find Philip at leas
that I return to your estate with you." His face r
mained expressionless, and she caught his barel
perceptible nod. She took a deep breath, her finger
twisting the silk of her dress. "And what if it
months? A year?"

"It won't be."

So sure! They measured each other across th
width of the carriage, and the air hummed with ur
speakable passion. Shane's eyes gleamed wit
banked fires, fires he was not hiding. He had neve
to her knowledge, looked at her so intensely befor
or with such heat in his gaze, even on the beach. H
let his gaze take a slow ride down her body, linge
ing on her breasts, which tingled with awarenes
then lower, where her intimate female parts surge

ldly, wetly. When he brought his gaze back up to
eet hers, it was filled with want and a faint amuse-
ent. The carriage seemed, suddenly, so tiny, so
ght; she could scarcely draw breath. Without even
touch, a word, a sound, she felt devoured. By his
ok, his intention.

When the carriage stopped, she was out in a flash,
ot even waiting for a hand down. She charged into
e theater, though she truly did not know how she
anaged to walk, her knees were so weak. Glancing
ack, she saw him following her in that long-legged,
ocky stride that made her heart turn over. She hur-
ed to the dressing room, but no one was there. The
eater was empty.

Shane came right up behind her, his rangy body
manating energy and heat. She turned and almost
ll against him, her heart pounding as she looked
p at him.

"No one's here," she said, her voice sounding
reathy and soft. The room smelled of greasepaint,
d the only light came in through one window,
anting in like a golden beam.

Shane smiled slowly. "Except you and me." His
oice was rusty with heat and his eyes glittered like a
at's in the dark, mesmerizing her, igniting fires in
er low depths. Oh, to touch him.

They heard the squeak of hinges, a door opening
om outside. Immediately alert, Shane shoved Eden
ehind him into the dressing room. They heard fa-
iliar voices, though, just before Franklin rounded
e corner and saw Shane.

Franklin froze, his face going hard. "You," he said
ith contempt.

Shane leaned back against the wall, hands thrust
to his pockets.

"Where's Eden?" Franklin rushed past Shane

into the dressing room, but Eden was on her w
out. The two collided, and Eden was jostled agai
Shane's rock-hard body.

"Oh!" She balanced herself with her palms on
chest, and his eyes flashed over her in one scorchi
look, a look of possession. She quickly turned
Franklin.

"Sorry, Franklin," she said. "Did I hurt you?"

"Oh, no, Eden." He sent Shane a dark look.
this *gentleman* had the decent courtesy to st
aside—"

"I am not in your way," Shane interrupted. "Bu
can change my plans if you so desire."

He did not give Franklin the chance to respor
for Sparrow had walked up to them, and he turn
to her.

"The man who dropped you the message. D
you talk to him? Get a good look at him?"

Sparrow looked uneasy. "Actually, I only saw hi
from a distance. The note was hand delivered to r
by a little mite, some street urchin, but I asked hi
who sent him and he pointed across the street to
bloke watching me. I guess he was making sure
received it, then he tore off. After he saw me read
that is."

Shane frowned. "What did this 'bloke' look like:

"Well, as I said, I could see him only from acro
the street. He was tall—not quite as tall as you, da
hair, beard. A little on the thin side." She shrugge
"That was it."

"Did he have anyone with him?"

"Alone far as I could tell."

Shane's frown deepened. The description cou
fit one of the thieves, but he did not yet know wh
the thieves looked like. He took Eden's arr
"C'mon." He began to lead her out of the theater

"Wait!" Franklin said. "Where are you going with her?"

Shane looked painfully persecuted. "Where, Mr. Director, do you think?"

Franklin ran a hand through his hair, distressed. "Eden, Eden, am I going to lose you? The show cannot go on without you, my darling, and we will either have to stop it altogether or find a replacement—something I loathe to do."

Shane tightened his lips. "Start looking."

Franklin looked stricken. "But Eden! The play you wrote for the orphans—"

Shane stopped, and Eden felt him tense. Franklin went on, obviously oblivious of the danger. "We have only seven days before the scheduled performance. And we promised. What are you going to tell little Tate? And Jessie?"

"Tate?" Shane said, his voice frigid.

"And Jessie," Eden added emphatically. "Two children at the orphanage. I even promised them roles in the play. They—" She paused and swallowed hard, agitated by his piercing stare. "They're brother and sister, eight and nine years old."

She felt a miserable lump of emotion knot her chest. She was thinking of him, of course, and his little sister, and he knew she was, as was he. She saw his mouth draw tight, his eyes turn so brittle, they looked like shattered glass. The other cast members had crowded into the corridor and were all watching avidly. Eden took his arm to draw him away from their audience.

"Shane," she whispered, "can I have a private word with you?"

He stared down at her for a moment, then nodded and escorted her back into the dressing room. He shut the door behind them, then turned to her.

"Proceed."

She took a deep breath, ran her palms down the sides of her gown, and made herself smile as brightly as she could. "I have a wonderful idea!" Judging by the bland expression on his face, she thought it might take some clever maneuverings to convince him that her idea *was* wonderful. "We can have the troupe come out to your estate and practice there—just for a week, so we can put on the performance at St. John's. Your estate is so huge, you'll never have to see us. The cast members can stay in the east wing."

"That idea," he said dryly, "is about as wonderful as the idea of child labor. The thieves contact us through the troupe. It would *not* be a good idea to remove them from the premises."

"Don't you have other assistants—like Simon—who could stay here and pretend to be the troupe?"

Shane's mouth twitched. "You'd like that wouldn't you? To send Simon as far away as possible. I need Simon for other purposes. He is very useful as a researcher. He found the connection to Forrest Steele very quickly, and he knows the man's exact location. And he has . . . interesting contacts."

Eden lowered her eyes and scuffed her shoe on the floor. She didn't much care about Simon's talents just then. "I don't know what I'm going to tell little Tate and Jessie."

She peeked up at him from under her lashes. His facial muscles had tightened, and she could almost see the battle going on inside him. At last he sighed and nodded. "They stay completely out of my sight. I do not want to see Franklin Pauls at all."

She smiled brightly. "Promise."

"And they are there only as long as you need—six ays to practice for the orphanage."

"Well . . . after that performance, we had lanned one at St. Frances's, and one at—"

"No."

She sighed. "I suppose we can postpone those wo. And I guess I'll just have to tell Franklin to find omeone else for Lysistrata."

Shane stared at her, then he was laughing and haking his head. "*You're* playing Lysistrata?"

The irony did not escape her. Here she had been rying to seduce Shane into kissing her, whereas ysistrata had done everything in her power to put a op to that sort of activity. She blushed and tried to gnore his humor-filled eyes. "Do you think we can ersuade the nuns at the orphanage to release Tate nd Jessie to us for the week?"

"I think," he said slowly, a kind of tenderness ghting his eyes as he caressed her cheek with his ough, warm fingers, "that you, Mrs. Lindsay, can ersuade anyone to do anything."

Shane felt her shiver, heard her soft intake of reath. She couldn't figure him, he knew it, and ooked trapped, scared, yet wanting. He couldn't fig re himself either, he thought, and smiled at her. Go on," he said quietly. "Tell them."

She turned and ran lightly out of the dressing oom, leaving a wake behind her of unaddressed assion. Of pounding, aching need.

The children swarmed all over him as Shane trode into St. John's dining hall.

"Mr. Shane! Mr. Shane! Can we come riding your orses soon?"

"Mr. Shane! Can we come swimmin'?"

Eden was astounded. She gaped as the orphan clustered around Shane, who ruffled their hair an smiled at them, and occasionally rested a big han on the crown of one's head. Speechless, she watche him so at ease with the children, starved for affec tion and attention and reassurance.

"Here, here now, children. Leave Mr. O'Conno alone and finish your meal." Sister Mary Franc fluttered her hands, attempting to scatter the chi dren, but they clung to Shane, until some of the caught sight of Eden.

"Are you going to read us a story, Miss Eden? one girl asked, racing over to Eden.

Both she and Shane stared at each other, his eye enigmatic, hers unabashedly shocked.

"You know these children?" she asked.

"Oh, Mr. O'Connor knows plenty of them," Si ter informed her. "Not all, mind you, for he is a bus man, and can visit only between cases, but, oh, ye see how they adore him. Children!"

A boy and a girl were pulling on Shane, urgir him to their table so he could share their meal wit them. Sister Mary Francis was mortified, but Shar gave her an almost imperceptible shake of his hea and she backed off. He allowed the little ones t make a great deal of seating him and offer him sandwich. Dumbstruck, Eden watched openly, ur able to speak. She and Shane had left the troupe t pack and find their way to the ferry, where the would later meet. Now, at the orphanage, on the way to speak with Mother Superior to seek permis sion for Tate and Jessie to come to Shane's estat they had stopped by the dining hall, where the chi dren were eating lunch.

"I do not believe this," Eden murmured.

Sister Mary Francis beamed at her from behin

er round spectacles. "What don't you believe, ear?"

"Shane. Here. With the children. I don't under-and . . ."

"You don't know him that well, I assume. Mr.)'Connor is the orphanage's major benefactor, and r years has sponsored some of the children—even rls—to universities, or has given them a start in life another way. Why, just last summer he brought vo youths, Brian and Michael, to his horse farm in aratoga as hands on his breeding farm. They write us and tell us how happy they are. Mr. O'Connor)unsels the children, invites them to his home)metimes to ride his horses, and helps screen fami-es to make certain they are well matched with the lopted children. Never, *never* does he allow the :paration of siblings. He would have nothing fur-er to do with the orphanage if we allowed that." he nun fanned her face just thinking of it. "He kes the boys on trips to the mountains, takes the irls out to dinner and to shows. Oh, he loves them, *ves* children, Miss Eden! How long have you nown Mr. O'Connor?"

"Not long," Eden murmured, her heart swelling ith emotion.

"Ah, then, that explains it," the sister said. "I sup-ose his keen interest in the home has something to) with the fact that St. John's made a huge blunder :ars ago with his baby sister."

Eden glanced to the nun's red face. She looked uly pained. "I know about that."

"Ah, so you know something of the man, then."

Yes, Eden thought, closing her eyes briefly, *I now. I know that my love for him grows every time I ›ok at him, think about him, hear about him.* She ad known all along, even before Liam and Camille

had verified the fact, that Shane had a deep an
sensitive soul beneath his aloof exterior. To see hi
with the children, relaxed and humored by them, h
tolerance far, far greater than what he had show
her, proved that he was the sweetheart she had su
pected. Instead of turning on St. John's with ve
geance or bitterness as most ordinary souls mig
given the circumstances, Shane had instead used h
wealth to make certain no other children at S
John's would have to suffer the pain he had.

Now, if she could only get him to direct some
that warm charm toward her. Of course, that woul
take some doing. Children were one thing, wome
another. Especially women who had made the fat
mistake of becoming actresses. Or who carried E
glish blood. Or were born rich. Lord, she had litt
chance of winning him over at all.

Sighing, she let her gaze linger on him. A little gi
sat on his knee and another clung to his arm. Othe
had clustered around Eden, though, tugging on h
skirts, begging for a story. She saw Tate and smile
at him. He was an intense child, not handsome, b
striking with dark eyes, a lean, wolfish face, and re
brown hair. His brown eyes were far older than h
years, yet were often lit with mischief, a kind
ironic humor at the world. His sister, Jessie, coul
have been his twin, save for the fortunate fact th
her face and eyes were softer, sweeter, revealing
gentler outlook of the world.

Tate worked his way through the others gather
around her and asked, "Forget about us, Mi
Eden?"

"Tate! You know I wouldn't. You're still to be
the play if Mr. O'Connor can arrange it with Moth
Superior."

"What's he got to do with anything?"

TEMPTING EDEN   273

Eden was becoming an expert at feeling jealousy,
d she recognized it instantly in Tate. She smiled
d put her hand on his thin shoulder. "You don't
ow Mr. O'Connor, Tate?"

"No. An' I don't see what he's doin' with you."

Tate had been at the orphanage for only three
onths and Eden supposed Shane hadn't gotten to
ow the boy yet. "It's a long story. But I haven't
en able to visit because of something personal that
s happened to me, and I have been staying at Mr.
'Connor's estate until the matter can be reme-
ed."

"His what?"

"His home. And he's going to see about you and
ssie staying with the troupe for about a week so we
n practice."

Tate snorted. "Fat chance, that."

"Why?"

"What's he want two street mites like us around
r? We might even steal his stuff."

"I doubt you would find much of interest to
al," came a deep voice from behind Eden. She
rned to see Shane, tempered humor lighting his
es. "I used to be a street mite myself—Tate, I take
"

Tate looked up at Shane skeptically, his gaze
ocking as it raked over this sophisticated man. "If
u were a street mite, I'll eat my shirt, mister."

Sister Mary Francis came up behind Tate and
gged on his collar. "You apologize to Mr.
'Connor, Tate McLaughlin, or you'll be washing
e corridor floors for a month!"

Tate squirmed, trying to loose her grip and retain
s dignity at the same time.

"Let him go," Shane said.

The nun immediately stepped back. "Just tryin to teach him some manners, Mr. O'Connor, sir."

"I know that. But Tate's not been here long, h he?"

"No . . ."

"And he's used to sizing a man up before I trusts him, aren't you, Tate?"

The boy edged his jaw up. "It ain't smart to l cozy with jes any ol' folks on the streets. But the you know that if you were a street mite—sir."

Shane smiled crookedly at him. "See, Sister, he learning his manners already. Sister Mary Franc didn't mean to hurt you, Tate, just wanted you respect your elders, right, Sister?"

"Yes, sir, Mr. O'Connor."

"Eden," Shane said, "tell the children the sto while I go talk to Mother Superior. Then we'll he out of here."

Eden had no doubt that they would leave with th children. Shane was authoritative and powerful, ar most people bent to his will. Just ten minutes late when she had finished one story and started anothe she glanced up to find him watching her from t doorway, an odd expression on his face. Fait accor pli, she thought, and knew that when Sha O'Connor made up his mind about a matter, would inevitably be that way.

" 'Tis a bloody castle!" Sparrow exclaimed as sl gawked at Shane's home. They were standing on tl curving drive in front of the stately mansion, and h head was tilted back as she gazed up at three stori of grandeur. She put her hand up to shield her ey and scanned the immaculately manicured gre lawns, the glimpse of ocean off to one side, then tl

ouse again. "There must be over a hundred rooms
ere!" she marveled.

"One hundred twelve to be exact," Shane said.
n elusive smile touched one corner of his mouth.
arge enough so that from this moment on, I will
ot have to lay eyes on any of you." He started
ward the front steps, then added without looking
ack, "Eden, I want to see you in my study."

He was inside before she could move, his aloof
emeanor leaving them all feeling a slight chill.

"Bloody rude bloke," Sparrow muttered, but Le-
ore reminded her that he was gracious enough to
ffer them his home.

"And quite a home it is!" Lenore added, staring
o at the mansion.

"I'll be with you shortly," Eden said, and headed
to the house. She made her way down the hall
ward Shane's study, but paused when she met Sion. He brought himself up several inches to look
own his long nose at her.

"You," he said, "have once again endangered Mr.
'Connor's life."

Eden felt it best she not talk to the man at all, but
e was curious. "I don't see how," she said.

"The man has received death threats for as long as
have known him. He should not go anywhere, I
peat, anywhere, without a bodyguard."

"But Shane does what he pleases," Eden rea-
oned, noting that Simon bristled when she used
hane's first name. "He shirks the idea of a body-
uard, sneers at death. Surely, Mr. Peterson, you
ould know that if you know him at all." With that
e turned and left the haughty assistant sputtering
nder his breath.

She decided to take a detour into the kitchen to
rab an apple, for she was famished. She was shak-

ing her head as she entered the room, and mutte[r]ing, "That man *really* does need a wife."

Mrs. Leahy turned from her task of rolling o[ut] dough. "Welcome back, miss. You must be speaki[ng] about Mr. Peterson."

Eden nodded and bit into an apple.

"I agree he needs a wife, but he will never marr[y,] not that one."

"Why not?"

"He was married once and his wife run off wi[th] their neighbor."

Eden gasped and choked on her apple. Nedd[ie] pounded her one on the back, clearing her air pa[s]sage, and she smiled at him, thanking him befo[re] turning back to Mrs. Leahy. "My God, that's aw[ful!"

"Wouldn't you have run off," Neddie asked wi[th] a twinkle in his eye, "if you were married to that ol[d] codger?"

Eden gave him a look of chastisement, and h[e] ducked his head and went about his business. H[is] brows drew together in a frown. She had been figh[t]ing with that poor man since the second they me[t,] and now she felt much remorse. "When did th[is] happen? *Why* did she run off?"

Mrs. Leahy shrugged. "Years ago. He used to liv[e] in London, and when she run off with their boy—h[e] had a son, y'know—he came to America. That's all [I] know."

Eden felt terrible. Of course, he had done h[is] share to provoke her, but now she could understan[d] his prickly nature. Oh, dear heavens, she would hav[e] to make it all up to him. Perhaps she could cook hi[m] a meal. Something from his home country. Yes, sh[e] thought, feeling better, that would be a fine gestur[e.]

Spencer appeared in the doorway, his eyes starin[g]

st past her. "Mrs. Lindsay," he said in lofty tones,
Mr. O'Connor is growing impatient in his study."

"Oh, I forgot! Thank you, Samson. Tell him I'll
e there presently."

Everyone in the kitchen, including Spencer, stiff-
ned, except for Mrs. Leahy. She leaned her fore-
ead against a cupboard and her shoulders shook
ith laughter. "Spencer, my dear, his name is Spen-
er."

Spencer had already stalked off, though. Eden
apped her palm against her forehead. "I have in-
lted that man one too many times. I should write
s name on my hand," she said, and the servants
uckled as she left the kitchen.

The doors to Shane's study were open, and he was
tting behind his desk, studying some paperwork
hen she walked into the room. "Sit down," he said,
d she wandered to the chair in front of his desk.
When I tell you I want to see you in my study, I
ean immediately."

Her spine stiffened. "You didn't *say* immediately.
nd don't you get my temper flaring, Shane
'Connor, for I have just discovered I have made a
orrid blunder."

Shane lifted an eyebrow. "And that is?"

"Why didn't you tell me Simon's wife ran off with
nother man? Why did you let me continue this ani-
osity between us? Why didn't you tell me he had a
n, and she took him too?"

Shane stared at her. "I didn't think it important,"
e said slowly. "Or any of your business."

"Wrong on both counts!" she said, surging to her
eet. "I thought he was just a mean, ornery old cuss.
ow I know the reason behind it. And you were
oing to let me go on believing the worst!"

"Edie," Shane said, and his voice was tender, surprising them both. "Sit down. You can apologize him, and hand him his watch later."

"Over dinner," she said, much calmer now.

"Are you sure you're not wanting to kill him Shane asked, obviously remembering the chili.

Eden took offense as she sank back into her cha "I'll be serving him English fare."

"Ah."

"Did you ever locate his wife?"

"She divorced him and married the other."

"And the son?"

"Is about my age. He never came back to see l father. Though Simon did try to contact him."

Eden lowered her lashes, swallowed the lump her throat. "Poor man."

Shane watched her face. She seemed genuine saddened. Could it be that Eden, so passiona about life, could immerse herself so adroitly into t emotions of others? Her warm rapport with the c phans had rocked him. Maybe he had been wron about her all along. His jaw tightened. It was best keep his distance from her.

"I want it clear," he said in a clipped tone, "th the troupe takes separate mealtimes, and that I c not want to even know they are here. Is that clear.

Her jaw went up. "I think you have made th perfectly clear. To the point of rudeness."

"And I don't want to know that you are here ther."

Eden stared at him in hurt puzzlement. Ho quickly he could switch from tender to detache Behind his flawless appearance and impeccab manners, was there truly a man with a warm hea or had he shut off his emotions so expertly, exce where the children were concerned, that the ma inside was frozen, almost cruel?

She stood, taking a deep breath. "Fine with me, Mr. O'Connor," she said. "I'll keep my distance. I'm sure if you learn anything about my brother, you'll inform me. I take it we can use the beach?"

He nodded curtly. She was dismissed.

Eden went to the doorway, her heart heavy, but then she turned, her gaze meeting his. "You might be able to pretend you have forgotten that kiss, Shane, but I know you haven't. Your heart pounded as hard as mine did, and like it or not, it was a lovely kiss."

The muscles in his hard jawline tightened. "It was more than a kiss, darlin'," he said in a soft, dangerous voice. "And therein lies the problem."

She lifted her brows at him.

"Are you saying you want another? Kiss, that is."

"I—" She truly did not know what she wanted. She was confused. This had never happened to her, this, heady need for a man. Kisses lead to . . . other things, and she was not a loose woman, or anyone's mistress. It was wrong to warm a man's bed if you were not married to him—at least that was what she had been led to believe, though Eden had never judged others for it. But then, she did not plan to ever marry again. Clearly Shane would never return her love. He was not that type of man. Knowing this, it was foolish to harbor love for him, but there it was, written on the secret chambers of her heart.

"Ah." He was on his feet and walking toward her in that curiously catlike way of his. She stood frozen in the doorway, her fingers gripping the frame. Her mouth went dry as she watched him come closer, stopping just inches in front of her. He put a thumb under her chin and tilted her face up toward the light. He angled his head as if to kiss her, but she stiffened. A cynical smile touched his mouth.

"No? Why not, little Edie?"

She tried to pry her chin from his grip, but he kept control, and she was forced to look into his hypnotic, soul-searing eyes.

"Self-protective," he said. "And that's good. You know why, mavournin?"

She could not even shake her head. "Because," he said, his voice going lower, rougher, "I'm a wolf."

She shuddered. He was so close she could feel his warm breath on her face, feel his heat, oh, his heat . . . Of its own accord her body arched toward him, but didn't touch.

"I devour women," he whispered, "and toss them aside, and I do it without a second thought."

"I know," she said.

"Do you want that, Eden? Do you want me to devour you too?"

She wanted him to kiss her again, to put that full, hard mouth to hers, to thrust his tongue inside. Staring at him, though, she couldn't speak.

His gaze raked over her. "I didn't think so. And that's why I do not intend to bed you. Because, for some unknown reason, I have a conscience when you're concerned, and you should be thankful that I'm using it, darlin', because if I chose to kiss you right now, you'd be on the carpet and under me so fast, you wouldn't have time to take a breath."

They were just inches apart. His mouth was but a pulse beat away. She felt everything in her lean toward him. She wanted the kiss that he threatened her with, excited her with. Every inch of her skin seemed acutely sensitized, yearning for his touch. Her eyes locked on his.

"You're trying to scare me," she whispered.

"Damn right," he said, and his breath was hot and harsh on her skin. His body edged nearer, heat and sexual tension snapping like a live wire between them. "Run, Eden. Stay out of my sight."

She closed her eyes, trying to shut out his power, his seductive allure. He spoke again, his voice husky and thick with pounding passion.

"I'm telling you, run now, Eden, or I'll have you in seconds. And I won't even shut the doors."

She felt the brush of his hips against hers, the flaming quick touch of his hardness. Her eyes shot open as she jumped back from the electric contact. And then she did run, the first time in her life she had ever run from anything or anyone. She darted out of the study and flew up the wide, curving stairs to her bedroom. She needed to think, to put some distance between them. To be rid of the mesmerizing, almost diabolical power Shane O'Connor held over her.

CHAPTER
FOURTEEN

*T*HAT EVENING SHE SOUGHT OUT SIMON AND RETURNE
his watch. She then asked him to dinner the follow
ing evening. The dumbfounded assistant could onl
stare warily at her.

"I swear to you," she said, "I'm extending th
olive branch. Please accept it. I was wrong to be s
harsh with you."

Simon began to back out of the library, where sh
had cornered him.

"Please, Mr. Peterson, do not be alarmed. I kno
this is sudden turnabout, but I've tired of the stri
between us. Will you accept my dinner invitation?
will prepare English fare."

Simon looked pale. "*You're* going to be cooking the meal?"

She smiled reassuringly at him. "Do not worry, Mr. Peterson, I won't poison you. I just would like to sit down and enjoy your company." Honestly, she did not think he *was* enjoyable, but in all fairness, she had to give him the benefit of the doubt.

Simon had backed out of the library, though, and was shaking a finger at her. "Stay away from me, do you understand? No shared meals, no conversation—" And he was gone, moving faster than she had ever seen him move. She sighed. Befriending Simon was going to take a great deal of effort, but she was determined to make good company with the lonely soul.

For the next several days Eden lost herself in acting. It was wonderful that the troupe was there, and they practiced on the beach and in the ballroom, with Shane's indirect permission. After hours of rehearsal they would swim and dive from the rocks, fish, then cook their catch over a campfire on the beach. The days were full and long, and it gave Eden a good deal of satisfaction to see Tate and Jessie turn golden brown under the sun, their eyes sparkling with energy and the wholesome life they were enjoying at Shane's estate. Sometimes they rode the pair of Shetland ponies Shane kept for younger riders, and Eden rode with them on the lively mare, Irish, she'd come to think of as her own.

It didn't seem fair to Eden that the children would have to return to the orphanage, and once or twice the children mentioned, wistfully, futilely, that they wished they could stay there forever.

She struck up a friendship with Sparrow too. Sparrow was a wonderful actress, and had a grand sense of humor. She moved like a cat, sleek and unusually graceful. She was even more gymnastic than Eden, and delighted the entire troupe with her hair-raising high dives off the giant boulders into the water. Though Eden felt a strong bond with her, there was something mysterious about Sparrow, something to do with her past.

Once, when Franklin had been busy directing the others and Sparrow was skinning a fish, Eden had asked, "Is there anything you don't know how to do, Sparrow? Where have you learned all these tricks no ordinary woman should know? I grew up on my grandfather's ranch in Texas, so I have excuses for being a hoyden at heart, but what was your child-hood like? You must have been a little roughneck!"

Sparrow's green-tinged eyes darkened, and she lowered her lashes to hide them. Flipping the fish into an iron skillet, she flashed a grin Eden's way. "I was a Gypsy," she said cryptically, and Eden felt there was some truth to her words. "And you, too, must be a Gypsy at heart—a fine lady like yerself takin' pleasure in such hedonistic desires. Blimey, but look at the way you're dressed! Franklin can't keep his eyes off you."

Eden laughed. She realized her new friend had turned the tables on her, but she let it go.

"I suspect," Sparrow went on, "Franklin tain't the man whose won yer heart."

Eden blushed, though she pooh-poohed the very notion. "Shane's cold-hearted and mean."

"I agree."

"And he's most patronizing."

"Yep."

"And acts superior. Hardly ever smiles."

"So, why d'ya like him? He tain't even hand-some."

Eden felt a tight knot in her chest. Oh, but he is.

she wanted to protest. She looked down at the sand, where the sun glinted gold on millions of tiny particles. "He's not handsome in the conventional way . . ."

Sparrow smiled. "Ah, you like the rough-lookin' type. The kind that look like streetfighters but are gentlemen to the core."

Eden's own smile was wistful. "Imperial too."

"Well," Sparrow continued, "I admit, he is rather . . . imposing." She nudged Eden's arm. "Cheer up! He's too stiff and formal for you. It'd probably take a whole artillery to melt him."

Eden glanced at Sparrow curiously. It interested her the way Sparrow mixed her phraseology, sometimes using sophisticated language, other times a cockney accent. It happened only when she was most relaxed. When with the troupe, she spoke only cockney. Eden shrugged mentally. Perhaps Sparrow really *had* been a Gypsy.

In those days she saw Shane only once. She had been racing on the beach with Franklin and Sparrow, and though Rattlesnake had taught Eden how to ride, she had to admit, Sparrow rode like the wind. They were neck-and-neck when they heard thunder behind them, the violent pounding of hooves on sand. Eden turned to look over her shoulder and slowed her own horse in awe. Shane was magnificent as he overtook them, riding his big bay as if he were part of the sleek animal, all power and violent speed. He galloped past in a blur, and Sparrow stood straight up in her stirrups to watch him disappear. Even Franklin stopped his horse to stare.

He should be painted in oils, Eden thought as her gaze followed him all the way down the beach, where sunset colors bathed him in red and mellow

gold. She closed her eyes against the pain of watch
ing him, of knowing he would never be hers.

Despite his vow to stay away from her, Shane was
fighting his own inner battle during those golden
late-summer days. He was keeping in touch with
Liam and had formulated a plan to lure the jewe
thieves out of hiding. He knew they would want to
get in touch with Eden . . . once they found her
So he would make certain she appeared someplace
where they wouldn't miss her. He would have pre
ferred to use a decoy again, but the closest female
assistant he had was Camille, and that was out of the
question. Eden was an actress, though, and a quick
study, and he would teach her some self-defense
moves. He was certain she would want to cooperate
She must be as desperate as he, he reasoned, to sever
their relationship.

Though he buried himself in a new project, even
hard work could not drive her from his mind. Too
often he found himself standing at his study win
dow, watching the gold-tanned and blond-white
brilliance of her on the beach. She was a stunning
actress, could mesmerize him from this distance
even without hearing her speak. He often saw her
with Tate and Jessie, saw how natural she was with
them and how they obviously adored her.

Once, after days of watching her dive and fish and
splash about on the beach, he saw Franklin lean all
too close to her and kiss her.

Fury poured through him. That she would allow
that panting, supercilious lecher—

He summoned her immediately to his study. Minutes later he heard her in the hallway, laughing and
chattering with Sparrow. His muscles tensed as
Eden came through the doorway, barefoot and
bright-eyed, her wild hair tangled, smelling of the

ea breeze and roses. Shane gritted his teeth, fighting
he urge to pull her into his arms and kiss her sense-
ess. The sight of Sparrow smirking in the doorway
made him scowl.

"I meant for you to come alone," he said coldly.

Sparrow raised an eyebrow at him, undaunted.
But Eden took one look at him, saw that his eyes
vere the color of icicles, and braced herself for another one of his dressing-downs.

"But now that you're here," he went on, walking
around the desk to stare Sparrow down, "I'm telling
you, no more diving off the rocks."

Sparrow only laughed at his order. "Aren't you
he bloody bossy bloke!" She looked him up and
down. "No one tells me what to do, got that?"

A muscle locked in Shane's jaw. Another rebel, he
hought. There was something disturbing about this
woman. . . . "I do not want to be responsible for
your death on my property. I will not be responsible
or fetching your body after it's dashed against the
ocks."

Sparrow glanced at Eden. "Ain't he the thought-
ul one?" She returned her gaze to Shane. "Tell you
what, mate. My corpse"—she winked at him—"is
my concern."

Shane frowned as she left the room, making a
grand show of her disdain by slamming the door
behind her. "There is something about that
woman . . ." he murmured, then looked at Eden.
"How long have you known her?"

"Sparrow?" Eden shrugged. "She's new to the
roupe. I haven't known her long at all. But we've
become friends. She's a wonderful actress—"

Shane cut her off. "Why didn't you tell me she
was new? That could be important."

"I don't see how. She's replacing—"

"It's not your responsibility to see how. But it . your responsibility to inform me of any changes i your life since your brother disappeared. I'm goin to have Simon run a background check on her."

For some reason, that angered Eden. "Why d you have to be suspicious of *everybody*? Sparrow's kind soul." Her brows drew together over flashin eyes. "Why don't you just run a check on everyon in the troupe, me included, so you can discover ev ery tiny detail of all of our lives."

"Not a bad idea, mavournin. I'll start with you. He moved to the sideboard to pour himself a whi key. "And in answer to your first question, I've a ready told you that it is an investigator's duty to b suspicious of everyone who crosses his path."

Eden's mouth drew tight. "Why have you sum moned me, sir? I thought it was your idea we kee our distance from each other."

His gaze flicked over her features while he sippe the whiskey. "And a fine idea it was." Suddenly, h slammed his glass down on the sideboard, the whis key sloshing over the rim. "But," he continued in voice taut as pulled wire, "I failed to finish dictatin my house rules."

His eyes narrowed and scoured a path down he throat to her breasts, obviously unencumbered be neath the boy's shirt she wore. "You are not allowe to wear that—that hideous getup one more instan Take it off."

Her spine stiffened with outrage. "I will not!"

"And burn it."

Eden felt such a violent unleashing of fury, sh couldn't even speak. Her mouth opened, but noth ing came out. She spun around swiftly, heading fo the door.

Shane was faster, though. Wolflike, he sprang. Hi

ig hands closed around her upper arms, turning
er and dragging her against him. She flinched at the
taggering contact, her hands pressing against his
hest. His eyes blazed down at her. She had to close
er own against his dark power, but the action only
ntensified the feel of his hard erection, a burning
nsinuation nestled against her stomach. The weight
nd heat of his throbbing arousal made pulses beat,
eat, beat against her pores.

"Look at me," he growled.

She couldn't. She would drown in him, this man
he both loved and fought. This man who could so
asily tilt her world askew, make her feel as though
he were cut off at the knees.

"I said look at me, Eden."

His voice uttering her name sent shock waves
hrough her weak body. Slowly, she dragged her
yes open to see his mouth hovering near hers. "You
aw the kiss," she whispered.

He released her abruptly. She hugged herself,
hivering as if he had thrust her out in the cold. "I—
don't see why it would matter to you, Shane."

He walked away from her, over to the window.
As soon as you are finished with the play," he said
n the same low, grating voice, "I will arrange for
ou to become visible so that the thieves can contact
s, and we can get this thing moving."

Her eyes widened. She wished he would look at
er, but he offered her only his rigid, formidable
rofile as he stared out to sea.

"The play is in two days," he continued. "That
ight I have an engagement, and the following day I
vill go over my plan with you. Shortly after that we
vill return to the city for good. I hope the plan will
vork. It's time you went home, Edie."

He turned to look at her then, and his gaze

reached across the shadows of the study to touc
her.

"I did not kiss him back," she whispered.

"You have a right to kiss whomever you please.

"I do. And I didn't. You know how I feel abou
Franklin, though you choose not to believe that
think of him only as a dear friend. He feels differ
ently, as you just witnessed. But I—" She lowere
her gaze, for forbidden words had almost rushe
out, words he would scorn and hate her for. Sh
lifted her eyes to his again. "But I will wear what
please while I'm here. You, sir, are not my guard
ian."

"He's a lecher."

She arched a brow at him as if to say "and you ar
not?" "Now," she said, "am I dismissed?"

Shane could only stare at her. He felt as if he wer
letting a precious gift fly away, a dove, an angel. Hi
throat tightened. Angel, he thought, to his Lucifer
She raised her eyebrows in question, and he nodde
tersely.

"I assume I will see you in two days?" she saic
"Will you watch our performance before your . .
engagement?"

"Yes."

She smiled. "That pleases me. I'm sure you wil
enjoy it."

With that she was gone, taking the promise o
paradise with her.

The play was a great success, and Eden was th
shining star. Of course, she was to think later, it wa
amazing she could perform at all, given her tor
mented heart. They had been up at dawn and int
the city on the first public ferry. Eden had invite

Simon to come along, and he did, although at first he declined. Shane, however, made his preference known that he'd like his assistant to accompany them so he could escort Eden home, along with two other bodyguards.

It wrought havoc on Eden's nerves to say good-bye to Tate and Jessie, and though she promised them she'd be back soon, Tate looked at her as if she were a traitor. She had never felt so stricken leaving a child. The brother and sister had secured a place in her heart, and she feared she would never forget them.

"I'll write you letters," she promised, but Tate scowled at her, and Jessie's big brown eyes had filled with tears.

"No one will read to me at night," she whimpered, and Eden promised her she'd be back. In the meantime, Jessie should learn her letters so she could read for herself.

"Not the same," Jessie said, sniffling, and Eden knew that of course it was not. The little girl craved the intimacy and affection of sitting on her lap more than the words. Tate put his arm around his little sister and led her away, not even deigning to say good-bye.

Later, Eden took Mother Superior aside and begged her not to put the children up for adoption. She was formulating a plan and needed to think about it some more.

The nun merely raised her brows. "That is for God to decide, don't you think, Miss Eden?"

Eden felt her heart wrench. "But—"

"They will not be adopted before I thoroughly screen the parents-to-be," Shane said, coming up behind her.

Eden's breath caught when she turned to look at

him. Already dressed for his evening engagement in a black suit with a wine-colored silk vest and cravat, he was devastating to her senses. His frilled white shirt was a startling clash against his sun-darkened face. "And Mother Superior knows that."

Mother Superior nodded in agreement and excused herself. Shane bowed to Eden, then crossed the room to where Tate was shooting him dirty looks. Eden didn't know what he said to the boy, but Tate brightened considerably, and ventured a smile when Shane lay a big hand on the boy's shoulder. He watched almost hungrily as Shane walked away, back toward Eden. She was being swamped by the troupe, who had come over to say good-bye.

"I'll be back in no time," she promised them, and glanced to Shane, who stood behind Sparrow. "Won't I, Shane?"

He didn't answer. Franklin scowled at him and took Eden by the elbow. "We'll wait for you," he said. "In the meantime I must have you replaced for Lysistrata, but the actress will understand you might be coming back anytime." He leaned down to brush his lips across her cheek, but suddenly Shane's big body was between them and Shane's arm got the kiss. Flustered, Franklin straightened, flushing red.

"I didn't know you harbored such feelings for me, director," Shane said, his deep voice tinged with humor. Franklin clenched his fists and warned him to take care of Eden, but Shane was already escorting her out, Simon on her other side and his two brawniest guards in front of her.

Outside the orphanage, Shane sent her off without so much as a fare-thee-well. Dismal and disheartened, she rode the ferry home without a word.

Even Simon recognized her mood as unusual, and when the carriage pulled up in front of the house, he

sked her stiffly if she would care to share dinner
vith him.

Stunned, she accepted his invitation, and together
hey dined on bay scallops with lemon and parsley,
ittleneck clams with a light thyme butter sauce, and
ysters in a smoky cream sauce. Various vegetable
lishes accompanied the meal, but Eden did not eat
vith her customary verve. She and Simon shared
eminiscences about England. It was only natural to
alk about Shane, too, and Simon expressed his dis-
ress over Shane's complete lack of regard for his
wn life. After all, he was like Simon's own son, and
ie worried about him.

"You'd think," Simon said, "he'd protect his per-
on much more carefully, but no, he mocks death
ind danger, doesn't think either can touch him. But
one day it will catch up, and I don't want to be
around to see that fateful day."

Optimistic man, Eden thought morbidly as she
stared into her wine. "I think," she said softly, "that
Shane feels it's all in a day's work."

"Hmmph, yes, I'm sure he does. Stubborn as they
come. And you, miss, are showing signs of strain." It
gave him great pleasure to pull out his pocket watch
and glance at it. "Past ten. Do you wish to retire?"

"Do you mind, Simon? It's been a long day."

"Mind, miss?" He stood to help her rise, coming
around the table to ease her chair back. "Of course
not. I'm going to retire shortly myself and read for a
while."

Eden glanced at his watch. "Where did you get
the watch, Simon? You mentioned it was special to
you."

He frowned slightly. "My wife . . ." He couldn't
finish the sentence.

Eden cried out as if he'd stabbed her. "Oh, my

Lord, I'm so sorry! I should never have taken it. ... was wrong of me, and I didn't know it had been ... gift from your wife."

Simon, startled by her outburst, patted her hand "Now, now, dear, mustn't fret. I shouldn't have taken your dagger either. I fear we let our tempers get the best of us." He smiled faintly. "I must say, didn't even know I had a temper until you burst onto the scene. Speaking of scenes, you were most delightful to watch today. You are a gifted actress.

Her gaze softened, and she smiled in return. That had been quite a speech for Simon. She was actually beginning to like him. "Thank you," she murmured

He led her to the stairs, then stopped at the landing and said, "You mustn't let him sadden you, miss. He is quite the private one, and has never treated women with more than amused tolerance, shall we say? In fact, other than Camille, you are the first woman I've seen him treat with any sort of consideration."

Eden's eyes sparkled with humor. "Really? You think he is considerate of my feelings?"

Simon looked flustered. "If he weren't, miss, he'd have tossed you out on your ear days ago. For certain he would have kept you locked in your room, given the fact that you try to run off at every opportunity. And look—he even allowed the troupe here. That in itself is extraordinary."

Eden smiled at him. Of course he would defend Shane, but she knew better. Shane was very eager to be rid of her. "Thank you, Simon, for a lovely dinner. Good night."

She ascended the staircase and gave Simon a final wave from the second floor balcony before continuing on to her room.

She might be gone the following day, she thought

she glanced around her grand bedchamber. Or
rtainly by the day after that. Shane was going to
xplain his plan the next day, and then they would
xecute it. She should be happy, Philip would be
ack. But his return now signified the farewell of
hane.

Sighing, she drew a bath for herself, then soaked
r a half hour. The room fragrant with floral scents,
he stepped from the bath and toweled off. Tonight
he would remember Shane as she would never have
m, a phantom memory. Later she would walk on
s beach, feel the wind in her hair, the salt spray on
er skin. But now she wanted to think, come up
ith her own plan of how she would force him from
er mind forever.

Slipping into her ivory silk wrapper, she went to
and by the open window. The warm wind fluttered
er damp hair, lifting it about her shoulders. It
ouched her cheeks, and she edged closer to the win-
ow, her arms crossed over her breasts as she stared
ut into the night. He was with *her* now, a woman
alled Genevieve. Without realizing Eden's presence
arly that morning, one of the kitchen servants had
et it slip that Genevieve was a past mistress of
hane's, and that they were attending a concert at
he Academy of Music. It was September, and Soci-
ty had returned to the city after its extended sum-
er holiday. Shane had always held a vital interest in
ulture, but it surprised the servants that he was es-
orting Genevieve there, and mingling with the elite
e usually shunned.

Eden was not surprised. She knew he was with
nother that night so he could slake his desires, the
esires she knew he felt for her.

The wind picked up. She took in a quick breath,
rasping the sides of her wrapper. The flame of the

scented candle on her bureau fluttered. She lean
out the window, saw the clouds racing across t
moon. A storm? Another heat wave had struck da
before, making everyone miserable. Would th
storm put an end to the sultry summer days that ha
succeeded only in weaving their heat through h
blood like an insidious, seductive serpent?

She closed her eyes. Shane. Even his name w
beautiful. It was strong, as he was, endless strengt
Dominant, intense, so confident and assured, he le
his brand on everything and everyone he touche
Just walking into a room in that quiet, graceful w
of his made everyone feel his power.

Suddenly she wanted to go home—away fro
him. She *needed* to go home.

From the corner of her eye she caught the lig
spilling in from the hallway. She turned slightly an
saw Shane standing in the doorway.

CHAPTER
FIFTEEN

ODEN'S BREATH CAUGHT AUDIBLY. SHE FOUGHT THE swift racing of her heart. Shane leaned against the door frame, his jacket slung casually over his shoulder, his waistcoat unbuttoned, his striped cravat hanging loosely around his neck. Even in the flickering candlelight she could see the glitter of his beautiful cat eyes, feel the powerful pull of his gaze. Her entire body tightened and her blood heated, surging, pulsing through her with warmth. She couldn't even speak his name; it was lodged in her throat.

He continued to stare at her, saying nothing. He had never done this before—he had never, ever come to her room. What did it mean? What did he

want? She swallowed, moistened her lips with t
tip of her tongue, but her mouth was so dry, she h
to wet them again. Still, her words were raspy in t
thick air, air fraught with tension.

"You . . . startled me."

His voice was rough too. "Did I?"

She began to tremble. "Yes. I . . ."

"I came to check on you."

She was surprised. "Why?"

Shane felt a sharp constriction in his chest. S
stood there, wide-eyed and looking frightened, as
he were going to eat her in one bite. Dauntless Ed
Had he done this to her? It panged him, her dul
ous surprise that he would even think to come a
check on her safety, as if he scarcely ever gave he
second thought, when in truth she was always on l
mind. And yes, now he had come to her, determin
not to act like the wolf he was rightfully reputed
be. Certainly he was there for his own selfish re
sons, but she desired him too. He knew she want
him; her lovely, responsive body did not lie. And l
could no longer deny himself.

One night with Edie was worth a lifetime
nights with any other woman.

As he had sat with Genevieve in the Academy
Music, he'd felt as pretentious as much of tl
crowd, a hypocrite—and there was no type of pe
son he disdained more. *She* had made him see th
about himself—take a good hard look inside—ar
suddenly he hadn't been able to tolerate one mo
moment of Genevieve's company. He wanted on
Edie. A startling and alarming thought, but it w
there just the same, and he had abruptly left Gen
vieve, arranged transportation home for her, the
made swift tracks to his own home, to the woma

ho had taught him how to laugh again, the woman
ho had loosened his taut control.

He hadn't been fair to her—not from the very
:ginning—and he was usually a fair man. She af-
cted him like a powerful narcotic that spilled
roughout his body, seeped into his blood, a nar-
·tic that was slowly killing him from resistance. So
: would give them this one night. He knew she was
woman whose memory he would carry with him
rever, but he also knew that Eden was a once-in-a-
etime experience. He would never know another
en vaguely like her. Tonight he would forget his
lf-imposed restrictions and worship her as she de-
rved to be worshipped, ply her, possess her, for
.e was his and always would be. Even after they
arted.

He eased away from the door frame and walked
owly toward her. "Why? I've come to check on
·u because you've been known to elude the
uards."

"I've—I've been very good lately," she said as she
acked away a step, toward the window.

He laughed. "Yes," he said tenderly, "you have
:en very good lately."

"Shane," she whispered. "You should do that
ore often."

"Do what?"

"Smile, laugh. It's so rare that you do. And it . . .
ianges your whole face. Lights up a room . . ."

Shane swallowed heavily. That he had kept this
om her too—his warmth, his laughter. He hadn't
id much to laugh about before she had come into
s life like a burst of sunlight blasting the darkness
om his soul. He smiled at her. "Does it, mavour-
n?" He came closer. "You mean I don't look so
uch like the ogre I am reputed to be?"

Eden could only stare up at him. His subtle ma scent surrounded her. She felt a fine film of perspi tion break out on her skin. "You know how intin dating your scowls are," she teased. "And your i stares. Not," she added hastily, "that *I* am ever i timidated by them." But she *was* intimidated by l slow, stalking gait, his purely seductive smile.

"Sure," he said, and she didn't know if he agre with her or was doubting her. "And you smile often, love."

Her heart hitched, as if caught on a wire. Lov How intimate that word sounded from his lips, at how certain she was that he'd used the endearme with countless other women. Still, the word wash through her with a sweet poignancy. "You're t close," she whispered, gathering her silk wrapper one hand under her chin. A gust of wind funnel through the room, almost snuffing the candle.

His eyes were a warm caress. "Not close enough he murmured, and stopped before her.

"I'm not dressed." She forced the words past t tightness in her throat.

He laughed low. "For you, darlin', tha dressed."

So close to him now, she noticed that he had loc ened the collar of his shirt and half his shirt stu were undone. She glimpsed a portion of his bro: chest with its covering of curly hair, and a surge emotion swept through her, so powerful she had grip the windowsill behind her. He reached out slide his warm fingers down her neck, then rest them in the quivering hollow at its base. She clos her eyes briefly, reveling in the forbidden thrill of l touch. But he took it away, and she felt bereft.

She opened her eyes. "You're home early," s. said, her voice a throaty whisper.

His eyes crinkled at the corners with his crooked
smile. "I am."

Her imagination, or had he moved closer? She
could hardly bear the tension, the pounding press of
heat between them. She searched his features in the
mellow candlelight. "Why?"

"I was bored."

"You don't like Genevieve?"

Warm amusement lit his eyes. "I like her fine. I
was just bored by her company."

"Oh."

"She is not you."

Eden jerked with surprise, and her breasts grazed
his chest. She pulled back, a jolt tearing through her
tautly wired body at the delicious caress. Yet . . .
as if of its own accord, her spine arched, and her
breasts were once again almost touching him.

A knowing glow in his smoldering eyes, he swept
his fingers across her cheek. His gaze was soft with
tenderness, yet burned with yearning. "I kept thinking of how you would have enjoyed the concert, of
how it would light up your face. . . ." His gaze
drifted across her features, lingering on her mouth.

"You are that, you know," he said softly, sliding
his fingers into the thick hair at her nape. "Light.
Light and laughter and—"

Shane caught himself before he said "love," but
she was that too, for she loved life, and found something to love in everyone . . . except him. And
how could he blame her for that?

He struggled against the raw emotion crowding
his chest, filling him with an ache he knew only she
could appease. Forcing down the rising pressure of
need that had been punishing his body for days, he
continued to twine her hair around his fingers.

"And I . . ." He laughed huskily. "I didn't lik her perfume. I kept smelling you, Edie."

He lowered his head and pressed his mouth to th side of her neck, where his fingers had been on seconds before. He closed his eyes, breathing in h scent, fighting the shudder that shook him, shoc him with the power she held over him. He felt h grip his shoulders, heard her soft moan. "Flowe tonight," he murmured against her skin. "No frui no spice, baby." He rubbed his face into the curv of her shoulder and felt her melt. "I feel like I'v absorbed you, Edie, I smell you everywhere. Yo scent clings to me, my clothes, my hands." His lip were burning a trail to her ear. He nuzzled her in th sweet hollow behind the delicate shell, and whi pered, "Maybe it's the heat."

Eden felt light as a bird, and poised on the edg of a bluff, ready to take flight with the whole worl beneath her, ablaze with color. His words—she ha never dreamed of such words from him! He wa tender, he was hauntingly sweet, his words, whi pered from his heart, were poetic. But then, he wa Irish, and the race was blessed with the silve tongue. No matter, a tiny voice murmured insid her, for the fairy-words had been given to her as gift from him. Sensations spiked her within, dartin throughout her, sizzling and popping over her skin tugging at the deepest, most intimate parts of he She had wanted this, his hands on her, his kiss, bu she was confused.

"Shane," she whispered, "where is she?"

He lifted his head to look at her, his breathin ragged. "Who?"

She smiled. "Genevieve."

He frowned as if he had forgotten the name, th woman, then the heat in his eyes melted to laughte

He shook his head, lifting a forefinger to trace one of her brows. "Artist's dream," he murmured. At her questioning look, he said, "Leave it to you to think of the other— She's with someone else. An old friend escorted her home."

Outside, the wind was whipping through the trees. The surf was rougher, the sea air cooler, less humid.

"There's a storm rising," she whispered.

"To be sure, darlin'. There's been a storm rising between us since the second we met. Thunder and heat."

He let his jacket drop to the floor and raised both hands to cup her face, touching her with grave reverence, as if she were a sacred chalice from which he would be honored to drink. His thumbs caressed her cheekbones, running lightly over the finely drawn lines and sensual curves. He brushed her thick lashes with his thumbs, wondering at their silky weight, their gilded tips. His heart twisted when she sighed.

"Reckless," he whispered. "You are reckless, my darlin', and that's a rare thing in a woman."

She opened her eyes, and they were the smoky blue of passion. He caught his breath harshly, feeling the sharp tug in his loins, already heavy and full and raging hot for her.

"Edie," he said hoarsely. "You know what I'm here for."

Yes, yes, she knew. She had to close her eyes from the hypnotic heat in his.

His voice was thick and raw. "Are you scared, darlin'?"

Only of everything. Only of the way she seemed to lose all control under his touch. He ran both hands down her throat to her bare shoulders, under the silk, caressing the fragile tendons, creating shivery thrills upon her skin, inside her. When he stroked back up to her jaw with his thumbs, she grasped his wrists and pushed his hands away.

"Don't," she said softly. "I—I know I've given you the impression that I'm fast and loose, but truly I am not."

"And why," he asked, a smile in his eyes, "have you given me that impression?"

His body radiated such potent heat, was so physically compelling, Eden felt his domination without even touching him. The current between them tugged at her, and even the cool, damp air gusting through the window did little to relieve the sultry throb of seductive awareness between them. She had to clench her hands into tight fists to keep from touching him.

"Why, Edie?"

"I—" A lump clotted her throat. She lifted her fingers to there, touching the hollow where her pulse knocked vibrantly. "I wanted you to like me. I—"

He inhaled sharply, cutting her off. "As if I couldn't," he said, the words sounding like a curse.

Startled, she raised her brows. "You like me?"

He put his hands on her small waist and pulled her toward him. His mouth, lowering, stopped a heartbeat from hers. "I didn't want to," he admitted, his voice gruff with emotion, "but, Edie, I like you very, very much."

He angled his head and covered her mouth hotly, urgently, catching her full bottom lip with his and sucking it, then running his tongue over it. Though he kissed her with alarming hunger, it was also with astonishing tenderness, and a wildness bloomed within her as her heart soared free. She wanted only

be closer. If she could have climbed inside him,
he would have.

He held her carefully away, though, as if the meeting of their aroused bodies would be too violent and
scorching a contact for him to control. He tormented them both by teasing her lips with his
tongue, not plunging inside, but keeping them both
out and aching for more. He murmured something,
something deep and rumbling, and she strained with
the need to mold herself to him. He let her go.

How could he do this to her? she thought franti-
cally, staring at him. Her body was as tight as a bow-
string, her breasts swollen, the tips stiff and aching,
longing for the brush of his hands, his mouth. She
closed her eyes, unable to look at him. Was he going
to torture her again, leave her wanting? Truth was,
she didn't know what she wanted—except that she
wanted him tonight.

"And what about you, Eden?" His voice, raw and
ragged, seemed to curl around her, seducing her
with its intensity. "Do you really hate me?"

Her eyes flew open. *"What?"* Hate him? She
loved him so powerfully, she felt she would die from

"That day on the beach," he said quietly, "you
said you hated me." He laughed slightly. "Many
times. And I don't blame you for it—"

She stopped his words by pressing her fingers to
his mouth. He kissed them, and she drew them back
as if stung.

"I was hurt and angry," she said. "Those things
you said—"

"I know." He moved as if to take her into his
arms, then stopped.

"But, no. I don't hate you." Her eyes lowered. "I
could never hate you, Shane."

"I've made many people hate me."

He said it with such pained sincerity, it startle her. "Deliberately?"

"Of course."

She took a step toward him and she reached up touch his jaw. "I don't believe it," she said fiercel

His smile was both self-mocking and tender. "A my little idealist, you don't believe that I've mac people hate me deliberately, or that many do?" N able to bear not touching her any longer, he reache out and jerked her to him, locking her against h body, molding her hips to his. Though she drew in quick breath and stiffened, he held her against hin one hand shifting to cup her bottom. There was on one way to get any closer, and his breathing quicl ened in anticipation of that. Her breasts were ne tled against his chest, and he could feel her nippl press into him. Her breathing was coming in quicl shallow flutters, her eyes were growing languid wit desire, but she was not to be distracted.

She put her hands on his shoulders and leane back in the circle of his arms, but the movemer only made their contact more intimate. "I don't be lieve either," she managed to say. "If you thin you've made people deliberately hate you, it wa only to protect yourself, Shane. I know."

Though her words made his gut wrench with stark, intense emotion, his mouth twisted with cyn cism. "Don't make me into some romantic hero lik those leading men in your plays, Edie. I'm not. I'r cold and callous and"—he gentled his words with faint smile—"I like it that way."

"You're not that way to children," she whispere as she caressed his shoulders, the back of his necl "I feel so bad about Jessie and Tate." She swallowe

rd. "We left them there with no one to love
em."

He saw the tears rise in her eyes, and his own
roat tightened. He felt too damn much for her.
ne was the weepiest woman he'd ever known—her
wn idealism made her cry—and he hated tears, yet
er tears always moved him. And this mutual con-
rn for children—orphans especially—pulled at
m.

"I'll take good care of them," he said hoarsely.

She again raised her hand to his face, resting her
alm on his cheek. "I know you will."

Her touch heated his body to a blistering degree.
e rocked his hips subtly against hers, loving her
ft moan. But he didn't want her thinking things
at were not true. "You know," he said, though he
d to force the words out, "I have only one inten-
on tonight. I'm going to make you mine."

Her expression was puzzled. "I—I thought—you
dn't intend to bed me."

"I didn't *intend*." He rubbed a strand of her hair
etween his fingers. "But here I am. I want you,
den."

The storm was coming closer. Eden could hear
e low rumble of thunder—and feel it, a seductive
rob that vibrated throughout her body. The waves
rashed the shore. The curtain behind her fluttered,
read like a full sail and swirled around her. She
ivered with both fear and anticipation. Yet Shane
emed to be warning her of something else.

He leaned close to nuzzle his face along her neck.
This will be our final night—our only night with
ch other. You know that, don't you, darlin'?"

Oh, she knew. She tilted her head back, shudder-
g with delight as his lips trailed down the sensitive
rve of her shoulder. He was holding her hands

now, almost as if he didn't trust himself to put the
on her body. And she was glad. She could hard
breathe, hardly stand upright. Tears fell inside her
she silently cried for what she knew would be the
parting, yet she was unable to turn him away. '
know," she whispered brokenly.

His breath was like fire, spreading flame along h
bare shoulder. She gasped, straining toward him
trembling need. Still, he allowed only the slighte
contact of their bodies.

"You know," he whispered against her skin, "ar
you risk." His tongue touched her ear, and sh
gripped his hands, swaying on her feet. "But darlir
let's see how much you hate me tomorrow."

"I won't," she promised.

"Listen to the wind." He lifted his head to sta
out the window. A sudden flash of lightning lit h
eyes, making them gleam with lambent fire. Oh, ho
beautiful his eyes were. She shivered and he glance
at her. "Are you cold, Eden?"

"No, I . . . we should close the window."

"We'll let the storm in," he said, and as if in a
swer, rain-chilled air swept into the room, taking he
breath away. The door across the room slamme
leaving them close and tight and alone. They cou
hear the waves tossing themselves roughly upon tl
shore, and there was no more light but from tl
flickering candle.

Shyly, Eden touched his chest. "You're very di
ferent from Wilbur."

Shane laughed. "I sure as hell hope so, mavou
nin."

His laughter was throaty and rich. It arouse
Eden in a powerful way. She stood on tiptoe and sli
her hands up his shoulders to join at the back of h
neck, then pressed her mouth to his, her tongu

ising his lips. He groaned, his arms going around
r as he met her ardent kiss, staggered by her bold-
ss. But he should have known she'd be like this,
rant with passion, unashamed of her appetite.
s arms tightened, drawing her up against him. He
ok control, his tongue burning into her mouth.
e gasped and leaned into him, wanting more.

The cold rain slashed in from outdoors, biting
eir skin with tiny needles. Shane moved his hands
the round swell of her bottom, squeezing the firm
sh, then pulling her tightly to him, against the
rd ridge straining the front of his trousers.

He pushed her wrapper off her shoulders so that
slid to her waist, then his hands were on her
easts, lifting them. His thumbs brushed her tight
pples, and she let out a gasping breath, shaking
ldly. They both watched the erotic sight of his
rk, masculine hands cupping the firm, soft
unds of her breasts, and their passion burned
gher, brighter. Shane pulled her to him again,
thering her silk wrapper in his hand, lifting it to
de his callused palm up her thigh. Firing his
od, she shifted to accommodate him. His hand
oved to her bare buttocks and caressed them. She
ifted against his hand, and he groaned. He wanted
go slowly with her, easily, but her wild response
s making that unlikely.

"Take my shirt off," he said against her mouth.
hen she stepped back to oblige him, her gown fell
an ivory puddle at her feet. In a sudden shy mo-
ent she bent to reach for it, but he caught her
ist, pulling her upright again. "Leave it," he com-
anded hoarsely, and his long fingers trailed to her
easts again, gliding over the peaked crests. He
nt her backward over one arm as his avid mouth

slid down her throat, following where his fingers h
gone until it closed over one aroused tip.

Eden moaned softly, arching her back. His tong
danced over her nipple, sucking and tugging till s
felt mad from the rhythm. He laved the other bre
with his warm, wet tongue, and she gripped t
sides of his head, her fingers lost in his hair.

"Shane, Shane . . ." She whispered the wor
like a song.

Shane's arms were trembling with restraint. I
had to stop or he would be too rough with her, t
savage. With enormous control he lifted his he
from her breasts and moved back slightly from h
"Undress me, Edie," he whispered. "Do it now."

Eden was limp, unsteady, her insides melting li
warm cream, sweet and thick and hot. So this, s
thought, was passion between a man and a woma
She had never known. Wilbur had been old and s
and gray. Shane was young and hard and dark, t
terly masculine, excessively virile. He burned w
seductive male fire. She was a little afraid of his hu
ger, the fierce light in his eyes, his excessive streng
But she loved him, loved him, loved him. Every pa
of her was filled with love for him. Bright, radia
love, love that she knew, sure as she stood the
naked before him, would never die.

Unable to keep her hands from him, she reach
up and tugged on one end of his cravat so that it s
around his neck and drifted from her fingers to t
floor. Then she pushed his waistcoat from his wi
shoulders and that, too, dropped. The top half of l
shirt was undone, and she spread her hands acro
his broad chest, reveling in the feel of its light fuzz
hair. His skin was warm and smooth, and she r
her hands over his shoulders and upper arms, ha
with bunched muscle.

"Oh, Shane," she murmured. "You're so beauti-
ul."

She laid her face against his chest, and beneath
er cheek she felt the savage pounding of his heart,
natching the rhythm of her own. His hand slid into
er hair, cradling her head, until she turned her face
)ward him and touched her tongue to his hard, flat
ipple.

He drew in a swift, sharp breath, his fingers flex-
ng in her hair. Rain and wind came swirling into the
edroom, and Eden began to shiver with the cold.
mpatient now, Shane tore his shirt off, then flicked
pen the buttons to his trousers. Startling her, he
ulled her hand to the hard, hot bulge at his groin.
hocked, she drew her hand back, but he grasped it
ightly, forcing her palm to press his throbbing
rousal. He made her rub him in a slow, sensual
notion, and when she began to move her hand of
er own accord, he groaned, pulling her close. He
issed her almost violently, thrusting his tongue into
er harder, deeper. Eden whimpered, returning his
iss with all the fervent passion she had stored for
im over the past weeks. Her fingers closed around
is magnificent length and squeezed.

His groan was harsh, male. His muscles shook
vith both restraint and insurmountable pleasure. He
vanted to get her to the bed, needed to get her to
he bed. To kiss her was not enough. His whole
ody throbbed and shuddered with the force of
eed that coursed through him. It was no use to
hink about the bed, though, for they were sinking
o their knees, unmindful of anything but each
ther. God, no, he didn't want to take her like this
—rough, on the floor—but there she was, stretched
ut beneath him, her silk wrapper somehow under

her. His hands were on her breasts, cupping them molding the firm flesh.

"Edie," he whispered, "I want to make this goo for you."

She stared up at him, dazed, touching his fac "You are," she whispered throatily in a voice tha sounded nothing like her own.

He fell upon her as if she were a feast. Though sh was slender, her body was voluptuously curvec firmly rounded. Her skin had turned the color of ol gold where the sun had touched it these past week on the beach, and where it had not, it was pal creamy silk that made Shane growl just to look at i Her breasts were quivering, the puckered pink nip ples a wanton invitation. Her legs were long an slim and graceful, and where her thighs met, pal curls formed a silky triangle that hid all her femal secrets. The candlelight licked flame there, catchin shining color.

Shane clenched his teeth. He wanted to thrus into her immediately, possess her, yet he wanted t take his time with her, explore her mysteries as h had ached to do for what seemed an eternity. Bu she was irresistible. He didn't want to wait anymor for her.

In a swift motion he shed his pants and boots.

Naked, he came over her, trusting himself to onl half straddle her, his throbbing hardness against he outer thigh. He had never been so eager to be insid a woman, yet he took care to lay himself on her, no in her, not yet. . . . Slowly he spread kisses ove her, feeling her soft sounds murmur up from th lowest regions of her body as she moved sinuousl against his mouth.

Eden felt the pulse of his heat on her thigh, sur as the pulse of her own heart. Passion-drenched laming with fever, she lay under him, steeped in him. All of this—hard man and the delicious sensation of his mouth exploring her body, the seething fire-river that curled through her, the liquid, pulsating shimmer of warmth that turned her boneless and open and sweetly yielding—was new to her. She felt light as a bird, wanting to fly and sigh and stretch and unfold for him. She let herself go, wanting to remember each moment afterward, never forget.

He captured both her wrists in one large hand, holding her arms above her head. Her breasts were thrust upward, begging for his kiss. He lowered his head and took one nipple into his mouth, sucking strongly. She arched into him, feeding his fierce hunger and he swirled his tongue around her taut, aroused nipple as his hand cupped and kneaded her other breast.

"Shane, Shane."

Hearing her chant his name drove the blood through his body in a pounding rush. The rain was slanting in on him, drumming over his back and buttocks where her hands were tightly pressed, and he could feel his own muscles flex against her palms. Her touch was magic, both gentle and firm, and he was so damn close to the edge, he thought he might burst. His chest hurt; breathing had become painful. His senses were bathed in her.

"Eden," he rasped as he slid his mouth down her firm, slightly rounded belly. He placed a kiss on the inside hollow of her hipbone. She writhed and lifted her hips toward him. "Your name means pleasure. Did you know that, darlin'?"

Under the onslaught of his mouth, Eden didn't care. But she felt his words like a searing imprint against her quivering flesh. He moved lower, circling his tongue around her navel, and his fingers brushed the curls at the juncture between her thighs. She jolted with the shock, remembering the same touch on the beach that day, but now he stunned her with fresh shock as he put his mouth to the moist heat instead.

"Shane!" she cried, arching with want, something she did not know.

"Shh, baby, don't be afraid." A ferocity gripped him at the knowledge that she had never been loved this way, and an aching tenderness. She looked petrified, and he promised, "I won't hurt you, darlin'." Before she could doubt him further, he gently parted her legs and, half mad with wanting her, he sank his tongue into her.

Oh, God, what was he doing? Eden wondered frantic. His tongue was licking a flame inside her sliding in and out of her in a magical rhythm that had her twisting under him, crying out. The rapture was exquisite, mind-hurtling. He kissed her and sucked her, washing her with his tongue. She clutched his head in her hands, pulling him closer His hands were on her thighs, fingers gripping her as she rose up under him, offering herself. He said something, and she felt his words inside her, a possession that shot skyward to her heart, her soul Then all sound was gone, all but the wind, and the surf, far off. She felt she was on a fast train ride speeding up over rocky cliffs, the wind rushing past her ears, hurtling her high, until she was screaming tossed through space, crying out . . . for him.

"I'm here, Edie. Let it come, angel, let it come." She was so damned passionate. Shane felt, just by thrusting his tongue inside her moist sheath, that he shared her ecstasy too. He was so hot, even with the rain pelting his back and shoulders. She opened to him like a flower at dawn, the petals satin-soft, and her scent was on his fingers. He could feel her pulsations, the rush of her ecstasy, and lost himself as her pleasure poured outward.

She was still quivering when he slid up her body and settled himself between her thighs, bracing his hands on either side of her. "Edie," he whispered, and smiled tenderly at her.

Wonder and rapture still darkened her eyes into deep blue pools. "I—I didn't know—"

His solid length against her swollen, damp flesh was almost unbearable . . . almost. "Eden, I want to take you to the bed," he said hoarsely.

She couldn't move, though. She felt drugged, a lazy languor creeping through her limbs, making them heavy. Oblivious of the storm raging outside, oblivious of anything but him, she now knew why men and women did this.

She slipped her arms around his neck, pulling him down. Shane pushed his hand between her legs, coaxing them apart. She flinched at the new touch, and his mouth sought hers.

"No more waiting, Edie."

She quieted, trembling, and he slid a long finger inside her, feeling her sleek muscles contract around him. She cried out and turned her head to his shoulder. Again he found her mouth, and hers opened as his tongue slid slowly into her. His thrusting strokes matched the rhythm of his finger inside her, and just as he felt the swell, the lift of her hips, he braced himself on trembling arms, poised at her entrance. He needed her now. His hardness probed the wetness between her legs. She jerked at the first blunt seeking of his body. He kept himself there, then began to slide into her.

She was so wet, so hot! He shifted, feeling her

resistance as he slowly pushed into her. Her body was a satin sheath, her inner muscles clasping and relaxing around him, pulling at his control. He clenched his teeth, striving for restraint, but his mind clouded with agonizing need, extinguishing everything but sensation. Her body stretched to admit him as he increased the pressure and slid his full, solid length into her tight passage. She cried out, her mouth pressed to his. A savage curse exploded from him. Buried in her, feeling the tiny gripping spasms along his throbbing length, he could not pull out. His jaws were clenched shut, his eyes fierce and glittering with want, he could only rasp out one word. "Why?"

Tears leaked from the corners of her eyes. She pulled him down to her, aching for the feel of his chest pressed to her breasts. "Take me, Shane, take me."

He was in desperate, violent need. It was the storm, driving him, driving him, for he could not go slow. He was mad for her, and she was his. She drew her legs up, pulling him in deeper, and he locked her to him. He wanted her to ride with him, but he could not slow. He wanted her to get used to the feel of him, but his body took control, and he began to move, easing back, then pushing into her again, his entry long, slow, solid. Waves of raw pleasure streaked through him, blotting his senses to everything but pure carnal satisfaction.

He began to say her name on each stroke, hoarsely, roughly. "Edie . . . Edie . . ."

It made her delirious. She tossed her head from side to side, chanting with him, her voice low and sultry. "Shane . . . Shane . . ."

His thrusts became harder, deeper.

She reached for his face, her fingertips touching

is clenched jaw. She matched each of his strokes, ising and falling with him as if she were made for his dance, only with him. And then she was reaching for something else—the rapture she had experienced before—and she found it, shattering in his rms.

Shane let the storm carry him. He had never lost control like this, never. But this was different. This vas Eden. Life-lover. He searched for the sun in her iot depths, searched for the light that made her so ibrant, so alive. Propelled by his savage need, he unged against her, and release came, blasting hrough him, his body tightening as he held the motion, shuddering, filling her with his powerful eruption, and uttering only her name.

CHAPTER
SIXTEEN

"YOU SAID YOU WERE MARRIED," SHANE SAID, RUNNING a lazy hand down the front of her body and letting his fingers splay across her firm belly.

Eden murmured, turning toward him, curling her arm across his middle and resting her head on his shoulder. Snuggling close, she absorbed his delicious body heat. She felt protected as his arms encircled her, drawing her even closer. After their heartbeats had slowed and their breathing had become regular, they'd lain on the floor awhile, dreamily descending into the misty euphoria of a pulsing afterglow. The rain had still been coming in the window, and she had begun to shiver. He had carried her to the bed tucking her under the covers, then closed the window.

Though the room was chilled and damp, and the storm still raged outside, Eden felt completely sheltered, drifting in a luxurious sense of peace.

Idly, she traced the vicious scar that wrapped around his flat, hard belly. She heard his tense, indrawn breath, then he grasped her wrist and lifted her hand to his chest. She felt his heart beating steadily, sure.

"I *was* married," she said.

He rubbed several strands of her hair between his fingers. "Honey, married people do what we just did. And obviously, you hadn't."

Hot color rushed to her cheeks, and she was glad he could not see her embarrassment. "Wilbur couldn't."

She felt his body tense. "Couldn't?" He spoke as if the very notion was a foreign concept to him. "I thought you said he was old, not dead."

Eden smothered her laughter, pushing herself up on her elbows to scold him. "Shane O'Connor, that wasn't nice! Especially since he *is* dead now!" She curled into him, sliding her body over his, letting their naked legs entwine. For a moment she feasted her gaze on his magnificent shoulders, so bronze against the crisp white sheets.

"Go on," he said. "Even if Wilbur *couldn't,* why didn't you tell me before I—"

"There wasn't time."

He laughed huskily, and the sound fired her blood.

"And," she added, "it wasn't the uppermost thing on my mind. In fact, I don't recall there being much of anything on my mind."

His shout of laughter delighted her, except she

didn't know what she had said that was so funny. She knew, though, that she liked the way he was regarding her now, his eyes warm with affection. "I would have gone slower," he said, "been more gentle with you."

Something clutched her heart, and she fought it. She wanted so desperately to tell him she loved him, it terrified her. This was a new reality for her. She had never suppressed her feelings, found it uncomfortable and pointless to do so, but this was Shane. He scorned emotion, soft feelings, weakness. So she swallowed and faced him with all the courage she possessed, hoping that nothing of her vast love for him showed in her eyes.

"You were tender and beautiful," she whispered, tracing his bottom lip with her forefinger. He closed his eyes as he cupped the back of her neck and pulled her back against his shoulder. His fingers rubbed her nape, and she wondered why he was so strangely quiet, what he had locked inside him too.

She reached up to slide her fingers into his hair, reveling in the feel of the soft strands. "No wonder," she whispered against his shoulder, "the women are mad for you."

His whole body tensed, then his laughter erupted again. She raised her head, indignant. "Well, it certainly can't be your charm!"

He laughed harder, and she made a face, pushing her fist against his solid chest. "I'm sorry now I told you I like your laughter. I take it back."

He rolled her over onto her back and leaned down to kiss her, making her lose her breath. "Good Lord, Edie, for an actress you haven't learned much guile. Time you did."

She looked at him, confused, and Shane was amazed he had offered her such cynical advice.

When his laughter settled, she swung over him, her hair sliding like a golden sheet over his skin. He could not believe this newly christened woman was straddling him like a practiced courtesan. Not that he minded . . .

"I want to touch you," she said. "May I?"

His eyes widened.

"Is that a yes or no?"

A wry smile curved his mouth. He reached up to outline the underswell of her breasts with his fingers.

"Oh . . ." She caught his wrist. "I like that."

"Mmm, so do I."

"But you have this backward. I'm to be doing the touching."

His smile became rakish. "Be my guest, my darling."

She shifted off him and pulled the coverlet down. Her eyes devoured him, running over his hard shoulders, his wide, strong chest. Candlelight made his skin gleam. She put her hands to his muscled ribs and felt his breathing quicken.

"How anyone can have muscles here," she murmured, then watched her hands ride the muscles of his powerful arms. She squeezed his biceps, unable to close her fingers completely around the bulge. "I'd hate to be behind your punch. How did you get such big arms?"

"I ride," he said, and his voice was curiously hoarse. "And swim. And fight."

"Fight?"

"Used to. I did some prizefighting when I was younger." He gave her a raffish grin. "I still punch a bag every now and then. Didn't you notice it hanging in the back of the stables?"

She shook her head. "No," she said, wondering at all the different, intriguing facets of this man.

"Sure. I used to make some money at it—me and my friend Kyle." He laughed shortly, huskily. "We were damn good at it—champs." His smile took on a cynical twist. "We drew great crowds—a couple of micks going at it—great entertainment."

Eden caught her breath. "It doesn't sound like entertainment to me." She ran her thumb over his knuckles and wondered how many times he'd had to use his fists. No matter. He was with her now, and violence had no place in a bedroom.

She kissed his knuckles, then inched the covers down farther, draping them just below his navel. She let one finger trace the thin line of hair that ran down his flat stomach and watched his abdomen go hollow under her touch. "You really are," she said in wonder, "very much different from Wilbur. He did not look anything like . . . this."

Shane had never been compared to another's lover aloud. Certainly not directly after making passionate, intoxicating love. And certainly never to an old man who "couldn't." Her inexperience was like an aphrodisiac, and as he watched her study him, he was becoming painfully, ardently aroused.

"Damn glad to hear that, Eden," he said in such a way that she giggled. "How long were you married to him?"

"Two years."

He couldn't imagine living two years in close quarters with Eden and not making love with her every morning, noon, and night. Seeing shadows darken her vibrant eyes, he frowned. "What is it, Edie?"

She shook her head, her hair moving like a cloud around her.

"What?" he urged.

She hesitated, looking everywhere but at his face

Her gaze finally settled, oddly enough, on his scar. She swallowed hard, then said, "He was a good man."

"You say that as if to convince yourself."

"No, he was. A good man."

"Then why don't you look at me and tell me?"

Her gaze flew to his. He stared at her, his eyes searching hers. She touched her throat. "I . . . he treated me kindly—never said a harsh word."

"But?"

She looked away again, at the flickering candle flame. "He couldn't consummate our marriage, but he touched me in other ways—with his fingers, and I—" She broke off, unable to continue.

Shane tensed, his muscles stretched tight. "You were married to him. He had that right."

She glanced at him. "I know." She shrugged. "I just didn't like it."

She was staring at him as if measuring him, perhaps to see if she could trust him, gauging his response. The candle flame was reflected in her eyes, turning them oddly catlike in the dimness. He pulled her down to him, stroking her jaw with his thumb. "What didn't you like about it?"

"He—he was so much older than me. So much, thirty-five years at least, maybe even forty. He made my skin crawl." She shuddered, thinking of his soft, probing fingers, his hairy white belly, pressing, rubbing, gloating. "I . . . was scared."

Shane was as rigid as rock. He crushed her to him, holding her tightly. He thought of her lying in the dark, his brave, dauntless sun goddess, afraid, having to endure an old man's touch, and everything swam in a red mist before him. "He's dead. You never have to go back to him."

"Shane, you're hurting me."

Immediately he loosened his grip, brushing her hair with his lips. "Try to get some sleep now," he murmured. He wanted to take her again, but he knew she needed time. Then he grinned. "It'll probably be nice to sleep in your own bed for a change."

She lifted her head to stare at him, blinking. "Huh?"

"Did you think I didn't know you've spent every night on the porch?"

She gasped, making him laugh. "I ought to turn you over my knee, you disobedient little brat."

Immediately she got her back up. "I have the right—" She softened, powerless under the impact of his smile. "It's so peaceful to watch the sun come up, listen to the beach at night."

"I know." His gaze lowered to her mouth. "There were many nights I thought of joining you."

"There were?"

He could tell she was flattered by that, and the thought made him smile. And suddenly he knew he couldn't let her go so early tomorrow. "There's a fair tomorrow," he said, rolling over onto her and nestling his hardness against the juncture of her legs. "I want you to come with me."

She stared up at him. "Are you asking me or ordering me?"

He rocked his hips against hers, and didn't have to say a word.

"Yes," she breathed, caressing his hair. "But I thought—"

He dropped kisses across her face. "Don't think."

She squirmed under him. "I love fairs! Rake used to take Philip and me—"

"Don't talk." His mouth closed over her nipple, tugging on sweet, aroused flesh. Eden moaned, arching into him.

"You have a beautiful body," she told him, her voice throaty.

He lifted his head to look at her, a flash of pleasure sparking through him at her words. Her eyes were a stunning, bewitching blue of the sea. "Thank you," he said. "I think."

She laughed. "Are you showing me how gentle you can be?"

"I'm trying," he said, then lowered his mouth to her navel.

Her slender body jerked under him and her fingers tugged at his hair. "Not that!" she pleaded, panting.

He swirled his tongue down low, touching it to the crevice where her thigh met her body. "You didn't like it?"

"Too much—" she managed to say, her fingers twining through his hair.

He came up over her, stopping at her breasts. He sucked at them with a strength that made her cry out. Tortured by the sight of her wet, puckered nipples straining eagerly toward him, he buried his face between her breasts, lifting and squeezing the full lobes that pillowed him.

Eden made soft sounds of pleasure under him. The candle guttered and went out. In the darkness his fingers found her, brushing her soft curls, finding her wet and ready for him. Staggering pleasure ripped through her, and she begged him to come to her.

"Edie," he said roughly, "we should wait."

Her body arched toward him impatiently. "I don't want to wait."

He growled and shifted, settling possessively between her parted thighs. He felt her moistness, her

dense heat. "You're ready for me," he whispere
thickly, and thrust into her.

She cried out, a high, thin cry. He drew out th
pleasure, fighting the insistent roar for release. Wit
every dreg of self-control he possessed he pulle
back, until the swollen crest of his manhood jus
brushed her throbbing entrance. Slowly, tormen
ingly, he plunged his hot, solid length into he
sweetly pulsing flesh again, driving them both ma
with the sleek, slow motion. Wild sounds burst fron
her as she surged upward against him. Violent shud
ders racked them both, but he kept it slow and ho
and long.

The ecstasy was unbearable. Just as she felt th
fullness, the tingling heat and quivering swells buil
in her melting loins, he would pull out, torturin
them both. She clawed at his shoulders, bringin
him down to her, and in his eyes and mouth she sav
an odd satisfaction and triumph, purely male.

"Let me!" she cried, and his mouth crushed her
as she arched up against him, hugging him in a fierc
grip as intense waves of heat consumed her, and sh
spun away toward the sun.

Eden slept as though drugged, and when sh
woke blue-gray light washed the sky. It was befor
dawn. She stretched and winced, all her muscle
sore and tight, inside and out. She reached out an
found him lying beside her. Turning her head, sh
saw he was awake and watching her.

"I thought you had gone," she said.

"Gone, all right. Honey, I've lost my mind."

She had climaxed many times after that secon
time, and he had held off, allowing her the use of hi
body, his own control like iron.

"Shane," she whispered, sliding a hand over his stomach, "I—" She broke off, blushing. "I wasn't fair."

"What do you mean?"

"I . . . enjoyed myself more than you did."

He chuckled and pulled her to him so that her curves were nestled to his rock-hard planes. "My pleasure was . . . immeasurable."

She smiled with delight.

"But," he added, "it's a good thing there was a storm."

Puzzled, she wrinkled her brow. "Why?"

He traced a lazy finger down the curve of her spine. "Otherwise," he drawled, his voice teasing and terribly arrogant, "I'm sure the entire household would have heard your . . . uh, enjoyment."

Her face grew warm. "Is that bad, to make so much noise? I couldn't help it."

He leaned over her, kissing her. "No," he said against her lips. "It is very, very good."

The wind, cool and gusting into her bedroom, woke her. Eden opened heavy-lidded eyes to a sparkling day, the window wide open, curtains billowing. She made a little sound of pleasure and snuggled deep under the covers, remembering. *Shane.*

She sat up abruptly. He was gone. Stricken, she stared at the empty spot beside her and felt the loss like a death.

"*Stop,*" she told herself, pressing her knuckles to her diaphragm to staunch the ache that cut off her breath. No regrets. *He was here, with you, for the night.* He had told her before he had taken her, gen-

tleman that he was, that they would have only one
night.

Slightly sore, she pushed the bedcovers aside and
pulled the bell cord, summoning Alice for a bath.
She went to the window and looked out. The day
was glittering, the cool, fresh wind tinged with the
scent of autumn. She put her hand up to shield her
eyes from the glare, her gaze skirting the shore. And
there she saw Shane.

He was lying on the wet sand, bare-chested, his
face up to the sun. His arms were tucked under his
head and he was letting the cool water wash over
him, soaking his denims. His boots lay several yards
away, and she guessed he had gone riding. My God,
she thought, gripping the windowsill, he was beautiful. And he would never be hers. The knowledge
made her throat ache and she fought the hot wash of
tears in her eyes. He was like a lazy, powerful animal
soaking up the sun, and she longed to run down to
him, to join him on the golden stretch of beach.

It was time for her bath, though. And today could
be the last day she shared with him, at least in lei-
sure. They were to go to the fair together, but first,
he had told her, he wanted to show her some street
fighting, and what to do when they lured the jewel
thieves out, so as to retrieve Philip.

She supposed she should be happy about that.
But somehow, as she turned to her bath, ignoring
the curious look Alice gave her, she felt only a hard
lump in her throat that she could not swallow.

Later, bathed and dressed in a raspberry-pink taffeta day dress, she descended the stairs and ran into
Simon. He took in her attire, her sparkling eyes, and
high color, and raised his brows at her. "Lovely
morning, isn't it, miss?"

"Lovely," she breathed.

He looked at her oddly, his head tipped to one side. "Mr. O'Connor thought so too."

As if that were a most peculiar situation, Simon shook his head and continued on his way.

"Simon," she called out, and he stopped. "Are you going to the fair today?"

"Fair? Oh, yes, I had forgotten about it. I might, miss."

She smiled radiantly. "I'm going with Mr. O'Connor."

Simon frowned. "He's taking you to the fair, is he?" he said, then his face cleared. Eden thought she saw the barest hint of a smile twitch at the corners of his mouth. "Very good, miss, very good."

She thought it was very good too. On her way to Shane's study, she ran into the butler. "Oh, *Spencer,*" she said with emphasis, startling him by remembering his name.

His usually dour expression turned beatific. "Yes, mum."

"Could you serve breakfast in the study, please? I'm to meet Mr. O'Connor there."

The butler bowed slightly. "As you wish, madame."

She assumed it would be quite a wait, for Shane had to bathe and dress. So she nibbled on strawberries and studied the bookshelves for titles. Not finding anything of interest, she wandered over to his desk and inadvertently read something he had written on a tablet.

"My heavens," she whispered. "He's writing a novel. And it's very good." Promptly sitting down, she became enthralled, lost in the detective story he had sketched out.

She heard him before she saw him. Across the porch his boot heels rang in his long, easy stride. She stopped reading, imagining instead his tight buttocks shifting up and down as he walked, the muscles bunching in his thighs. When she then heard only silence, she looked up to see him standing at the study doors, obviously having paused there on his way to his room.

He was still damp, water beading in silver drops in the hair on his chest. His hair was slicked back off his forehead, throwing his rugged features into sharp relief—blade-clean and granite-carved. Her gaze traveled slowly up and down his body, and she wished she could touch him. When she met his eyes, though, she felt guilty.

She jumped up out of his chair. "I didn't mean to read—Shane, I didn't know you were a writer."

He smiled wryly. "Neither did I."

"You're a wonderful writer. The story is so *good!*"

"Do you see what kind of influence you are on me, darlin'?"

Not sure how to take that comment, she looked down, fidgeting with the pages of the tablet.

"How are you this morning?" he asked.

A flush burned her cheeks, and he laughed softly. He looked relaxed, at ease, and all she could think of was him over her last night, thrusting inside her, his hands on her breasts, his mouth covering hers. She shuddered, and knew that one night with him had not been enough, that a hundred nights with him would never be enough. She wondered if he felt the longing, but doubted it. Shane was not a man to wish for things he could not have.

"I'm fine," she said, thinking how absurdly she used the word to describe the indescribable rapture she had experienced in his arms. "And you?"

His eyes glinted. "More than fine."

She caught her breath. "Are you going to bathe—shave?"

He looked amused. "Soon." Reaching behind him, he pulled the doors shut, then his gaze flicking over her as if she were a tempting morsel he would like to savor, he started across the room toward her.

He paused by his desk, glancing to the tray of strawberries, and he touched one with his finger. "Strawberries," he murmured.

"Yes."

He glanced at her, smiling slightly. "Have you eaten?"

She swallowed hard, unable to shake the feeling that his words meant something else. "No. I was waiting for you."

With the hint of a smile still in his eyes, he let his flaming gaze flash over her. "Wise choice." His eyes focused on her bare feet peeking out from under the hem of her gown, and laughter rumbled up from his chest. "Eden honey, do you ever wear shoes?"

Her toes curled into the thick carpet. She shrugged. "It feels good to be—" She cut herself off, for he had edged closer to her, and the smell of seawater and man and wind was suddenly overwhelming. She felt a swift pull in her belly; her heart hammered hard and fast. Already she was aroused, could feel the sweet pulsing in that secret place where only he gained entry.

His sensual mouth curled up at one corner, as if he knew what he was doing to her. "Are you ready to practice my plan?"

"What—" She stopped to clear her throat. "What do you want me to do?"

"A loaded question," he murmured. He trailed one finger down her neck to her bodice, where he traced the upper swell of her breasts. She gasped as he pressed his fingers over her wildly beating heart. "Do you know," he said, "that I told myself I wouldn't touch you this morning—that we had all last night, that you're still probably recuperating, that we are to be parting company soon."

Eden felt her insides splinter. She took a step back, for his rugged virility pulled strongly at her even as she fought it. But she could not tear her gaze from his.

"But then I saw you," he said. He moved closer to her, almost touching her. She stepped back again, but the desk hit the backs of her thighs and she was trapped. The light in his eyes turned wolfish. "And you look so beautiful, darlin'." His gaze drifted to her mouth and his voice turned husky. "Like a piece of fruit, ripe, eager to be plucked"—he lowered his head to put his warm mouth to her neck—"and eaten."

She made a murmuring sound, shivers of delight streaming down to her loins. She put a hand to his chest, shivering at the feel of his water-cool skin against her overheated flesh.

"Shane," she whispered, trying to shrug him away. It was no use. He kept his mouth against her, sliding it up to her jaw. "You're dripping on the carpet."

"Mmm" was all he said.

"This is—" She gasped as his tongue touched the corner of her mouth. "This is the second carpet you've ruined."

"You helped me ruin the bedroom carpet," he said. He lifted his head to look at her, amusement in his eyes. "Should I make you pay?"

You already have, she cried inside herself, her heart twisting.

In a sudden move that surprised her, he grasped

er by the waist and lifted her to sit on the edge of
he desk. "God, Eden, I can't keep my hands off
ou."

"I noticed," she said, tipping her head back as he
an his lips down her neck, all the way to where her
breasts swelled above her bodice. He slid one hand
nside the dress and was just able to touch a taut
nipple, stroke it into a tight, throbbing peak. Eden
moaned, going limp against him. '"Oh, Shane, stop.
You must stop."

"Why?" he asked, and lowered his head to suck
her nipple through her dress. She cried out, grasping
his hair, her vision dimming.

"Someone might come in," she pleaded, past car-
ng if anyone actually did.

"No." He slid his hand to the outer curve of her
breast, pushing it high so that her nipple popped out
and into his mouth. He grasped it between his teeth,
tugging, then sliding his tongue over the rigid point.
Her throat arched backward in abandon.

"Someone might, Shane."

Breathing hard, he lifted his head to stare into her
glazed eyes. "No one bursts in here without knock-
ng, except you." He grabbed her hand and pressed
t to the front of his trousers, forcing her to rub his
rigid erection. "Feel that," he said, his eyes ardent
and hot on hers. "After how many times last night?
And I still want you, honey. You're like a madness,
an addiction, pounding in my blood."

His raw words, the throb of his hard arousal, hot
and pulsing in her hand, made Eden shudder and
burn. He took a plump berry from the breakfast tray
and pushed it at her. "Eat it."

Stunned, she took the strawberry from him and
put it in her mouth. He made a low sound in his
throat, his gaze fixed on her lips.

"Now," he said hoarsely, "give some to me."

At his words, ardent and coarse with throbbing sexual undercurrents, desire and heat exploded through her body. She never knew that eating strawberries with a man could be so erotic, but putting her fingers to his lips and feeling the contrast of their damp heat against the cool, ripe fruit sent her nerve ends skittering. His tongue touched the tip of her finger, and boldly she slipped her finger into his mouth.

Then he was pushing her backward, the tray, books, papers crashing to the floor as he swept them aside to make room for her, his need savage and urgent.

"Shane!"

His hand went to the front of his trousers, where he jerked the buttons open, freeing his throbbing manhood. "Do you know," he growled, "I dreamed of doing this to you that first time I saw you eating those strawberries. Damned fruit—"

He lifted her skirts and deftly unfastened her undergarments. His fingers glided up her thigh, teased her moist curls, then slid into her honeyed sweetness. He shifted, meeting the arch of her body as he came over her, into her, penetrating deep.

Eden clung to him, shaking, cresting almost immediately as he surged powerfully into her. She was lost in him. There was a pained sweetness to their lovemaking, a desperate urgency. Knowing it would be their last time, she took his hard thrusts eagerly wrapping her legs around his waist, oblivious of her back being pressed unrelentingly to the desk. She ran her hands over his damp back and shoulders feeling the muscles shift and swell. Through passion dimmed eyes she saw, beyond the window, the blue sky pitch with every thrust of Shane's body. The sun

s like a gold, pulsing heart, retracting and ex-
ading, the sea gulls graceful arcs that drifted upon
ir own ecstatic ride. She closed her eyes to every-
ng but him as he lifted her higher. Some part of
 mind was aware that he was tender, but she
In't care if he was or not. This pain would ease.
e loss of him would not.

Shane gave a final tremendous thrust, and cli-
xed in violent, shuddering relief, pouring himself
o her, bringing her with him once more up over
h white cliffs to a place where there was no pain,
 loneliness, only exquisite ecstasy and peace,
eet peace.

CHAPTER
SEVENTEEN

*T*HE DAY WARMED, WAS CLEAR AND SUNNY WITH
high, deep-blue cloudless sky. The fairgrounds we
crowded with a variety of people, some obviou
wealthy and exquisitely turned-out, others of a mo
rural appearance. The air was fragrant with salt
and warm, sweet-smelling hay. Pungent anim
smells and the savory aromas of home-baked foo
stuffs drifted on the balmy breeze. Eden, strolli
the grounds with Shane, inhaled deeply, indescr
ably happy to be at his side.

He was dressed comfortably in a jacket and tro
sers of midnight blue, his fine linen shirt open at
throat. Eden was wearing a dress of pale blue la

prigged with cream-colored rosebuds. Comfortable
d slippers cushioned her feet, and she'd swept her
air up into a casual twist at the back of her head.

She was pleasantly lazy, sated, delightfully aware
f sore muscles in her softest depths where Shane
ad buried his hard length. As she strolled alongside
'm, she basked in his pleasant company, refusing to
ink about the evening, when he would take her
to the city and they would hang about the theater,
ping to draw out the thieves.

It was a plan they had reviewed that morning to
eticulous extent, after they had eaten breakfast out
1 the porch. Shane had told her that he felt the
ieves were still in the area, that they still wanted
e jewels and were most likely waiting for her to
sume her normal life-style.

"They'll think you've relaxed your guard by
w," he said, "and we'll let them believe that. Trust
e, everything will be fine."

"I trust you," she said, and he narrowed his eyes
her. He heard more to her words than just a blithe
sponse.

"Edie," he said, reaching across the table to touch
r face, "don't imagine more than there was for us,
arlin'. We'll be leaving each other very, very soon."

He had excused himself immediately thereafter to
upstairs and dress for the fair. She was left to
onder his words, to feel the hot ache settle in her
est, filling her with a sadness and haunting pain
at would not ease.

Now, though, as they browsed among art displays
d stalls of handiwork, livestock and horticultural
hibits, booths laden with cheese, preserves, pies
d cakes and breads, the trotting track and stables,
e delighted in the moments, in the souvenirs he

bought for her, in the food they shared. They paused in the stables to look over the horses.

Standing by a golden mare, Shane took in her lines. "Regal," he said, and ran his hand down her silky flank.

Eden shuddered. His big dark hand against the mare's body was sexual somehow, especially since she knew what magic those hands could provide.

"Fine-boned," he went on, ambling around to the mare's other side. His piercing eyes found Eden's over the horse's back. Her lips parted slightly, and her skin tingled. Somehow, she had the feeling that he was talking about *her*. "Elegant. Aristocratic. Spirited. She has fire. It's in her lines."

Eden was breathing quickly now, the fecund stable scents and pungent hay, the soft stroking whisper of his voice making her pulses dance, her blood heat. She tore her gaze from Shane's and turned to put her hand on the flank of a great gray.

"Powerful," she said. "No doubt, exceptional movement. An inordinate amount of stamina and endurance." She was aware of Shane walking around the mare to stand behind her, but she continued her examination. "Fluid muscles, yet like steel." Her voice was a scraping whisper. Shane's body pressed lightly against her back, and she felt hot and weak. "High desirability as a sire."

His hand covered hers, and she jumped. He put his mouth close to her ear. "I'm hard for you."

Sweet, thick honey melted in her loins. She wanted to turn into his arms, mold herself against him, let his mouth crush hers.

"Shane! Shane darling, is that you?"

Eden could feel him turn slowly at the sound of sultry, excited female voice, but Eden whirled, face burning. Shane's arm slid around her possessively an iron band around her waist even as she struggled to be free.

"I thought that was you from behind, though . . ." The woman's gaze slid deprecatingly to Eden. "I wasn't certain."

Immediately Eden's chin went up. They were facing a stunning woman in an exquisite gown of buttercup yellow, her heart-shaped face protected from the sun's harsh rays by the lace-edged parasol she carried. She twirled it, keeping her gaze on Shane and smiling prettily at him. "Fancy meeting you here." She reached out and touched his forearm. "Haven't seen you in ages!"

Eden squirmed, nauseated by the woman's fawning manner. Shane's grip tightened.

"Hello, Charlotte."

A past lady love, Eden guessed, torn between amusement and a horrid feeling that Shane had shared his beautiful body with her. She was somewhat reassured to see that he looked annoyed, barely tolerant of the woman's intrusion.

"Charlotte," he said, "I'd like you to meet—Eden, what the hell is wrong with you?"

She was tugging at his hand, still attempting to free herself, unable to look at the woman, who was watching them with a catlike gleam in her eye. She smiled weakly at Shane, then stood on tiptoe and whispered that she had to use the fairgrounds more intimate facilities. He let his probing gaze run over her face, then nodded.

"Hurry" was all he said, and she flew.

She had no need to use the facilities at all. She just wanted to escape that woman, her hungry look, the reminder that Shane would return to such women as soon as she was gone. Fighting the thick emotion cramping her chest, she headed for the opposite side of the grounds, to an open target range where a number of men were lined up to try their hand at bull's-eyes.

She watched for a while, then stepped up to try her hand. The man in charge, who guarded the rifles as if they were gold, was vehemently opposed.

"Yer a woman, miss—it just ain't done!"

She was outraged. She put her nose to his and said, "I am here as a guest of Mr. Shane O'Connor. If you do not give me a rifle this moment, I will have him throw you in jail for refusing to take my money!"

The man looked baffled. "Can ya do that?" He glanced to the spectators behind her, who had paused to watch this unorthodox creature, all of them shrugging.

"I'll make certain it can be done!" she said, snatching a rifle from his hands. "What's more, I'll wager you one hundred dollars a man that I can soundly beat anyone who challenges me!"

"You're on!" shouted several men, and there began the loudest and most scandalous ruckus the county fair had ever experienced.

She was reloading her rifle after having bested twelve men, when she heard a warm, amused voice behind her right shoulder. "Still the finest shot in the county, little sister. Even if it is a different county."

She froze, her heart stopping. Everything around her seemed to freeze too—the men holding rifles poised, the targets, the crowd in their colorful clothing that had come to watch the spectacle. Slowly she turned to look behind her and saw a tall man with dark hair and a beard.

"It's me, Edie," he said quietly. "Philip. In disguise."

She almost screamed. It *was* Philip! Thinner,
shaggier, but those were his unmistakable hazel eyes
above an oddly-colored beard that had to be fake.
She wanted nothing more than to fling her arms
around him, hug him, but she read his warning look
and kept her composure.

"Game over," she said to her competitors, who all
loudly groaned their disappointment, but she was
adamant. "And I'll be back to collect my money!"

Once she had relinquished the rifle, she tugged
Philip behind one of the booths and threw her arms
around him. She wept against her brother, clinging
to his shirt. "Oh, Philip, you're alive."

His hand was in her hair, soothing her. "Shh,
Edie, of course I'm alive. You know me—a cat with
nine lives."

She was torn between hugging him forever and
punching him. "You don't know all the grief you
caused me—all the worry—"

"And I'm sorry about it all, Edie, but there's an
explanation."

She pulled back to scold him. "There always is
with you." She reached up to tug on his beard.

"Ouch!" he yelped.

"I thought it was fake. Actually, it *must* be fake—
that color."

"It is, but I've glued it on."

"What!"

"Never mind, Edie. I wish I could stay here with
you and chat, but I've got to go—in minutes actually—" He craned his neck to look around. "Where
is that investigator fellow you've got shadowing you?
I'm shocked he's even let you out of his sight."

Eden was both confused and relieved. That Philip
was indeed alive and kicking was a shock in itself,
but now he was telling her he was leaving again, and

was demanding answers of her. Well, she needed some answers herself. "Are you involved with the theft, Philip?"

"Not in the way you think."

Which, of course, made her think only the worst. Suddenly unutterably weary, she sank to the worn milk stool propped against the side of the booth. She stared up at him, took in his spare frame, his hunched shoulders, and thought he looked nothing like the dapper, elegant rakehell that had disappeared.

"What has happened, Philip? Please, tell me from the beginning."

Squatting down in front of her, he took both of her hands in his. His eyes beseeched her, and she felt that old feeling of half-dread, half-exasperation, when he used to beg her to cover his tracks for him so Rake wouldn't tan his hide over a prank he had pulled. Of course, Rake had never laid a finger on him, but the threat had always existed, and that was enough to keep Philip's mind cooking for new and better schemes.

"First," he said earnestly, "tell me, where are they?"

She cocked her head to one side. "Why do you want to know?"

"I want them of course—" He broke off when she gasped, then he shook his head with vexation. "Edie, don't lecture me. It's not what you think! Now, where are the gems?"

Warily, she answered him. "Shane has them."

"Shane? Is he the tough bloke who looks somehow sinister and completely proper at once?"

"He's the one."

"Police?"

"Investigator, Philip—to find *you*!" Her temper as rising.

Philip scratched his wig. "Sounds Irish."

"He is."

They stared at each other, her gaze challenging, s intrigued. Then he said, "Mama wouldn't like "

"Mama doesn't like anything I do."

"That's true." He rubbed his false beard. "You ve him?"

Eden felt as though she had been punched. But it ad always been this way between the two of them, is silent understanding that just a mere glance uld convey. Even after having been away from ach other, they cut right to the heart of the matter. he looked away, her vision blurred by sudden tears. Yes, but it's no use. We are parting."

"Well, he's a bloody fool."

She laughed through her tears, pleased by his loyty. "Philip, please tell me what this has all been out."

"You've got to understand, Edie, this was supose to be a much smoother operation than it rned out to be. And I'm sorry for worrying you— d for making you feel you had to hire an investgator. Although it did turn out rather nicely for u— Ah, yes," he said when he caught her rolling er eyes, "the jewels. I'm going to attempt to make a ery long story very short. Now, one night a couple f weeks back in a billiard hall—"

"Which one?"

He gave her a strange look. "O'Shaunessy's."

She snapped her fingers. "Missed that one."

Philip went on. "I overheard a very interesting onversation. Two men I hadn't seen before, and ho had gotten thoroughly drunk, let loose their

tongues and talked about the jewels they had re
moved from a certain very wealthy man in London."

"Forrest Steele."

He looked impressed. "Yes. I—" He had the
grace to blush. "I asked one of the women who
worked there—"

"A tart."

His flush deepened, then he grinned. "Yes. Mi
randa. I asked her if she would please, as a favor to
me, one of her most gracious and loyal clients
squeeze some information from these two thieves so
I could locate where they were keeping the jewels."
At her disapproving frown he hurried on. "Right
from the start, Edie, the thieves had mentioned the
name Steele, and because of his power they had to
move the gems quickly. I knew Steele would offer
reward for those gems, and when I saw them I knew
the reward would be substantial—enough to pay of
all my debts and get married."

"Married!"

"That's another story."

"Philip, did you get that tavern girl—Elizabeth—
with child?"

"Oh, no, is she claiming that again? She does that
at *least* once a month. I haven't been with her fo
three. And I did *not* sleep with her. She's got he
gents mixed up."

Eden sighed. "Never mind. Please, do go on."

"Well, I found the jewels, brought them home
and planned a trip to England to receive my rewar
and—" He sighed. "I suppose to pop in on Mam
too. But then, what happens? I go down to the ship
ping office to buy passage and I get nabbed—by th
thieves, of course. There are actually three of them.
He scowled. "That third saw me talking to Mirand
and made her squeal on me. These were roug

chaps—I'd like to make them pay for how they hurt Miranda—but that will have to come later. They were rough with me too—bound and gagged me, left me in a warehouse. Once they knew I'd left the jewels at home, they went back for them, but, of course, you had taken them." He smiled at her. "Thanks, Edie. I should've known you'd do the right thing."

"I didn't know *what* to do."

"Well, you know most of the rest. The night on the pier, they hired a half dozen thugs, promising a reward, but I really don't think any of them got a penny. I wasn't there, but they told me you had a broad-shouldered bloke with you, and another woman." He laughed. "I didn't know who they were, but when one of the thieves was moaning about a knife wound, I knew you were there. Edie, you shouldn't take such risks."

"But when did you escape, Philip? We had another note from them and no one showed at the meeting place. I thought . . . you might be dead."

His gaze softened on her. "I didn't mean to put you through that. I escaped—got a piece of glass and worked on the ropes. Rattlesnake taught us some useful tricks, didn't he, sis? I knew I had to get to you, and I escaped, but didn't know they had followed me. Actually, the ringleader was glad to be rid of me, I heard him say he wanted to be more than once, but the others chased me. If I had known, I never would have endangered you, Edie. I went to the house, and saw you there—with the Irisher—and they took a shot at me."

She gaped at him. "I thought they were shooting at Shane or me! And please call him by his name, Philip. Irisher is impolite."

"I don't know him well enough to call him by his first name. I'll call him by his last."

"You know it?"

"Yes, I'll tell you how in a minute. Let's have some kind of order to the telling of this story, shall we?"

She waited.

"To answer your question, right, the bullet was meant for me. I knew then I had to stay away from you. I ran, but was frantic with worry, afraid you'd been shot. I figured O'Connor would take care of you, and later I returned to the house. But the servants were gone, and so were you. After that, I figured contacting Franklin or one of the troupe was the best idea. I gave a message to some woman at the theater and she promised to deliver the note to you. I followed her to a flat—some big bloke's with red hair—"

"Liam."

Philip raised his brows. "Another Irish—sorry. So I watched this bloke—Liam's—place for a while, figuring he was some sort of contact, but he's a sly one. The only time I saw him come out of his flat was to buy groceries, and when I followed him, I lost him. At last I wrote the final note, pretending I was the thieves, to lure you into the city so I could talk to you. O'Connor showed up. He was with that other woman, and Edie, I know a wig when I see one. Actually that woman doesn't quite have your same build. The thieves might not know that, but I'm your brother and I can detect a fake twin when I see her."

Eden smiled. "That was Camille, Liam's wife. She's a very nice person."

"Well, I planned to trail them back, figuring they'd lead me to you, but I was so bloody tired, fell asleep while waiting for them to leave. I decided after a while to return to the theater, but no one was there. Only that big red-headed bloke and, I guess, his wife. I *did* go to St. John's, knowing you had a performance there at some point, and the Mother Superior told me you were coming in that day. That was yesterday, Edie. I followed you to the docks, and once I saw you leave on that private boat, I thought, forget it, I'll never reach her. But I asked the ferry boat driver who the other boat belonged to and he went on about O'Connor. That's how I know his last name. Well, once you had gone inside that fortress of a castle, I didn't know how to get you out. And then it was night again. I had to sleep outdoors, during that godawful storm, and I don't mind telling you I long for a bed. You've certainly worn me out, little sister."

"*I've* worn *you*—" It wasn't worth arguing about. Philip had his own peculiar way of thinking. "But why the disguise?"

"At first I wore it to hide myself from the thieves. I didn't know if they were still trailing me. I lost them, but then they found me once hanging about the theater. Now I don't know. Have you heard anything from Steele? Now that I know you are all right, I'm going to take the jewels back to London."

"I'm not sure Shane will go along with that."

"He doesn't have to. They're not his. They're *mine* to return."

Eden sighed. "We'll still have to talk to Shane. The gems are at his home, and—"

"Don't you see, Edie, he won't want to give them to me. He'll just want to give them back to the authorities, and I won't get my reward. I'm heavily in debt—"

"I know. I met Mr. Camponelli."

"Campon—" Philip paled.

Eden saw a movement out of the corner of her eye, and she paled too. Shane was coming toward them and looking exceedingly angry—that icy anger that hardened his already glacial features. "Oh, dear."

"What?"

She smiled weakly at Philip. "You can discuss this with him yourself. Just don't exacerbate—"

She stopped as Philip stiffened, the barrel of a gun pressed to his back.

"Stand up," Shane said. "Slowly."

Unfolding inch by inch, Philip rose to his full height.

"Shane," Eden said, leaping to her feet as well, "this is not what you think!" She didn't know what he thought, but judging by the fury on his face, it was not what she hoped. "Shane, he's—"

"Shut up."

She flinched at the chill in his eyes and voice. "Now," he said to Philip, "who the hell are you?"

Philip glanced over his shoulder at Shane. "I'm Philip."

Shane tensed. His fierce eyes narrowed on him, then flicked to Eden. "Goddammit, you said he was . . ." Of course, he thought. A wig. A false beard. Damn.

Hearing the commotion by the target field earlier, he'd figured Eden was in that vicinity. He had trailed her there, watching proudly as she bested a man. But then this man had leaned down to whisper something in her ear, and the two had scurried off behind this booth. Shadowing them, Shane had been furious as she hugged the man, and he'd believed himself betrayed once more. When it was clear they were well acquainted with each other, he had headed over there, ready to tear the man apart with his bare hands. Now he wasn't quite sure what he wanted to do with the man who had eluded them so well.

Philip slowly raised his hand and pulled off his wig, revealing hair as thick and white-blond as Eden's. "See?"

"I see," Shane drawled sarcastically.

Philip extended his hand. "Hello, sir. Eden has told me something about you in these brief moments, and I have to say that though I am surprised at her choice in men, it's difficult to become too alarmed with Edie's choice about anything."

His hand hung in midair as Shane glanced at Eden. "Choice?"

"Philip, be quiet! Shane, shake his hand and get it over with. I'm glad you two have finally met."

After their brief handshake, Shane put away his gun. "Remove the beard," he said.

"Oh, but that will take some doing. You see, I've glued it on."

"What?"

"Yes, I'll need some hot water, to say the least."

Oh, my God, Shane thought, a male Edie. He shook his head as if to clear it.

"Turpentine would be good," Eden suggested, perfectly serious.

Philip smiled as if her idea was brilliant.

"Now, why didn't I think of that?"

"Probably," Shane drawled, "because it will leave nothing of your face but blood and bone."

"Shane! Must you be so graphic?"

He looked down at her. She was at his elbow now, and he wondered if he could trust her after all. But her brother was a distraction as he continued talking.

"Perhaps I'll find something in the stables, or—"

"You're staying here with us," Shane said. "And we're heading back to my estate. Now. You have a great deal to explain, mister."

Philip brightened. "That is *exactly* what I had in mind, O'Connor—"

"Philip," Eden interrupted, hoping to delay his telling Shane about his plan. "Why don't we—oh, wait! I left my souvenirs by the target range."

She dashed before either man could stop her. Too late, Shane broke into a run after her. A burly man with curly dark hair rushed toward her and grabbed her, circling a muscular, hairy arm around her throat and lifting her clear off the ground. In one meaty fist he held a knife, and he pressed its point to her skin.

"Move and I kill her," the man growled.

A collective sound of fear and shock rose from the spectators around them, and Shane froze, feeling the barrel of a gun at his back. He swore inwardly, though he was the picture of cool composure. He saw a man at the back of the crowd run off as if to fetch a policeman, but he knew that would take too long.

"Hands on top of your head," the man behind him said.

Slowly, without any intention of keeping them there, Shane obliged him. His captor removed the gun from his waistband and tossed it to the ground. The crowd "oohed." Another man had captured Philip, and Shane assumed these were the thieves.

"Now," said the cold voice from behind. "You are going to lead us out of here real nice like and give us the gems, or we slice your beauty's throat."

Shane tensed and the man from behind laughed. He tipped his gun toward the sky and pulled the trigger. Women screamed. Men scrambled.

"Get outta here—all of you!" he shouted, and the
owd scattered.

As confusion swirled around them, Shane's and
len's gazes connected. She moved suddenly, a
ckward jerk and kick that he had taught her just
at morning. Her captor dropped his weapon and
rsed, one hand covering the eye she had punched.

"Get his knife, Edie!" Shane shouted as he
nched his own assailant in the face. The man went
wn, and Shane tackled Eden's brute, though she
d done a fine job of bringing him to his knees on
r own. Philip was having some trouble, so both
len and Shane went to help him. By the time all
ree thieves were on the ground and moaning, the
lice arrived. Philip identified the men as jewel
ieves and kidnappers, and Shane explained how
 was working with Scotland Yard. Since the police
re familiar with the highly respected Shane
'Connor, they agreed with his decision to keep the
ms locked in his safe at his home until he could
nd them over to Forrest Steele's representative. In
e meantime, they would jail the thieves until the
ndon authorities arrived.

Shane, Eden, and Philip returned to the estate
d celebrated with Simon over a light meal. Eden,
wever, could not fight off her conflicting feelings
joy that her brother was home and the bitter grief
at she would be leaving Shane the next day.

She was aware of him watching her over dinner,
are that she only half listened to Philip's engaging
ries. She was glad her brother had retrieved
ke's watch and Grandmama's earrings, but it
dn't cheer her for long. Bleakly she stared out the
indow and sipped her wine, wondering how she
uld live the rest of her life without ever setting
es on Shane again.

Leaving the dinner table early with the excuse that she was exhausted, she went upstairs to pack. She dismissed Alice, tossed a few articles of clothing into her trunk, then drifted over to the window to stare out. Idly her fingers stroked the silk curtains and with a pang she remembered the night before. If only she didn't love him. If only she could stay there forever. If only—

The door creaked, and she turned to see Shane standing on the threshold. "Edie."

She turned quickly to hide the wetness in her eyes. "I'm packing," she choked out.

He came up behind her, putting his big, warm hands on her shoulders. "Good," he said, nuzzling his lips to her cheek.

She swallowed. "Good? Are you so eager to be rid of me, then?"

"Ah, Edie." His warm body brushing hers sent fiery streaks through her. "You put up a good fight today."

She tensed. "You taught me well."

He released her and went to the armoire. Taking out her dresses, he threw them on the bed. She glared at him, her misery fast escaping and healthy anger taking its place.

"Excuse me, sir, what do you think you're doing?"

A smile touched his eyes. "Helping you to pack."

"I can do it myself!"

He laughed soft, low. "What kind of mother could have raised such belligerent, outrageous children?"

"She didn't raise us. Rake did."

"Ah."

She stripped him of the lace undergarments he held. "What does that mean? Ah?"

His eyes crinkled at the corners. "Honey, don't you have anything but silks and lace? Other than that ridiculous exploring-the-beach outfit."

"Well, what, pray tell, am I supposed to have? Trousers and jackets like yours?"

"Well," he said, "I do admit to noticing that your derrierre does interesting things to a pair of breeches."

"It is cruel of you to tease me now."

His gaze was tender with affection, and she turned away. "Don't," she said, hurting.

"Don't what?"

"Don't look at me like that and then send me packing."

"Mmm," he murmured, apparently not in the least troubled about sending her off.

She flipped a chemise into her trunk and managed to look at him with feigned nonchalance. "I guess you plan to move on to Charlotte?"

He laughed, and the sound made everything in her tighten painfully. He pulled her into his arms even though she struggled to be out of them. "I like the idea of you in trousers," he said.

She pushed at his chest. "Then you're an odd one."

He laughed again, white teeth gleaming. Eden caught her breath at the riveting power of his smile. He lowered his head to brush her lips with his own. When he lifted his mouth from hers, his gaze was warm and seductive. "In trousers I can see all your curves. And here." He cupped her bottom with one hand, bringing her against his hardness.

Sweet agony tore through her, and she fought to pull away. "Leave me to pack."

He smiled. "We're sleeping together tonight."

"I—no—"

"I just want to sleep with you, Edie. I won't touch you."

She looked at him, incredulous, as if that were the joke of the century. To sleep with and not touch? She had learned enough to know that wasn't likely.

"I don't want to sleep with *you*."

He seemed amused. Already he was undressing her, his long fingers undoing the buttons of her dress. "We have to get up early in the morning."

"You can't wait, can you? I'm surprised you're even going to see me off."

"I'm not."

She fought down the sharp pang in her chest. "I didn't think so. Please, Shane, let me go so I can finish packing."

"There's nothing left for you to pack."

"What? I have—"

"Not where we're going."

She held her breath, her puzzled gaze searching his.

"After every case I go away—somewhere. This time I'd like you to come with me. I have a cabin in the Adirondacks." He smiled down at her. "Honey, you're going to need trousers where we're going. I'm bringing you to the mountains."

CHAPTER
EIGHTEEN

IT WAS COOLER IN THE MOUNTAINS, AUTUMNLIKE, AND the maple trees had already begun to turn. Eden had watched out the window in awe as the train wound up along its narrow track toward the railroad station several miles from Shane's cabin. The scenery was magnificent, breathtaking—the awesome, rugged peaks of gray rock that had been carved by glaciers and running water, the dense forests of evergreens, birches, and maples, the woodland ponds and inter-connecting lakes and streams. Shane told her of the Iroquois and Algonquin tribes that had traveled through this region, hunting and fishing and living off the land. There were all kinds of game in the mountains, he went on, deer and elk and moose, as well as wild predators such as the lynx, and panther, and the wolf.

"Then you fit right in," she teased, and he laughed.

She had caught glimpses of extravagant estates and lodges on the fringes of blue lakes, but Shane owned a small, rustic log cabin with just one main room, beam-ceilinged and dominated by a huge gray-rock fireplace with a bearskin thrown in front of it. A few rag rugs were tossed on the wide-planked floor, and a bed stood against one wall. At the back of the cabin was a small separate kitchen, complete with a table and two chairs. Though they had brought a few provisions, there was coffee and tea and flour and sugar, beans and salt pork neatly stacked on shelves over the cast iron cookstove.

"Do you cook?" she asked him, surprised.

He set down his bags and smiled. "Sure," he said. "Did you think I brought Mrs. Leahy along when I come up here?"

Eden blushed, her skin tingling under the warm intimacy of his gaze. "I—I didn't think—"

"Are you hungry now, darlin'?"

It was almost sundown and she was famished. But somehow, she was also shy as well. She didn't understand why, could only suppose it might have something to do with that one bed and knowing he would want her to share it with him. Oh, what had she done! Suddenly panic-stricken, she lurched away from him, wanting to run outside. He caught her, his fingers closing around her upper arm. "I'm hungry too, darlin'," he murmured.

"I didn't say I was hungry."

"But you are." His fingers were in her hair, freeing the pins, and he groaned as the thick satiny mass cascaded over his hands. He buried his face in it, breathing in her fragrance, then suddenly he lifted her, crossing the room in quick, long strides and laying her down on the bed.

They tore at each other's clothing, and he came into her almost immediately with one long, powerful thrust. She cried out, taking all of him into her, his strong manhood filling her to completeness. She undulated beneath him, her aching need turning to flooding warmth, crashing, shattering about her till consciousness dimmed, and she came slowly back, floating like a feather on the wind. She reveled in his savage thrusts, the powerful muscles in his back flexing and bunching under her hands, the harsh, rough sound in his throat before he, too, shuddered violently, burying his seed deep inside her.

Shane's heart thundered against his ribs, and his breath came in harsh rasps as he held her close. He stroked her hair, shaken by the intensity of their joining, and by the even stronger desire to keep his seed deep inside her, to sire a child with her. He clamped back on the emotion surging wildly in his chest. He was mad! But it was there, the almost aching longing for a tiny, golden-haired son or daughter, with Edie's sunny nature and flair for life.

She was gazing up at him, a questioning look in her blue-green eyes. Sunset colors spilled across her face, claret-red and autumn gold. He began to thrust his hips gently against her, the rocking motion slowly bringing him to full arousal again. It seemed that a mere touch of her fingers, a whisper of his name, could easily send him over the edge. He had never wanted a woman more. Would never want a woman as intensely again, and he knew this as sure as he knew he was from the land of Eire.

"Edie, Edie," he chanted softly as he rocked her.

He caught the glimpse of pain in her own eyes and knew she felt it too, that every time they joined it would be all that much harder to part, but he couldn't, wouldn't, release her one moment sooner than she had to go.

For days they hiked the mountain, explored the verdant forests, fished in clear streams, cooked trout over an open campfire. Shane showed her the falls, a beaver house, the loons diving for fish. She kept an even pace with him, dressed like him in denims and soft chamois shirts—clothes that he kept in a trunk for the orphan boys he sometimes brought up there.

"Do you think," she asked him one day as they cooked lunch over a campfire by a clear brook, "that you might bring Tate here sometime?"

"Sure," he said easily.

"And you don't take the girls up here?"

"Not very feasible without a female chaperone."

"Hmm, it's too bad they can't enjoy this too."

Shane rubbed his jaw. "Somehow I can't see me and Mother Superior sharing the same sleeping quarters."

Eden laughed. "She might like it."

Shane's amused gaze drifted to her mouth. "Hmm."

"And how many boys do you bring up here at a time?"

"Usually six, no more than eight. It does them good to learn how to live off the land. Some have only seen city. Some never want to go back."

He spoke softly, but she caught the hint of wistfulness in his tone. She studied his face, but he was concentrating on the fish in the skillet. "I still think it's unfair the girls can't come up here," she said as

e spread the tablecloth on the grass and set their
aces. "They would enjoy it just as much as the
oys. It might be the only freedom they're ever al-
wed in their lives."

"Well, honey, why don't you stay here and I'll
nd some up?"

She caught her breath and glanced over to him as
e flipped the fried trout onto the plates. He did not
ok as if he were joking. When she didn't speak, he
anced at her, and half smiled. "I didn't think so.
o stage up here."

" 'All the world's a stage,' " she murmured.

"Mmm, so it is. Pour the wine, darlin', I want to
rink with you."

As he raised his glass to her in silent salute,
hough, Eden felt a sharp ache in her chest. She
oked away, then felt the gentle rasp of his thumb
n her cheek.

"What is it, mavournin?"

She turned to him. "Why *didn't* you ever marry,
hane? And have children? You're so good with
em."

He frowned. "I told you why. My livelihood does
ot permit it . . . and I have yet to find a woman I
ould want to spend the rest of my life with."

If he had slashed her with knives, the pain
ouldn't have hurt more. She pushed it away, telling
erself he hadn't meant to be cruel, just honest, and
e wondered if he was scowling more at himself
an at her. She was convinced of it when, in one
wift move, he twisted her onto her back and leaned
ver her, his hard body straddling hers. He stared
own at her a moment, then bent his head and ran
is tongue around the outside of her lips. She jerked
nder him, and he raised his head to look down at
er again with his mesmerizing silver eyes.

"Darlin'," he said huskily, "once I wanted what every man wants—a wife, babies—but I learned real young there're enough hurtin' babies in this world, and too goddamned many cheating, frivolous wives."

He pinned her arms high over her head, and his eyes gleamed with some strange emotion before he leaned down again to kiss her. He let one wrist go and brought his big hand under her chin, gently squeezing her jaws to lift her mouth more into the kiss, and their hearts were pounding.

"Forgive me," he whispered, his voice harsh and plaintive at once, "for not being a sentimental man."

She started to protest, but he crushed her lips under his own, and soon, with the sky blinding blue above her and his hands on her bare flesh, he made her forget everything but loving him.

She cherished the talks she had with him. As he chopped wood, or they prepared meals, or lazed on the riverbanks, they shared bits of their pasts—and carefully avoided discussing the future. She told him what it had been like, being plucked from a pampered aristocratic upbringing and thrust into a less pampered but certainly unrestrained and overindulged childhood in the heart of Texas. Her grandfather was irascible and outrageous, she told him, and had once shot a man right off his horse for ogling his precious fourteen-year-old granddaughter.

Shane laughed at that.

"Shane, it was savage!"

"But did Rake kill him?"

"No . . ." she said slowly. "Just a flesh wound."

"Aha. And did the man ever bother you again?"

"I never saw him again."

Shane laughed again, straightening to look at her. She was sitting on a pile of wood with her legs drawn up under her, nibbling on an apple and watching him as he chopped wood. "If you were my granddaughter, I would've done the same."

Eden stopped eating to stare at him, but he had started chopping again. He was shirtless, and riveting to watch, his muscles rippling and bulging and glistening with a fine film of sweat. His hair had grown longer, even a little shaggy, and he hadn't shaved that morning so that beard stubble shadowed his compelling face.

"You look like a ruffian," she said.

He stopped again, propping the ax handle against his crotch so he could run his hands through his hair, trying to smooth it back.

"And you have beautiful hair," she murmured. Tossing aside the apple, she slipped off the woodpile and walked over to him. His arms slid around her waist, and she reached up to twine her fingers through his soft locks. "Why do you always smooth it back, as if you're trying to straighten it?"

"Do I?"

"Mmm-hmm."

"Curls are for girls."

Startled, she blinked.

He laughed. "It's what my old friend Kyle used to say—he and Liam teased me something unmerciful about my curly hair when I was young. I guess— Lord."

She saw the raw pain that flashed into his eyes just before he removed her arms from around his neck and turned away to take up the ax again. He swung it with more force than he had previously.

Later that evening he told her about Kyle. They were naked and entwined on the warm bear rug before the crackling fire, lazy and sated from lovemaking, and Eden had run her finger over the scar that cut into his belly. This time he did not remove her hand, only stared down at her when she asked, "When are you going to tell me, Shane?"

He watched the flame reflected in her sun-colored hair, turning it to gold. Feeling an ache in his throat he wrapped his fist in her hair and tilted her head back so her gaze met his. "He was like a brother to me."

"He's dead, then."

He closed his eyes briefly. "There was no bloody reason for it. But I caused his death, Edie, and his ghost rides my soul every day of my life."

His gaze drifted to the fire. "Kyle," he said, and laughed shortly, harshly. "Just the sound of the name makes a person feel like he wants to dance. That was Kyle—full of life, so fucking—" He caught himself, his fist clenched in her hair. "So alive, Edie, like you. I met him on the streets, chasing a girl, for crissake, when we were ten years old. He liked her red pigtails, and she was screaming for her mama."

"Hmm, sounds like you two had a lot in common, right from the start."

He laughed again, his hand unclenching to stroke her hair, running up and down her bare back in an idle caress. "He and Liam and I were a trio—vowed forever friends. We prowled the back streets, played stickball in the summer, and had snowball fights in the winter. We were hellraisers—fought and stole and conned folks for money and food. But Kyle was the most proficient shyster of all. He was a born politician. He spoke with a silver tongue—had the art of conversation and argument down to an art.

"He was big and blond and green-eyed—his eyes were greener than Liam's. He grew up faster than both of us, though he was almost a year younger than me. He lived with his older brother in a tenement, but his brother was hardly ever there—and they shared the flat with a half dozen others. Kyle stayed with us on the streets more than he went to the flat. His brother drank and he'd hit Kyle if he didn't come home with food or money."

Shane's jaw tightened, then relaxed. "Kyle didn't let it bother him too much. Said it toughened him up, and he was able to take punches better on the streets."

He was quiet for a moment, staring into the fire, his hand resting on the small of Eden's back. "He went to the coal mines in Pennsylvania with Liam and me, worked in that black pit for two years before we couldn't take it anymore. It was so black, the sun hurt our eyes when we came out, and the dust was so bad, we'd be coughing as we worked. It was hell, and we suffered a cave-in, lost a lot of friends, some younger than us."

Eden caressed his cheek. "You saw too much death for a young boy."

He tightened his arms around her and inhaled the fragrance of her hair, sun- and flower-scented, tinged with the faint odor of woodsmoke. She was lithe and beautiful, and so vibrantly alive. And he was talking with her as he never had with any other woman—as a friend.

"Yes," he said, and kissed the curve of her shoulder. He wanted to run his hands over her, pull the soft bearskin off her lovely body and touch her everywhere, but he was remembering the past and the friend he had thought of as his younger brother. The brother he had failed to protect.

He went on, his voice sounding hoarse in the warm, snug room. "We came back to the city, and that was when I lost Meggie. After that, well, something changed and we became tougher, fought more, until Kyle and I were lured by school. We attended when we could, but we had to work to live." He laughed suddenly. "Kyle seduced the teacher."

"What?"

"It's true. She wasn't much older than he was, but she fell for him, and that was the end of that. Oh, he was a natural seducer, he was, of both women and men, though in a different way, of course. He told Liam and me he was going to buy a saloon with his prizefighting money and his smooth talk—and then become the first Irish mayor of New York. If he had lived, no doubt, he would have."

"What happened?"

His jaw clenched. "I met a woman."

He felt her tense in his arms, and automatically held her closer to him. "She was older than me by a few years—I was eighteen. Her name was Alexandra Whitney. She was of English descent." When Eden moved in his arms to protest, he stilled her. "I don't judge by that so much anymore, but it does seem they have a bone to pick with the Irish, and we have every right to feel the way we do toward the Brits."

"Ah, so you do admit some prejudice," she said, and grinned up at him. "So it's a good thing I'm half Norwegian."

He laughed and hugged her. As she snuggled against him again, he continued. "Her father was a high-ranking politician. I was to learn just how much influence he had later. Kyle and Liam and I were living in an old abandoned shack by the piers, and we raised hell that summer. Kyle came home one afternoon, having learned of some guns coming into the city illegally and being shipped to England to use against Ireland. Being an idealistic type, Kyle wanted make his contribution to the city and thwart the operation. It wasn't the first time he'd tried something like this—we had a gang, always ready for any ction. Well, Liam and I agreed to it, but I found out e day we were supposed to sabotage the shipment at the operation was run by Alexandra's father. I und out through her. One of our gang had been ught spying on the loaders down at the docks, and e spilled his guts to her father, the boss. Her father, e told me, was going to find every last one of the ng and have them arrested. But that's not what he d.

"The gang member Randall Whitney had caught ld him some names—one of them was Kyle. Alexdra told me that much, but she did nothing to op her father. I went home and tried to warn Kyle at Whitney knew, that we should call off the bust, ut Kyle wasn't there. Liam and I couldn't find him ntil dark, and he was down at the docks with the ther gang members. Just as we called out to him to et the hell out, that Randall was going to have him rested, Randall's hired thugs opened fire. He must ave taken half a dozen bullets, and as he went own, he looked at me like I had turned him in. As —"

Shane broke off, laying an arm over his eyes as he emembered. Kyle, arms spread wide in a grotesque, ozen pose, jerking as the bullets kept hitting him, d himself yelling, "Nooo!" His cry had seemed to ll out over the harbor, but Kyle never heard him. e would never hear him again.

He felt Eden's hands on his chest, felt her soothg touch. But it was still hard to swallow, even arder to talk.

"Bullets were spraying the dirt around me as I nelt over Kyle. His hair was blood-soaked, and I

heard Liam screaming at me to get out of ther
move, they were going to kill me too. The fun
thing was, at the time, I didn't much care if they di
But somehow he got me to my feet. I was staring
the others—some were dead—our gang, runnin
some hurt bad, then I took a bullet in the thigh.
went down.

"Two thugs were on me instantly, and one did t
damage you see tonight. He wanted to kill me. H
left me there bleeding, my guts spilled on the stree
Cops were coming from somewhere—one of t
loaders had summoned them—and everyone w
running except Liam, leaning over me and Kyl
sobbing, for crissake. I was fading, and the last thi
I remember was Liam's crying.

"Later, in the hospital, she came to see me. Sl
pretended to cry, to act like she felt bad about t
whole incident, but I knew she'd done nothing
stop it. She might have even known that her fath
hadn't intended to arrest us, but kill us. I told her
get the hell out, I never wanted to see her again, ar
that's when she called me an uppity mick who didr
know his own place."

He stopped, lowering his arm from his eyes ar
staring up at the wood-beamed ceiling. The roo
was silent except for the occasional spurt and hiss
the fire.

Eden laid her cheek on his chest. "I'm so sorry
she whispered with a heavy ache in her voice, "th
you ever had to go through that." Tears leaked fro
her eyes, wetting his skin. "I love you, Shane."

He stiffened, but then he clasped her tighter
him and rubbed his jaw against her temple. "Yc
shouldn't tell me that, Edie. I'm not an easy man
love."

She lifted her head rebelliously, her eyes flashir

ith fire and love. "Are you going to tell me not to
ove you? You cannot control my emotions, Shane
)'Connor! When are you going to learn that?"

His grin was wry. "Now, I guess."

"Damn right!" And she dissolved into tears again,
eeping against his chest.

"Edie, Edie," he crooned, rubbing the back of her
ead with his hand, "why are you crying, darling?"

"Because of your life! What a miserable existence
or a little boy! And then, oh, Lord, you almost died,
ke that—and your friend, like a brother . . . oh,
ow I would have liked to have met him."

She sat up abruptly, and Shane caught his breath.
Ier hair spilled over her beautiful shoulders and
reasts. She was like a golden princess, both furious
nd heartbroken at once, and he had never felt such
nguish in his chest. He knew then that life without
er would be vast, impenetrable emptiness.

"Edie, come down here, darlin'. We can't change
he past."

She covered her face with her hands, weeping
gain, and it shook him that the tears were for *him.*
God! He reached for her, his fingers touching her
vrist. "Edie," he said hoarsely. "Don't cry."

She lowered her hands and faced him, her eyes
ortured, drenched with tears. "I know you don't
ke me to cry, but I'm not *her,* Shane, and I can't
elp it. I think of you getting off that ship with a
aby in your arms, only to lose her years later. And
ll the heartache you've suffered, the friends you lost
—and that woman—" She broke off, her eyes
blaze. "Where is the witch now? I'll make her wish
he'd never known you! I'll—"

Shane cut her off with a laugh. "Edie, so fierce! I
lidn't know you could be so bloodthirsty."

She burst into tears again, and he pulled her down

to him, feeling a strange jerk in his chest as her sob racked her slender body. "Hush, angel, you're making yourself ill. Shh, Edie, don't. You're tearing m up inside." She didn't seem to hear him, so he said "I killed her."

She jerked her head up, and he grinned. "I had t say something to make you stop."

She sighed and lowered her head again, her chee rubbing his chest. "You are a very easy man to lov And I will love you whether you like it or not."

Oh, Edie, Edie, how am I going to leave you? Th thought tore at him. "Your life wasn't all that speci either, Eden."

Surprised at his observation, she came up on he elbow to stare at him. "What do you mean? I had lovely life on the—"

"Ranch with your grandfather," he finished fo her. "And with a brother who left you to come t the city long before you wanted him to go."

He saw her lashes lower and knew he'd hit nerve. When she opened her mouth to protest, h continued, almost harshly. "And what about you mother? What kind of mother was she, for crissake absent all your life?"

"Not—"

"Not when you came to New York to see them. know. Did she ever, since you were transplanted a the age of five, come to see you?"

"Why, I—"

"No, of course not." He went on ruthlessly, forc ing her to take a hard look at herself and what she' thought was the perfect life. "Because she was selfis and self-centered, and was relieved to unload yo two burdens on Rake."

She stared at him, then stiffened her spine, he expression indignant. "Well, sir, if you would be s

nd as to *allow* me to respond to the questions you
ready answered for yourself—" She paused,
arching for a scrap of fabric to wipe her nose on,
d it was enough time for him to wind up again.

"And then she marries you off to a man old
ough to be your grandfather."

"Not quite. And will you let me speak?"

He lifted a brow at her.

She drew in a deep breath. "Wilbur was—"

"I know," he drawled, "a good man."

"Shane!"

He grinned impudently at her.

"You're wrong on all counts."

He drew his fingers across her cheek. "Am I?" At
r nod, his gaze turned tender. "Edie, why don't
u just admit that you felt like an orphan too?"

Stricken, Eden sprang to her feet. "I had Rake!"
e cried. "He did not abandon me."

"No, but your mother did."

"Mama's sickly. Ask Philip." But her voice broke.
h, yes, she had longed for her mama as a little girl,
d missed her terribly. Especially after Papa had
ed. She had lain awake nights, listening to the
ickets chirp and aching for her papa. Big, blond
apa. "He used to swing me up in his arms, and I'd
ream, scream, scream with laughter."

"Who, Edie?"

She glanced down, almost surprised to see Shane.
Papa." She lowered herself to her knees, then lay
own on her back, her head pillowed on Shane's
oulder. And she began to talk, about her father,
r mother, the love in the house before he had
ed. She fell asleep eventually and woke in the mid-
le of the night to the hoot of an owl and Shane's
ft breathing.

She studied him, his hard profile, the line of his

sensual mouth, the thickness of his lashes. To watc
him sleep was a gift. To smell him, feel his warr
body, and to have learned the secrets that ha
haunted him made her feel a protective rush of eme
tion, and she wondered how she had ever bee
happy before this man had come into her life. Lov
welled inside her, gripping her heart.

"Shane, Shane," she whispered, desolate at th
thought of their parting. He hadn't even responde
to her telling him she loved him. She hadn't ex
pected him to, not really, but the confession wa
between them now, open and raw, like a wound tha
might never heal.

She closed her eyes, trembling as she swallowe
her pain. She ran her hand over his chest an
thought of his forceful magnetism, his beauty. Ol
she loved him! She turned her lips to his skin an
touched him with feather-light, tender kisses. Sh
hugged him, stirring him awake, and he was in
stantly alert, his expression intense. As he realize
his surroundings, his gaze softened on her and h
mouth curled in a slow smile.

"Darlin'," he said, his voice raspy from sleep.

Lazily he ran the backs of his fingers down he
cheek. She smiled back at him and leaned close:
laying her palm flat above his navel and feeling hi
breath quicken.

"Who's Lombard?" she asked mischievously.

His eyes narrowed, and his voice went razor
sharp. "What?"

She lay on top of him, fitting her softness to hi
hardness. Resting her forearms on his chest, sh
gazed laughingly at him. "You talk in your sleep."

"Like hell."

"No, honestly, you do! Where else would I con

ıre up the name—and why have you reacted so
ırongly to it?"

"Damn," he muttered, and looked furious with
imself. "What else did you hear?"

"Oh, that this Lombard fellow has something to
ɔ with stocks and bonds, and that—"

He swore, and she laughed.

"It's not funny, Eden." His eyes had gone hard,
is tone serious. "I've never allowed myself to sleep
ʋith a woman. I have *never* stayed the night in a
ʋoman's bed since I became a detective. Do you
ınderstand what I'm saying?"

Her brows snapped together in an impatient
ɾown. "Of course I understand, Shane. I'm not a
ınny." Still, she had trouble quelling her smile.
How long have you had this talking-in-your-sleep
ɾoblem?"

He didn't answer.

"You know," she said, leaning closer to him and
ɔoking straight into his eyes, "that is a truly fine
ɾick you have developed."

He frowned. "What the hell do you mean?"

"That trick you do with your eyes." She put her
ace up close to his so that he had to drop his gaze
lightly to meet hers. "It's quite a wonderful trick for
detective to have acquired. The way you're able to
ɔwer your eyelashes to hide whatever might show in
our eyes."

He looked disgusted. "Eden, what the hell are
ou talking about?"

She flashed him a dimpled smile. "Oh, I suppose
t's become second nature to you now. But, in the
ɔeginning, when you became a detective, you must
ıave realized that anyone—especially a woman—
ould read what you were thinking just by looking

into your eyes. They are most revealing, you know. Truly, Shane, your eyes do reflect your soul."

His lashes dropped.

She laughed with delight. "See?"

"I *don't* see," he growled just before he pulled her down to him and thrust his tongue into her mouth, filling it with lusty, dancing strokes. She moaned, making his body tighten and throb, and when he tore his hot mouth from hers, they were both breathing raggedly. "You're too damn smart for your own good, you know that?"

"How can someone be *too* smart," she murmured, moving her hips sinuously against his.

"I want you," he said thickly.

She smiled, a sultry smile. "I want to wait."

His loins were pounding. She looked like a golden tigress, hungry, yet teasing her mate. "Why?" he got out. His hands cupped her bottom and pulled her firmly against his hardness.

"Because," she answered, her voice low, "sometimes it's just more . . . suspenseful if we have to wait."

"What a lot you've learned," he said almost wonderingly. "But you've got to get off me, sugar, if you want to wait. Because looking at you, feeling you— don't have that kind of restraint—"

Eden made a small, agonized sound as she slipped off his body and lay next to him, her heart sounding like the roar of rapids in her ears. She closed her eyes to still the wild, throbbing hunger that tore through her body and blood. Waiting, she knew, would only intensify their pleasure, and she was savoring her power, the yearning.

"Tell me," she said, her voice strained, "how you became an investigator."

"After Kyle died," Shane said, "it took me some me to heal. I was in the hospital for a long time, nen Liam got me out. He'd rented a cheap flat over n the West Side, and he—he took care of me." He wallowed, remembering the humiliation, the pain of eing so weak and dependent on his good friend. While I was healing, Liam was training to become a op. I called him a damn traitor, but he said he was oing it to get Alexandra and her father." He ughed shortly, sardonically. "I told him that was ny privilege, but Liam went on about his business. Ie was bigger than me, and stronger now that I'd een hurt, and all I could do was work on increasing ny strength. When I did, I left Liam's and was even vilder than before. Pretty soon I was jailed for mur- er."

She jerked her head around to look at him. "But ou weren't guilty."

He turned toward her. "Edie, why is it you always ive me the benefit of the doubt? If you could have een me then—a hard-ass bastard, leader of a gang nvolved in all sorts of unsavory dealings, merciless, itiless—I doubt it would have even crossed your nind that I was innocent."

She rose on one elbow, gazing earnestly at him. But you were innocent, weren't you, Shane? I *know* ou wouldn't kill unless in self-defense."

"Don't be so sure, darlin'," he said flatly.

"You haven't," she exclaimed. "I refuse to believe t! Of course, your profession calls for that sort of hing on occasion, but you're not a murderer, Shane, ou just aren't."

He reached out and took a strand of her hair be- ween his fingers. "So certain," he said softly. "No, weetheart, I didn't kill the man. But I was going to

prison for it, until Liam used his influence and se
me Johnny McKay." He chuckled.

"Who was Johnny McKay?"

"Chief of police. He straightened me out b
good. We made a deal. He wouldn't send me
prison if I worked for him—on the streets—as
detective. At first the notion repelled me, then Lia
reminded me how prison would repel me more, an
I could see the logic. Besides," he went on, his voic
growing quiet, "I'd been looking for Meggie a
those years, searching for any clues, and this ju
honed my skills."

"And you've become the most famous detective i
the country," Eden added, liking the end of th
story.

He smiled at her. "Now, come over here," h
said, and hooked an arm around her waist, pullin
her down on the bearskin rug.

"Mmm," she murmured, sinking into the war
fur. She arched as he put his hands on her, liftin
her so that her breasts met his mouth. She made
tormented sound in her throat as he tugged at on
nipple, his hand sliding to the curls between he
legs. He slipped one finger inside her silky wet hea
and they both shuddered and moaned. She coul
feel her thick, sweet honey moist on his fingers, mak
ing her open and ready and wanting him.

"Shane, Shane," she whispered.

"Turn over," he said hoarsely.

"What?" She was dazed, staring into his torri
eyes. But he was urging her over himself, so that sh
lay on her stomach.

"Christ, Edie, you're beautiful."

The dying fire bathed her body in glowing gol
and Shane's gaze ran over her curves, the sweep c

her shapely back, her firm, rounded buttocks, the long, graceful legs. He groaned and bent to kiss her, starting at her feet and moving up to her shoulders, then, slowly back down again, stopping to linger on all her acutely sensitive points—the sides of her full, flattened breasts, the curve of her spine, down low in the small of her back, and in the cleft of her full, firm buttocks. He pushed the soft mounds aside with his hands and slid lower, between her thighs, his tongue finding her petal-soft folds. She bucked under him, and he pressed her down as his tongue searched, found, stroked her.

"Shane!"

Her body was silken and wet and languid, yet taut and hammering with mindless need. Erotically stimulated, all she could do was moan under his decadent touch, his probing tongue. He was touching her in ways she'd never dreamed, never even thought possible, and now there was no thinking at all. Pressure built in her, hot and unbearably sweet. She shuddered, drowning from want. Wanting him, full and hard, inside her.

"Oh, please," she moaned.

Shane was wild with need. It was a raging force in his loins, and his blood was hot with the lust. He pulled her up on all fours, and, reflexively, she pressed her bottom against his erection. He braced her with his hands and eased into the dark-sweet heat of her. Her cry and the indescribable ecstasy of their joining nearly sent him over the edge, but he waited for her, his hard, full thrusts against her bringing her to quick release. He could feel her sweet pulsations tugging at him as he drove into her again and again with a force that made him mindless with need. He took her down onto the fur, hearing her soft love words that blasted the shadows from his mind and soul. A wild thrill surged through him as he poured himself into her with savage, shuddering release.

But with the thrill, Shane felt an agony too.

CHAPTER
NINETEEN

THEY SLEPT WELL INTO THAT NEXT · DAY, WHICH
turned out cold and damp, with rain rushing down
in sporadic bursts. The fire had died low, and they
lay entwined on the bearskin, gray light seeping in
from the slatted shutters. They made love slowly
when they woke, exquisitely, as if it would be their
last time. Afterward Shane held her in his arms, and
they stared into the dying embers. There were few
words between them, as if enough—too much perhaps—had been said already.

Unable to shake the despondency that weighed in
her heart, Eden rose at midafternoon and fried some
sausage and hotcakes. It was cold, and she had put

on only her flannel shirt, so she huddled near the stove. Shane came up behind her and slid his hand up under her shirt to her breast and cupped it, making her sigh and lean back into him.

"I never thought an old shirt could incite me to animal lust," he murmured, holding her now with his hands on both her breasts, his thumbs circling her stiff nipples.

She made a purring sound and let her head drop back against his shoulder, her eyes half closed. "Heaven," she murmured. "I'm tempted to stay here forever." She could have bitten her tongue as soon as she said the words, for she felt him tense behind her, then he stepped away from her.

"I'll go get some wood," he said, and was out the door before she could protest.

Well, he had warned her and she had known when she first had lain down with him that he would leave her in the end. Her eyes had no business filling up with tears, and she had no reason whatsoever feeling the awful crushing pain in her chest. As she went to pull on her trousers and boots, she thought of all they had shared in the night—not only their bodies, but words, private thoughts, secret longings, past hurts. He had trusted her, for a time, but she knew he was regretting even that and was becoming once again, closed and detached.

She was setting the table when he came back in with an armload of wood. His hair was wind-tousled, his cheeks ruddy from the cold, and raindrops dampened his clothes. Even if he did have regrets, she thought, he would never be able to take back what they had shared. She loved him, would always love him; there would never be another man for her. She knew that as he stood watching her with those probing silver eyes that would forever haunt her soul.

Rain and cold wind swirled in from the open doorway behind him. She heard the haunting cry of a loon and shivered. He noticed and kicked the door shut.

"Breakfast—dinner—supper is ready," she said.

He smiled slightly. "Sure. Let me get this fire built."

They were introspective throughout the meal. No easy conversation, no caresses. It was time to go. Even as she thought it, Eden's heart twisted with real pain. She set down her fork and said with typical bluntness, "If I carry your child, I will raise it on Rake's ranch. Texas is a wonderful place to raise a child, whether it be a boy or—"

"If I have gotten you with child," he said fiercely, "you will inform me immediately. I want to know about that baby *before* it's born and you start raising it."

Eden went white. "You will not take that baby away from me." She felt as fiercely protective as a lioness of its cub.

"It will not be raised an orphan."

"Excuse me? If *I'm* raising it, the child will not be raised an orphan."

He drew in a deep breath and ran his hands through his hair. He seemed to be trying to relax, but his eyes were still hard. "Edie, if you are carrying my child, please do not put it in an orphanage."

"I just told you I would not, sir."

"You're an actress. You travel. A child would be a burden. And when you travel, I'm sure you wouldn't want to take the child along, and Rake is an old man. You could tire of the responsibility. Please, contact me first."

She leapt to her feet and glared at him. "How little you think of me, even now, Shane O'Connor! As if I would put a child of mine in a home!" She swept the plates off the table and carried them to the counter. He didn't want her in his life, but how quickly he would claim his son or daughter—like a prize of war! Stubborn fool! Arrogant male! With her back toward him she drew in a deep, steadying breath and said with wavering calm, "You are not going to take my child from me."

"It would be mine too!"

She turned to scowl at him. "Shane O'Connor, this subject may very well be moot. Chances are I am *not* carrying your child, and if I *were,* I have the advantage of hands on first! And—and maybe I *won't* go to Rake's. Maybe I'll find a flat in London, or France, or maybe I'll just be a traveling Gypsy and raise our child the same. If that were the case, it might be hard to find us, don't you think?"

She had gone too far with the last, she knew. Shane's face went rock-hard, his eyes turned to ice, but she stood her ground. Slowly, Shane unfolded his tall body from his chair and strode toward her, his boot heels scraping the rough-planked floor. He stopped inches in front of her.

"I am a detective, remember? I will hunt you down to every corner of the earth, and when I find you I—"

"Stop." She put her hands on his chest. "Let's not argue about it, Shane. I love—"

His mouth crushed hers. Shane felt a keen ache, the pain so sharp he was losing his breath. He took her face in his hands and tempered the kiss, his tongue stroking the warm velvet of hers. He could never take too much from her, for she always had so much to give. He should say something cruel, he knew, to end it, but he couldn't even think the words, never mind speak them.

He dragged his mouth from hers and pressed his lips to the curve of her neck. She gasped, falling against him, and he fought the tenderness inside himself that beat for her. They were wrong for each other, and he should never have touched her. He was hard and cynical, and she was life and love and magical enchantment. Yet, selfishly, he wanted to keep her in his life—but how, and as what? Certainly not as his mistress. She wouldn't have it. And that arrangement would drive him mad within a week. He would want her with him always. She was his obsession, stamped into his soul, his blood. It was time to part company.

When he lifted his head to stare down into her eyes, he saw that she knew it too. *Ah, Edie,* he thought, *we don't need words. We can see everything in each other's eyes.*

"I'll do the dishes," she said quietly. "Why don't you pack?"

He put his forefinger under her chin, tilting her face toward the light, and kissed her softly once more.

"Your name suits you perfectly, you know. Garden of Eden. Full of irresistible temptations."

"I love you, Shane. I know you don't like me to say it, but you can't stop me."

He said nothing, just brushed his thumb over her cheekbone and walked into the other room.

Eden washed the dishes and sometime later wandered into the main room to join him. He wasn't packing, but was scribbling on a pad.

"Are you writing?" she asked him eagerly.

He glanced up, looking distracted, as if he'd forgotten she was in the cabin with him. He nodded then bent his head to write some more.

"I find it interesting you are left-handed."

He did not respond, just kept his head lowered over his work. She understood that. When she was working on a play, nothing and no one existed except for her story and the characters in it. But she was curious.

"What are you writing?"

He looked up again. "Character description."

She edged closer to him. "Oh? Male or female?"

He compressed his lips, obviously impatient. "Female. It's about you, Edie."

Startled, she touched her fingers to her throat. "Me?"

"You, darlin'. I don't want to forget some"—a faint smile touched his mouth—"some—certain attributes about you. I want to use them in my story."

She felt something dance inside her. "Well, that's very flattering."

"You might not think so if you read it."

She drew herself up straight, frowning. "Shane O'Connor, what are you writing about me?"

"Ah," he teased, laughing softly, "that's a writer's privilege, to keep everything under wraps until the end."

"That's not fair!"

He laughed. "Of course it is. And you as a writer know it. Ah." He scribbled something else on the tablet. "I forgot to include your enormous storehouse of vanity—though I don't see how I could, it being such a vital part of your personality."

More than ever, Eden wanted to get a look at that tablet. She sidled toward him, but he tensed and was off the chair as fast and deadly as a fired bullet.

"Shane—"

His quick gesture silenced her, and in three strides he was at the front door. He flung it open and disappeared into the storm outside. How could he have heard *anything* over the wind and rain? she wondered, her heart pounding as she stood frozen in the center of the room. She didn't know whether to tear after him or stay put, but she didn't have the chance to decide. Less than a minute later Shane reappeared, his gun in one hand, her brother in the other. Shane had him by the collar, and he shoved Philip across the room, where he landed on the sofa.

"Egad, man! Loosen up, would you?" Philip cried, drenched and visibly shaken. He clutched his valise to his side.

Shane kicked the door, and it slammed, shutting out the wind and its fury. It was nothing, however, compared to Shane's black mood. He advanced toward Philip, his gun by his side, his other hand curled into a fist as if he might need it to land a punch.

"I knew," he said through his teeth as he came closer, his shadow making a hideous, dancing pattern on the wall, "that there was something I didn't like about you."

"Shane!" Eden exclaimed, then shrank back as he cast her an accusing glare.

"Did you two set this little game up between you? That he would come up here and hold me at gunpoint so you could get your hands on the jewels and take off with them?"

"What?" She was outraged and hurt that he would think that. She flew at him, startling him, and he swore as he dropped the gun.

"Goddammit, Edie!" He grabbed her by both arms and spun her around so that her arms were

pinned behind her back, not hurting, but re-
straining.

"How could you?" she screeched. "How could
you accuse me of such a thing?"

"Calm down," he said, noting that Philip had not
charged for the gun. Perhaps he had made an error
in judgment after all.

"I don't want to calm down!" she raged, squirm-
ing and trying to break free so she could attack him
again.

"What the hell am I supposed to think when a
man is skulking around the cabin! Normally that's a
little odd, don't you think, but given our situation
more dangerous than odd."

"I did not," Philip said haughtily, "want to interrupt a private moment."

Shane sliced his icy gaze at him. "How thoughtful
of you, you thoughtless bastard."

Eden broke free and spun to glare at him. "Apologize this instant—to both of us!"

"Like hell."

She glanced at the gun, but he was upon it before
she could move. He stuffed it into his waistband, his
narrowed eyes warning her. "Honey, you *ever* think
of pointing a gun at me, it would be the worst mistake of your life."

She could not believe he was talking to her like
that, could not believe she had actually considered
lunging for the gun, though she knew she would
never use it on him. Nor could she believe her
brother had followed them up there.

"The both of you are incorrigible!" she shouted.
"I'm going to leave you alone so you can fight out
your grievances in your stupid male fashion."

She'd taken only two strides before Shane was
upon her, wrapping his arms around her waist and

auling her backward. "Dammit, Edie, he *is* a self-centered, thoughtless bastard who has endangered your life one too many times—"

"What!" Philip sprang to his feet, his face flushed ed.

"Sit down!" Shane ordered. He pushed Eden down too, gently but forcefully, into an armchair. "Stay!" he barked as she made to rise, and she glared ferociously at him.

"I did not mean to endanger Eden's life in any way," Philip protested, and turned his apologetic gaze on his sister. "Really, Edie, I didn't."

"*I* know that," she said, still scowling up at Shane. He towered over her, looking immense and threatening, his hands planted on his narrow hips, his face tight with impatience and vexation.

"What the hell do you call dodging bullets on piers and outside your own home, and at the fair, for the love of God?"

"Stop shouting, Shane."

"I'm not shouting!"

But he was. Calm, controlled, unruffled Shane O'Connor was shouting once again, thanks to the bewitching and thoroughly exasperating Eden Victoria Lindsay. He shook his head and stared at the floor to collect his thoughts—not an easy project with these two in the room.

And Philip was winding up again. "I tell you, sir, it was never my intention to place Edie in any sort of danger—"

"Then why the hell did you bring the bloody jewels back to the house once you robbed the thieves?"

"I—I didn't think—" Philip started.

"No, for the love of God, you *didn't* think! And are ya thinkin' now, I'm askin'?"

They all looked stunned at his brogue, even Shane

himself. He cursed, and she and Philip exchanged looks.

"Right musical sound, that," Philip said in that same strange way Eden had of sometimes mixing her Texan lingo with her British. Then Philip pulled himself up straight. "*I'm* the one who should be outraged at *you*, O'Connor, for bringing my sister up here like she was some hussy! Why don't you just take an advertisement out in the newspaper, for the love of Pete?"

"The matter did not concern you before," Shane said. "Why are you mentioning it now? Have you even apologized to your sister for your thoughtlessness? She spent her life savings on trying to find you, and I have yet to hear you thank her for it."

Philip looked truly shocked. "Your savings, Edie? On me?"

She cast a chastising look to Shane. "Not nearly half of it, Philip, really. Don't worry your head over it."

"He's not," Shane drawled, and both twins glared at him.

"Philip," Eden asked, "why did you come up here? Is everything all right?"

"Everything is fine. I came up here to get the map from you before I return to London with the—" He stopped and cleared his throat.

"Map?" Eden repeated blankly.

"You know, Edie, the map! It was with the jewels —and it's reputed that Forrest Steele values it more than the jewels, for it leads to other treasures, and that map is the original."

She shook her head. "I don't know what you're talking about, Philip."

He looked stricken. "Surely, Edie, you would not withhold that from me." He turned to Shane. "It's your doing! She would never have withheld it from me in the past."

Shane's brows snapped together. "What the hell—"

"Philip, please, I don't *have* a map."

"It was with the jewels, Eden. A packet of papers tied with a ribbon—"

Eden shot to her feet. "I know! Why, yes, I'd forgotten." She frowned. "But I don't remember where I put the papers."

"Think, Edie, think."

She chewed on her bottom lip. Feeling Shane's stare on her, she offered him a weak smile. "Philip wants to return the jewels to Steele himself, Shane. He thinks he's entitled, since that was his initial intention when he took the jewels from the thieves."

"Oh, he does, does he?" Shane ambled across the room, stopping barely a foot from Philip. "Let me repeat what I think I'm hearing here. You think that because you stole jewels from the thieves, you're entitled to the reward."

"That's right," Philip said. "But I need the map too."

Shane rubbed his grizzled jaw, and the sound of his whiskers rasping against his palm shredded Eden's nerves as his gaze flicked her way. "And what might you think of this plan, darlin'?"

She glanced apprehensively toward her twin, then back to Shane. "Not a *bad* idea," she said. "It makes a good deal of sense that he should collect be-cause—"

The door burst open and she screamed. In flew a wild-haired woman with a gun trained straight on her.

"Drop it, O'Connor!"

Shane had already drawn his gun and cocked the trigger before she hammered out the order.

"Drop it or I shoot her!"

Shane swore through his teeth. The woman's own gun was cocked, and he knew she meant business.

He dropped his gun.

"Now kick it clear across the room. Hands up, all of you!"

Eden and Philip obliged her. Shane didn't. "Goddammit, it's you." It had been hard to tell at first, with the wind swirling into the room and her hair tangled about her face, but now that she'd slammed the door shut, he could see that he knew her.

Ping! She fired a shot that blasted through a ceiling beam.

She grinned wickedly at him. "That's right, it's me."

"Sparrow!" Eden cried, both shocked and horrified that her new friend was wielding a gun. And pointing it straight at her heart.

Sparrow's pale eyes narrowed. "I said, kick the gun, O'Connor."

"Give me a good reason."

"Stop stalling. It won't buy you time. I'm trained to take down men like you in the blink of an eye. Now, kick the bloody gun across the room!"

Eden's blood ran cold. What was the woman talking about—"trained" to take men down? Her gaze went from Sparrow to Shane, and she saw that he was simply staring at the woman.

"Shane," she pleaded softly.

But Philip moved, kicking the gun so hard across the room, it sang as it hit the wall. Shane swore and took a swing at him, connecting with his jaw. Philip sprawled back onto the sofa and pressed his fingers to his cut lip.

"Goddammit, O'Connor, I've taken just about enough from you—"

He struggled to rise, but Sparrow fired another shot.

"Stay where you are," she snapped. She flicked her gun back toward Eden. "Now, you," she said, "and O'Connor, on the floor."

"Like hell," he growled.

"Sparrow," Eden pleaded, "why are you doing this?"

Sparrow laughed cynically. "Oh, cut the games now, princess. I have to admit, you did a fine job to finagle O'Connor in on this deal, but—" She turned her disdainful gaze to Shane. "You should bloody well be ashamed of yourself, mate. You fell head over heels for her and lost all your objectivity."

"You got your facts wrong, lady."

Shane was cursing himself up and down, left and right. Something about this woman had nagged at him from the start. Even now he wasn't quite sure what her game was, but he was intent on finding out. He took a step toward her.

"Don't!" Sparrow kept the gun on Eden.

Shane kept moving forward, tempting fate. "There're three of us," he said, "and one of you, mysterious lady from England." He saw her tense, and thought, *good,* a raw nerve. "And you have no backup."

"Don't come one inch closer, O'Connor, or she's hurt very badly. I've shot folks before."

"Oh, I don't doubt it," he murmured. "But, still, after she's shot, you'll have to deal with me."

The gun went off. The bullet whistled past him, actually skimming his shirt-sleeve, and lodged in the windowpane behind him. He froze, then inclined his head slightly. "Either you're a very good shot, or a very poor one."

"It was a warning. Next one finds your heart."

"Impressive words."

"Accurate ones too."

"Shane, please," Eden begged, "do what she says."

But Sparrow surprised them all. "I'm from Scotland Yard."

Shane stopped. Eden gasped. Philip went pale.

"You?" Shane said.

"Yes, me, O'Connor, you bloody traitor. Did you think I was stupid? The Yard did not inform you who I was because I told them I had my doubts about all of you. Normally, you're a fine detective, but this time, as I said, you had a slight distraction. I knew, though, that you can sniff a tail a thousand miles away, so I didn't bother following you. I knew where you were. It was him." She jerked her head at Philip. "I knew he could help me unravel your whole sordid little scheme. He's a greedy bloke—wants the map too."

"He is not greedy!" Eden exclaimed. "Philip is returning the jewels to Forrest Steele."

"Ah, is that what your story is? Well, it's a good one, I'll give you that. But I don't think Simon Peterson will agree."

Shane tensed. "What about Simon?"

"Quit the innocent act, O'Connor. You bought into this deal, didn't you? You know damn well golden boy over there tied up your good friend and made off with the jewels."

"What?"

Shane spun on his heel to face Philip, who looked as if he had a terrible stomachache. "You did *what?*"

Philip sank back against the sofa. "I told you I was going to return the jewels. The old man was not . . . er, exactly cooperative. I asked him nicely at first to give them to me." He cringed at Shane's lurid, hissing curses. "My God, man, I didn't tie him tightly. And if he hadn't hesitated—"

"Why, you—" Shane was upon him, his hands closing around Philip's throat, mindless of Eden's screams. Only another gunshot snapped him from his fury.

"Dammit!" Sparrow shouted. "I will *not* waste another bullet! Now, all of you, shut up!"

Shane spun to face her. "Drop the goddamn gun."

"I want you on the floor."

"And that's one place you aren't going to get me."

Sparrow did not answer. She strode quickly across the room to the sofa and opened Philip's valise. Upending it, she dumped its contents onto the bearskin rug. Philip groaned as the jewels spilled out, brilliant, endlessly faceted. Shane cursed, watching Sparrow as she scooped the diamond up and held it toward the firelight. When the fiery brilliance struck her, he sucked in his breath.

"Meggie," he said hoarsely.

Sparrow stiffened as if speared in the back. She looked at Shane as he caught her chin in one hand, turning her face to the light. He could see the beat of her pulse in her throat, fast and frightened as a rabbit's.

She yanked away from him. "No!" she shouted, backing away as if she'd seen a ghost. "What game is this you play, O'Connor?"

He shook his head. "Meggie," he said again, pained by her cry of protest. "It's you, it's you. I don't know how it's you . . ."

She continued backing away from him as if he were demented. "What do you want with me, O'Connor?"

She was terrified, he realized, absolutely terrified. It infuriated him and baffled him at the same time. His little sister. There was no mistaking those eyes, and he wondered why he hadn't seen it before. Of course, he hadn't really been looking at her before, but now, *now* . . .

"Meggie—" He reached for her, and she stumbled back against the sofa.

"Get away from me! What do you want? Who *are* you?"

He swallowed against the ache that rose in his throat. He'd held this woman in his arms more than twenty years ago, made sure the nuns found a wet nurse for her, had even fed her himself—and here she was, her eyes hard with hatred, so scared, so defiant. "I'm your brother."

She looked stricken, then her eyes narrowed with hate. "I don't have a brother."

Shane felt a clamp around his heart. He reached for her, but she darted away from him. "Yes, yes, Meggie, you do."

"Stop calling me that!" she shrieked. "I'm not Meggie! I'm Sparrow, and I have no brothers, no sisters—no bloody family you son of a—"

"Is that what they told you?" He spoke softly, as if he were gentling a frightened filly. "How else would I know your name?"

"You're a detective," she snapped.

"That I am. And it's been a curse, in its way, for after all my investigations, I've never been able to find you."

"Ha!" she laughed, the sound snide. "Some detective."

"You take that back!" Eden said suddenly. She glared at Meggie. "You take those words back. He is the finest detective around, and he looked for you for years. The orphanage destroyed all the documents pertaining to you."

Meggie only sneered. "He should've looked overseas. I'm a Brit, he's a mick, and that's an obvious fact none of us can close our eyes to."

"You were *raised* as a Brit," Shane said. "And if you call me a mick again, so help me God, I'll wash your mouth out with soap."

"Spoken like a true brother," she said scathingly.

He let out an exasperated breath. "Why would I lie about this? What's in it for me? Why would I invent some ridiculous story about having a sister if I didn't?"

The questions gave her pause. She stared at him, the firelight throwing strange flickering flames into her eyes. "Impossible," she whispered. "They told me—" She stopped, pushing an errant curl off her forehead, only to have it spring forward immediately.

"What did they tell you?" he asked softly.

She looked away from him into the fire. Her long, slender fingers touched her throat. "They told me my family had died."

"Most of them did," Shane said. "Our parents and brothers and sisters. You were the youngest and I was the second oldest. And we are the only ones who survived. I have a photograph of the two of us at home in my study."

"Oh, yes!" Eden said. She walked over to Meggie, took her hands, and pulled her into the light. Meggie stood under their scrutiny, seeming numbed and dazed. "And you resemble each other. You do! Philip, don't you see the similarity between them?"

"It's there for certain," he said.

"Both of you have such light, striking eyes, as if they can see right through a person." Eden laughed. "And that! The way you both shield your gazes with your lashes when you don't want anyone to read what's in your eyes. And curls! You both have glorious curls."

Shane made a disgusted face and ran his hand through his hair.

"And these blond strands," Eden continued, lifting a hank of Meggie's hair off her shoulder. "Shane's are dark gold, yours are lighter, but it's another sign you are related."

Meggie snorted. "That means nothing."

"You were blond once, Meggie," Shane said, and saw her stiffen, alarmed that he knew even that about her.

"And you both have a bump on your nose, in the exact same spot!" Eden said.

Both shot her a withering look and drawled, "Thanks, Eden."

Startled by their same reaction, they stared at each other as if they were children seeing their reflection in a mirror for the first time.

"And you have a faint strawberry birthmark on the back of your left shoulder," Shane said.

Meggie was obviously shocked. She wrapped her arms around her stomach as if to shelter herself from pain and slowly, with her back to the wall, she slid to the floor. She stared in numbed disbelief at the fire, seemingly oblivious of those in the room.

Shane walked over to her, kneeling before her. "Meggie." He touched her face, but she flinched.

"Leave me alone," she muttered, and dropped her forehead to her drawn-up knees.

He stared at her bent head, his throat locking up.

"Meggie, what's happened to you? Who took you away?"

He had never thought to look overseas—and the very last place he'd think the nuns would allow her to be carried off to was England. Or maybe they hadn't known at all. He swallowed thickly, studying the crown of her head, the errant curls and sparkling blond strands weaving through the rich dark mass. He wished he had the photograph of them with him. He wished he could show her. Who was she? What was she like? Other than feisty. Scotland Yard! What kind of woman had she become? Odd, that they had both become involved with the law . . . and maybe not so odd after all.

He wanted to know everything about her, her adoptive family, her upbringing, the schools she had attended. Surely she had been raised in wealth. The nuns had told him that, at least. But England! It left a bitter taste in his mouth, a taste hard to swallow.

He tried to see all this through her eyes—to understand her fear and shock, and rejection. It was hard for him, though, because he wanted, so badly, to hold her.

He took one of her hands in his despite her attempt to yank it away. She brought her head up sharply, and he felt a sharp twist in his gut. It was like looking into his own eyes, only with a greenish tinge. There was pain in them, though, a pain so deep it tore at him. That she had suffered any type of pain hurt him, for he had failed to protect her from it.

"Will you kindly, sir, let go of my hand?"

He almost grinned. In some ways she reminded him of Eden. "Will you kindly, ma'am, come sit on the sofa and talk to me?"

She looked away.

He took a deep breath. "We had three brothers and a sister," he said. "Seamus was the oldest, then me. Padraic was next. Colleen was our sister. And Danny was the youngest. All of them"—he swallowed—"all of them died on our way to America."

Meggie spoke, her voice muffled. "I don't want to hear anything about them. I don't want to know."

"Why not, Meggie?"

Frowning, Meggie looked back at him. His voice was soft and gentle, but his words hurt her. *Because* she wanted to scream, *it doesn't matter now!* How could it matter after what she had lived through? After she had suffered so much? And he, this famous investigator, her *brother*? No, no, no! She fought the moans that choked her throat. She fought the tenderness in her brother's eyes.

"I have to leave," she said.

She saw Shane tense, then he did something so incredible, she was too shocked to react until it was over.

He gathered her in his arms and lifted her. *Her,* wildly independent, highly qualified, perpetual risk taker, the only female and the youngest undercover agent in the Yard, who *never* accepted any kindness from any human being without suspecting an ulterior motive behind it. He carried her to the sofa and set her down.

"I'll put on some tea," Eden said, and was quickly off to the kitchen, her brother following her.

Minutes later, surrounded by her solicitous audience, with a cup of hot tea in her hands and swaddled in a thick quilt, Meggie tolerated their numerous questions.

"Is it true," Eden asked, "that you're an agent for Scotland Yard?"

Meggie smiled. "I am," she admitted. "But

von't talk much about it. I'm an undercover agent, and I wear many disguises."

"But you're such a fine actress!" Eden said. "You know stage directions."

Meggie sipped her tea. "I have some theater experience." She stirred uncomfortably under her brother's keen stare. She would have to be careful of his one, she thought. He didn't miss a trick. And he was sure he was storing bits of information to examine and interrogate her with later. Deftly, she turned the subject to the jewels, fixing her gaze on Philip. "I want to hear your story," she said, then warned, "and tell it to me straight. I can spot a liar at a hundred paces."

Philip explained what had happened to him, finishing with, "And I came up here to ask Edie for the map, but she can't recall where she placed it."

"I have it," Meggie said.

The twins gasped, and she grinned as she set her teacup on the low table in front of her. "That's right. Do you remember that first day we met, Eden?"

"Yes," Eden said slowly. "It was also the first day I had met Shane." Her eyes brightened. "How interesting."

Meggie nodded. "I had just finished another case here in America when I was contacted by the Yard about the jewel theft. The thieves were expected to dock in New York or Boston soon. Another agent was sent to Boston, but they came here. I followed them off the ship—there were six of them at the time, too many for me to handle alone, but they split up. I followed the two with the case. That night they went to the billiard hall, and that's where I first saw your brother—and later saw him steal the jewels. Curious, I followed him, wondering what his role was in all this, but it became convoluted when *he*

was kidnapped. Anyway, I backtracked Philip's con
nections and found you, Eden. I knew you were a
actress, so I arranged to join the troupe."

"How ingenious," Eden said. "I should write
play about this!"

"I already am," Shane said, then grinned at he
which made her blush.

Meggie rolled her eyes. "Anyway," she went or
clearly disgusted by the passionate exchange c
glances, "I searched the carpetbag you brought t
the theater that day and found Steele's papers. I sti
have them."

"That's a relief," Philip breathed.

Everyone turned to stare at him.

"I have the rights to the reward!" he exclaimed
"I stole the jewels from the thieves—took all th
risks—got beaten up for it too!"

They couldn't help but laugh, even Shane.

"I suppose," Meggie said dryly, "you're entitled
You can travel back to London with the Yard au
thorities as soon as they come for the thieves."

Philip relaxed back in his chair, all the tensio
leaving his face. "It'll be nice to pay off the debts.

"Then what are you going to do?" Eden asked.

"I'm going to buy a gaming room in London an
get married."

"Who is she, Philip? You have yet to tell m
about your affianced."

He blushed. "Well, that's because she is not m
affianced yet. But—but she will be!"

Shane shook his head and excused himself, mut
tering something about needing some air.

He went out the back door for a smoke. It ha
stopped raining, and the air was chill and damp. H
rolled a cigarette, then lit it and inhaled deeply. Th
smoke tore at his lungs, and he exhaled slowly, hi

yes narrowing through the smoke. *Meggie,* he thought, a sharp pain cutting him like a knife in his chest. She was as British as the people who had oppressed their race for centuries. She was beautiful, too, in her own odd, quirky way, that funny bump on the bridge of her nose, her thin face expressive, interesting, dominated by her huge, soulful eyes. He sensed there were many layers to her, layers that could take years to uncover, because she sure as hell *was* covering, and the pain in her past could be anything.

His fingers shook as he drew once again on the cigarette. She was in his life now, to be sure. Leaning his head back against the log wall behind him, he stared up at the purple twilight sky and thought of his mother. *Found her, Ma,* he said silently. Or actually, in a strange way, they had found each other.

When he went back inside, the other three were all laughing by the fire. Meggie was still wrapped in the quilt, her eyes darting back and forth from Eden to Philip as they regaled her with tales from their childhood. And Edie . . .

He couldn't remember feeling so much emotion in his life as he did at that moment—his sister and his love in the same room, she so happy to have found her own brother. When she turned her shining eyes on him, his heart filled up with so much love, it hurt.

"Come over here, Shane."

She jumped from her chair to grab his hand and tug him across the room. With her hands on his broad shoulders, she urged him to take a seat, then she plunked down onto his lap. Not that he minded. He had never experienced such open, easy warmth, and there was something acutely satisfying about talking and laughing with people he cared about, even if one of those people would soon be going away.

They talked long into the night, drinking black berry wine. Eden was the first to drop off to sleep and Shane carried her to bed. Philip stretched out on the floor and was soon snoring, but Meggie remained awake, staring into the fire.

"Can I get you more tea?" Shane asked.

She glanced up at him, looking startled, as if she had forgotten his presence. "No, thanks, I'm fine."

"Are you, Meggie?"

He lowered himself into the chair across from her and leaned toward her, his elbows braced on his knees. "I know it's a shock to have learned you've got a brother, mavournin." He laughed softly. "I'm more than shocked to see you too."

Her brow puckered. "What's that word mean?"

"Which word?"

"Mavournin."

A sharp jab of pain lanced Shane's forehead right behind his eyes. He was angry, furious actually, with the nuns, for having robbed her of her own heritage and for the agony he kept glimpsing in Meggie's eyes. But he softened his voice, feeling only tenderness for his little sister. "It's an Irish endearment."

Her lips twisted bitterly. "I was taught to hate the Irish."

"And do you?"

She looked away, pressing her fingers to the bridge of her nose. "I—" Her voice broke. "I can't believe this—that you are my brother—" She swallowed hard and lifted her head, fixing him with those haunting eyes. "I don't even *want* a brother. don't want anyone—"

Her words stabbed at him, but he understood

After shutting yourself off for so many years, it hurt like hell to feel anything again. "I know," he said.

"You know? How can you? You live in that beautiful home, and you have someone in your life that loves you very, very much."

It was his turn to look away. "She is not in my life for long. And I do not want to talk about her."

"And I," Meggie said softly, "do not want to talk about us."

His jaw tensed. "Tell me one thing."

She waited.

"Did the family who adopted you tell you you were adopted?"

"Oh, yes," she said, her voice brittle. That was all she said, though, and her gaze challenged him to question her further.

"Stubborn Irish," he murmured, and stood. "Get some sleep, Meggie. Before dawn I'm going hunting, and after breakfast we'll head back. You've got to put some meat on those bones."

"Spoken like a true brother," she said, but her voice was softer now, and a crooked smile pulled at her lips.

In the morning, though, when he came back with some wild game, Meggie was gone. Eden and Philip were just rising, and there was a note on the chair where Meggie had slept.

I had to go. I cannot get used to the idea of a brother after all these years. I'm sorry if I've disappointed you, but I have a life to live, and I like it that way—always traveling, always busy. I've kept Steele's map and will return it to him myself. The bloke has me curious. As for the jewels, I'm sure you will see that they are properly returned, and that Philip receives his reward. Tell Eden good-bye for me. She was, for a brief time, a good friend.

It was signed, simply, *Meggie.*

Furious, Shane balled up the note and threw it into the fire. "Goddammit," he roared, making Eden and Philip flinch. This time he would find her if it killed him. She was running, and he couldn't let her run anymore. He had to find out what had put that deep sadness in her eyes. It was, after all, a brother's responsibility.

CHAPTER TWENTY

T WAS EASIER THIS WAY, EDEN KNEW. WITH SHANE hut away in his study, dashing off telegrams to Scotand Yard, obsessed in his search for Meggie, it was easier for her to pack and slip away without the pain of a face-to-face departure. He'd made it clear that he hadn't wanted her to stay with him.

That last morning in the Adirondacks they had packed quickly and taken the next train out, but Meggie was long gone, without a trace. Shane had followed up on two leads, but Meggie was an expert at escaping those who trailed her. She'd said in the note she was going to return Steele's map to him, but Steele was no longer in South America *or* London.

Eden packed as soon as they returned to Shane' estate and left on the ferry with her brother. H opened the house up and recalled the servants whil she went to the orphanage to visit Tate and Jessie They were delighted to see her and asked abou Shane. Afterward she went to Mother Superior t see about adopting them and taking them to Texas She felt it was a solid plan, and Mother Superio said she would consider it.

Back home, she began to pack her bags for Texas while Philip got ready to go to London. Every au tumn she returned home so she could spend Christ mas with Rake. Her heart just wasn't into acting and she would have to explain to Franklin that sh would rejoin the troupe the following spring. As sh packed, all she could think of was Shane. He didn' want her anymore, but oh, how she loved him. Ho she would give anything to spend the rest of her lif with him.

That was hopeless, though. She was certain tha he loved her—it showed in his revealing eyes. But h was stubborn, hard-headed. Though she hoped h needed only time to miss her, that he would come t his senses and follow her to Texas, the realist in he mocked her, telling her that Shane had no intentio of coming after her, nor would he ever. The onl way to let go of him was for her to leave.

She had that chance sooner than she might hav expected—and in a much different way. The follow ing morning a telegram came from Uncle Monty i London with an urgent message for her and Philip Mama was doing very poorly, her heart weakening every day, and Monty urged them to seek passage t

England as soon as possible, for he thought that, truly, this time she was dying.

They were able to book passage almost immediately. The shipping agent took pity on their plight and granted them tickets that same day. Later that afternoon, from the deck of the ship as it made its way out to sea, Eden watched the New York shoreline growing more distant. And with it, her bittersweet memories of Shane.

A cold November wind howled outside the house. Shane rubbed his eyes wearily with one hand. Dammit, he thought. Once again Meggie had disappeared off the face of the earth.

"She's one of our best agents, old chap," Meggie's boss at Scotland Yard, Jake Fielding, had informed him when they had met two weeks before. Fielding had been in the States to confer with American agents in Washington. He'd clapped a big hand on Shane's shoulder and added, "Wouldn't take it personally. Ha, we'll be lucky if *we* find her, she's so elusive. She does this from time to time—goes off on her own ventures—and then she's back. I don't know where she goes, except that I know she's been all over the world, and I don't know why she goes, but she does, and no one can stop her. Mysterious Meggie we call her. A free agent. And a damn good one. I'll contact you when she returns."

But Shane did not want to wait. And he did take it personally. The only good thing about Meggie's disappearing act was that searching for her helped him to escape the pain of losing Eden. Every time he thought of her, pain and fury blazed through him like a white-hot knife. She had slipped out like a thief in the night, without even so much as a good-bye. And within two days she had disappeared a immaculately as Meggie. Eden and Philip ha tricked him after all, for they had taken the jewel with them, and he felt like every kind of fool. Whe he'd realized she had left his home, he had gone int the city and stormed her Fifth Avenue home, but th servants were keeping mum about her whereabouts He had threatened them with everything from bein tossed out on their ears to outright murder, but nc one of them had divulged Eden's destination. He' finally realized she probably hadn't told them.

He had considered sending a trace to Texas, bu doubted she would turn up there. He doubted sh would appear anywhere he might expect. In the enc he decided it was best that he didn't know. H wasn't concerned about the jewels—Forrest Steel would get them back; he had the power and th money to do it. And hadn't he wanted this, her ou of his life? Yes. He had been a fool to let her get s close in the first place. He did wonder, bitterly, cyni cally, if this had been her plan all along—to escap with the gems—or if her conniving twin had ar ranged it for her. Either way, he was bloody tired o the whole mess and was glad to wash his hands o her.

Only he couldn't sleep at night, he could hardl eat, and his temper was shot to hell. She pervadec his blood, his sinew, the pit of his belly. Mrs. Leah clucked about his weight loss, about the lines o strain and tension etched into his face, but he couldn't forget her. Eden *was* unforgettable. He lovely features were seared into his brain. Her ow special, evocative scent seemed to linger in the hous —on the staircase, in his study, in her room where he sometimes went to torment himself, imagin them entwined on her bed. She was wild and fre

nd so goddamn passionate. He'd never met a
woman like her, nor would he ever again.

He tried ridding his mind and body of her with
hard physical exercise, pounding up and down the
shore on the back of his most powerful mount. He
threw himself into his detective novel, but the female protagonist was uncannily similar to her. There
seemed to be no respite for him.

When he went for long walks on the beach he
would glance at the huge boulders rising up and
back from the rocky shore and remember her upon
them, diving from them, her body like a flashing
golden arrow as it cleaved the deep dark sea. All he
had to do was close his eyes to picture her racing
along the shore on the chestnut mare she favored,
her golden hair flying like a banner in the wind.
Edie, Edie, he would think, *where the hell are you?*

She'd shown him how to laugh again—magic he'd
lost as a boy, magic she had sprinkled over him like
a fairy angel, so indulgent with her gift. And now she
was gone. Of course, he had made no promises,
could not make promises, and their parting was inevitable, but it was the way she had cut out of his life
that so infuriated him. Sometimes he wondered if all
they had shared at the cabin had been a lie, but his
instincts told him no. No one, not even Edie, could
act so well.

He became more reclusive as the winter wore on.
Mrs. Leahy and Simon fretted, but Shane stayed
locked in his study, writing long into the night. He
took time to visit with Tate and Jessie, even brought
them to the house for Christmas, but they asked him
about Eden and why she had left them, and he
couldn't give them a decent answer. The Mother Superior had mentioned that Eden had requested
adoption consideration, and though it confused him,

Shane had laughed bitterly at that. Besides, where Tate and Jessie were concerned, he had plans of his own.

In January he took them up to Saratoga. The first draft of his novel was finished, and he needed to get away. But he couldn't escape his memories of her that crushed him, like a dead weight on his chest. And as he lay alone night after frozen night in Saratoga, he knew, with a grim, bone-jarring realization that he would never forget his passionate little life lover, Eden.

Mama had died. She had lingered for a few days after Eden and Philip had arrived, but after the first week she slipped away. Though Eden had never felt close to her mother, she did feel as though her last hours with her had been peaceful, and that Mama, in a way, had made peace with her two "irreverent" children.

After her death there were estate matters to settle which only added to their wealth. And, yes, Mama had left a goodly portion of her possessions and bank account to Philip as well as Eden. Philip was especially delighted that his income had increased considerably since he had collected his reward from Scotland Yard. At first Eden was horrified to learn that he had carried the jewels with them overseas, but once she'd realized his intentions were honorable, she'd breathed easier.

All the time she was in England she missed Shane dreadfully, and wondered if he had come to his senses yet and realized that he loved her. He certainly had had enough time to mull it over. She wished he were with her in London. She wished she could feel his strong arms around her at night, and sleep, feeling his warm breath on the back of her neck. To think that he might have already found another woman tore at her. The morning they had left New York, she had given a note to Franklin to bring to Shane so he would know that she had been called home, that Mama was dying, and that she would be in touch with him as soon as she returned.

That was why, one brittle, late-January afternoon, she stood on his front doorstep, swaddled in her coat and hood. After a grueling journey from London during which she'd lost more meals then she'd kept down, she had made her way directly to Shane's estate. She had had no problem gaining entry to the estate, for the guards had recognized her immediately. She pounded on the door with her fur-mittened hand and waited for the butler—what was his name?—to answer the door.

He did, seconds later. And he stiffened visibly when he saw her.

She grinned up at him. "Hello, Livingstone!"

He straightened even more sharply, and she was crestfallen. Wrong name.

"What," he asked loftily, "does madame want?"

Though a stony feeling settled in her chest at his cold tone, she kept the smile on her lips. "Madame," she said, striving for cheerfulness, "wishes to see Mr. O'Connor."

"He's not here."

"Oh. When do you expect him home?"

"He is not *expected,*" came a frosty voice from behind the butler, "for a very long time."

Eden's eyes lit up when she saw Simon. "Simon! How are you?"

Simon lifted his nose. "Mr. O'Connor," he continued as if she hadn't spoken, "is out of the country."

Staring at him in hurt puzzlement, Eden puckered her brow. "And you can't tell me when he might return?"

"If I could, I would not."

Stricken, she swayed on her feet, and had to grab the doorjamb. Why was his reception so chilly? She didn't understand. "Simon—"

"I advise you to get on, Mrs. Lindsay. Mr O'Connor wants nothing to do with you. And to be honest with you, I'm not sure what *you* want with *him.* You've played your little game, got the jewels made off with them, and, frankly, I'm surprised you're not incarcerated. When I shut this door, I will notify the authorities, and let them handle the situation."

"The situation," Eden cried as he began to close the door, "has been handled! Philip returned—" But the door was shut. She glared at it, incensed at Simon's rudeness, then pounded on it with her fist. "Open up! Simon!" She pounded and pounded until one of the guards came forward and took her by the elbow. She squirmed away from him and skidded down the sweeping front steps. Reaching down, she scooped up a fistful of snow, packed it between her hands, and hurled the snowball at the door. It made a muffled thump and dropped, harmless. Before she could pack another, she was escorted to her carriage and off the property.

How could he! How could Simon just lock her out without giving her a chance to explain? she fumed all the way to the city. She had to tell Shane about the baby. At the ferry landing she hired a hack to take her to Franklin's flat. When she arrived she confronted him, fury simmering like a hot coal deep inside her.

"You didn't give Shane the note, did you?" she demanded. "Why didn't you, Franklin?"

"Eden, I couldn't." At her outraged gasp, he took her hands in his, pleading with his eyes. "Eden, please. I couldn't see you throwing your heart away on that man. He—"

"And who assigned you my caretaker? Oh, Franklin, how could you? I thought you were my friend!"

His expression grew fierce. *"Friend?"* He gripped her upper arms, torment and love storming in his eyes. "I *love* you, Eden! I've loved you for the longest time, and you can't even see past your—your *infatuation* with that cold bastard." He stopped at the shock in her eyes and let her go. Walking to the window, he stared outside, his body and face tense.

"Oh, Franklin, I'm sorry." She walked over to him and touched his arm. "Sorry I don't love you. I love Shane. I'll always love Shane, and you, dear Franklin, will always be my friend. I'll be back next spring and we'll—" She cut herself off, knowing she wouldn't be back, at least not so soon.

But Franklin already knew. "Go home, Eden," he said wearily. "Write me if you wish. I'm certain we will connect again sooner or later."

At the door she turned and smiled. "I just want you to know one thing about Shane. He's not a cold bastard. He, too, is a good actor, Franklin."

Her final stop before boarding the train for Texas the next day was at the orphanage to see Jessie and Tate. But they were gone. To Eden's shock, Mother Superior told her that the children had already been adopted.

"By whom?" Eden demanded.

"I am not at liberty to say," Mother Superior said, but her blue eyes were searching and perplexed.

Eden boarded the train with a heavy heart. She

had so wanted to take the children to Texas, she had so hoped to see Shane again. Oh, she knew he was doing his best to ignore her, ignore the fact that he loved her, but she was not going to give up so easily. He just needed a nudge. And they had the little matter of her pregnancy to settle, but she would leave that to the last, after she had persuaded him to come to the ranch. Her traveling days were over for a while, and much as she hated to admit it, she was bone-weary.

Her heart soared when she first saw Rake. He hadn't aged a bit, his thick hair still a shock of snow white, his fiery blue eyes ablaze. Those sharp eyes took in her appearance, her wan face, and he immediately sat her down, fixed her a huge meal, and demanded she tell him what had happened.

After she had related everything, even her unrequited love for Shane, Rake handed her an envelope. "Came fer you in the mail a week ago."

It was from Shane. Fingers trembling, she opened it, and out fell her fifteen-thousand-dollar check which he had never cashed. Accompanying it was a terse note telling her that he did not require payment for services rendered, seeing as the case had taken on a personal tone. That was it. No words of endearment—he hadn't even wished her well.

Stewing, she crumpled his note and threw it into the fire. "I have never in my life met a more unreasonable, pigheaded fool!"

"What?" Rake squawked. "Because he returned your check?"

"No! Because he won't admit he loves me!"

She insisted right then and there that Rake take her to town so she could hammer out a note of her own and send the check back to him. She didn't believe for a minute that Shane was out of the country. Still, she had to wait two weeks for a reply. He returned her check yet again and sent no response to the note she had written.

"Damn him!" she raged, stalking into the kitchen and waving the check under Rake's nose. "He returned the check, Rake!"

Rake, truly puzzled that she would be having such a conniption over a returned check, reached for his rifle. "I'll go flush him outta that New York castle for ya, Edie. I'll *force* him to take that check and eat it, if that's what you wish, little one."

Eden hugged him tightly. "Oh, I love you so, Rake. It is kind of you to make such an offer, but I want Shane to realize his love for me on his own."

"How much time do you plan to give him?"

"Not much," she admitted. "Then I have to take drastic measures."

Rake pulled away to look at her, and his eyes burned with a ferocity that spoke of dire consequences to be suffered by O'Connor if he did not cooperate with his granddaughter's plan. "By God, he better respond the right way this time, Edie, or he'll wish he never messed with a granddaughter of mine!"

She smiled and patted his hand reassuringly. "Don't worry, Rake, he'll respond."

But after she'd sent two telegrams, he hadn't responded, except for two terse words. *Stop writing.*

When Rake returned to the ranch house at suppertime one March day, he found Eden angrily pacing the porch.

"Look at this!" she exclaimed, waving a telegram under Rake's nose. "Drastic measures are called for! In my last telegram I demanded he respond to my proclamation that he loves me and he wrote back—this!" She read aloud Shane's cold response. *"You, Mrs. Lindsay, are living in an delusional world Enough of this ridiculous game. I tire of your notes, and have responded to them only out of common courtesy. In the future, if you persist in harassing me, I will have to take legal action. Now, please, carry on with your life as I wish to carry on with mine—in peace."*

She raised her head, and her eyes were bright with fury. "Do you believe the utter pomposity? Supercilious, arrogant—"

"Where's my gun?" Rake roared. He stomped off toward the kitchen, and Eden chased after him, catching up with him in the main room and tugging on his arm.

"You can't shoot him from here, Rake!"

"Goddammit, I'd like to! The bastard. Where does he get off using that language with my little lovely? I'll shoot his—"

"Granpapa, please," she said, using the name she had used when she was very young. "Remember, I love this man."

"I can't see why, the stubborn mick—"

"Don't call him that!"

Rake softened, circling his arm around her shoulders and squeezing her. "Shh, shh, Edie. I just can't stand to see you upset. He doesn't come out after your next telegram, then I go out to New York, and I mean it."

Wearily, Eden leaned her head against her grandfather's shoulder. She knew he would. Though she was tired, she was angry too, angry at Shane for being so blind and so stubborn. She also knew that if he refused to come to Texas after she sent her final telegram, she would have to move to England.

To live in the same country with him and not to have him was simply too painful for her to contemplate.

"Pack my bags," Shane told his valet.

The valet stared at him. "But sir, it's—"

"Yes, I know, it's snowing. Pack up."

The valet pursed his lips and did as instructed. The master just hadn't been the same since that woman had come into—and left—his life.

Shane was well aware of his servants' opinion of his state of mind. They would think he was even more unbalanced when they learned he was going to Texas to see Eden.

At first her notes had annoyed him. He'd wanted nothing to do with her, and had wanted to cut her out of his life as cleanly as possible. But as time had worn on, he'd found he could not be rid of her. She had left him with memories, and they were unbearable. She was etched into his heart as surely as an engraving in stone, and would always be a part of him, a brand he wore inside. After he had sent his final telegram, he'd taken out hers again, reread them, and known that he must go to her. Yes, it was time he told her. Time he took her into his arms and said the words she had so longed to hear from him. He could only hope she hadn't tired of waiting. That she hadn't gone again.

As he made his way down the stairs, his valet behind him carrying his bags, there was a knock on the front door. Spencer opened it to a messenger. Another telegram.

Shane took the envelope, frowning as he tore it open.

SHANE, I THINK IT IS ONLY FAIR THAT SINCE YOU HAVE
REFUSED TO BECOME PART OF MY LIFE IN ANY FASHION,
THAT WHEN OUR CHILD IS BORN I HAVE THE LIBERTY TO
NAME IT AS I SEE FIT. IF OUR BABY IS A BOY I PLAN TO
CALL HIM SHAKESPEARE. IF IT IS A GIRL I WILL NAME HER
OPHELIA. ENGLISH NAMES, I GRANT YOU, BUT, AGAIN,
THAT IS MY PRIVILEGE SINCE I WILL BE RAISING THE
CHILD. THANK YOU, EDEN VICTORIA LINDSAY.

For a long moment Shane simply stared at the
telegram as if he hadn't just read the words that had
jarred him right to his bones.

"Sir?"

He lifted his head to see Simon standing before
him, looking greatly concerned.

"Shakespeare," Shane whispered.

"I beg your pardon, sir?"

The telegram drifted from Shane's fingers to the
floor. "She wants to call our baby Shakespeare."

Simon blinked, obviously stunned, but Shane
quickly composed himself.

"Spencer, see to my bags." He was laughing now.
"Holy sh—Simon, I'm going to be a father."

Stunned, Simon watched him fling open the door
and head out into the ferocious snowstorm, bare-
headed and without a topcoat.

Spring had come to Texas, the fields freshly tilled,
the sun blazing hot. Shane stood on the front porch
of Rake's ranch house and knocked twice on the
door. There was no answer. Leaving his bags on the
porch, he strolled around back, taking in the land,
smelling the rich earth, looking out to where the
earth touched the sky. There was a bunkhouse some
distance off, the stables, and the backyard itself with

its small garden plot, the turned-up soil glistening and brown.

And then he saw her, crouching down by a decrepit wagon, placing a saucer of milk before a mother cat and her four kittens. His heart slammed against his ribs. Just seeing her caused such a violent physical reaction in him, he couldn't move for a moment.

She did, though, straightening, and sweat broke out on his brow. Edie, Edie. She was round with child, his child. How far along was she? God, she looked almost ready to have the baby. He felt remorse and self-contempt for having allowed her to go through her pregnancy alone. Not that he had known, of course, but that did not mitigate his pain.

He could only stare at her, at this woman who had turned his life upside down. Yes, he loved her with an intensity close to agony. He ached to pull her into his arms, ached to tell her he had never meant to hurt her, but she looked so heartbreakingly beautiful that he did not want to shatter the moment.

Suddenly he stiffened, feeling the barrel of a gun shoved into his back. "All right, you slimy son of a bitch!" came a rough, snarling voice behind him.

Hearing her grandfather's voice, Eden whirled, her hand flying to her throat as she caught sight of Rake with his gun on Shane. Stunned, her mind not registering what she saw, she could only stare.

"Fine time for you to show up, you thievin' heartless bastard! Just in time for my daily bout of target practice. Get over there, right by that tree."

"Rake!" Eden shouted.

But Rake was reveling in his victory. "No, Edie, I want this varmint off my property. Stand back now, I'm going to shoot him."

"No, you are not!" She rushed to her grandfather

and pushed the gun away. "Do not upset me, Grandpapa. This is my business to deal with alone." Her gaze softened on him. "You can watch from the window if you like, and if he makes an unseemly move, you can do what you wish."

This seemed to satisfy him, at least temporarily. He stalked off, grumbling, and Eden turned to Shane. He was regarding her with a raised eyebrow, the expression so arrogant and typical of him, she was torn between laughing and crying. As impeccably dressed as always, he wore a gray suit, a pristine white shirt, and a silver brocade vest that matched his eyes. Her gaze scanned his harsh, beloved face, and she noted the tension lines about his chiseled mouth.

"What are you doing here?" she whispered.

Shane wanted only to touch her, to hold her in his arms, but she was not his to touch—not yet. He saw the pain in her eyes and he cursed himself, knowing he was responsible for that pain.

"Edie," he said. "I'm sorry."

She turned and strolled away, idly touching a flower in the window box by the toolshed. "Really?" she asked mildly. "For what? That you impregnated me?"

He deserved that. And Eden had always been so brutally honest—a trait he loved about her. "Sorry I hurt you, darlin'."

"Oh? What makes you think that you did?"

He walked over to her. "You have always been so brave." He stared again at her belly and felt such a keen longing to put his hand there, he had to drag his gaze back up to her face. She was even more lovely than he remembered, her features soft and radiant with her pregnancy. How perfect their child would be, how lively and strong. "Why didn't you tell me earlier?"

"About the child?" She shrugged. "I didn't want you to come out because of that. I wanted you to come out to see me."

Eden drew in a deep breath and released it on a shaky sigh. It was clear that her pregnancy *was* the reason for his appearance, and the fact hurt. "But since that is so obviously the reason, I suppose you would like to talk about the baby's upbringing. I do think raising it here—"

Suddenly his arms were around her, holding her tightly against him. He pressed her head to his chest, and she heard the thunder of his heart. Tears gathered in her eyes and overflowed onto her cheeks. She swayed against him, the feel of his hard, rugged body so intimate, so *wonderful,* so temporary. She should pull away, she knew, for delaying their inevitable parting would only cause more anguish. Oh, but she loved him. So much. She breathed him in, the faint masculine scent of his spicy cologne, musk and leather. She ran her palms over his powerful back, twined her fingers through the thick, soft curls at the back of his neck. The baby gave her a startling kick, and she jumped, but Shane pulled her closer, his arms tightening around her.

"I felt that," he said huskily. "Edie, already you're a wonderful mother. And you're not raising this child alone." He pulled away to look down at her. "I was on my way here when I got your final telegram. If you don't believe me, sweetheart, you can ask Simon. I didn't know you were carrying my child when I made my decision to come to Texas."

"But your telegrams—"

His lips tightened as he muttered a curse. "I'm a scarred and cynical man, Edie." Shaking his head, he laughed a little. "What the hell do you want me for?"

She simply stared up at him, unable to believe what she might be hearing.

"Yes," he said somberly, his fingers gliding over her cheek. "I do love you, Eden. I've loved you for a very long time, I think, and these past months have been hell without you. Marry me, Edie. Even if you weren't carrying my child, I'd want you to marry me. I never thought I'd say those words to any woman— and I know I'm asking a lot, putting you in danger with my profession, but I want to do more writing anyway, and—"

She pressed her fingers to his lips. "Hush. That has to be the longest proposal in history."

Shane pulled her to him. The baby kicked again, and Shane did what he had been wanting to do. He laid his hand on the side of her belly.

"Lord," he breathed, and he found her mouth, kissing her hungrily. "Say yes," he begged as his hands slid over her body. He reacquainted himself with the feel of her curves and soft mounds—filled out now, lush and ripe with the swelling of their child.

"I can't breathe," she whispered, and laughed when he loosened his hold. "Yes," she whispered when he looked down at her. "Yes, forever, Shane." She flashed a smile at him. "But in the Adirondacks you told me you had yet to meet a woman you'd want to share your life with—"

"Until you. I knew it then but didn't want you to know, Edie. You'd always talked about how you would never marry again."

"Until you," she murmured, staring up at him with adoring eyes. "But . . . there are some conditions."

He lifted a brow at her.

"First of all, that you don't shut me out. Second, that you stop worrying so much about the risk I'm at because of your profession—"

He cut her off. "I'll have to make some adjustments, some changes, not take so many high-risk cases, but that's just as well. Writing books is something I want to do more of. And Eden . . . I want to get married today."

She gaped at him, and he grinned.

"With your grandfather watching me out the window back there, it might be a good decision after all, don't you think?"

"I haven't finished my list of conditions."

"Well, hurry the hell up, honey. I want to get you alone."

She giggled, but then sobered. "I went to England because my mother died, and I asked Franklin to give you a note, which he didn't—"

"Son of a—"

She shushed him again, this time pressing her mouth to his. "And Philip took the gems without my knowledge. He returned them—"

"I know. Scotland Yard informed me."

At the mention of Scotland Yard, Eden frowned. "Have you found Meggie yet?"

His lips tightened. "Not yet. But I will." Once again he pulled her close to cradle her head against his chest. "I'm sorry about your mother, Edie. Was it terribly hard for you?"

She snuggled into his arms. "Mama and I made peace at the end. It was best she go . . . and be with Papa. She was never happy once he had died, and perhaps that was why she had such little tolerance for Philip and me."

Shane laughed softly.

Eden leaned back in the circle of his arms. "Have you a different opinion on that, sir?"

"I prefer to keep my opinion to myself, Mrs. Lindsay, soon to be Mrs. O'Connor forever."

She smiled up at him, loving the sound of that name. "There is something you should know. The doctor said I cannot travel until I have the baby. You have to stay in Texas awhile."

His gaze flicked toward the house.

She laughed. "You'll just have to make your peace with Rake."

"Hmm" was all he said.

"And another thing.

Doc says the baby might be bab*ies*. There is a strong possibility that we could have twins."

Shane paled.

Eden laughed and reached up to touch his cheek. "Shakespeare *and* Ophelia."

"Like hell." He leaned down to kiss her mouth, but since they were both laughing, he nipped her nose instead. "Colleen and Patrick."

"I can see," she murmured, lifting her mouth to his, "we are going to have to compromise."

"I have a condition of my own," he said.

"Oh?"

"Yes." He pulled her close, breathing in the fragrance of her hair—jasmine now. "In the future, when you become pregnant, I forbid you to keep it from me for so long. You must tell me as soon as you know. Every time."

Eden held her breath, then let it go, trembling with the effect of his words, his insinuation. Her eyes shining, she stood on tiptoe and touched her lips to his, whispering against them, "Yes, darling, I promise. Every time."

EPILOGUE

$\mathcal{S}$HANE LAY ON HIS BACK IN THEIR BED, HIS ARMS around Eden, the sound of the surf lulling them to sleep after their passionate lovemaking. The twins, nine months old, were sound asleep in the nursery, and just that day he had heard that the publisher he had sent his novel to wanted to publish it. Eden had just finished writing a play, and soon she would take up acting again.

Lazily, he ran a hand up and down her spine. Her body was as firm and slender as it had been before she had given birth, but with more curves now, all soft woman. "Edie darlin'," he whispered, not even knowing if she was asleep. "You've made me the happiest man on earth."

She smiled, snuggling against him. "I love you, Shane. Today was a perfect day, wasn't it? With Liam and Camille and baby Michael sharing our celebratory meal—I can't believe she's expecting again!"

He laughed. "They have to catch up with us."

"They won't," she murmured. "Not unless she has triplets. Tate and Jessie are so happy too, aren't they? And so wonderful with the twins. It's like they're Austin and Angel's blood brother and sister." She slid over him, caressing his mouth with her fingers. "I was thinking . . ."

"Edie . . ."

She laughed and hugged him, rubbing her face against his neck. "Do you know Jackson from the orphanage?" She heard him catch his breath as she cupped his manhood in her hand.

"Dammit, Edie, that kid is trouble. He's twelve years old—" He lunged up and twisted, rolling over and pinning her beneath him. "Don't think you can have your way with me by touching me like that either."

She pouted. "You don't like that?"

"I like it too damn much, and you know it. But honey, we can't adopt a twelve-year-old."

"Why not? With a little love and care, and a wonderful man in his life to teach him how to behave, he'd be a gem. Anyone can see he's a diamond in the rough."

"Anyone, huh?"

She made a sinuous move beneath him, feeling his arousal hard and throbbing-hot against her stomach. "Shane, I love you. With the nanny to help out, you know it won't be much trouble at all."

"But Jackson? He hates the whole world."

"Not for long, he won't. Shane, don't you see? You could have hated the whole world too. But you didn't. Teach him that. Teach him that no matter how ugly situations can get, there is always hope."

He gazed down at her, his heart seeming to grow in his chest. God, he loved her. She was so brimming with love, she'd rather die than not share it. He smoothed the hair back from her brow, then lifted himself on his forearms and pushed slowly into her. She gasped, breathing his name, her face lighting with pleasure.

"I'll consider it," he promised, and began to move in and out of her with long, measured strokes.

Eden took all of him into her, wrapped in love, flooded by his power and his tenderness. She was lost in him, ecstatic with happiness, and knew that before long they would be blessed with a third son, a hungry orphan boy called Jackson.

ABOUT THE AUTHOR

MAUREEN REYNOLDS is the winner of the 1988 Best New Western Romance Author award from *Romantic Times* and the *Affaire de Coeur* Gold Certificate, and was nominated the 1990 Most Sensual Romance award from *Romantic Times*. She spent her childhood in Massachusetts and lived in New York and Indiana before moving to her present residence in Miami.